MW01200975

THE
ONE AND ONLY
VIVIAN STONE

THE
ONE AND ONLY
VIVIAN STONE

MELISSA O'CONNOR

G

Gallery Books

New York   Amsterdam/Antwerp   London
Toronto   Sydney/Melbourne   New Delhi

G

Gallery Books
An Imprint of Simon & Schuster, LLC
1230 Avenue of the Americas
New York, NY 10020

For more than 100 years, Simon & Schuster has championed authors and the stories they create. By respecting the copyright of an author's intellectual property, you enable Simon & Schuster and the author to continue publishing exceptional books for years to come. We thank you for supporting the author's copyright by purchasing an authorized edition of this book.

No amount of this book may be reproduced or stored in any format, nor may it be uploaded to any website, database, language-learning model, or other repository, retrieval, or artificial intelligence system without express permission. All rights reserved. Inquiries may be directed to Simon & Schuster, 1230 Avenue of the Americas, New York, NY 10020 or permissions@simonandschuster.com.

This book is a work of fiction. Any references to historical events, real people, or real places are used fictitiously. Other names, characters, places, and events are products of the author's imagination, and any resemblance to actual events or places or persons, living or dead, is entirely coincidental.

Copyright © 2025 by Melissa O'Connor

All rights reserved, including the right to reproduce this book or portions thereof in any form whatsoever. For information, address Gallery Books Subsidiary Rights Department, 1230 Avenue of the Americas, New York, NY 10020.

First Gallery Books trade paperback edition July 2025

GALLERY BOOKS and colophon are registered trademarks of Simon & Schuster, LLC

Simon & Schuster strongly believes in freedom of expression and stands against censorship in all its forms. For more information, visit BooksBelong.com.

For information about special discounts for bulk purchases, please contact Simon & Schuster Special Sales at 1-866-506-1949 or business@simonandschuster.com.

The Simon & Schuster Speakers Bureau can bring authors to your live event. For more information or to book an event, contact the Simon & Schuster Speakers Bureau at 1-866-248-3049 or visit our website at www.simonspeakers.com.

Interior design by Julia Jacintho

Manufactured in the United States of America

10 9 8 7 6 5 4 3 2 1

Library of Congress Cataloging-in-Publication Data is available.

ISBN 978-1-6680-7483-1
ISBN 978-1-6680-7484-8 (ebook)

To Shawn,
the reason I believe the best love stories
come with a healthy dose of humor.
Thank you for always making me laugh.

CONTENT WARNING

While I hope *The One and Only Vivian Stone* makes you smile and swoon, it also explores some of the darkness of Hollywood and the entertainment industry at large.

If you would like a spoiler-free reading experience, please move on to the story now.

For those who would like to be prepared:
This book contains an off-the-page abortion; an off-the-page stillbirth; brief depictions of sexual abuse; and mentions and brief depictions of drug and alcohol abuse.

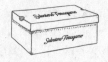

CHAPTER ONE

Margot

now

I'll admit it: I'm a creature of habit. Change scares me.

Or maybe it's less that change scares me and more that familiarity is reassuring. Living a couple of hours away, I don't often drive through my old neighborhood in Long Beach, but whenever I do, it's like rewatching my favorite movie. Knowing what to expect means being able to savor the details.

There's something charming about how the Pete's Hardware sign hangs slightly crooked. And the mist puffing out from the decorative mug above the door to Blossom's Bakery.

Even the red-and-white awning as I pull up to Ruiz Music is the same. It's been twenty years since I stepped inside, and I wouldn't again if not for the old shoebox I discovered this morning while cleaning out my grandma's attic. Inside was a note—a love letter—to and from people I'd never heard of, alongside cassette tapes. Probably mixtapes, but I couldn't check. The player I also found was broken.

But I knew who could fix it.

Before I can weigh the merits of being a coward, I gather the cassette player and the shoebox from the passenger seat and walk through the music store door. The bell above jingles, and nostalgia at being here again tingles down my spine. To the left are rows of sheet music books. Guitars hang from the wall above, while amps and keyboards sit in a display on the floor. Classical music pipes through speakers.

To the right, a man stands behind the counter, his back to me. Broad shoulders stretch a black T-shirt, his forearms tensing as he transfers an amp to a nearby table. Though I can't see his face, how he moves is distinctly familiar.

"How can I help—" He turns toward the door, his words coming to a halt as his gaze meets mine.

My stomach tumbles like it's in a cocktail shaker.

I don't know what I expected Leo to look like after all these years. Identical, I suppose, like he'd been frozen in time. For the most part, I still see the boy from high school in a man's body. The brown eyes I used to know like the back of my hand are the same. So are his lips, which very well might be the best part of his face, with their soft slope and gentle peaks.

Other things have changed. He didn't used to have stubble I wanted to run my fingers across. Or a voice so low and gravelly, it sent goosebumps down my arms. He abandoned the close-cropped haircut he once favored, his dark strands longer now, swept back in waves I didn't realize he had. And the last time I saw him, his arms were bony—not muscled with biceps that more than fill his sleeves.

Teenage Leo was cute. This Leo is a wildfire. If I'd known he would look like this, I don't think I would have summoned the courage to come inside.

Deep breath in. Breath out.

"Hi." I force a smile, stepping forward as if drawn by a magnet, and set the shoebox and the player on the counter between us. "It's been a long time. I wasn't sure you still worked here."

Very cool, casual. If my throat were gripped by a vise, that is.

His gaze slides over my brown curls, my face, then down my body. He studies me with the kind of deep concentration he used to have when fiddling with electronics.

"Margot."

That's all he says. I suppose he's forgotten how we used to spend so much time together, our moms had a running joke about paying each other rent. Or all the times we sat on the roof outside his bedroom, talking under the stars. How he once kissed me like it was more vital than air.

Then he rounds the counter, closing the distance between us, and wraps his arms around me. "You're back."

I rest my cheek against his chest and return the embrace, oxytocin rushing through me as I inhale. The familiar scent of his detergent is an addiction I've never overcome.

He pulls back but doesn't let go, holding my arms. "It's so good to see you. I've been thinking about you." Before I can consider why, he adds, "I saw the obituary for your grandma. I would have come to the wake if there'd been one."

"Mom and I decided to keep it small."

As small as my family. I don't have aunts or uncles. No cousins. Gram never married. Without her saying it, I sensed that her relationship with my absent grandfather hadn't been a loving one.

Same story with my dad. He left when I was a baby, claiming he wasn't ready to be a parent, so Mom and I lived with Gram. Ironically, three years after he moved to Arizona, he got married, and within a decade they had three kids. He's never shown an interest in my life.

"I'm sorry." Leo's lips press into a thin line. "I stopped by the house a while back, hoping to offer my condolences to you or your mom, but no one was home."

"It's okay," I whisper past the lump in my throat. "Gram had a long, full life. I got more time with her than most people get with their grandparents." But she was more than a grandparent. She was like a second mother.

It's been two months since she passed, and I keep obsessing over the last time we spoke. If I'd known, I wouldn't have rushed her off the phone, eager to keep reading a romance novel. I would do anything to get back that last conversation and let it stretch all night. To have one more piece of her to hold on to.

"How old was she again?"

"Ninety-three."

He lets out a low whistle, releasing me. "And she was still driving."

"How did you know?"

"She stopped by once in a while. Brought me cookies on my birthday."

Gram had a calendar with special dates she meticulously transferred over every year. I hadn't realized his birthday was one of them.

"Everything is exactly the same." I walk a few feet to a keyboard and test a few keys.

"Do you still play?"

I curl my hand away. "No."

Leo scans me again before shifting his attention to the counter. "So what brings you in? I'm guessing there aren't cookies in here." He points at the shoebox.

There's no ring on his finger. I shouldn't notice. It shouldn't matter. But I do, and it does.

I want to ask what he's been doing with himself. If he ever thinks of me. Instead, I go over to the box, all red save for *Salvatore Ferragamo* printed in cursive on the side and top. According to my research, it's a luxury Italian fashion house that's been around since the 1920s, which is odd. Gram wouldn't have been able to afford anything from the brand.

An unfamiliar scent wafts into the air as I lift the lid. "I found this in Gram's attic."

"Talk about a blast from the past." He smiles wide, thumbing through the cassette tapes, and a melody of soft-strumming guitars plays in my chest. "What's on them? Some Fleetwood Mac? Guns N' Roses?"

"Gram was more of a Beach Boys lady, and Mom likes Mariah Carey." Spiderweb-like cracks spread over the plastic case I pop open, the tape labeled *1 of 8.* "See that? There should be eight, but the last one is missing."

"Have you listened to them?"

I flip the player and open the battery compartment to show him the powdery mess inside. "Not yet. I don't have a spare one of these." I give him a knowing smile. "But I used to know a pretty handy guy when it came to electronics. I'm not sure if you still tinker—"

"All the time." He pries out the batteries, then brushes the loosened corrosion aside. "I can clean this for you."

"That would be great, thanks." At the risk of sounding impatient I say, "How long do you think it will take?"

He shrugs. "I can do it later today and text you with an update. Is your number the same?"

"Yes." He still has it? Interesting.

"If you leave the tapes, I can test those too."

"Could there be something wrong with them?"

"Maybe. They're probably fine, though. It's also a way to make sure the player works. If you don't want to leave them, I have a couple of tapes around here."

I don't know why I'm hesitating. He's my best chance at getting everything to work. "Okay, but don't listen to them."

A mischievous eyebrow raises. "Why? Afraid there's something embarrassing from your childhood on here? The Margot DuBois Diaries? Am I going to find out you secretly smoked pot? Or who else you had a thing for in high school? Ten bucks says whoever it was turned out to be a loser."

His use of "else" tells me he hasn't forgotten what he once meant to me.

I give his arm a playful shove. In this second, it's like no time has passed. "Your trash talk is as stellar as ever, but I think you're in for disappointment. They're probably mixtapes."

"What's this?" He motions to the letter in the box, and I nod my permission. It's weathered, like it's been folded and unfolded many times. Leo spreads it out on the counter.

My Dearest TDH,

I need to get out something I'd never voice. The truth is, I love you madly in a head-over-heels, last-person-I-think-of-before-bed and first-person-I-think-of-when-I-wake-up way. I'm trying to stop, but it's not easy. When I'm with you, I'm a blazing fire. When I'm not, I'm crackling embers. Distance helps, but I don't want to stay away. I love hearing your thoughts on everything big and small. As soon as you're near, though, the fire roars back to life.

Every day I imagine your laugh. Every night I think of your lips. But if all we can have is friendship, I'll take it. Because the only thing worse than not being with you would be not having you in my life.

Love,

Vivian

Leo glances at me. "TDH? Are they initials?"

"I assume so, but I don't know whose. Gram's name is Ginger. Mom's is Diane. Even my dad's name, Lucas, doesn't fit. And I don't know anyone named Vivian."

He folds the letter and sets it back in the box. "Sounds like you have a mystery on your hands."

Though this feels like a natural break in the conversation, I'm not ready for it to end. I want to ask him everything I need to know to catch up on his life. I want to take a trip down memory lane and linger there for hours. I'm tempted to ask if he'd like to grab something to eat or have a drink. Instead, I lift a hand in goodbye and walk back to my car.

Hours later, I'm driving to Gram's old bungalow after dropping off some clothing donations. My phone vibrates with a text at a red light.

> Sorry, I couldn't get the player to work. But I have an alternative. The first tape wasn't clear, so I cleaned it.

I voice-to-text a response.

> Did you listen to it?

> Only enough to make sure it worked. I'm free tomorrow. Text me your address and a good time to swing over with it.

I don't reply until I'm in the driveway and out of the car.

> I'm at Gram's for now. Any time after 6 works.

Gram had a reverse mortgage we didn't know about until she passed. Mom is paying it from DC, but she can't afford to keep doing it, so while I'd rather preserve the house exactly like it is, I offered to clean it out and meet with a real estate agent. My boss is letting me work remotely for the next month, which should be all I need.

A month to say goodbye.

When I used to pass the overgrown poppies along the walkway and cross the threshold, I knew I'd be met with the lingering scent of Gram's perfume: a mix of lavender and baby powder. Dozens of antique teacups in floral patterns rested in the hutch where they'd always been. Cookies cooled on a wire rack, chocolate chips warm and gooey.

Poppies still spill onto the walkway as I reach her front door. The scent of lavender clings to the drapes, fluttering above an air-conditioning vent. Teacups sit in neat rows on their saucers. But the wire rack is empty.

My phone buzzes.

> Great. I'll bring something to eat while we listen.

> Who says you get to listen?

I'm wondering if the joke will come across when he answers, and my worries disintegrate.

> I cleaned the tape and have your only available player.
> That's my price.

I think through possible responses, typing, deleting, then retyping before hitting *send*.

> Deal.

CHAPTER TWO

Margot

now

Dust tickles my nose as I reach the attic the next day after work.

I tug a dangling cord, and light stretches to the edges of the room, illuminating a patchwork of household history: a yellow rotary phone sitting on a stack of college encyclopedias. A VCR and a tote labeled *Disney movies*. My Care Bears lunchbox. Inside is a pile of photos next to a disposable camera.

Once, as a teenager, I tried to live up here, deciding I needed the entirety of the top floor for my personal sanctuary. A space where I could blast Britney Spears and read endless V.C. Andrews books. Between the low-pitched ceiling and the stifling heat, I didn't make it an hour.

This time, I don't have a choice but to power through. Partly because I need to keep cleaning but mostly because I'm hoping to find another clue about TDH and Vivian, whoever they are, and Gram's connection to them. Some uncovered piece of her life to soften the sting of missing her.

I dig into bins and flip through photo albums without a single lead. Just before six o'clock, I haul a tote filled with more cookie cutters than anyone should own downstairs. My phone rings as I set the bin aside.

It's my real estate agent.

"Hi, David." I check my reflection in the hall mirror and use my thumb to swipe away the dirt smudge under my eye.

"Hey, how's it going?" Before I can answer, he says, "I'm calling to schedule a time to take pictures. Would a week from today be too soon? I've been thinking about the market, and we should list the place ASAP. Summer is a great time to sell."

The house is still furnished but more minimally than it used to be. While Mom and I were here for Gram's funeral, we started cleaning it out. At least the most obvious things—clutter we didn't have to think about tossing and whatever Mom wanted to bring back with her.

"That should work." If David notices the hesitation in my voice, he doesn't mention it. It's only a house. Not Gram. Still, it feels like erasing what's left of her.

"Perfect. We'll get it sold for you in no time."

A knock comes on the front door as I end the call.

Years ago, Leo knocked as a courtesy and walked in. He also felt comfortable going into the fridge for a snack. The boy never stopped eating. When I pull back the door to find him hugging a full paper bag, it's clear that part hasn't changed, yet I'm hit by the stark difference in how his large frame fills the doorway. I wish I had been here to see him become this: all man.

I step back to let him pass. "Hungry much?"

He toes off his sneakers, his attention drifting over the mudroom and toward the rest of the house, likely noting the small differences since he was here last. "I wanted to get options. I wasn't sure what you liked these days." In his other hand he grips the handle of a boombox, black and silver, with big speakers.

"Is that what I think it is?" Seeing one for the first time in decades has wistfulness growing in my belly.

"Sure is."

Leo follows me through the kitchen to the dining table and sets the bag and boombox next to a Cheez-It box. I'm ashamed to admit it's been there for days while I keep grabbing handfuls when my stomach rumbles.

"Looks like your diet continues to be the picture of health." He shakes the near-empty box.

"Cooking meals isn't worth the effort when it's only for me." I wonder if he will offer something in return—a detail about his personal life—but he doesn't. I snatch the box and squint at the ingredients. There has to be some nutritional value I can rub in his face. "Look at that. Made with real cheese."

As if knowing what he offers is infinitely superior, Leo pries open a takeout box so the scent of spices drifts into the air. I grab the beef lo mein and sit, laughing as a memory taps at my mind.

He sits next to me, bumping my knee with his. "What's funny?"

I skip the chopsticks—never could get the hang of them—and grab a fork. "Do you remember how we used to spend hours lying on the roof outside your bedroom window?" When we first started, there were a couple of feet between us. But as we grew more comfortable with each other, the space narrowed.

"Do I remember? You used to sniff my shirt. It's not the kind of thing you forget."

"Did not."

I absolutely did. When the breeze caught right, a scent floated over, and I thought it was subtle when I turned my head toward his shirtsleeve.

"Liar." He digs a fork in and twirls some noodles. "One time you tried to make me forget it happened by tickling me—"

"Are you still ticklish?" To verify, I poke his side.

He lets out a laugh like the Pillsbury Doughboy, only husky, and bats me away. "Cut it out, you freak."

"Rude."

"It was rude when you tickled me on the roof. I almost fell off."

So dramatic. "You didn't almost fall. Just slid a little."

It's a relief, knowing what to expect from him. His appearance may have changed some, but he's the same.

"I have to tell you," I say, "it was such déjà vu seeing you behind the counter at your dad's music shop again."

"It's my shop now." Pride gleams in his eyes. "Although I almost changed my mind in college and went in another direction."

"Which direction?"

"Accounting." When I make a gagging noise, he laughs. "I know. Not me at all. I realized I love the store and can't imagine being anywhere else." He glances sidelong at me. "I kind of thought you'd come back after college too."

If it hadn't been for Ben, I probably would have. We met in a creative writing course and were together for seven years. Unfortunately, I know what it's like to live with a man day in and day out, trusting him implicitly, only for him to leave without batting an eye.

"No one is more surprised I didn't end up back here than me," I say. "But I really like Santa Barbara."

"And what do you do to keep the cupboards stocked with Cheez-Its? Do you still write?"

I hate talking about this. When you write, people tend to assume publication is inevitable. Only a hop, skip, and a jump away. It's become a sore topic.

After we got our creative writing degrees, Ben used his trust fund to pay his bills so he could write all the time. I edited for a magazine and wrote in my spare time. While he got an agent, a six-figure book deal, and a spot on the *New York Times* Best Seller list, I had nothing to show for my efforts.

I stopped trying to get published. He stopped trying at our relationship.

Instead of unpacking it all, I go for simplicity. "No, that didn't work out. I used to work for a magazine, but now I edit for a higher education publisher. I really like it." I tack on the last part when he furrows his brow, and it's true. I like it well enough. "What have you been doing besides running the store?" I ask like I'm mildly curious rather than dying to know. "Any girlfriend in the picture? Kids?"

He tilts his head, noncommittal. "There was someone. Amy. We got married."

Of course he got married. Look at him. I bet the body he's hiding under those clothes would render me speechless. The Leo I remember was funny and thoughtful and smart too, and it doesn't seem like that's changed. But he said—

"*Was?*"

"We're not together anymore." His eyes catch mine. "We divorced."

"Oh. I'm sorry."

"Thanks." He shoves a big bite into his mouth. It's nearly a full minute until he says more, like he needs time to work up to it. "We wanted kids, but it wasn't working. It took a lot out of us. Too much."

I can't decide which is worse: wanting kids, like I do, but not having the opportunity, or having the opportunity but not being able to. But I quickly decide it's not a contest of whose situation is more painful.

"It's been a couple of years," he goes on. "I'm okay."

"You deserve to be happy."

"You too." He gives a tight-lipped smile, pushing his container aside. Somehow, he scarfed down the whole thing, while I barely put a dent in mine. He reaches for the boombox. "Ready to start the tape?"

I stop him from pressing a button. "Why am I nervous?"

He studies my hand over his, the air thickening alongside the increased tempo of my pulse. "I think the word you're looking for is 'excited.'" His gaze drifts over my face. "It looks good on you."

A flush creeps up my chest as I let him go. His hand flexes before hitting *play*.

The boombox's knobs spin for a few seconds, a moment of static, then the audio starts.

"I know getting these tapes will come as a shock, but I don't know what else to do. I'll admit, I'm getting desperate. But I keep thinking if you would only hear me out, you'd—well, I don't expect you to forgive me. I do hope you'll understand why I did what I did all those years ago. That's not the kind of person I am, but I simply didn't— You know what? Let's start at the beginning. At least the beginning as I see it: Los Angeles in December of 1951. I don't expect this to fix everything, but maybe when you hear it all, you'll give me a chance to make amends before it's too late."

A chill rolls over me as I peer at Leo. "This isn't Gram or Mom."

"Then who is it?"

I shrug and rest an elbow on the table, chin in my hand.

"I'm sorry in advance if this goes a bit long. I tend to ramble."

Tape One

CHAPTER THREE

Vivian

then

I twisted the knob on my car radio, silencing a Bing Crosby tune, and reached for the crumpled audition form sitting on the passenger seat. Maybe I'd overlooked an encouraging word the first time I read it. I smoothed it against the peeling leather of my steering wheel and checked the notes scrawled at the bottom.

Can't act. Needs to lose the accent. The raspy voice is good for sexy roles, but she's not curvy enough for them.

My stomach clenched, and I balled up the form and tossed it onto the back seat.

I'd read it all before. Each time, I slapped the rejection onto the nail sticking out of my bedroom wall. The stack had to be 85 or 99 or 122 pages deep now. I'd checked it that morning before leaving for my waitressing shift and determined that another sheet would not hang on that trooper of a nail without slipping off. Which I'd taken as a sign that today's audition would be different.

It wasn't.

All I wanted was to go home and soak. My feet screamed from spending the day on paper-thin soles. I hated to break it to them, but we had an hour more to go. My best friend, Ruth, wanted me to meet her new boyfriend. She was a revolving door with men but talked about this one so much, it had to be serious.

I opened the door of my beat-up Ford coupe, its hinges creaking as I stepped out. Razor-sharp pain zinged through my feet. I bit the inside of my cheek and strode down the Sunset Strip, each click of my heels emulating a word in an evil mantra: *can't act, can't act, can't act.*

Bright lights illuminated Mocambo. Remember it? You must. It was one of LA's celebrity haunts with a Latin American flair. A line of stylish people congregated under its green-and-white-striped awning that night, making me conscious of the pitiful state of my sleeveless dress, its remaining sequins hanging on for dear life.

With my next step I squeezed through the crowd, my foot falling awkwardly with a snap beneath it. My balance faltered, my heart lurching as I toppled.

A strong hand caught me around the arm before I could go down. "Whoa."

I tipped my head back to gaze at the man steadying me.

He was tall, about a foot over my five-three, and had a pompadour hairstyle—greased on top and slicked back on the sides. With strands an inkier black than his suit, the high shine only deepened it.

Lord, have mercy.

I'd been around my fair share of attractive people. It was a consequence of the industry I was trying to break into. Usually my heart skipped a beat for a fella in a leather jacket and blue jeans. But this man made the description "tall, dark, and handsome" fall woefully short. I guessed he was a bit older than my twenty-two.

"You all right?" He bent to retrieve the stump of my heel.

I gasped, scooping up the pitiful black chunk and holding it like it was a baby bird. "No, no, no. These are my mother's lucky heels." Not that they'd ever been lucky for me.

"It can be fixed, right?"

How sweet for this dreamboat to care. "I suppose." The entire heel had broken off, so it could be reattached. But there wasn't money in the budget for a cobbler unless I resorted to a bread-and-water diet for a couple of weeks.

The man leaned in so I could hear him over the crowd. "What are you going to do now?"

I inhaled the woodsy scent of his aftershave. With a hint of vanilla, it wrapped around him like a gift. "My, you smell good."

His dark eyes danced with delight. "What was that?"

My face flamed.

When I was seven, my father suggested a muzzle to stop me from sharing private thoughts and information. It happened during a rare occasion when he'd taken me to the hardware store, and I'd gotten into a conversation with the clerk and told him my parents slept in separate bedrooms.

Instead of answering his last question, I circled back to the previous one. "I'm supposed to meet a friend, but I can't go in there like this." I demonstrated, bobbing up and down a few inches with every step. "See?"

He put a hand over his mouth to hide his smile. "It's not that bad."

"*Not that bad*? I must look like a walking pogo stick."

The man knelt, studying my shoes like a mechanic might inspect a broken engine. Though I couldn't picture him knowing anything about car repairs, to say nothing of how to fix my damaged heel. I imagined he had spent the adult portion of his life advertising Brylcreem hair products and Old Spice shaving soap. When he prodded the heeled portion of my intact shoe, I held his shoulder for balance and lifted my foot so he could get a better look.

With one hand on the heel and the other encircling my shoe, he asked, "May I?"

He was suggesting breaking the other one? No. They were my only heels. I needed them for auditions, and fixing two would be more expensive than fixing one.

Leaving and letting down Ruth would nag at me, but I couldn't go inside barefoot or lopsided.

What other choice did I have? I squeezed my eyes shut. "Okay."

Within a second, he snapped off the other heel, leaving me in flats. I tested them out. They were a little uneven but better than I'd expected.

"It worked." I stared at him in awe and collected the other heel.

"You sound surprised."

"I am. That kind of thing doesn't happen in real life. Let me guess: You can also clear a forest with a single swing of an axe."

"That's Paul Bunyan." He flashed perfect teeth in a smile.

I liked that he found me amusing. "This will be moot if I don't find my friend."

"Maybe she put your name on the list."

A thrill melted over me like butter. "I've never been on a *list* before."

"You're not an actress?" He crossed his arms, assessing me.

"I'm more familiar with the beloved pastime of standing behind studio gates with a sea of people in the hopes of getting chosen as an extra for no more than a blip of screen time."

He winced. "I remember those days."

Not to sound entirely pathetic, I added, "I did have a stint on Broadway," leaving out the bit about how small my part was. "So you act, then?"

"Here and there."

I flipped through my mental Rolodex of films, unable to recall seeing him before. "What studio?"

"MGM."

A warm breeze picked up a stray piece of my brown hair, loose from where I'd pinned it to the side. He reached for the strands at the same time I did.

Our hands met, then our eyes—locking for what could only have been seconds but stretched out like minutes. When I dropped my hand, he swept the wisps behind my ear, brushing a spot on my neck while an electric current hitched a ride on my nerves.

"Vivian!" Ruth's head poked through the dozen people by the door. With her blonde bob and elegant style, she was a dead ringer for Grace Kelly.

She whispered to the man next to her, likely her boyfriend, Dean Keller, and waved me over. He had sandy hair in a perfectly straight side part and wore a charcoal gray suit. A director in his early thirties with several successful films under his belt, Dean had hit it off with Ruth when she hung around his set as an extra.

She drew me in for a brief hug. "You came."

"Broken heels and all." I skimmed my hands over the fur coat she wore. "Is this a mink?"

She raised the collar to snuggle into it. "A gift from Dean. I told him how much I missed my old one."

With Ruth's background, I wasn't surprised that she used to have one. But it made more sense when she lived in New Jersey, where winter brought an abundance of snow.

I turned, finding the man from the line next to us. Was it illogical to assume he wanted to talk more? Because I wanted that too.

Ruth stepped toward him. "Hugh, right? So good to meet you." She lifted on tiptoe and kissed his cheek. I hardly had time to hinge my gawking mouth shut before she gestured to me. "Fellas, this is my best friend, Vivian Mackenzie. Vivian, this is my boyfriend, Dean, and his friend, Hugh Fox."

When she said it fast, Hugh's name sounded like "you fox." If it was a stage name and some Freudian psychology on the studio's part, it was a little on the nose. But it worked for him.

I blinked away my confusion and connected the dots: Hugh wasn't standing there because he wanted to talk to me more. He was there to meet Ruth like I was there to meet Dean.

Mimicking Ruth, I kissed Dean on the cheek, then Hugh. The latter's hand came to the small of my back, and I couldn't help but inhale his scent again. "Pleasure to meet you."

My voice had gotten a bit raspier. I must have lingered too long, because when I drew back, Dean gave Hugh an *Attaboy* smirk.

Ruth took Dean's arm as they went inside, while Hugh offered his. "Shall we?" he asked.

I reached for him, finding solid muscle, and fought against squeezing. Though it didn't stop me from imagining what he looked like under that button-down.

The low-lit room hummed with energy as we walked in, the air hot and conversation roaring. A live band played a rousing song near the front, where couples did the jitterbug.

We sat at one of the last empty tables near the corner of the room, and I wiggled my feet against the pain.

Stripes painted the walls while fringe balls hung from the ceiling. At the room's edge, glass cages held cockatoos, macaws, and parrots. This wasn't simply a place to unwind but an experience where everyone wore their Sunday best and no expense was spared.

"Champagne," Dean said to a nearby waiter.

"What are we celebrating?" I rarely drank but had a glass when the occasion called for it.

"We just wrapped a movie. This guy's first lead"—Dean motioned to Hugh—"and it's going to be a smash hit."

If someone pointed at me while uttering those words, I'd swoon. Preferably onto a chaise longue with a hand over my brow, only to be roused by a housekeeper with smelling salts.

Ruth gave a coy smile. "Maybe you'll be directing me someday."

"Why wait? I'll direct you tonight, honey," Dean said, playful as his eyes dipped over her body. The waiter returned, depositing a metal ice bucket and the champagne. "You can leave it." Dean positioned the bottle away and pushed the cork until it popped, liquid bubbling from the top.

I handed over my flute and turned to Hugh. "Your first lead? That's big."

Bigger than he let on. While he'd been humble, I had made a fool of myself with my broken heel and by admitting I'd only ever been considered as an extra.

When Dean handed the flute back, I took a sip. Cool bubbles skated across my tongue, fizzing on the way down.

"That's what they keep telling me." Hugh flagged over a cigarette girl in a saloon-style skirt. "I'm grateful, but bigger roles come with more pressure and rules." He handed her a quarter in exchange for a pack from the tray strapped around her neck.

"How was your audition?" Dean asked Ruth, handing over her glass.

"Awful. It was a recasting because the woman who got the part wouldn't take pills to lose five pounds before filming. They asked if I'd take them to lose ten in the same amount of time."

Ten? I was offended on her behalf. Ruth was slimmer than me.

I swear, I never knew what casting directors wanted. I wondered if *they* knew what they wanted. One would claim I wasn't curvy enough, only for another to suggest I drop a few pounds. No one had mentioned pills, though. "What'd you say?"

"I asked why not five like the other woman. They didn't like the question." A hard line formed between her eyebrows as she played with the clasp on her black clutch. "I'm giving myself three more years to get somewhere."

"How about you?" Hugh asked me.

"I don't have a deadline." It broke Mom's heart when my father made her give up ballet to stay home. The way she spoke about being onstage, she never stopped mourning the loss of her dream. I refused to live with the same remorse. "I don't think I could stand the idea that if I'd tried a little longer, I might not have failed."

"Giving up isn't a failure if it means putting what's best for you first," Ruth said. "I'm all for tenacity, but relentlessly pursuing it will eventually make you miserable."

Maybe. But quitting would too.

Hugh bent closer, allowing us a more private conversation. "So you're stubborn?"

"I'm passionate. I've always wanted to act." Smiling, I recalled one of my earliest inspirations. "After seeing *Gone with the Wind*, I pestered my mother into using one of our drapes to make me a dress. It was nothing like Scarlett's, the fabric brown and green in a Western motif. Cowboys and lassos."

He rested an elbow on the table. "I imagine it looked more like you were about to attend a rodeo than save the family plantation."

"Exactly. My father had this bored look when I insisted on showing him my reenactment. He was snoring by the time I raised my fist, pretending to be Scarlett, and said, 'As God is my witness, I'll never be hungry again.'" I imitated the action.

Hugh stared at me. "You're different, Vivian Mackenzie."

I hummed with a roll of my eyes and took a sip.

"It's not an insult. The girls I go out with are—"

"Talented?"

"Dull. But it comes with the job."

I'd heard about the sham dates studios set up for their stars to generate a certain image and increase interest in their films. I always wondered when I saw a picture in the paper if it was real or set up.

"And I'm, what, entertaining?"

He paused as if choosing his words carefully. "You make an impression."

"What kind of impression?"

In an industry where looks trumped talent—where boring but beautiful got you a contract—I wasn't the impression-leaving type. With dark brown hair falling past my shoulders, a proportioned figure, and hazel eyes, I was more girl next door than starlet. Back home I turned heads. But this wasn't home.

"I mean you're memorable." His attention drifted over my bare shoulders, my neck, my face. "Maybe a one and only."

Chairs scraped against the floor as Ruth and Dean stood. "We're going to dance," she said. "Care to join?"

Hugh offered me his hand. "What do you say?"

The face of his wristwatch caught my eye, and my heart sank. I hadn't planned on staying long.

One dance wouldn't hurt.

Who was I fooling? One would lead to two, three, four . . . "Actually, I should go."

"It's early," Hugh said.

"Not when you work the breakfast shift." I waved as Ruth and Dean walked toward the dance floor.

"Where you headed?" Hugh stood. "We could share a cab."

"You're leaving your celebration?"

He let out a huff, smiling. "We celebrated last week. I wasn't expecting anything tonight, but maybe I should have. Dean can be extravagant. I came to meet Ruth."

Sharing a cab would give us an opportunity to talk more, but I had my car. "I drove here." Champagne fizzed down my spine. Would it be too forward to have him take me home? "But if it's not out of your way . . ."

His gaze latched on mine. "I'll drive you home."

CHAPTER FOUR

Vivian

then

My car's rusty passenger door screeched as Hugh opened it for me, making me inwardly cringe, and then he handed me a paper cup.

On our way out, I'd caught the scent of a freshly brewed pot of coffee and remarked how good it would taste if it wasn't so late, so he'd troubled a waiter for a cup of decaf. Because he couldn't only be tall, dark, and handsome—TDH. He had to be a perfect gentleman too.

As he got in on the other side, I couldn't decide if it was more embarrassing or more comical for an actor who could have any woman he wanted to drive this hunk of junk. My car roared to life, and I mentally sighed while soft piano notes came from the radio alongside Nat King Cole singing "Too Young."

"Where am I going?"

I motioned ahead. "East."

Neon signs from the rows of stores and restaurants lit the night sky as he pulled onto the street. I sipped my coffee, the warm liquid spreading to my belly.

"Is it any good?" he asked.

"Yes."

"I should have gotten one. Can I try it?"

I gave him a bright smile. "No."

Why was I playing hard to get?

He grinned, slowing for a car pulling out of the Sunset Tower Hotel. "I feel like I'm playing *Twenty Questions*. Have you heard it on the radio?"

"Maybe," I sang, using one of the other answer choices on the show.

"You want to play?" His gaze snapped to mine. "But instead of choosing something to guess, we ask about each other. I bet we can get to twenty by the time I get you home."

Why would a man like him want to know about someone who had been too awkward to talk to boys in school and who served pancakes for a living?

There was only one boy in my grade I had ever approached, and only because he was good at shop class. I was about fourteen when I asked him to fix my bike—my primary means of transportation. He agreed in exchange for a kiss. Which I didn't give him. Not then, at least. Instead, I took my bike to Willie, who owned a repair shop. When the cost to fix it was more than I had, I bartered a deal: I kept the lonely old man company while he did the repair.

"All right." I unglued my thighs from the leather seat and turned toward him. Answering questions would be worth it if I got to ask my own. "But let's make this more interesting. How about each question gets a follow-up that doesn't have to be a yes, no, or maybe answer?" I pointed for him to turn right.

He nodded. "Fair enough."

"Are you originally from the West Coast?"

"Yes."

"Where?"

"San Diego," he said. "How about you? East Coast, right?"

"Yes." The obvious follow-up hung there, and I thought of my audition notes: *Needs to lose the accent.* Instead of trying to hide it, I'd lean into it. If he laughed, it would be because I wanted him to. "Long Island."

He smacked the steering wheel. "I thought Boston."

I choked on a sip, unable to find it in me to be offended. "The nerve."

"Sorry." His face scrunched in a smile that could only be described as sexy.

My heart flipped, which was sure to negatively affect my health. I was bound for embarrassment in the afterlife when everyone found out my heart attack had stemmed from the sight of someone's smile. "Are you under twenty-five?"

A strand of black hair swung across his forehead as he shook his head. "I *am* twenty-five." At a red light, he pinned me with calculated eyes. "Twenty-two?"

Casting directors often pegged me for eighteen, so Hugh's assessment took me by surprise. "Nice guess." I pointed for him to turn left onto Santa Monica Boulevard.

"Ruth told Dean, and he told me."

I feigned dismay. "You *cheated*?" Because Ruth hadn't mentioned we'd be meeting Dean's friend, I'd assumed Hugh didn't know about me either.

He did the scrunched-face smile again, rolling down the window, then withdrew a pack of cigarettes from his coat pocket. "Prior knowledge isn't cheating. That was your question, by the way." When he held the pack in my direction, I took one. "Can you grab one for me too?"

"Yeah." I tugged out the car lighter and lit both. "And that was *your* question."

"Damn." He blew smoke out the window. "All right, your turn."

A warm breeze swept through the car as I rolled down my window and debated my next question. "Did it take you a long time to land a contract?"

I'd gone through an eternity of waiting. The rise and fall of the Roman Empire had to have been faster.

"Define 'a long time.'"

"More than four years."

He hesitated. "No. A few months. Three or four."

Three or four *months*? I laughed. Not because it was funny but because it came so easily for some people. I didn't resent him for it, but still it hurt. Laughing made it hurt less.

Sometimes I felt stupid for attempting to make it big, especially because I wasn't getting anywhere. My mother needed help back home.

She worked at a rinky-dink factory arranging industrial parts on a conveyor belt. Every day she wore coveralls and a bandanna over her hair like some down-on-her-luck Rosie the Riveter. But I felt sick whenever I thought of giving up. I couldn't let the savings she gave me, which I'd used to get to LA, be for nothing.

Hugh only gave a sad smile. "Have you gone to a lot of auditions since moving here?"

"Define 'a lot,'" I mimicked.

"Let's say over twenty."

The stack of rejections hanging on the nail in my room came to mind. If more than twenty was a lot, I'd become hopeless. "Yes."

When I opened my mouth to ask my next question, he lifted a finger. I'd forgotten his follow-up.

Hugh slowed as a couple hurried across the street and to the sidewalk in front of the Formosa Cafe. "What kind of roles were they?"

"Dramas." I lowered my voice a little as I gazed at him from under my lashes. "I'm a serious actress."

"How about comedy? You're funny."

"Amusing isn't the same as funny."

Amusing I could agree with. Funny? No. But it didn't matter. Who wanted to slum it in comedy when there was the refined world of drama?

I was raised on matinees with Mom, where I became engrossed in the latest picture and escaped my life. There were no parents fighting, like at home. No screaming, no crying. Instead, I became immersed in a world where the good guys won and the bad guys got punished. Dreams were reached and true love prevailed.

I desperately wanted that: to be someone else—anywhere else.

Acting gave me that ability. The ability to be in a picture-perfect world where everything was scripted and there were no surprises. I knew my role, and while everything might go topsy-turvy, it would right itself by the end. It gave me some semblance of stability, if only for a while.

"I'd be willing to take you to the studio and show you around." He stubbed out his cigarette in the ashtray. "Introduce you to some people."

I stubbed mine out too. "You would?" Dean hadn't even offered introductions to Ruth. "I don't want help getting a role." Help came with owing favors. I'd been down that road and wouldn't go back.

"I couldn't get you one even if I wanted to." He pointed at my coffee, raising an eyebrow in question, and I let him have it. After taking a sip, he peered at the cup, and the tip of his tongue caught a drop on the rim.

My throat went dry.

When I gestured for him to go right, he turned onto my road, past a CINEMA sign with a flickering red M.

"My apartment's there. The peach one." It was the new but inexpensive dingbat style popping up everywhere. Women-only but not the stuffy, chaperoned dormitory kind. "Want to come up to call for a taxi?"

As soon as the words were out, I pictured the state of the apartment. Were any of Ruth's stockings or my bras out?

"Yes." We got out of the car and he handed over my keys and coffee. "Did that count as your question?"

"Yeah, but so did yours. Is your new film a drama?"

"Yes." He followed me up the stairs, close enough for the inviting heat of him to roll over me.

"Did you have to kiss anyone in it?" With only the glow of the lampposts, it was easier to ask awkward questions.

His eyes darted to my mouth as we reached the landing. "Yes."

I'd never brought a man here, and my nerves rioted with the desire for it to mean more than it did. Even unlocking my apartment door with him beside me felt intimate.

I flipped the light switch.

Nothing. Off, on. Off, on.

"Problem?" Hugh asked.

It would have been less embarrassing for someone to put me out of my misery, leaving me to the ghosts' ridicule, than to explain the problem to a man I'd already put on a pedestal.

"Ruth lost her job." Again. I headed to the living room and set down the keys and coffee. "We got behind on the electric bill."

He scanned the room, too shadowed with the faint streetlight coming through the windows to allow him to make out the scratched legs of a secondhand chair or our sofa's faded fabric. "Did she tell Dean?"

"I doubt it." She wanted him to see her as responsible. I motioned to the phone on a table next to the sofa. It was the last bill I paid, so it would work. "Help yourself."

While ordering a cab, Hugh picked up a pen and scrawled across an old *Life* magazine with Esther Williams on the cover. He hung up and tucked his hands in his pockets. "Have *you* kissed anyone in a role? Like when you were on Broadway?"

"No. Did you have to prepare to kiss your co-star?"

"No."

"Why not?"

"Because I already know how to kiss." He stepped closer. "Are you afraid to kiss in front of the cameras?"

"Yes."

"Why?"

I'd be a disaster. Laughed off set.

I waved him off. "Oh, I don't know. It would be awkward with everyone watching."

"Remember, no lying."

"Fine." I found the perfume I'd left on the coffee table and misted my wrist to occupy myself with anything but his reaction. "I've never really kissed anyone."

Not according to Ruth, who said pecks didn't count.

The car I'd saved up for by graduation needed work, and Willie couldn't repair it out of the kindness of his heart, so I went back to the boy who was good at shop. He made the same offer. This time I took it. It seemed like a decent trade for our lips barely grazing here and there. But when he shoved his tongue in my mouth, I slapped him, and he stopped helping.

Not long after that, I met my agent, Walter Row. A man who left me with no interest in being physical with anyone. Until now.

"You're serious? Men must have wanted to kiss you." Hugh said it with such confidence, a shiver ran through me.

I shrugged a shoulder. "Have we finished twenty questions yet?"

"I could show you what to expect if you'd like." He took my hand and brought my wrist to his nose, inhaling, then lightly hummed.

The sound zipped up my spine. "Okay." My heart pounded so hard, it came out as a whisper.

He blinked at me for a moment. Was he truly surprised I'd taken him up on his offer? Not only did I need to learn, but I wanted to know what it was like to kiss him.

"There are two kinds. The film kind and the real kind." He stepped back, letting my hand fall. "In the picture I just finished, I played a soldier who came home from war believing the woman I loved had moved on. When I found out she'd waited for me, this is how I kissed her."

It was like a clapper board snapped and someone called, *Action!* In a moment, his eyes widened like he hadn't thought he'd see me again. With one step, his arms encircled me and his lips crashed against mine.

Goosebumps rushed down my arms. The woodsy scent of his after-shave surrounded me as he held me like I was all that mattered in the world. Though I'd seen none of his films, his acting was impressive, because in those few seconds he convinced me I was precious.

When he released me, I brought a hand to my heart to check if it'd come loose.

It was exactly like the kisses I'd seen in pictures a hundred times, when violins played in the background, rising to the moment the doe-eyed dame and the hunky gent could no longer hide that they were gone for each other.

His chest rose and fell. "That's a film kiss. If you have to do it, let your co-star take the lead. They never last longer than three seconds."

I brushed my fingertips across my lips. "You said there was an-other kind. How is it different?" Of course, I'd seen kisses outside of movies, but I was dying to hear him describe it.

"You'll want to be more"—his gaze traveled down my body—"involved."

"Such as?"

"Touching." He took my hand and brought it to his chest. My fingertips slipped under his suit coat. "It's not like in films. Your hands can move. Explore." His sights locked on my mouth. "Lips part and tongues meet."

I'd stopped breathing normally. "It sounds very orchestrated. Lots of moving parts."

"It's not complicated. It's less thinking and more—"

"Doing?"

He smiled. "I was going to say 'fun,' but yes."

My chest constricted with the need for everything he'd said. I tipped my chin up, bold in the dark. "Show me."

His smile fell as he looped one arm around my back. It was like the world slowed to half speed. I fisted his lapels as he kissed me.

It was softer this time, more experimental—like learning the exact curve of each other's lips. The top, then the bottom. His mouth was patient as it led the way, the rhythm of pulling back and coming together again forcing any worries over how well I could do this to melt.

He drew me flush against him while his tongue skimmed the seam of my lips, coaxing them apart to dip inside. A breathy groan left him at the contact, and sparks flew down my body.

Hugh kissed with expert, sensual care. Like every second, every stroke, every nibble and glide of his mouth, was purposeful.

I never wanted to stop. Who needed to eat or work or sleep when there was *this*?

He slid a hand into my hair, tugging gently to allow the perfect angle for his mouth to explore my neck. I dragged my hands down, and when his coat fell open, I searched the firm expanse of his chest and stomach.

"This is how all kisses should be." I fingered a shirt button, willing myself not to undo it.

"I know. But Hollywood doesn't want to scandalize the masses." He left a trail of kisses up my neck to a spot below my ear. When I gasped, he replaced his lips on mine.

The soft glow of headlights filtered up from the street.

Hugh made an inch-wide gap between us, though it felt like a mile, and stared at my lips like he might kiss me again. He propped a hand on the window frame and peeked out. "Taxi's here."

I deflated but nodded, hugging an arm around my middle. "Thanks for the practice."

He smiled softly—still sexy without the scrunch—as we moved to the door. "If you need more, you have my number."

"I do?"

"I left it on the magazine. And call if you want to see the studio." He took my hand and pressed a kiss to the back of it. "That's a film kiss I do like."

The next moment, he was out the door.

CHAPTER FIVE

Vivian

then

The front door clicked shut the next morning as I grabbed my apron, checking the pocket for my pen and pad, then I smoothed a hand over the buttons of my blue shirtwaist dress uniform to make sure they were all secure.

Ruth was filling a kettle at the sink as I walked out. After setting it on the gas stove and lighting it, she turned toward me and startled.

I smiled. "Boo."

"Jeepers." She brought a hand to her chest. Shadows were under her eyes, not helped by the mascara settled there. "What are you doing up already?" She opened a cupboard, then another. It was the kind of searching someone did when they weren't familiar with another person's kitchen.

"I have work. What are *you* doing up?" I couldn't imagine what time she and Dean had left Mocambo. I tossed my apron on the counter and found a mug. "Forget where we keep them?"

Her head fell with a small groan. "I haven't slept, but I have to leave for an audition in a couple of hours, so I can't now."

I checked the clock. I had five minutes. "Did Dean keep you too busy with his directing? And several encores?"

The corners of her eyes crinkled with her grin. "He's very good."

"At directing or sex?"

"Both."

"Well, now you're just bragging." The reason I knew anything about intimacy was because of her.

"We dug through some boxes of old costume attire and acted out an erotic storyline."

"Like Tarzan and Jane?"

"Or Superman and Lois Lane."

"Cinderella and Prince Charming." I pinched my lips but couldn't fight my laughter.

Ruth came from a wealthy family. She'd had everything: a housekeeper, a chef, a driver. A tennis instructor and piano lessons and a French tutor. But her parents cut off financial support when she left to pursue acting. Her father said it was for easy girls.

"It's not the kind of performing Daddy thought I'd be doing when I packed my bags." She wiggled her eyebrows. "But all experience is good experience, right?"

I brought a hand to my mouth in mock horror. "Floozy."

She grabbed a floral tea towel and flicked it against my hip. "Virgin. I'd love to see you find someone you liked so I could hear about *your* dalliances for a change."

My heart pounded alongside flashes of last night. Hugh's mouth on mine. His hand in my hair. My gasp when he—

Ruth's gaze narrowed. "Why are your cheeks red?"

I fetched the instant coffee and propped a hip against the counter to get a good look at her reaction. "We kissed."

"'We' meaning . . . Hugh?" Her jaw went utterly slack.

"You look ridiculous."

"I'm surprised."

"You kissed Dean on your first date." I rested my chin in my palm. "Come to think of it, you did more than kiss."

The kettle whistled. "But you weren't on a date. Besides, this is you we're talking about."

"Practically a leper, I know." I stepped around her and turned off the stove.

"That's not what I meant. You must like him."

She made no move toward her mug, so I scooped out a portion of coffee, noting there were about two servings left, and poured the water. "What's not to like about TDH?" When she tilted her head, I added, "Tall, Dark, and Handsome."

Ruth stared. "You gave him a nickname."

I tipped my hand back and forth in a *Sort of* motion. "It's more of a descriptor."

She picked up her coffee, an uncharacteristically contemplative look on her face.

"What, you hate it?" I asked. "We can come up with another name."

"No. It's perfect."

It didn't sound like she thought it was perfect. "What aren't you saying?" She stirred and stirred. "Ruth."

"We're going out again tonight," she blurted. "Hugh's taking his co-star, Peggy Harris. Dean said the studio wants to show a budding romance between them."

Ice pricked my heart.

Pretending Hugh would risk his image so he could go out with me would have been delusional. Like Marlon Brando dating, I don't know, a seamstress. Even if he wanted to, the studio wouldn't have approved of him being with a nobody like me. Of course, as a director, Dean wasn't subject to those rules.

"I'm not sure he has feelings for her," Ruth went on. "Apparently, Hugh was in a serious relationship with a woman from back home until about a year ago. She broke his heart, and he hasn't dated seriously since."

"It's all right."

Her hand stilled. "You sure?"

It was easy to pretend I was fine. I used to do it all the time with my mother.

Mom never knew how deeply everything between her and my father affected me. I wanted to protect her, but there was nothing I could do, so I pretended not to hear plates shattering or doors slamming. Never questioned the times she told me to pack my things, saying we were leaving, though we never made it out the door. I would have done anything to alleviate her burden, and if I acted fine, she didn't have to worry about me.

"Of course." All I needed was to forget how Hugh's lips tasted and the press of his body against mine. Easy-peasy. "Honestly, I could use another friend." There was even the perfect excuse to call: He'd offered to show me the studio.

Since there was no reason to play it cool, I rang him that afternoon when I got home from my shift. His voice sent a flutter to my belly I attempted to swat away as we made plans to go out the next day.

Ruth walked in, flipping on the kitchen lights as we hung up.

The power was on.

Normally I'd have asked how her audition went, but this couldn't wait. "Did you go down to get the power turned back on?"

Her eyes were half-open. She must have been exhausted. "They shut it off?"

Apparently, she hadn't.

I rang the electric company to thank them for turning it back on with an assurance I'd have a portion of what we owed that week. But the woman on the other end said it was already paid in full.

Her lips smacked like she was chewing gum. "Handsome fella sorted it all out for you, ma'am."

There was only one man who knew our power was off.

Why would Hugh do that? I didn't know anyone who would do something so kind without motivation.

I let my head fall back on the sofa. It didn't matter. I'd pay him back.

◆

The next day, after another shift, I changed into a simple polka dot dress with a wide black belt. A knock came at the door as I walked into the kitchen.

I'd hoped to meet Hugh downstairs so he wouldn't see our apartment in broad daylight, but I should have known a gentleman like him wouldn't simply honk the horn.

"Come on in." Ruth opened the door for him. "Don't mind the mess."

"Don't mind the mess" was something her mother said when guests came over. The ironic part was that because they had a housekeeper, there never *was* a mess. Our apartment, on the other hand, was in perpetual disarray.

"It's fine." Hugh stepped in wearing a casual short-sleeved button-down, the top button undone.

"Don't say that." I hid dirty mugs in the sink. "She needs to be gently bullied into doing something around here."

Ruth crossed her arms. "If that's what you've been doing, you've been too gentle, because it went over my head." She glanced at Hugh. "Vivian is the best. Did she tell you how she took me under her wing in New York?"

"No. Is that where you met?"

She nodded. "At rehearsal. We were both cast as replacements in *Annie Get Your Gun*."

I only got a bit part because of my agent. He knew the casting director, and I needed a leg up, so he offered an introduction. Said the fella owed him one. It was a carrot dangling in front of me and, starved, I latched on to it.

The favor came at a cost. At that point in my life, I was familiar with bartering pieces of myself to get what I needed. Walter said he wanted time with me. I was too naive to know better.

"Technically, we met in the ladies' room." I was running late after stopping at my agent's office. I kept telling myself, *It was worth it*. All I could do to keep from crying. When I reached the rehearsal studio, I headed to the ladies' room, needing to splash my face.

Only someone was already in there.

"I was sobbing because I had nowhere to go," Ruth said. "I'd worn out my welcome with every friend in the city. But the alternative was to give up acting and go home."

I gave her a small smile. "Between the sniffling and the hiccupping, I couldn't understand half of what she was saying. She kept talking about a doll collection."

"I was asking if you thought I should sell them." She pointed at three porcelain dolls sitting on a shelf in the living room. "Those are the only ones I could fit in my suitcases when I left home."

Hugh's gaze caught mine, eyes going wide as he brought a hand to the side of his face so she wouldn't see him mouth, *Really?*

I held back a laugh. If only he knew how many she'd accumulated since then.

"And you said no?" he asked. There was an unspoken *Why?*

I lifted my hands at my sides. "I thought she was trying to give them to me."

Ruth wiped the corner of her eye, like she was seconds from shedding a tear over the thought of their loss. "Vivian said I could stay at her place until I got on my feet."

But she never really did.

I bet you're thinking Ruth took advantage of me, since she couldn't hold down a job, so she rarely contributed financially. You have to understand, though: I was in a bad place when we met, and she was a ray of sunshine, convinced things would work out for us. I needed that kind of optimism at a time when I'd lost my self-worth.

When the Broadway production ended, we left it all behind. I might not have had any confidence, but I was still determined to give myself the life my mother didn't have—in my career and, someday, in love.

Until we crossed the country, I wondered if at some point Ruth would give up and go home, where she wouldn't have to worry about running out of food or the possibility of being evicted. That she rarely complained told me all I needed to know about how much she wanted to reach her dream.

"Sounds like a good friend." Hugh smiled in a way that snatched the air from my lungs.

"Like I said: the best." Ruth looked at me with soft eyes. "You'll love her."

CHAPTER SIX

Vivian

then

Hugh's cornflower-blue Pontiac had a white roof and no rust. A stark contrast to my Ford jalopy. He pulled onto the road and motioned to the red shoebox sitting between us. "For you."

Inside lay an elegant pair of black pumps. I slowly turned to him. People weren't that nice. What did he want?

He peeked at me. "You're looking at me like I murdered your entire family."

"A second cousin, at least."

He let out a short laugh. "I felt bad for breaking your other shoe."

"Oh." My insides melted as I brushed my fingertips across the satin heel. "You have impeccable taste."

"That's all Ruth. I phoned to see if I could take the others to a shoe fixer—"

"A *cobbler*." I bit my lip to hold back a smile.

"—because you said they were your mother's lucky heels. But then I thought maybe you could use a new pair." He eyed me with a grin. "Make your own luck."

Ruth must have been happy to supply my size, because when I kicked off my flats, the heels were a perfect fit. For the first time, I looked refined. At least from the knees down.

I leaned over to kiss his cheek. "Thank you."

I would get my mother's fixed eventually. She bought them after we moved into our apartment. They were the first purchase she made without needing my father's approval.

When she was exhausted from work or overwhelmed with bills, Mom slipped on her heels and put on an upbeat Billie Holiday tune for us to swing dance to across the linoleum floor. The shoes represented a new beginning, and as Hugh drove through the studio gates, I admired my new ones and decided he was right: I was ready to make my own luck. Maybe, like Mom's, they would represent my new beginning.

Hugh cruised around the backlots, pointing out New England Street and the Railroad Depot. Verona Square, first used for a *Romeo and Juliet* adaptation, and a boat dock. Copperfield Court and Billy the Kid Street.

Finally, we circled to the main lot, where Hugh led me to the soundstage where most of his recent movie had been shot. He flipped a couple of switches on metal spotlights as we walked in, and I wandered to the set of a gymnasium decorated for a school dance.

"What scene happened here?" I lifted my arms at my sides.

"It's where Peggy—she plays Marcia—and I have our first kiss before we graduate high school and I go off to war."

He reached for a record player on a nearby table off set. Louis Armstrong's "A Kiss to Build a Dream On" filled the air, and I twirled, letting my dress flow around me.

Hugh held out a hand as he came up to me. "We never got a dance the other night."

Without a thought, my hand was in his, and he drew me close to sway alongside the jazz song's low trumpets.

"Thank you again for the heels. And for getting my power turned back on."

"You're welcome," he murmured in my ear, holding me close.

"I'm not used to people doing favors for me without expecting something in return."

"I don't expect anything"—he stepped back to twirl me—"but it doesn't mean I'm not already getting something."

The urge to kiss him spread through my chest like a blaze, which was dangerous, given what Ruth had said about him going out with Peggy. Sham or not.

When he made to twirl me again, I let his hand go and faked a smile. "Tell me more about your movie."

His face fell, his hand still hanging in the air before slowly dropping to his side. "All right." The song screeched, coming to a stop as he lifted the tonearm, and then he plopped into a chair marked KELLER and rested an elbow on the back. "Dean would kill me if he saw me sitting here." He pointed at a stack of papers at the edge of the set. "There's a script."

Excitement tore through me. When I was a child, I wrote my own stories. Most of the time they were original. But once in a while a film didn't resolve how I wanted it to, so I would change it. I never cared for tragic or bittersweet endings—I had enough sorrow in my own life—so my versions were only happily-ever-afters.

"How about"—he thumbed through another one—"page eighty-two. Wanna try it?"

I read the introduction to the scene—not the one in the gymnasium but one where his co-star climbed ten flights of stairs to see the man she loved waiting for her at their special place on the rooftop. I motioned around me. "There are no stairs."

"You're an actress, right?" He raised his eyebrows in challenge as he grabbed a clapper board. "And—action." He snapped it.

Spotlights beat down on me, sweat beading on my neck. He had to be kidding. But he only crossed his arms, waiting with a faint smile.

I tossed the script aside. If he was going to be a smart aleck, I would give it right back.

Craning my neck, I tented a hand over my brow to shield my eyes from the light and peered up, whistling like there was an endless back-and-forth of multiple flights of stairs. He chuckled while I mimed shoving my sleeves up.

This couldn't be how the character had been played, but I didn't care. Arms swinging, I made a show of dashing up the stairs. At the "top," I ran my hands over my hair and patted wrinkles out of my dress. I charged up the next flight, only stopping to fake pulling out a compact and powdering my nose. His continued laughter urged me on.

After another flight, I staggered and caught my breath, wiping my brow with the back of my hand. Then, using a railing that wasn't really there, I dragged myself up step after step, each one more agonizing than the last. Halfway up, I groaned.

Hugh laughed so hard, I almost cracked a smile.

Something came over me when he snapped the clapper board. His laughter consumed me. I wanted more.

With my hands on my knees, huffing and puffing, I glanced up once more. I let my knees give out, dropping to the floor, and clawed my way up one more flight. Finally, I moaned and collapsed like I'd fainted.

Footsteps came near. When he nudged my leg with the tip of his shoe, my eyes snapped open.

He smiled down at me. "You only made it halfway."

I pointed at how far I'd come. "After all that?" I waved him off, my voice weary. "You're not worth it."

Clapping and hearty laughter came from the darkness behind the director's chair. A middle-aged woman stepped into the light wearing a pillbox hat, a purse slung over her arm.

I sat up, my heart jumping in every direction.

"Shit," Hugh whispered, then pasted on a charming smile. "Mrs. Mills."

"For the last time, it's Judy." She redirected her attention to me. "You are quite the comedian."

Mills? As in Eugene Mills, the head of MGM Studios?

Judy must be his wife, and I'd made a fool of myself in front of her.

"We were only clowning around." Hugh helped me up. "This is my friend—"

"Vivian Mackenzie." I offered my hand and she took it.

"Pleasure. You have a little . . ." She motioned to my head, then brought a fist to her mouth to conceal a grin.

I reached up and found a colossal dust bunny attached to my hair.

Judy wiped the corner of her eye. "I haven't laughed that hard in ages."

Hugh aimed a scrunched-face smile my way. "Vivian is a serious actress." He lowered his voice like I'd done the other night.

"Under contract?" she asked.

I shook my head like a bobblehead.

She scrutinized me for a moment. "Well, I was only passing by. My husband never stops working, so I dropped off some supper. Nice to meet you, Vivian." She chuckled again as she walked back through the darkness.

I turned to Hugh. "What was that?"

A few days later I found out exactly what it was when Hugh rang to say Judy Mills had told him about a role her husband was having trouble casting and I should audition for.

You have to understand, no one asked me to do auditions back then. And it wasn't just anyone who'd asked but the studio head's wife.

My behind nearly missed the chair when I fell onto it. "What kind of film is it?"

"A comedy."

My excitement nosedived. "I don't do comedy."

"You did when Judy watched, and you're good at it."

What Judy had seen was me goofing around. "I'm amusing."

"You're hilarious." When I kept quiet, he went on. "Listen, what's the worst that could happen? You don't get the part? Then you don't get a part you weren't sure you wanted."

He had a point, but I wasn't ready to give up my dream, which didn't include a lick of comedy.

"Think about it. A producer named Gerard Donovan is going to be getting in touch with you soon."

CHAPTER SEVEN

Vivian

then

"Soon" turned out to be two weeks later. When Gerard's secretary phoned to schedule an audition, I agreed, but in the meantime Dean mentioned a *Julius Caesar* remake I should try for.

Julius. Caesar.

It was exactly the kind of film I hoped to land. Problem was, auditions were in the middle of my shift. I'd skipped work for one last month, and my boss had said if I did it again, he'd fire me.

I mulled it over with Ruth.

Standing in the kitchen, wearing the fitted white shorts she'd used to play tennis in, Ruth set a bottle of ketchup and half a loaf of bread on the counter, then gazed back into the fridge like a ham roast might appear. "You have to do it. We'll figure out the money part."

She said *we* when *I* would have to figure it out. And what if this time I didn't find another job? How desperate would I get? I'd hit rock bottom before and couldn't again.

"You know those . . . photos," I said. "The ones I did for money."

She aimed an intense stare at me. "You're never going to have to do that again. I wish I'd known you then. I would have . . ." She rested a hand on mine. "I would have helped."

I squeezed her hand, knowing it was true, though back then she had left home and didn't have money either. We were both alone. At least now we had each other.

Ruth gave me a squeeze too, then went back to the fridge.

"What exactly are you going to make?" I narrowed my eyes at the ingredients on the counter.

She found a chunk of cheddar and held it up, triumphant.

"Grilled cheese?" I flipped the ketchup bottle onto its top so the remaining half-inch could slide down.

"And tomato soup."

"We don't have any."

"Dipped in ketchup is close enough."

I scrunched my nose at the combination.

"You really only need to eat every other day." She set a pan on the stove. "It's called fasting. Scientists in Chicago discovered it and tested it on rats."

All the food talk made my stomach rumble. "Scientists discovered it? It's in the Bible, Ruth. It's millenniums old."

"Well, if it's good enough for God, it's good enough for me."

"I don't think you're the picture of purity he's looking for."

She stuck out her tongue and handed me the remaining cheese after her two meager slices. "Eat and go to the audition."

My stomach was too tense over the probability of losing my job. "I'll hurl."

"Then save it for after." She motioned to my dress pocket.

I sputtered before landing on a reply. "You want me to channel Shakespeare while stowing cheddar in my dress? *Julius Caesar* with pocket cheese?"

Regardless of the consequences, I decided to go. I was in LA to be an actress. To do drama. I'd risk anything to get it.

———————— ◆ ————————

I stood in line with a dozen other women outside a closed door, fidgeting with a loose thread on my dress while I studied the script.

A woman with a clipboard came out and called a few names. It wasn't until she went through them a second time that my name registered.

"That's me."

I trailed her and two other women dressed better than me into a room. A bright light shone in the middle while, in front, three men waited behind a desk with a stack of paper, blue-gray cigarette smoke curling around them.

Sweat dotted my back. I slowly exhaled.

A young woman with auburn hair went first and, with a natural Southern accent, delivered the lines fairly well. She seemed sweet. Soft-spoken and exuding an innocence akin to that of Doris Day. Once finished, she gave a winning smile.

The casting director peered at her over his glasses, the cigarette between his stubby fingers dropping ashes outside the ashtray. "Where you from, honey?"

"Georgia."

"Georgia," he said under his breath like a curse, pushing his glasses up the bridge of his nose. "And you thought a Southern belle could be in *Julius Caesar*?"

Jiminy Cricket. He was one of *them*. The kind who would eat you for breakfast.

"I . . . um . . ."

"Luckily for you, I happen to know a guy looking for a Georgia peach," he went on. "If you can string a sentence together, I might pass your name along."

She clasped her hands. "I'd be grateful for the opportunity."

The man standing to one side of the casting director dragged a thumb up and down the inside of his suspenders. "She'd be real grateful." To the casting director's other side, a man wearing a tweed vest and a bow tie snickered like he was in on a joke they all knew.

My blood surged, my pulse flickering in my wrists.

They dismissed her and called the next girl, a brunette named Betty with a smattering of freckles across her cheeks. She walked up with the kind of confidence I could never replicate. Within seconds of her starting, I forgot where I was. It didn't matter that there were no cos-tumes or sets. She sold me on the part with her timing and delivery. I wanted to run over and hug her; she was that good.

The casting director crushed out his cigarette, then reclined in his chair with crossed arms. "Where you from, doll face?"

"Los Angeles." Betty tipped her chin up, pride in her voice, and the men gave each other knowing nods, like being born here was a reasonable explanation for her talent.

You've heard of Betty, right? Betty Burke. Not long ago, it came out that she was the result of an affair her mother, a makeup artist, had had with a high-profile actor with prominent ears. She'd had her daughter's ears pinned so her husband wouldn't suspect she wasn't his.

The casting director wrote a note on his clipboard. "All right, next."

As Betty and I switched places, the casting director tilted his head like he was mildly intrigued.

I could do this. If I wanted it badly enough, I could do it. And I wanted it more than anything.

I cleared my throat. Quieted my mind. Then began.

The lines appeared in my head, one after another, as if a typewriter clacked out the words the second before I needed them. I could almost hear the margin bell alerting me that I was close to the end. The next part flowed, my voice straining to deliver it to the best of my ability, then—

My mind went kaput. Completely, utterly, blank.

Shit. *Shit.* I knew this. *Back up.*

My hands trembled so hard as I raised the script, my eyes couldn't focus.

"You can stop right there."

My heart thudded. I could have done better. I should have.

"I don't even have to ask, but how about you tell me." When I didn't immediately respond, the casting director arched a graying eye-brow. "Where're you from?"

"Long Island."

"You ever have any voice lessons? Acting lessons?"

"Yes. Acting." Not since living in Manhattan, but he didn't need to know that.

He folded his arms on the table. "Here's what I'm gonna do. And don't take this the wrong way, but I'm doing you a kindness, 'kay?"

"Yes, sir."

"You can't act. Can you sing?" He shrugged. "Doesn't matter, because you can't act."

I flinched.

Can't act. Can't act. Can't act.

I blinked back tears. Despite having grown a thicker skin, hearing that I was terrible at what I loved never got easy.

He glanced at the man in suspenders. "Anything else?"

Yes, please go on. I wasn't yet mortified enough to tear up the floorboards and hide.

The man hooked a thumb into his waistband and leered at me. "She's pretty."

"You are," the casting director said. "You're real pretty. Would make some fella a lucky husband. Can you cook?"

Betty let out a high-pitched cackle from where she stood against the wall, making my insides ripple with embarrassment.

"I've never really tried." When my mother started working, I became responsible for my own breakfasts, lunches, and dinners, but they were simple, like sandwiches or tinned spaghetti.

The director nodded like he'd come up with a solution he was quite proud of. "Here's what you're going to do. You're gonna go back home and sign up for cooking classes. Then you're gonna have your mother tell all her friends you're available. They'll tell their sons, and I bet my bottom dollar you'll be married by the end of the year."

Twist the knife a little more, why don't you? I hadn't quite bled out yet.

I wanted to get married someday, but not so I could cook and clean and be a pretty little wife. I wanted a bigger, fuller life. Maybe I would never have the adventure or grand love of the movies, but after so many years imagining fictional worlds, ordinary wasn't an option.

"Betty?" The director motioned for her to step forward, effectively dismissing me.

I didn't wait to grab my rejection. The nail in my bedroom wall wouldn't have held it anyway.

———————— ✦ ————————

I wallowed. Went to the restaurant to check if I still had a job.

I didn't.

Money had always been tight, but never like this. We were down to a handful of canned goods: green beans and cream of mushroom soup and tinned fish.

Once I summoned the mental fortitude, I brushed myself off and went to my audition with Gerard.

It started like all the others. Studying the script. Filling out a form for him to litter with comments about how I couldn't act. It would sting, but not like the previous one. Mostly because I couldn't take it as seriously.

While waiting in line, I opened my purse and withdrew a notepad and pen.

Dear TDH,

I have to be honest, I'm not sure why I'm writing you. I suppose because I need to get these thoughts out, but I'm too embarrassed to share them. Writing to a diary seemed juvenile. So here we are.

I'm so disheartened over my last audition. It wasn't much different from my other ones, but this one felt final, for some reason. A nail in the coffin.

Will you think I'm pathetic when you find out how lousy I did? Will you think it when I goof up this next one too?

I know we haven't known each other long, but I value your opinion. Maybe it's silly, but I want to impress you, and—

"Vivian Mackenzie?" A woman looked up from her clipboard.

"Yes." I shoved the notepad into my purse and followed her and the two other women also called—one with chestnut brown hair and the other a strawberry blonde with cat-eye makeup. We walked into the same kind of room as all the others with the same kind of man as all the other directors and producers.

Gerard, tall and round, asked me to go first.

My nerves were settled. Calm.

As I delivered the lines, I pictured Hugh there. He'd get a kick out of how, when the script said a door slammed, I stumbled to the floor with a bewildered look on my face, my character assuming it'd been a gunshot. I yelled an annoying "*Ah! Ah! Ah!*" as I dug my heels into the floor and pushed back until I was several feet away.

When the typewriter in my mind tripped over the exact wording of a line, I made it up. Though it was only a mildly amusing ad-lib, Gerard could hardly catch a breath amid his laughter. I worried he would keel over. It was the third time he'd done that since I had started, but he must have been easily entertained.

He swiped a tear from his eye. "Where have you been hiding?"

"Pardon?" Was this the part where he wanted to know where I came from? An underhanded jab at my accent?

"You could have saved me some time by auditioning weeks ago. Before I started losing my hair."

To be fair, he'd lost most of it already.

A producer liked me? It wasn't Hugh or Judy, whose opinions didn't ultimately matter when it came to landing a contract, but someone of importance in hiring.

Gerard grabbed his clipboard and called up Helen, the one with strawberry blonde hair, then moved on to the last woman. They were both funny enough that I smiled. After, he asked me to stick around while the other two were excused.

I'd never been asked that before.

"I want you in my picture. It's called *In Your Eyes*." He slid paper-clipped pages across the table. "I can offer a two-year contract."

My heart pounded like I'd reached a mountaintop. So this was a contract. I'd started to believe their existence was a myth. But there was my name in thick, black handwriting.

"It's all standard," he went on as I flipped through the stack. "MGM can put you in whatever films they want."

"And this?" I skimmed the next section.

"Oh, morals clause. All it means is you won't degrade your image. You know, affairs. Breaking the law. Anything that could negatively impact how the public sees you." A reassuring smile. "Not a problem for a sweetheart like you."

No one could know by looking at me what I did when I thought I had no choice. If the studio found out about the photos—*nude* photos—I'd be finished before I got started.

At my silence, Gerard's gaze narrowed. "Unless there's a skeleton in your closet?"

My hands shook. I closed them to hide it and chuckled. "Little old me?" Not a denial, but his smile returned all the same.

Despite how badly I wanted a contract, I never expected to actually get one. I still was reeling from the idea that a producer *liked me* when the reality of what he offered sank in.

Comedy.

All the times I'd pictured this moment, it had never involved what came from me next.

"Can I think about it?" Turning it down would be hard, but this wasn't the dream. Would Monet have been happy drawing cartoons? I was no Monet, but it didn't change my reservations.

Gerard's nose wrinkled. "What's there to think about? It's more than the blip of a role we usually start people with. We need to get you with Hair and Makeup to decide on your look right away, so I can only give you until tomorrow."

Those words were like hanging a steak in front of a ravenous lion. I cycled through ideas of what they'd come up with and how they'd change my appearance. "Understood."

There was a chance leaving would give him time to second-guess picking me, but taking the contract meant saying goodbye to drama. I needed to make a strategic choice.

I left the room. Before I reached the end of the hallway, my name came around the corner from the nasally voice of the strawberry blonde who had tried out for the same part. Helen.

"She's a less talented Fanny Brice is what she is."

I stopped cold.

"Hey, that's not fair. To Fanny, I mean," said another woman with a laugh. Probably the brunette we'd auditioned with.

I slouched against the wall, my breaths coming and going so fast, I became dizzy.

Of course, I wasn't a comedian. I only got a chance because of Judy's influence. Which meant I might not get another if she thought I'd squandered my opportunity.

Maybe this contract could be a stepping stone. Accepting must lead to something better than what I had. It was a foot in the door. After establishing a rapport with the right people, I'd have leverage to push for something else, even if it took several films to prove myself.

What was the alternative? To keep being told all the things wrong with me? To keep getting rejected? Besides, this was a guaranteed paycheck.

I turned and went back, finding Gerard collecting papers off the table. "I accept."

He held out a pen. "Good decision, kid."

Ignoring the heaviness in my belly from knowing that if anyone found out about the photos, this would all fall apart, I took the pen and signed.

HUGH'S REVOLVING DOOR . . . NO MORE?

Up-and-comer Hugh Fox has been busy making a name for himself at MGM—and among Hollywood's leading ladies. *Gentlemanly, kind, dreamy.* Those are the words these dollies use to describe him after their memorable nights on the town. But if they're so memorable, why hasn't Hugh been seen with any of them more than once?

Let's take an example: Sources say last month Hugh was at Mocambo with director Dean Keller and two skirts. Things looked very cozy on the dance floor between one of the broads and Dean. Hugh, on the other hand, was seen sneaking out with the other, the two driving off in a clunker.

The very next night, Hugh was seen with another woman! None other than "Pretty Peggy" Harris. When we heard they danced the night away, then went their separate ways, we figured that was it for the pair. Yet, only two days later, they were seen together again, this time for dinner at Ciro's. Then later that week at a party.

Maybe Hugh has finally met his match!

CHAPTER EIGHT

Margot

now

Once the tape stops, I grab my phone from the table and type "Vivian Mackenzie" in the search engine. "I was worried she wasn't going to do it."

"Do what?" Leo reaches for his phone too.

"Accept the offer." The whole time Vivian deliberated, I kept thinking, *What are you doing? Don't walk away!* "She was so adamant about drama, I didn't think she'd cave."

"Realistically, how could she turn it down? She was *broke*."

I know a little about what that's like. Growing up, I didn't own brand-name anything. We never took a vacation. Rarely went out to eat. But I never went hungry. Never had to worry about my clothes or shoes falling apart like Vivian did.

We're quiet, both staring at our screens, when Leo lets out a short groan. "Do you know how many Vivian Mackenzies are on social media?"

"She might not have socials. Gram didn't." I scroll through a staff directory before retreating to my search results. "We'll probably have better luck with obits. We're assuming she died, right?"

"Probably. What about Hugh Fox?"

"What about him?" Modern audiences might not recall most of his films, but they'd recognize his name. "He's classic Hollywood. We know that already."

"I don't think I knew that." He turns his phone toward me, displaying a black-and-white photo of Hugh's handsome face.

"Oh!" A thought startles me, and I nearly drop my phone. "Vivian's letter to TDH."

He smiles, making the connection. "It's Hugh."

"I wonder if Vivian made the tapes for him." If so, why did Gram have them? Did she know Hugh? The questions won't stop prodding me, and I hate that Gram isn't here to ask.

"Maybe. How old do you think they are?"

"Gotta be decades." I do a quick search on my phone. "They're probably from between the mid-'60s and mid-'90s."

That means when Vivian recorded these, she was recalling events from over a decade prior, at least. Yet, when she described her auditions, she had fresh emotion in her voice.

That was the most relatable part. I know what it's like to have such a deeply rooted desire, it becomes part of you. How failure follows you like a shadow.

It occurs to me I didn't see Leo walk in with the shoebox. "Where are the rest of the tapes?"

"Back at my place. I need to clean them before we can listen."

My shoulders slump. There's no hiding my disappointment. I want to listen to them all now. Or as many as I can tonight and the rest tomorrow. There is something to uncover here. A connection to Gram to make. It's the piece I've been hoping for, the one to make up for our last missed conversation.

"Is that okay?" Leo sits straighter. "I can go get them now if you want. I just figured—"

"No, it's fine." It's not, and I doubt I'm fooling him, but I have to accept it. I don't know how to clean tapes and can't risk damaging them. "I appreciate your help."

"I'm invested now." He drags the boombox close. "I've got a full day tomorrow, so how about we listen to the next tape the day after?"

In the meantime, I have the last one to find.

The heat of a new day warms my arms as Leo and I walk the path along Rainbow Harbor. Two women wearing joggers and pushing strollers power walk past. To the right, whale watching boats rock idle, while, to the left, restaurants nestle among large swaths of trees and plants.

It feels good to be talking to Leo again. Not that we've communicated much since he came over. Only a couple of texts with the kind of pleasantries I wish we were beyond and an update that I searched Gram's room top to bottom but couldn't find another tape or letter.

He asked if I'd been to the harbor recently, and when I admitted I hadn't, he suggested we come here to listen to the next tape so I could see how the area has evolved since graduation.

Squinting at the sunlight reflecting off the water's surface, I push my sunglasses off the top of my head and slide them over my eyes. "I can't get over how much has changed."

While Gram's isn't far, I didn't consider coming here when I visited. Now I wish I had. There's a twinge in my stomach at seeing how life has moved on without me. At the same time, I'm proud of its developments.

Kind of like how it feels to see Leo again.

"It brings in more tourists, which is good for business," he says. "But it still feels like home, you know?"

A group of kids on bikes speeds toward us. In an instant, Leo turns to me, his hands on my upper arms and his back to them, like he might shield me from an accidental collision. His body presses against mine, my cheek brushing the soft cotton of his shirt. I inhale the familiar scent of his detergent—and something else. Something that wasn't there when we hugged at the music store. Is he wearing cologne?

The kids zip past, neither of us pulling away. My face grows hot with how close we are, his heart beating hard under my ear while the bikes become a faint whir of spinning wheels in the distance.

Leo stares down at me, his eyes dark and stormy, and I recognize that look. It's the one I analyzed at sixteen when his hands glided over every inch of my back, covering me with sunscreen at the beach. At seventeen, after his family returned from a six-week road trip over summer break, and I was so happy to see him I jumped into his arms, my legs encircling his waist. The look I finally understood at eighteen when he peeled my shirt off.

Stop. I shut my eyes and will the images to fade.

I knew cleaning out Gram's place would be full of complicated feelings, and reconnecting with Leo has been an unexpected but welcome reprieve. Hopefully, by the end of the tapes, we'll have a rekindled friendship we can maintain when I leave. Considering anything more is pointless. It'd be a short-lived fling, and then we'd be back to where we were before I came home.

When I straighten, he blinks, stepping back.

"I called my mom yesterday to ask about the tapes," I say as we start walking again.

"And?"

"She's not familiar with them and doesn't know anyone named Vivian."

"Maybe Vivian and your grandma were old friends."

It's possible. "Vivian could have left acting and ended up a switchboard operator like Gram." I always wondered if she listened to anyone's calls. I would have been too nosy not to.

"Or what about long-lost sisters? Vivian's dad left. He could've had children with someone else."

"It's what my dad did."

The idea that Gram—that I—could be related to Vivian hits me with a flash of excitement. A relative who *kissed* Hugh Fox.

"I asked my mom too," he says. "I thought Vivian could have been someone local. But she hasn't heard of her."

An image of a woman with the same eyes as Leo floods my mind. "How is your mom? Does she still quilt?" I have one of her creations folded across the back of my couch. It was a graduation present and has only gotten cozier with age.

"On and off. Sometimes she'll mix it up with something else, like crochet."

A gasp passes between my lips. "That Mrs. Ruiz always was a rebel."

Leo laughs. "How about your mom?"

"She's good. Still in DC." Mom moved after I left for college. The consulting job fell into her lap, but she would have turned it down if Gram hadn't insisted it was a great opportunity and said not to worry, she'd be fine on her own. And for a long time, she was. Until she wasn't.

On the phone yesterday Mom offered to come out for the weekend to help with the house more. But with her hours and the flying, she'd only be here for a day. Didn't seem worth it.

He eases his hands into his pockets as he turns slightly toward me. "I haven't been to Santa Barbara in forever. How do you like the beaches there?"

"I honestly don't spend much time at the beach."

"What about surfing?"

I love that he remembers how into it I used to be. "I haven't been on a board in years." When I was younger, Leo called me a daredevil. I sought adventure. Anything to get my adrenaline coursing. "I suppose I've become risk averse with age."

"You make it sound like you're too old now." He frowns, scanning the water. "Piano. Writing. Surfing. You stopped them all."

While I would take my toes in the sand any day, Ben found the sensation irritating and the beach boring. After a few years, work got busy, and all my free time was spent writing.

Ben and I would turn on soft classical music and sit in our respective chairs, laptops open. He would set a timer, and we would see how many words we could write in an hour. If we reached our goals, we rewarded ourselves with sex or takeout or an episode of whatever TV show we were in the middle of.

It didn't feel like a sacrifice to pull back on surfing to dedicate more time to my other beloved hobby. The one that always meant more. At some point, though, Ben stopped calling his writing a hobby, but he never stopped calling mine one.

"They were fun, but I don't have time for hobbies." The last word burns my tongue. "Besides, my body is out of shape."

He assesses me head to toe. "Looks good to me."

Smiling, I glance down, unable to meet his gaze when he's looking at me like that. I forgot what a flirt he could be. Now I remember why I used to think about him before falling asleep.

"I just mean things hurt now that didn't used to." Before he can say more on the topic, I segue. "How's your dad?"

"Good. He planned on retiring last year, but he still comes in a few days a week to give lessons."

Mr. Ruiz is the nicest father I've ever met. I can recall more than one occasion when Leo got frustrated at a restoration project and his dad reassured him, "For every question there is an answer. If you dig long and hard enough, you'll find it."

He was the same way when he gave me piano lessons as a teenager, telling me mistakes were not a big deal and that he made them all the time. Then he would describe some recent misstep of his that had me laughing. Not that the assurances kept me from quitting when I decided that, if I wanted to be good, I should have started when I was younger.

We stroll past a man selling ice cream out of an umbrellaed cart. Leo motions to him while looking at me. "For while we listen?"

"No, thanks." I'm suddenly too eager to get to the tape to wait any longer.

He removes his drawstring backpack and takes out a Walkman and two sets of old-school headphones.

I let out a barking laugh. "You're kidding."

"Swiped them from my dad's collection at the store." He connects the headphones to the Walkman's two jacks. "Ready?"

I slide a pair over my ears and give a thumbs-up.

CHAPTER NINE

Vivian

then

As soon as I left the studio, I went home to call my mother.

Her glee when I shared the news of my contract was so loud, I pulled the receiver from my ear while Ruth breezed into the living room with two steaming mugs and set mine on a *Life* magazine. From where I reclined on the sofa, I transferred the mug to a nearby doily so as not to spoil Hugh's phone number with a coffee ring. I traced a fingertip over his handwriting.

"This is such big news!" Mom said, her words coming out as nearly a shriek.

"I know." My cheeks hurt so much from smiling, I massaged them to relax the muscles. "It came down to being in the right place at the right time."

Ruth made a dismissive click of her tongue as she sat and pinched the edge of the magazine, bringing it closer to set down her mug. I slapped the cover before she could and dragged it back, staring at her. She grabbed the corner, but I snatched it free and gave it a victorious shake.

"It came down to your talent," Mom said.

After so much rejection, it was hard to believe. "So you think it's the right choice? Despite it being comedy?"

"I wasn't the one who needed you to do drama."

"But it's what we love."

I still recalled the thrill of walking into the cinema with Mom and finding our seats. We saw Judy Garland in *The Wizard of Oz*. Joan Fontaine in *Rebecca*. Humphrey Bogart in *Casablanca*. Even with money scarce, we made moviegoing a priority. If the choice was between seeing a film or eating lunch, I'd have picked the former any day. It simply filled me more.

Ruth lifted my mug from the doily and scowled at a coffee stain. I hugged the magazine to my chest as if to say, *This is why we can't have nice things.*

"I might have steered you in that direction unintentionally because ballet feels like drama," my mother said. "But destiny sometimes finds you; you just need to listen. Comedy might be your destiny."

I held back an eye-roll. "As soon as I get paid, I'll send a check." It would be small but better than nothing.

"I don't need money. I'm fine."

"You work in a factory."

"Don't do that. Don't talk down on my job. It supported us fine for how long?"

"You deserve better." I imagined my mom at my age, wearing slippers and a tutu. Doing a graceful pirouette on pointe. Not with grime caked under her fingernails.

"A lot of things happen to us we don't deserve. But really, Vivian. I'm fine. Now tell me how you're going to celebrate."

Ruth blew over the top of her mug, pretending not to eavesdrop.

I lowered the receiver from my mouth. "How are we celebrating?"

She scooted to the edge of her seat. "I thought of setting up a dinner with Hugh and Dean." Before I could poke a hole in that plan, she said, "Don't worry, they'll cover the tab."

I didn't like letting people pay my way. It felt like they held something over me. I owed them. But I had little choice if I wanted to go out and celebrate.

After my mother went on and on about making sure I didn't forget to be happy while chasing my dreams, we hung up so Ruth could call Dean, which was how the four of us ended up at Romanoff's.

My outfit—a navy flared skirt with white piping and a matching sleeveless blouse—was unremarkable though mildly saved by a designer scarf tied into a bow around my neck to hide a snag. It was a grand find last year at the secondhand shop near our apartment.

We sat at a round table, talking about Gerard and the picture I'd be working on, while I tried not to inhale my food. It'd been a while since I was truly full.

Once the conversation had been thoroughly exhausted and our plates taken away, talk turned to Hugh's upcoming premiere while Dean filled our flutes with champagne.

"I'm terribly jealous," I said, playful. "I want a premiere."

Hugh clinked his glass with mine. "But now you'll get one."

I hadn't thought of that. The realization made my eyes and smile go unnaturally wide.

"Put those away." Ruth motioned to my face, then to a nearby table. "You'll frighten the children."

Hugh brought a fist over his mouth to hold back a laugh.

"You must tell me what everyone wore." I bumped his arm with my shoulder. When he stared blankly at me, I shook my head. "On second thought, never mind. You don't care about clothes."

"Who says? I happen to have a nice"—Hugh pointed at his coat's breast pocket—"whatever the fabric doodad is that goes here."

"I knew it." I dropped my hand to his forearm, turning to Ruth. "See?"

Not that men couldn't be interested in clothes. My favorite designers were men. But when I'd asked Hugh what to wear to the studio, he'd said "any old dress" would do, like they were all the same.

Ruth smirked at where I held on to Hugh. "Yeah, I see."

How dare she call out how I couldn't keep my hands to myself? It was like primary school all over again.

I reached for my drink, smiling sweetly. "All I heard is you'd like to be suffocated with a pillow in your sleep."

She made a clawing motion in my direction and hissed.

Dean quirked an eyebrow before focusing on Hugh. "Speaking of the premiere, you need to drive with Peggy."

Hugh grinned. "I know."

A kernel of jealousy popped in the heat of my chest. Had he grown feelings for his fake girlfriend, or did the smile mean he found Dean's reminder unnecessary?

It didn't matter. I needed to stop dissecting his reactions like an overenthusiastic biology student with a frog.

A couple walked past. Dean grabbed the man's arm, standing to shake his hand. "Heyyy. Look what the cat dragged in."

The man had brown hair close-cropped on the sides with soft curls on top, a few pieces hanging over his forehead, and wore a white button-down rolled to the elbows, with a loosened tie. Slightly rough around the edges, he was the kind of good-looking that made fellas want to turn in their letterman sweaters for leather jackets and girls cut out his picture to paste in their notebooks. Surrounded by little pink hearts.

If Hugh was the quintessential dreamboat, this man was a stud with a capital *S*.

Dean dropped a hand to Ruth: "This is my girlfriend, Ruth Phillips." Then Hugh: "And you've heard me rave about Hugh Fox."

The man bit the edge of his lip to stifle a smile. I wanted to smack his arm. Fox was a stage name, for crying out loud.

Dean pointed at me. "And this is Vivian Mackenzie. Everyone, meet Christopher Pierce."

"Please, call me Kit," the man said. "Nice to meet you all. This is a good guy to have in your corner, here." He rested a hand on Dean's shoulder.

"He's only saying that because he's in my next picture." Dean shook a finger in Kit's direction. "Look out for this one. He's gonna be a big deal someday. Mark my words."

He'd be a big deal based on looks alone, and Dean didn't work with people who weren't fantastic.

Considering how Kit failed to introduce the lovely woman on his arm, though, he was rude. And that look about Hugh's name? Arrogant. Because "Kit Pierce" was so much better?

Actually, it was pretty good.

Kit offered a quick goodbye, and Dean went to refill our glasses. I raised a hand to stop him from topping off mine, smiling with an "I'm swell, thanks." I could justify one celebratory drink. Thoughts of more made my chest tight. Not because I had a problem but because it made me think of my father.

When the check came, Dean threw some money over as he whispered in Ruth's ear, practically nuzzling her as a shoe accidentally grazed my shin.

They were playing footsie like teenagers, weren't they? This was a classy establishment. No sly maneuvers under the table allowed.

Hugh added several bills to the pile.

"I'm going to pay you back." I fidgeted with my cloth napkin.

"For one dinner?"

"For everything. Besides, it's not like this is a date. We're friends, right?"

His gaze dipped to my mouth. "Do you usually kiss your friends?" He said it so low, only I could hear. The goosebump-inducing spark that resulted was anything but friendly.

"That was practice and one time. You're seeing someone now." I smiled so he'd think I was all right with it.

Hugh stared at me for a moment, then pushed the check and cash to the table's edge as if the matter was settled. "We're celebrating you tonight, so it's my treat."

I had a feeling he'd continue to foot the bill, and I mentally tallied how much I owed him.

"Did you call home to share your news?" he asked. "I bet your folks are proud."

My heart warmed that the thought had occurred to him. "I phoned my mother. She went on and on for so long, I pretended the call got disconnected so I could hang up. I haven't seen or talked to my father in"—how long had it been?—"seven years now."

His face fell. "The way you told the Scarlett O'Hara story, I assumed—"

"No, he left. My father had many vices, chief among them booze and other women. My parents fought whenever he came home smelling of either." I shrugged, not nearly as nonchalant as the action implied.

I used to walk and bike all over town, staying out until the streetlights came on. Maybe it was cowardly, but half the time I had dinner at my friends' houses so I wouldn't have to be there when my father got home from work, since I never knew what his mood would be.

Sometimes I wondered if my mother would meet someone new, but I worried if she did, he'd be another version of my father.

"What about your family?" I asked. "Loving and supportive, or . . . ?"

"Pretty much. My father was always home by five thirty. After dinner, we'd play catch or work in the garage. My mother doesn't know how to drive, so on the weekends we headed into the city as a family for groceries. We didn't always have sugar, you know, when there was rationing. But if we did, Mom let my sisters and me bake a treat."

I smiled, happy for him. "Sounds like a good childhood."

"It was."

To smooth the pity off his face, I joked, "Now you can see why I'm not in a hurry to date when I had my parents for an example." Had I gone too deep for dinner conversation?

He tapped his fingertips on the side of his glass. "The studio might make you someday."

The "might" and "someday" hinged on me being important enough for my relationships to matter.

I almost said, *Like they're making you?* because I wanted to know how he felt about Peggy. But it would hurt to hear he cared about her, and it would hurt to hear he didn't but had to date her anyway. Neither was a good option, so I bit my lip and looked out the window.

No matter how stormy my insides were, in sunny California it was always another beautiful day.

Sometimes I wished it would rain.

———————◆———————

My first client meeting happened early the following week. An MGM publicist decided my look would be the "girl next door, America's sweetheart" type, and the team got to work.

Makeup artist Sandy Wilkinson made over my face, shaping my eyebrows into defined arches and darkening them with pencil. Lipsticks were compared to my complexion until she found the right one and recorded it as "mine." It was the only one I could wear for events where photographers would be. The idea that photographers might someday follow me around was laughable. But, swell, "Cherry Red" it was.

A hairdresser cut and styled my hair while I had my first lesson to get rid of my accent. My raspy voice was to be my defining feature, and the lessons would help make it more pronounced.

After taking my measurements, a stylist brought in a variety of brassieres from Frederick's of Hollywood. In the right size for the first time and wearing a push-up, I had more cleavage than I knew what to do with.

With my big brown waves dusting my shoulders and my makeup complete, I came out in a scoop neck teal dress and matching felt hat. At the click of my heels, Gerard turned.

"Well, I'll be damned." He crossed his arms, assessing me. "America might have to adjust its standards of what the girl next door can look like."

As the final piece to the transformation, I got a new name: Vivian Stone.

CHAPTER TEN

Vivian

then

Hugh and I had made plans to meet at the nearby soda shoppe after my session.

A bell above the door rang as I walked in, faint over a Hank Ballard tune coming from the jukebox in the corner. Hugh sat on a red pleather stool in the back, sipping a milkshake, not noticing I'd walked in.

When I stood right next to him, he glanced up. His eyes widened before shooting down my body and back up again with such speed, I would have laughed if I wasn't so nervous, even my lips shook.

"Christ." There was no playfulness in his tone, only undiluted shock as he spun toward me in his seat. He appraised me again, more slowly this time.

Arms spread wide, I twirled, my dress flaring. "What do you think?"

"You're a knockout."

I motioned up and down. "Is it too much?" I wanted his honest opinion but had trouble speaking with the way my chest kept heaving, especially because every time I managed to take a breath in, his attention flicked to the swell at my neckline.

"There's no such thing in Hollywood." His mouth transformed into a beaming smile. "You look like a movie star."

"A star? I'm not the one with a lead." I sat across from him and took a small sip of his milkshake. There was no reason to get my own. Before leaving, Gerard had said to watch what I ate and to smoke a cigarette if I got hungry. As if I hadn't learned that trick years ago.

"You'll get there." He dragged the milkshake closer to him. A red tinge from my lipstick marked the straw. It was impossible not to notice, but he rested his mouth over it and sipped.

The sight unleashed a kaleidoscope of butterflies in my stomach.

He nodded at the milkshake. "You don't want one?"

"I shouldn't."

"No? How do you feel about cake?"

My mouth watered. "Do you have an hour?"

"My sister's wedding is next month." Hugh tapped his lips as if thinking. "She said something about buttercream and lemon curd."

I groaned, waving a hand. "Stop, stop. I'm powerless against the lure of sugar and citrus."

"So you'll come?"

I hesitated. "You aren't taking Peggy?"

He held the base of the glass and gently spun it. "It's a little soon for meeting the parents, I think."

But it wouldn't be for a friend.

Maybe the invitation had something to do with Hugh's last girlfriend, the one Ruth said broke his heart. He wouldn't want to get his family's hopes up about him finding happiness with someone else by bringing a girlfriend before he was sure about it.

I swallowed the envy that someone else got to be more than friends with him and pasted on a smile. "Wild horses couldn't keep me away."

————— ◆ —————

One month later, and well after midnight, Hugh's car jostled.

We were halfway home from his sister's wedding, where he had introduced me to his family, encouraged me to have a second slice of cake, and thrown me over his shoulder to carry me back to the car like a sack of potatoes in a poofy blue dress because my feet hurt.

He curled his hands around the steering wheel and cursed as the shaking continued.

"What's wrong?"

The road was dark and deserted as he pulled off to the side. "A flat, maybe."

There have been a few times in my life in which I've been grateful to be a woman rather than a man. Having to deal with mechanical problems is one of them. Men have it easier, wouldn't you say? Establishing a career, making money, gaining respect. Even urinating is more convenient for them.

They would never comprehend the frustration of being in a ladies' room, elbows pinning a bunched dress to one's hips while shimmying down panties and hovering above the toilet so as not to let one's skin touch the seat. They would crumble under the pressure.

We stepped out and walked around front, headlights shining as Hugh studied the tires.

He pointed at the driver's side. "Looks like it's this one."

"Do you have a spare?" That was all I could add to the situation: asking the obvious.

"Yeah, but not a jack."

My next question—*Can you fix it?*—was now moot. We were stuck.

Hugh scanned the quiet road. "We'll have to wait until we can get someone's attention. Hopefully, they'll have a jack." He released a heavy sigh. "Sorry."

To our right was the shadowed darkness of rolling hills and dry earth, while from our left came the ebb and flow of waves on the beach, the scent of salt hanging in the air. A faint glow came from the crescent moon.

"Don't be," I said as we rounded back to our doors. "There are worse places to be and people to be with." Which was less bizarre than saying I'd force a diaper onto a cheetah for the opportunity to be stuck with him.

"Just wait, you haven't heard me snore yet, and we might be here till morning."

I sat on the brown leather bench seat and removed my heels while Hugh turned off the ignition, the headlights going out, leaving us in darkness.

"This feels like a sleepover." I curled my legs under me. "I used to have them with my girlfriends when I was a kid." At their homes, of course.

"A sleepover. I'm intrigued. What did you do at these sleepovers?"

There was nothing for my senses to focus on but the low timbre of his voice, the sound sending tingles down my body.

"The usual," I said. "Braided each other's hair. Gossiped about cute boys. Sang."

"Oh, right, you were in that musical. You must be pretty good."

My smile likely would have terrified him, had he been able to see it.

I opened my mouth to sing the first tune that came to mind: Hank Williams's "Hey, Good Lookin'," my voice catching and flying off-key.

After a few lines, he said, "Oh. Gee. That's . . . wow."

"What? I'm not ready for *The Ed Sullivan Show*?"

He sucked in a breath through his teeth. "I don't want to hurt your feelings, but I'm afraid a lie that big would smite me on the spot."

I tried to scoff but laughed instead. "Bad enough to make the wolves howl, huh?"

"Howl? They'll think you're a stray and herd you home." He reached over and locked my door, so close his vanilla scent wafted past me. "Better safe than sorry."

I pinched his side, making him jump back and chuckle. "I suppose now would be a good time to tell you my part in that musical was *small*. In-the-back-where-no-one-could-hear-me small." I knew I couldn't sing but had hoped one role would lead to another. "How about you? Can *you* sing?"

Hugh took over where I left off but with his own rendition, his voice turning soulful. After several seconds, his words trailed off.

I blinked, trying to adjust to the darkness. "Are you good at everything?"

"No."

"Name one thing."

"I'm forgetful. I have to go over my lines a lot—*a lot* a lot. I don't have a jack. I had one, but I lent it out and forgot to get it back or to buy a new one. I'm a workhorse, on set an hour before hair and makeup. Schmoozing at parties when everyone else is taking it easy."

I let out a theatrical gasp. "I can't believe I befriended someone with such loathsome qualities. Then again, spilling secrets is a sleepover tradition, so I'll overlook it." In the darkness, sharing came more easily. "But you have to admit those aren't so bad."

He laughed, the sound nearly self-deprecating. "Well, I'm awful at long-distance relationships."

My pulse picked up a notch. "Oh? What happened?"

"It's . . . complicated."

I wanted him to tell me but wouldn't push. "You don't have to explain."

We sat in silence for a long moment before he spoke again. "I had a girlfriend back home but got really busy when I moved to LA. Going to auditions. Working. I didn't call enough. Didn't visit like I should have."

"Did she know how hard this all is? How much work it is?"

"No one can unless they're in it. I was going to get settled, then we were going to get married, but everything happened so fast. My contract, the schedule. I couldn't keep up and wouldn't set a date. I didn't want to start our marriage with me always working."

I waited, patient, for him to continue.

"I guess time got away from me. A year later, I had a handle on the expectations, but it was too late. She'd started seeing someone else." Almost to himself, he added, "Said she never knew if I loved her or my ambition more."

A strange sensation spun in my chest, sensitive to his pain yet sympathetic to her. "She could still change her mind and forgive you."

"No, she's married now. It took a while, but I'm happy for her." His tone turned resolute as he said, "It's better this way, I think. Focusing on my career."

Even though Hugh wasn't still brokenhearted, his story—his perspective—broke *my* heart a little.

"Now tell me one of your secrets," he said, lighter. "One you haven't told anyone."

I'd been an open book with him. He knew about the painful memories of my father, my insecurities toward drama, my financial difficulties. "I can't think of something I haven't told anyone. Ruth knows all my secrets."

"All right, then tell me something you've only told Ruth."

Memories hurtled back, paralyzing my tongue. I forced the thoughts away.

"I used to lie to my father." I curled and uncurled my fingers to release some tension. "When he asked me why I was never home."

"Lying to your old man? That's your biggest secret?"

"No." I conjured my most vulnerable moments, and the air thickened, making it harder to breathe. "The truth is a bit heavy."

"Then don't carry it alone," he whispered.

Static coursed between us. Something told me I could share anything about my past and he wouldn't shy away.

"I was eighteen when I moved to New York with stars in my eyes. It's where I learned to waitress. Walter was one of our regulars. He was nice. Kind eyes, encouraging smile. Good tips." I shrugged. "He asked if I ever considered modeling and gave me his card."

"You called," Hugh filled in softly.

"I did." It had felt like my big break. I'd been "discovered." "He filled my head with assurances of his connections and promises that, with him, I would reach my goals. I trusted him wholeheartedly. When he booked me one modeling gig after another, it felt like my trust was well-founded. Yet every audition for every theater I went to ended in rejection. I needed acting lessons, but modeling stockings didn't pay enough. I took my concerns to Walter. He'd become a father figure, and I poured out my worries. He had a solution."

I squeezed my eyes shut, a memory playing in my mind that felt out-of-body. Like it hadn't happened to me but to another woman in a horror movie. Soon, someone would rescue her.

Only life doesn't work that way. A white knight didn't come to save me. No one did. I had to save myself.

"What was it?" Hugh's voice strained, shocking me from my trance. When I didn't respond, he said, "I'm prying, aren't I?"

I trusted him. I had the same gut feeling when I met Hugh as I did with Ruth. My secrets were safe with him.

"I posed nude. No one had ever seen me like that before. I hadn't even had a proper kiss. Yet I wanted my dream so much, I was willing to sacrifice a piece of myself to get there."

Hugh probably thought that was the worst of it, but it was only half. The easier half.

"Vivian . . ."

"Do you see me differently now?" I knew better than to think he'd call me names. Still, I needed to know what he thought of what I'd done.

"Yes. You're brave. Braver than me by far."

Those names I didn't expect him to call me, I'd been calling myself, and with his words, he took an eraser to some of them, lightening their intensity. Though it was hard imagining that this man, tall and broad-shouldered, could be anything but brave. "For going through with it?"

"For not crumbling afterward. For continuing to chase your dreams. For acknowledging what happened when voicing it must have been hard." His hand found my cheek. "Thank you for trusting me."

My heart jumped like it wanted to thrust me into his arms. I gasped, holding back.

His hand fell away. "Are you okay?"

"Mm-hmm. Just tired."

"Get some sleep." He shifted away. "And shove me if my snoring keeps you awake."

Within minutes, his breathing grew shallow. I couldn't understand how some people fell asleep so quickly. For several minutes, I listened to each steady exhale.

I inched closer. "Hugh?" When he didn't respond, I got nearer still.

Maybe it was terrible, but I was only human and completely flawed. I scooted close enough to make out the perfect angles of his face and pressed my lips to his in a whisper of a kiss.

It wasn't enough, but it would have to be.

CHAPTER ELEVEN

Vivian

then

Filming for *In Your Eyes* began in the backlot's Small Town Square, which had been modified for the film to give it a European feel. Interconnecting storefronts with pale blue, cream, and peach façades displayed signs boasting bakeries and bookshops. Striped awnings hung over patios, while flower boxes held imitation begonias and chrysanthemums. My heels clicked on the path under a stone archway with sprawling ivy, adrenaline pumping through my veins.

I knew this was coming, but to actually be here? I must have wandered into an imaginary world where things like this happened to people like me. Drama or not, at that moment it didn't matter. What mattered was the overwhelming awe and the breath-snatching fear that I could lose it.

One of the leads, Chester Hale, spoke to the director. Chester was well into his forties and looked a bit like the "King of Cool," Dean Martin, with big brown eyes and a baritone that could give a woman on her deathbed a second wind. Although he probably hoped they were *young* women. According to *Confidential*, his current girlfriend was eighteen.

The other lead, Evelyn Summers, tall and slender with pouty lips, was off set, getting a last-minute powdering of her nose. She was known as Hollywood's "Party Princess" due to her bar- and bed-hopping.

Once Makeup left, Evelyn withdrew a prescription bottle from her purse, shook a couple of pills onto a table, and used the bottom of an empty water glass to crush them. She slid the granules into her palm, then ran her tongue over them.

The sun beat down on my neck, and I wiped a damp strand of hair from my temple. I'd never seen anyone take medication that way.

Within fifteen minutes, the director, Mario, called everyone to get started. Gerard came up to him, arms crossed.

"Hiya, honey," Evelyn said as she met me on set, wearing an off-the-shoulder brown dress. It wasn't supposed to be off the shoulder—her measurements had been taken wrong—but she preferred it that way and asked to keep it. "Ready to go?"

Her demeanor had changed since rehearsals. Her mouth moved faster. She had a twitch.

Admiration waned as I tried to piece together what had happened. "Yes."

The boom operator rested the pole on his shoulders, a microphone at the end, while the cameraman leaned into the eyepiece and flipped a switch. We found our marks.

"And—action," Mario called.

Chester, wearing a fedora and a scowl, cornered a gunman in a shop, saying, "Not so fast," while I ran out the door. It slammed shut with a bang. Convinced it'd been a gunshot, I stumbled to the ground and clawed away, yelling, "*Ahh!*" Dust got in my mouth, and I coughed, exaggerating its severity with a grimace.

An ad-lib, but Gerard let out a deep chuckle.

Evelyn ducked behind the fountain. She missed a line, so I improvised, tripping over my feet to dive behind her. I peeked over her shoulder when more commotion came from the shop, Chester and the bad guy trading punches.

"He's gonna need a"—Evelyn paused to recall her line—"an alibi."

"Easy." I lifted my hands at my sides in a show of innocence and in a sweet voice said, "*We were together the whole night, Officer. Playing bridge.*"

By the time we cut, most of the crew was laughing, and I caught a smile from Mario. I fought against taking a bow, my ears ringing as pride washed over me.

We managed the scene in about twelve takes—which could have been five if not for Evelyn's mishaps.

The situation was still on my mind later at home. I mentioned it to Ruth.

"They had to be pep pills," she said, her heel propped on the coffee table as she painted her toenails bubble gum pink. "What Evelyn took."

"Let me guess: They put some pep in your step?"

Ruth didn't laugh. "Too much pep. They're meant to keep leads working. Up to seventy hours, I heard. Then they get carted off for a nap before going again."

If I was at all curious how some movies got made so fast, this was it.

I popped a couple of my new prescription pills and washed them down with a gulp of water.

"What are those?"

"Oh." I set the bottle on an end table, still embarrassed over what had happened. "Just something to help me lose a few."

After filming today, Mario said there was a prescription for me at the studio hospital. Something to help keep my weight in check. He'd noticed I looked a little fuller than usual. The studio doctor had me step on the scale to confirm it: I'd gained ten pounds.

Shame filled me as I went home, half of me humiliated to have been called out like that—to have even let the weight gain happen—and the other half kicking myself for accepting the pills.

I should have said no, but it wasn't that easy. The only reason I had been eating better was because I had some money, and I only had money because of my contract.

Agreeing to take the pills wasn't the same as the other sacrifices I'd made. It wasn't like the nude photos. It wasn't like what had happened with Walter. At least, that was what I told myself, because I didn't want to believe I was being taken advantage of again.

That night I tossed and turned. My heart raced. I probably slept only forty-five minutes. Instead of being exhausted the next day, I got to work early and paced around the lot to burn off some energy. My brain cranked so fast, I struggled to get my words out in the right order, my thoughts already on to the next thing.

Despite having dropped a few pounds, by the end of the second week I dumped the pills, deciding I needed to find another solution to my weight issue.

It wasn't until recently that I learned that the pep pills and diet pills the studios handed out like candy were stimulants.

The rest of filming went the same. When we finished, talk turned to the premiere. My *first* premiere.

Usually single lead actors went together, but since I wasn't a lead, I didn't have to. But I couldn't attend my red-carpet debut alone. Gerard suggested that Hugh and I go as friends, saying it was good publicity. Of course, he said it right in front of Hugh, and I hoped my agreement looked like a strategic decision and not like I was pathetic for not having a legitimate date.

There was no overthinking it. It all got settled within five minutes.

The night of my premiere, I shimmied into a clingy cream off-the-shoulder dress, my cups overflowing, making me look like a sexpot. An oversize satin bow in the same cherry red as my lipstick was tied around my waist and cascaded to the floor. Opera gloves finished the look.

A knock came on my door. I slung the stole I'd borrowed from the studio over my arm and opened it. Hugh stood there, dapper in a tux.

His eyes widened as he walked in. "Wow."

I pressed a kiss to his cheek in hello. "Bad or good 'wow'?" There was a bit of lipstick left behind. "Where's your hanky?" I dug into his coat pocket for it and dabbed his cheek.

He paused, glancing sidelong at me. "Good."

I replaced the hanky. "You took a minute to come to that conclusion."

"No, it's—" He motioned to my chest, then caught himself, placing his hand in his pocket. "You look gorgeous."

"But it's more of my cleavage than you're used to seeing?" I teased, handing him my stole. "My stylist seemed to forget I'm supposed to be the girl next door."

He draped it over my shoulders, the brush of his fingertips on my skin causing miniature fireworks to burst down my arms. "I suppose if you lived at a gentlemen's club."

I nudged him and met his gaze over my shoulder, holding it for several long seconds.

When we were stuck on the side of the road, Hugh had said I was brave. But bravery wasn't confidence. Telling him how I felt despite the obstacles of his girlfriend, of my nearly nonexistent image compared to his, and of him never uttering a word to prove he cared for me, was senseless. Not only because it could make a friendship I desperately needed uncomfortable but because I could manage rejections from directors and yet I couldn't handle one from Hugh.

Deciding enough was enough, I mentally built a wall of thorny vines around my heart with the hope that the sharp prick would stop me from fantasizing about the idea of us.

Flashbulbs from photographers went off like a heated panful of popcorn kernels as we walked the red carpet. Never having had cameras aimed at me before, I flashed a bright smile while my heart lay buried in my throat, worrying over whether they'd snap unflattering photos.

"Hugh! Hugh Fox!" A photographer waved to get his attention.

"Hey," one shouted. "Can we get a shot, Hugh?"

I loosened my grip on his arm. "Go ahead."

He set a hand over mine, keeping me from slipping away. "This night is not about me. It's about you. I don't give a hoot whether they get a picture of me, and if they're smart, they'll get plenty of you. Because they're going to be worth something someday."

A light flashed as I stared at him.

His insistence didn't change what photographers thought of me, but I shoved the fears from my mind, turning to the cameras and smiling.

After a handful of photos, Hugh whispered, "Your turn." He disengaged himself and walked toward the doors. I missed the reassurance of him at my side as I rested my hands on my hips.

If no one took my picture, the embarrassment would eat me alive.

Pop. Pop. Pop.

Cameras went off in my direction.

"Over here!" someone shouted.

"Let's have a smile, honey," another encouraged.

I tried but my lips trembled too much for it to look natural. The photographers were only doing this to appease Hugh, but I let them. I would take this moment for all it was worth.

A limousine pulled up to the curb. Chester Hale extended a hand for Evelyn Summers as she stepped out in a red-and-gold-studded gown. All eyes were on her.

Someday I would have that. Everyone's attention on me.

"That's some dress." Hugh snickered, nodding in Evelyn's direction as I reached his side. "How long is her train?"

"Long enough that she's going to have trouble using the ladies' room. She'll have to sling it over the stall door." I mimed tossing it over.

His eyes gleamed as he chuckled, and my heart tested its newly formed walls, wanting to leap for joy. And during the movie, when he told me how wonderful my performance was. Again when he did the scrunched-face smile I loved.

After he dropped me off at my apartment that night, I found a piece of paper, needing an outlet for all the feelings I held inside so I could finally put them to rest.

My Dearest TDH,

I need to get out something I'd never voice. The truth is, I love you madly in a head-over-heels, last-person-I-think-of-before-bed and first-person-I-think-of-when-I-wake-up way. I'm trying to stop, but it's not easy. When I'm with you, I'm a blazing fire. When I'm not, I'm crackling embers. Distance helps, but I don't want to stay away. I love hearing your thoughts on everything big and small. As soon as you're near, though, the fire roars back to life.

Every day I imagine your laugh. Every night I think of your lips. But if all we can have is friendship, I'll take it. Because the only thing worse than not being with you would be not having you in my life.

Love,

Vivian

I tucked the letter in an envelope, scrawled his name on the front, and stuffed it in the top drawer of my vanity. With it, I stowed a secret that I was sure would never see the light of day.

JUNE 20, 1952

"PRETTY PEGGY" MEETS THE PARENTS

Dreamboat Hugh Fox took the monumental step of introducing his girlfriend, Peggy Harris, to his parents.

The group lunched at the Windsor, where they emerged a little over an hour later with everyone all smiles. Peggy must have charmed Hugh's parents, but with her gentle demeanor and stunning style, it's not hard to see why.

Only last week, he attended a premiere with newcomer Vivian Stone, where we caught them making eyes at each other. We couldn't help but wonder if there was a new relationship on the horizon for Hugh. But our sources say he attended as a friend, and things are serious with Miss Harris.

If we're being honest, Hugh and Peggy make more sense.

CHAPTER TWELVE

Vivian

then

"You're playing a monster at Martha's Vineyard," Gerard said from behind his desk.

Were monsters funny? I probably made a similar moaning and groaning when my alarm went off in the morning, so if I stayed perpetually sleep-deprived I could pull it off, and I'd have dark circles to boot.

I crossed my legs in my seat. "Who's directing?"

"I'm kidding about the monster. It's supporting actress as a nosy next-door neighbor. But it does take place at Martha's Vineyard. If you'd been listening, you'd already know."

Supporting actress. I could do that. It was a step up. "That's swell."

"You don't sound happy." He rested his elbows on the desk, hands steepled. "You know you ain't ready to be a lead yet. It'll take some time."

"How long?" A lead was the best way to prove I deserved my chance at drama.

"As long as it takes to knock Eugene's socks off and convince him to go for it." He checked his wristwatch and frowned. Apparently, I'd overstayed my allotted time in his busy schedule. "Speaking of Eugene, he wasn't too happy about the *Hollywood Reporter* article."

"We got great reviews."

"I mean the one where your relationship with Hugh was called into question."

I'd seen it. "Making eyes" at each other? What they'd caught was us joking about Evelyn's train.

"He put a lot of effort into making Hugh and Peggy's relationship a fairy-tale romance. Then you throw a wrench in it. Make people question things." Gerard stared for a beat, but I read between the lines: The head of MGM wasn't happy with me. For clowning around, of all things.

I was building a rapport with producers and directors, but when it came to my next contract, Eugene's opinion trumped them all. "I didn't do it on purpose." Not to mention that going with Hugh had been Gerard's idea.

He walked around his desk, toward the door. "For future premieres, let's get you out with one of our available actors. Being seen with Hugh is great for your image, but it's a delicate balance of portraying the *right* image, you know?"

That image probably didn't include the times Hugh phoned to make sure I was keeping up with my bills. Or when he dropped by with takeout, saying he was in the area and had ordered too much. Or even the note he left in my dressing room during my first week of filming that said, *Break a leg.*

I grabbed my purse and followed Gerard. He had a point about going out with available actors. Not only to boost my image, which would help me secure a better contract next time around, but because I might like one of them.

He held open the door. "We've set the tabloids straight about Hugh's love life, but don't do anything that could be misconstrued."

I assumed having dinner out with Hugh, Dean, and Ruth was acceptable, but I wouldn't press my luck by asking. Better to ask for forgiveness than permission. "Of course."

It was a marvel those two words didn't sound like a curse.

I couldn't remember the last time I'd asked permission for anything, even as a child. I was more responsible than those twice my age. I had no choice. Once my father left, Mom was always working, so she trusted me to make sure I got my homework done and had clean clothes ready for school.

Those nights when she got home, smelling of industrial grease, she'd hug me and say, "We're in this together." She meant it to be encouraging, but I carried it like a burden. I didn't want to be in it together. I didn't want the responsibilities that forced me to grow up faster than everyone else. I wanted to be a kid.

At the same time, I saw the difference between Mom and other mothers. Though she had polished nails, her hands were calloused. Her house dresses were perfectly pressed but faded. In the rare instance when she had an event, she went to the Revlon counter and let the girls make her over. She never went to the beauty salon to get curlers put in like other moms.

So I pretended we were in it together. Because I think she needed to feel like she wasn't alone.

Gerard shut the door with a resolute click, leaving me in the executive hall, where photos of every big shot in the studio lined the walls. At the end, Eugene's door flew open so hard it hit the wall as someone stormed out.

I recognized that head of inky hair.

"Hugh!" I called, and he stilled, jaw tense and eyes blazing. I'd never seen him like that. I caught up, searching his face for explanation. "What's wrong?" The collar of his short-sleeved button-down had flipped up. Strange, as Hugh never looked anything but put together.

He pointed at his chest, seething. "I'm not my own person." He threw a hand at Eugene's office. "He's been telling me what to do for years. He owns me, and I'm *sick* of it."

Hugh must have had a conversation similar to mine. I took his arm and tugged him out of earshot of Eugene's office. "Did he ask for a meeting to talk about us?"

"What? No." He opened the door leading to the stairwell. "I asked for the meeting."

So we weren't talking about the same thing. "What happened?"

Our voices echoed as we went downstairs, Hugh slowing to match my pace.

"We got into an argument." He swung sharp eyes on me. "He's threatening to ruin my career. More than my career."

Eugene had that power. One word, and Hugh would be blacklisted.

"He thinks I just need to blow off some steam on location for my next picture," he said as we turned down another flight, a lightbulb flickering above us. "As if that will help."

"Where are you filming?"

"Hawaii." He said it like he was being forced to share an igloo with a polar bear rather than visit a tropical paradise. "I still have to wrap my current film, but then I'll be gone for *months*."

At the next landing I grasped his shoulders, stopping him. "Hawaii? You can't be serious." Panic bled into my voice. "However will you handle all the fresh air and beaches? You'll be knocking sand out of your shoes for *months*."

He flashed a soft grin. "All right, smart aleck."

Someone opened the stairwell door next to us, but I didn't pay them attention.

"We'll make a list of all the things you need to do before you go. Just in case." I cupped Hugh's cheek, his five-o'clock shadow grazing my hand.

"In case what? I kick the bucket?"

I stepped back, indignant. "How can you be so insensitive at a time like this?" I rested a hand on the banister but lost all pretense when my hand slid a couple of inches, making me gasp.

The man next to us chuckled. He wore pin-striped slacks and held a stack of papers to his chest. It was the casting director for *Julius Caesar*.

"A funny broad." He smirked, nodding in my direction. "Snagged a role after all, huh?"

Apparently, he was still a nitwit.

"Gerard has a good eye when it comes to talent," Hugh said as we started down the next flight. "Whoever was dumb enough to pass her up will kick themselves when her name is in lights."

I peeked over my shoulder and bit the inside of my cheek to stifle a laugh at the look on the director's face. We walked out the doors to the lobby. "I'm surprised he remembered me," I said.

"I wasn't lying when I said you make an impression."

That was sweet, but the only impression I left on that guy was *can't act*. "Listen, I don't know what happened with Eugene, but don't let him ruin your career. You were meant to act, and it'd be a crime against motion pictures for you to stop." I smoothed his collar back in place. "Hawaii is a great opportunity. When you get back, we'll all be here exactly how you left us."

———◆———

Over the next several months, MGM kept me busy with one small role after another. A next-door neighbor. A nurse. A chorus girl. A chicken with its head cut off.

All right, not the last one. Sometimes it felt that way, though, trying to keep my schedule straight. Jumping from one lot to the next. I was never needed for an entire film, so as soon as my part was done, they sent me to another.

I clipped every article with my name in it and bought copies to mail to my mother with a check. I also sent one to Hugh, finally paying him back, right before he left for Hawaii. Not that I was convinced he'd cash it.

One day I knocked and poked my head into Dean's office. "You asked to see me?"

He stood and motioned for me to sit. I tried very, very hard not to stare at his desk.

Last night, Ruth waltzed in and told me they'd had the best sex in months on his desk. "He laid me out on top of all the scripts and contracts," she'd said with a sly smile. Now I was face-to-face with those stacks of paper. *Contaminated* scripts and contracts.

"I'm gonna be directing this romantic comedy called *Sunday Circus*," he said. "It's about an uptight businessman and his boss's daughter. He can't stand her because she's always getting in the way at the office, and she thinks he needs to let loose."

"Does her father own a circus?"

He tilted his head slightly. "No."

Of course not. A ridiculous assumption on my part.

He pushed the papers aside until he found the one he was looking for. "We're casting now. The lead's yours."

I waited for the punchline. It didn't come. "You're kidding."

"I'm not."

My heart grew wings, and I threw my hands in the air. "Yes!" I erased the distance over the desk and embraced him. "Yes, yes, yes."

A *lead*. With Dean directing, it'd be a hit, and I'd finally prove myself to the studio. It couldn't have aligned more perfectly with the remainder of my contract.

Blood rushed through my veins. I could picture my renewal meeting already: sitting with Eugene while we negotiated what I wanted. Which he'd be more than happy to supply. Why wouldn't he? I'd be a verified success. He wouldn't want to lose me.

Dean patted my back. I let him go and braced myself on the desk. "You're not giving it to me because we're friends, right?"

Shit. I'd touched the tainted scripts.

He shook his head. "It was something Judy said one day when Eugene and I were discussing options. She called you a pistol."

Of course. Judy loved me. Whenever I saw her, I asked about her figurine collection and if she'd gotten her hands on the sugar-glazed porcelain cat she'd been hunting for.

I made my hand into a gun and flicked my thumb. "Bang."

I was gloating but didn't care and continued to do so when I went home and told Ruth.

After a round of high-pitched squealing, she promised to beg Dean to pick the most handsome single actor MGM had to play opposite me. Knowing her, she felt guilty about packing to move in with him and wanted to make it up to me. She cared more about being with Dean than what people might whisper about her.

The phone rang about a week later while I washed dishes.

"Are you sitting down?" Ruth asked, out of breath and with nary a formal greeting. "You should sit down for this."

I rinsed a floral plate. "I'm sitting."

"I found out who you're playing opposite. You met him before. That dreamy curly-haired fella Dean introduced us to at Romanoff's."

I rolled my eyes. "Oh, for Pete's sake."

Sure, he was one of Hollywood's most handsome. He was also rude and arrogant.

Christopher "Kit" Pierce.

CHAPTER THIRTEEN

Margot

now

"Should we assume the woman on the tapes is lying?" I take off the headphones, both of us sitting under a tree near the harbor. "It's a prank?"

Leo pulls his down around his neck. "Do you really think your grandma was the kind of person who would have prank tapes in her attic?" The face he makes says I should know better.

I try to convey my most *Don't be ridiculous* look. "Leo."

"Margot." A soft smile. "Check this out." He holds up his phone, a Wikipedia page open.

I scroll past a black-and-white photo of a beautiful woman—dark hair, high cheekbones—and read from the summary. "Vivian Stone, born Vivian Mackenzie on September 12, 1929, is an American actress originally from Long Island, New York. She's the only child of the late Susan Mackenzie, a ballerina, and the late Stephen Mackenzie, a stockbroker. She currently resides in Los Angeles, California . . ."

"There are too many details to be a coincidence *or* a prank." Leo pockets his phone.

That would make her—I do the mental math—ninety-five. It's almost her birthday. "Why would Vivian record this? And why would Gram have the tapes?" Those are the parts throwing me. Well, the whole thing is throwing me, but those are the ones I keep coming back to.

"The same reason we said before: They knew each other. Sister, friend . . ."

"If Gram knew someone famous, there'd be more evidence of it among her things."

He squints at me like I'm the delusional one. "Enough denial. We don't know why or how, but your grandma knew Vivian Stone, Hollywood legend."

A woman in hot pink leggings walking a goldendoodle must have heard him because she stares over her shoulder as she passes us, her mouth partially open.

As much as the pessimist in me wants to keep poking holes, my gut tells me he's right.

Why wouldn't Gram have told me about Vivian? There were so many times when I was young that we sat at the breakfast table with our teas and she told me pieces of her life. She never thought to bring Vivian up then? Or during our weekly conversations after I moved out?

I kick a stone, frustrated once again that Gram isn't here. Without her, I'm afraid of never learning the answers to my questions, and this piece of her I thought would give me comfort will remain a loose end.

———————◆———————

The next two evenings after work I clean the guest room and the kitchen. The only things I don't pack are two plates, two glasses, and two forks, spoons, and knives—wishful thinking that Leo will be over again—along with mugs, tea, and some miscellaneous kitchen supplies.

No tape.

I don't let myself linger on memories of Gram thumbing the worn pages of her cookbook. Or the familiar clank of her well-loved measuring cups. Those are for a day with greater emotional bandwidth.

The following night, I'm pulling into a parking space at my old high school, the lot dark and empty save one other car, when my phone rings.

"Hello?"

"Hey, Margot. How are you?" David's voice radiates energy. "Sorry for the late call, but I have great news. I was talking with some new clients, a couple that's looking to relocate, and I mentioned your place. I know it's not on the market yet, but it matches their needs, so I brought it up. People love when you tell them about unlisted properties."

"And?"

"They're interested! You should have heard them. I didn't have any photos, but they did a drive-by, since they're in town, and they love it. Those petunias out front really drew them in."

"They're poppies."

"Even better."

I brace an elbow against the car door, head in my hand, and massage my temple. There's nothing wrong with people driving by, but it feels intrusive.

David must sense my apprehension, because a little more calmly he says, "I gave them the list price we talked about, and they're willing to pay more to keep it from going on the market. Quite a bit more. Assuming they like the inside, that is."

"Now what?"

"They're going to be in town for another week. Came down from San Francisco to visit family. Any chance you could have it ready to show before they leave?"

He knows I planned on having it ready because we were going to take pictures. But I assume the question is, am I ready for strangers to come through the house I grew up in?

This is the plan. Someone needs to buy the house so Mom doesn't have to pay the mortgage. I certainly can't afford it and my rent. "Sure, we can make that work."

"Perfect. Oh, one last thing. They want to speed up closing, but I told them that wouldn't be a problem since it's vacant."

A fist grips my heart. Gram's place is not *vacant*. I'm there. Hell, it still smells like her perfume.

I release a breath, telling myself to be grateful. One couple will come through instead of who knows how many between open houses and showings.

"Text me a date and time." I open the car door, ending the call. The football field lights are on even though school is still a couple of weeks away. Leo stands in the middle of the field, holding a football, as I walk up. "Look at that. Number Six is back."

Seeing him here again brings back a memory of the first time I saw him.

We went to a big school. It was impossible to know everyone.

One evening during our junior year, my friend Kiyana and I were in the stands, waiting to watch the varsity game. She was into one of the guys who played trumpet in the pep band.

Her long braids brushed my arm as she angled toward me. "He's cute, right?"

I peeked over my shoulder, unable to pick out which boy she meant. "Sure." They all looked similar in their feathered hats. Those were cute, at least.

"It's starting." She bumped my shoulder with hers and pointed at the field.

The other team's quarterback threw the ball to a tall kid, who charged fast down the field. Everyone cheered and shouted for our team to catch him. The excitement was nearly deafening as Number Six from our team gained on him, going for the tackle. Then *bam*.

The player with the ball slammed headfirst into Six's chest, sending him down. Hard. A few others were caught in the mix, and the play stopped.

I squinted at Six, flat on his back. "That doesn't look right."

A coach ran out, and everyone on the field knelt. Someone started CPR. Gasps and whispers came from the crowd.

"No." Kiyana reached for my hand. "Something's wrong."

Sirens pierced the night, red and white lights flashing as an ambulance arrived, and they carried Six away on a stretcher. Parents, students, fans, were saying, "Is he dead?" and "Got him right over the heart." But it all blended, becoming a hum like the power lines made.

Please don't die. I shut my eyes. *Please don't die.* It didn't matter that I didn't know him. He was a classmate. He lived in my hometown. And he was far too young.

As I lay in bed that night, I kept seeing the impact. Over and over. *Bam. Bam. Bam.* Helmet to heart.

The next day Kiyana called to share what she knew: The boy was Leo Ruiz, the kid whose dad ran the music shop. He'd suffered cardiac arrest, and CPR had saved his life. I found his picture in the yearbook, trying to recall if we'd ever had a class together.

A note had been taped to the music store door saying, *Closed until further notice.* When it reopened a couple of weeks later, Gram made some cookies and asked me to drop them off.

I didn't expect to see Leo sitting behind the front counter. At the jingle over the door, he glanced up from a disassembled laptop, screwdriver in hand.

Cute. He was definitely cute. Slim but not gangly. With dark eyes that made me feel exposed somehow. Like he wasn't just noticing me but *seeing* me.

"Shouldn't you be in the hospital?" I forced one foot in front of the other until only the counter separated us. I'd heard he was on a ventilator.

"I was released a few days ago." He set down the screwdriver. "They did all sorts of tests. My organs are stable. 'Miracle recovery,' some are saying." He made air quotes with his fingers.

It must have felt strange for him. Everyone knew who he was now. He'd made the news.

"Can you walk?" I didn't see a wheelchair.

"With help." He tipped his head toward the back of the store and the screech of a violin. Someone must have been taking a lesson. "I get a little better every day."

I set a tin on the counter. "My grandma made you cookies. I'm sure you don't want cookies from some lady you don't know, but, trust me, hers are the best."

He pried the lid off and shoved a cookie into his mouth. "And you are . . . ?"

"Oh, I'm Margot. Margot DuBois. We go to school together." Mom would have scolded me for not offering my hand to shake, but it was sweaty. The longer I looked at him, the cuter he got.

He wiped his hands together to free a few crumbs. "Well, Margot DuBois." He rested an elbow on the counter, pointing at the tin while giving me an earnest stare. "That was the best cookie I've ever had."

I lit up. "Right?"

A few weeks later, Leo came over, having found out where I lived from a friend of a friend, to return the tin. Gram only filled it with more cookies while Leo and I talked about school. The next time he came back, Gram gave him another refill, and I learned his hobbies: football, music, and restoring electronics. He learned mine: surfing and writing.

Rinse, repeat.

Eventually we made plans to hang out without a cookie segue.

"How did you manage that?" I say now, gesturing to the floodlights.

"I'm the coach." He backs up and tosses the ball to me in a perfect spiral.

It slips from my hands as I try to catch it. "Shut up. Since when?"

"Five years ago." He lifts his hands, signaling me to throw the ball back. "I missed it. Besides, I was getting soft." He dives two feet to the left to catch my terrible pass.

I burst out laughing. "Sure you were."

Hugging the football to his chest with one arm, he walks backward. "Go long."

"I can't do this." Still, I take several steps back, a warm breeze whipping around us. "I'll fall on my face."

"If I can learn how to change the engine in my car, you can learn to catch a football."

Before I can prepare myself, the ball whizzes through the air, straight at my chest, and I grasp it. "I did it!"

"Yeah!" He gives me an air high five, which I return. Like we used to.

The toss back to him is a little better than last time, but he still has to jump to catch it. A sliver of his stomach shows. Enough for me to tell it's muscled.

Soft, my ass.

"How did the housecleaning go today?" he asks.

Thoughts of David and the ticking clock on all that needs to get done send the heavy pumping of my heart to my eardrums. "You know when you lose something, and you say to yourself, 'It'll turn up eventually'? I don't have that luxury. I can't wait six months, a year, for the last tape to turn up when I'm least expecting it."

"You'll find it."

"What if I don't? What if, at the end, there's nothing? No tape or memento?" Each word comes out more clipped than the last. I'm getting worked up, but I can't help it. One more thing; that's all I want. Some special piece of Gram. A detail I never knew.

"I can only imagine how hard it is, missing your grandma and having to decide what to do with her things."

I stretch my neck to one side, then the other, to loosen the tightness in my shoulders. "Searching for the tape or another letter is the only thing keeping me from breaking down."

"Can I do anything to help?"

"No." We pass the ball back and forth while I work on swallowing the emotion clogging my throat. "Let's talk about something else, please."

"Okay," he says after a few seconds. "So there's this corkboard at the store—"

"I remember." It's the kind people use to advertise their businesses with cards or flyers.

"The mom of one of my students pinned up something about a short story contest. Thought you might be interested."

His next throw isn't perfect, forcing me to bend to catch it. "I told you I don't do that anymore." The Notes app on my phone, full of story premises, says otherwise. But I've never been able to stop jotting down ideas I'll never use.

"How many rejections did you get when you were writing?" he asks. "You don't have to say if you don't want to."

"Six years. Five manuscripts. Forty or so rejections for each . . ."

"Vivian had nearly that many, didn't she?"

"I don't remember." I do. My count is higher. "I wonder if she would have kept getting rejected if she hadn't met Hugh."

"Maybe. But I think the difference was she found what she was good at. What she loved."

I throw the ball. "She loved drama."

"How many times did she talk about how it *felt* to make someone laugh? She might have liked drama, but she loved comedy."

It's clear he wants me to rethink writing with an eye toward finding what *I* love, but I'm not taking the bait. Six years is a long time to dedicate to something that involves continuous rejection. It destroyed my confidence. Now I can't think about writing without feeling like hands are squeezing my lungs.

He nods at the bleachers, where the boombox sits. "Want to listen to a tape and find out who's right?"

We go and take a seat on either side of it as a gust of wind blows my hair into my face. I sweep it away at the same time that Leo reaches up to free a strand from where it sticks to the ChapStick on my lips.

At the touch, I still, a shiver sending goosebumps down my arms. His entire focus narrows to my mouth while he strokes his thumb along the edge of my bottom lip.

A little voice in my mind says if I lean forward, he will too. I can learn how twenty years have changed the way he kisses. Considering how everything else about him has aged like a fine wine, I imagine one brush of his mouth on mine would make me drunk with want.

Bad idea. The older I get, the less faith I have in dating. I had hesitations from a young age, knowing what Gram and Mom went through. But I still gave it a shot, hoping my experience would be different. It wasn't. My breakups with Leo and Ben were so traumatic I decided it wasn't worth getting serious about anyone.

Leo and I made great friends, though, and I think we're getting back there. As long as we don't complicate things.

I curl a hand around his wrist and gently tug it down. "I'm really glad we're talking again. You were one of my best friends in school. I'd love to have that back."

"Me too." His eyes catch mine, and there's such sincerity there, I know he means it. He wipes his palms across his shorts, then motions to the boombox. "Ready?"

In the spirit of the movies, and to move past the awkward moment, I give my most serious expression and say, "I was born ready."

Tape Three

CHAPTER FOURTEEN

Vivian

then

Ruth invited me to Dean's movie wrap bash at their new place in the Hollywood Hills later that month, the house white and stately, with vaulted ceilings and a grand staircase. Kit was supposed to be there, and I wanted to spy on the person I'd be working long hours with to get a sense of how big an asshole he was.

Ruth and I were getting ready in her bedroom, both in our bras and underwear, while the front door continuously opened and shut downstairs with people streaming in. A Frank Sinatra record played, the music muffled.

"Your closet is huge." I'd never seen one big enough to walk inside, with a rod that went all the way around, stuffed with dresses. I clipped my stockings to a garter belt. "I should pay you rent and move in here." It honestly wasn't much smaller than my apartment in New York.

She motioned to the left. "A roll-away cot over here." And to the right. "An electric kettle over there. It's got potential."

Never mind that they had a few spare bedrooms. She'd un-packed her dolls in the only one with furniture so far and set them row after row on the bed. Dozens of eyes, staring at you. Some were porcelain collectibles in elegant dresses, while others were the same kind of rosy-cheeked babies she left behind in New Jersey. Don't get her started on her favorites. I made the mistake once, wanting to understand the appeal of such a peculiar collection, and it was an hour-long stretch on the merits of Betsy Wetsy versus the Shirley Temple doll, during which time I wanted to bash my head against the wall.

I love her, but it's true.

"Pick whatever you want." She slid a dress off a hanger and threw it on. "Something with a deep V. It'll make your boobs look fantastic. I'm so jealous."

"At least no one tells *you* to lose weight." I carried such guilt, such embarrassment, over how my weight yo-yoed, it took the enjoyment out of eating. At home, I finished every crumb on my plate because I couldn't stand good food going to waste, while at work I stuck to coffee, not wanting the studio to look too closely into whether I was still taking the pills.

"Give it time." She checked her reflection in a gaudy gold-framed mirror attached to the closet wall, opposite the door, and fastened on a pearl necklace. "They will."

Last week Ruth secured a contract for musicals. She listed the apartment as her address on the studio paperwork, not wanting them to give her a hard time about living with Dean, sure he would pop the question any day.

"I'll see you out there," she said, turning to me. "Or do you want me to wait?"

Because of Dean's connections, he often brought home dresses actresses had worn once for events but never would wear again. Ruth wasn't too proud to be seen in them. Considering how little I made, I didn't have the money for anything as nice.

I waved her off as I picked through the options. "Go ahead. I need to try on a couple of these." Despite what the size said, they were tailored, so there was no telling if they'd fit.

The bedroom door clicked shut behind her, and I pulled a pale blue satin dress off its hanger, *K. Hep* handwritten on the tag, and tried it on. It fit but was too long, so I stripped it off and found a black velvet one, labeled *N. Wood*, which matched my lucky heels.

The door hinges creaked.

"I'm still not ready." I searched for a zipper to loosen so I could try it on. "Exactly how much boob should I show? This one looks really low-cut."

"Fucking hell," a deep voice whispered.

My lungs seized, my breath catching in my chest as I slowly turned. A man in a white T-shirt and a leather jacket propped his hands against either side of the closet doorframe.

Kit Pierce.

When I found out we'd be working together, I read some articles about him. The papers liked to focus on his sky blue eyes, saying he'd "pierce" you with his dreamy gaze. With how those eyes flew like a slingshot over my body, dimples sinking as he smiled, they weren't wrong.

I held the dress against me as heat spread from my cheeks to my chest at the horror of my future co-star seeing me like this.

He pointed at himself. "If you're asking me, the more boob, the better."

"What are you doing here?"

"Dean said the john was upstairs. I guess I picked the wrong door." He tilted his head, studying me. "Or the right one."

"Don't you know who I am?" We were going to work together, and he seemed clueless.

"Oh, shit." He straightened. "This isn't some sort of surprise, is it?"

"Surprise?"

"You know? Birthday or bachelor party." He wiggled his eyebrows suggestively as he stepped forward. "It's supposed to be a wrap party but . . ."

"You think I'm a stripper?"

He took another step closer. "Do you prefer 'exotic dancer'?"

"No."

"Striptease artist?"

"No."

"Burlesque queen."

I straightened my shoulders. "Does the name Vivian Stone ring a bell?"

He narrowed his eyes. "Yeah, she's supposed to—"

"She's me." I took some pride in his face falling.

"This is going to be a problem." Resignation hung in his voice as he glanced behind me.

I followed his gaze over my shoulder—to the gaudy mirror reflecting my backside. My head spun, yet he only shrugged like what he'd seen was accidental.

Get this under control.

I'd have screamed at him to get out except I didn't want to appear "emotional." You know how it is: A woman has to work twice as hard to be taken seriously, and when she stands up for herself, she's considered difficult. I didn't know what Kit was like, and I worried making a fuss could impact my reputation. And if we didn't work well together, the cameras would pick it up. Which meant I wouldn't prove myself, and my contract renewal wouldn't go as well as I hoped.

"Turn around. I'm getting dressed," I said. His shoulders sagged like wearing clothes was a crime, but he complied. I cleared my throat. "Now, why is this a problem? Surely, with your knowledge of every possible term for 'stripper,' you've seen a woman in a state of undress."

"Well, yeah." His tone said it was ridiculous he needed to confirm it. From what I could tell, he was around my age. Exactly how many naked or nearly naked women had he seen? "But we're doing a romantic comedy."

"So?" I threw on the dress and checked the mirror. "All right, I'm decent."

He turned and studied me. "With that neckline? Not a chance."

No wonder the papers called him a playboy. "You were saying?"

"We're going to have to kiss."

"And?"

"After this I'm not going to be able to kiss you without imagining you in a bra and panties."

My pulse hummed.

I couldn't control my body's reaction. It only happened because, objectively, he was very attractive. That whole leather-jacket-and-blue-jeans style was exactly the type I had used to daydream about, and the way he looked in them bordered on sinful.

"Sounds like *your* problem. If someone needs to back out, it'll have to be you."

"*Back out?*" he slowly enunciated. "You know how many films I had to do to get a lead?"

"Well, *I'm* not backing out." Not that we really could without bringing down the wrath of MGM by forcing us into B-list movies or loaning us out to subpar studios.

He smiled. "I like you."

I reached for my back, my fingers grazing the zipper. "I don't like *you*." The lie burned my tongue. Something about his unflinching candor was intriguing.

"Let me help." He spun me at my shoulders so I faced the mirror, his warm breath skating across my neck as he bent his head.

The bedroom door clicked. "Pick a dress and let's go. I haven't seen Kit yet, but—" Ruth stopped short as she took us in, my zipper still open.

"Found him." I hoped my wide eyes conveyed how outrageous I thought this was.

Ruth either didn't pick up on it or chose not to. "Oh." She gestured between us. "I'm probably going to have flashbacks of you two in here, sweaty and naked, from now on, but—"

"I'm not sweaty." I peered down at myself. "Or naked."

"Anymore," Kit added unhelpfully.

"No, it's fine." Ruth raised her hands and backed out of the closet. "Have a ball."

Really?

When the bedroom door shut, I motioned to my dress. "I have to go explain. Can you . . . ?"

After Kit zipped me up, he followed me downstairs, where the party was in full swing and the air was hazy with cigarette smoke. A woman in a tight sweater over a bullet bra attached herself to his side, handing him an old-fashioned. He opened his mouth to say something, but I eased into the crowd.

People congregated in different areas, clinking martini glasses and nibbling on hors d'oeuvres. Oysters Rockefeller, canapés, pimento cheese balls, deviled eggs.

Debbie Reynolds sipped a Manhattan with a few others near the dining room's floor-to-ceiling windows, which offered uninterrupted views of LA's skyline. In the living room, Kirk Douglas animatedly regaled a captive audience on the yellow corduroy sofa with a story.

Ruth was in the kitchen, eating a lobster croquette. Dean stood next to her, talking to another man as he walked his fingers up her back. It was so simple. An effortless kind of love.

I explained everything to her.

She pouted her bottom lip. "Nothing happened?"

"No."

A cheer came from the living room, where a man in a sweater vest passed a box of cigars around. My attention flicked right, snapping to Kit. He gave a faint smile, eyes never leaving mine, even while the woman at his side tried to engage him in conversation.

"Maybe next time," Ruth mused, following my gaze.

"Don't hold your breath."

Though it would have been nice to see him in only his underwear. Fair was fair, after all.

CHAPTER FIFTEEN

Vivian

then

During the days leading up to our rehearsals, I decided that how Kit and I met in Ruth's closet wouldn't affect my performance.

My palms sweated that first day, with me knowing how much of my future rested on this film's success. Yet Kit walked in like it was any other day, popping cheese cubes in his mouth while he talked to one of the crew, then an extra, as if there were no unspoken hierarchy of importance on set. When he caught sight of me in a director's chair with our script, he came over.

"How?" I asked.

"How what?"

"How are you not nervous?"

"Who says I'm not?" He popped another chunk of cheese into his mouth as I caught sight of Helen, the strawberry blonde with cat-eye makeup, walking across the room. She was cast in the film too—a small part, thankfully. Seeing her made my skin itch with memories of her pettiness.

I tried to ignore her, focusing on Kit. "You don't look it."

"I'm an actor." He winked. "But, honestly, I'm losing my mind."

"A little advice?" I nodded at his hand. "Don't save any of that in your pocket for later. It's bad luck."

He scoffed. "What has cheddar ever done to you?"

I cracked a smile. "How long do you have?"

After tossing the last piece into his mouth, he wiped his hands together. "You're a little goofy, you know that, Stone?"

The studio doctor, a short man with thick glasses, walked in and lifted a hand to get our attention. He shook a prescription in my direction. "For you." It sounded like he had a frog in his throat. "We'll adjust them once in a while, depending on the day."

"What are they?"

"A little moxie in a bottle." The doctor pushed it into my hands. "Keeps you bright-eyed and bushy-tailed." When I hesitated, he said, "We wouldn't want a lackluster performance, right? Our top clients take them. Perfectly safe."

I thought of Evelyn Summers, twitching and talking fast. Then of not sleeping when I took the diet pills. Of such endless energy, I thought I'd burst out of my skin.

There was no way I could take these, but I couldn't let him know. I would rely on more coffee.

As the doctor walked away, Kit said, "Doctor's orders," mimicking him down to the frog in his throat. The dam broke, and I laughed, which only set the stage, so to speak, for rehearsals.

If Kit hadn't started ad-libbing here and there, I wouldn't have either, but once we got going, there was no stopping us. Clowning around felt natural by the time we started filming.

During a scene where we danced cheek to cheek in a ballroom, tango music in the background, I accidentally stomped on his foot— part of the script. Kit was only supposed to fight a grimace. Instead, he keeled over, grabbing his foot. For good measure, I bumped him with my hip, sending him to the floor.

The crew erupted in laughter, the sound sending my confidence soaring.

Another day, a scene had us arguing in an alley.

I shot wide eyes on Kit. "How could you do that to me? Do you want me to be jobless? Homeless?"

"You sound a little *breathless*, sweetheart." His voice was off, having an accent.

I bit my lip to keep my composure, already knowing it wouldn't work for long. "And you sound like a Scottish laird, but you don't see me complaining."

"Oh, do I now, lass? Maybe we need to take a wee trip across the pond to be sure." He threw me over his shoulder, and I squealed, reaching desperately for a cameraman.

"Cut." Dean dropped his head back, chuckling. "For the love of God, cut."

It didn't feel like acting. Acting was supposed to be toiling to get the mood right. Agonizing over the delivery of lines. This? It was too easy. Like playing around.

I'd learned how to turn it on and off. Even if I wasn't in the mood to be funny or was having a bad day, once the cameras rolled, it was like a veil lifted. I became my character.

A month later, we filmed in the lake next to the Waterloo Bridge on Lot 2. After I drove my vehicle most of the way into the water, Kit came to the rescue, but my character wouldn't leave without her beloved car.

In the sequence that followed, Kit grasped a rope attached to the front of the car and gave comical heaves. The cameras focused solely on him, with me only a haze in the background, sitting on the car roof. Since there was no dialogue here, and music would replace all sound during editing, I took the liberty of goading him, knowing that nothing I said would make it into the final cut. And honestly? We had been at this for hours. I'd become bored.

I lay on my belly and kicked my legs up behind me, crossing them at the ankles. "Where are your muscles? I would have had this done by now."

Kit gave a slight shake of his head, holding back a smile, and yanked again. He wore suspenders with his shirtsleeves rolled up to his elbows. His forearms tensed as he tugged.

Maybe if he'd had no muscles to speak of I wouldn't have teased him, but seeing him in a white tank whenever he changed his dress shirt gave plenty of opportunities to notice that wasn't the case.

"Easy for you to say from your perch," he said over his shoulder so the cameras wouldn't see his lips moving. "Why'd you drive this car into the lake, anyway?"

"I hoped a big, strong man would come along and sweep me off my feet." I sat on my knees, pointing at a cameraman. "Have you seen one?"

"So that's what you're looking for?" Kit asked.

"Looking, looking." Tenting a hand above my eyes, I made a show of searching the set, a few chuckles coming from the crew. "I'll probably have to get down and find one myself."

Kit turned his back to the cameras as he continued yanking the rope, the curls around his hairline damp with sweat. "I'm not really a sweep-you-off-your-feet kind of guy, but I'm sure I could figure something out."

I couldn't tell if he was playing.

As much as I didn't want to admit it, when he smiled, my heart did the kind of flutter that might have needed medical attention. It hadn't done that since meeting Hugh.

Unfazed by everyone listening, he went on. "Let me guess: You like flowers? Romantic dinners?"

"Can we take five?" I called to Dean, who waved his agreement, turning to give the crew a break. I slid to the hood of the car, careful to keep my dress from riding up, so I was right in front of Kit. "We're not doing this."

He nodded at the top of the car. "You could have said no from there."

"I won't discuss my personal life in front of everyone. And I'm not dating a co-star." Dating another actor was fine, but dating a co-star felt sticky. "Whatever it is you're thinking? Don't."

Since he didn't argue, I assumed we were on the same page.

------ ◆ ------

A couple of weeks later, Kit caught up to me as I reached my dressing room.

Dark circles under his eyes showed through the makeup Sandy had used to cover them. "I've been trying."

"What do you mean?"

"After the lake, you said to stop thinking what I was thinking." He raked a hand through his hair, ruffling his curls. "I'm trying, but it's not working."

His continued interest surprised me. "So what do you want?"

He blew out a breath. "You said you don't want to date a co-star. To be clear, and no offense, I don't want to date you either."

That stung a little more than I would have thought.

"Don't get me wrong," he went on. "You're beautiful and funny. But I don't really date, and the only thing I know about you is you like to hang out in closets."

That stung a little less. I placed my hands in the pockets of my pedal pushers, waiting for him to continue.

"Look, we have, what, three hours before our next scene? I don't know about you, but I'm bored out of my mind sitting in my dressing room every day during breaks." He pointed at mine. "You can either go in there or you can come have a drink with me."

"I don't think so." I opened my door.

"How about a smoke?"

I peeked at him over my shoulder. "You know what they call people who keep doing the same thing, hoping for a different response?"

He smiled, and, boy, did those dimples dip in the most delicious way. "Optimistic?"

"Insane." At the lake, he'd suggested supper, then today drinks, and now a cigarette. "You know, every time you ask me out, you offer less."

"I'm not asking you out, remember? It'll only be two people enjoying each other's company."

"Who says I'll enjoy it?" I teased, shutting the door a little too firmly. "Let's walk." I held out a hand and focused on the silver case he held.

Kit popped it open and handed me a cigarette, then grabbed another for himself and lit both. He brushed a thumb across a dent in the case as we left my dressing room behind to wander the lot. "See that?"

"Yeah."

He brought it to his chest. "Saved my father from a bullet in World War II."

"You're kidding."

After returning it to his pocket, he held up three fingers. "Scout's honor."

"Why do I have a hard time believing you were a scout?"

"Probably that morality bit of the pledge." He blew out a puff of smoke as a trolley drove past. "I've been wondering. 'Vivian Stone.' Is it a stage name?"

"Yes. Is yours?"

"Nope. Studio let me use my real one."

"They must have known the papers would gobble it up."

His lips curved into a playful smirk. "You been reading about me, Stone?"

"You flatter yourself."

"Well, someone has to."

I glanced at my feet, fighting a smile. "Considering this is your first lead, you're already getting plenty of praise in the gossip rags for your last film."

He dipped his chin, meeting my gaze. "So you *are* reading about me."

Fell right into that one.

We went around the corner of a building, where an old black Ford with bullet holes along the side was parked. I imagined the cast members were gangsters in fedoras and two-toned shoes.

Kit kicked a loose stone. "What'd you have to do to get your first role?"

"*Do?* I auditioned." I shot a blank stare at him. "If you didn't even have to audition and got a contract because you're gorgeous, don't tell me."

"You think I'm gorgeous?"

"Well"—I gestured to his face—"even you have to think so."

"I didn't know you thought so."

There had to be a point to his question. "I don't know what you're asking. I auditioned and I got a part."

He snapped his fingers. "Just like that?"

"No, not just like that. I'd been trying to catch a break for years. Why? What'd you think I might have done?"

He was quiet for a moment, squinting against the sun. "There's talk about Eugene Mills and actresses."

"What kind of talk?"

"I guess his secretary walked in on him with a young woman on his lap. One of his new clients, looking uncomfortable."

Tension climbed up my back. "That's awful."

"It's Hollywood." He withdrew a flask from his pocket and took a swig.

It wasn't isolated to Hollywood. "I didn't sleep with anyone to get my contract. I promised myself when I got here I wouldn't. Even if it meant I never got a single role and had to head back to Long Island."

If the choice was either never achieving their dream or giving away a piece of themselves to reach their goal, I never judged someone for what they did. I judged whoever put them in that position. Because it wasn't really a choice, was it? It was an abuse of power tied with the pretty bow of alleged consent.

Walter Row was not the type who cared much about presentation, though.

"Can't you do something?" I asked. "About Eugene and the women?"

"Like what? Who's going to listen?"

"You're a man."

He threw a hand in the direction of the executive building. "And he's the head of the biggest studio in the country, with more money than God. I make an accusation to the press, and not only does he pay them off"—he curled his hand into a fist—"he squashes me like a bug in the process."

If Kit couldn't help, what good would I be?

"Someday," I said, "when one of us has a bigger voice, let's tell someone about Eugene."

He nodded as we reached my dressing room door.

"When you showed up, you said you'd been trying to stop thinking about something." I turned to him. "Tell me what it is."

"I don't know if—"

"Say it."

His gaze ping-ponged from my eyes to my lips, then lower. "I'm very attracted to you. And I'm pretty sure you're attracted to me too."

"You said you don't want to date me."

"You don't want to date me either."

"So what do you want?"

He rested a shoulder against the wall, invitation in his eyes. "We could have sex."

A nervous laugh fell from my lips, stunned by his frankness. "I'm not sleeping with you."

"I didn't think so."

Twenty hours awake hit me at once, the multiple cups of coffee worn off. I had to catch a couple of hours of sleep before they had us going again.

I twisted my door handle. "Let's keep things professional."

Professional, I repeated to myself.

CHAPTER SIXTEEN

Vivian

then

Dear Hugh,

Ruth just left, and I have to tell someone what happened. I keep going over it again and again.

It wasn't long after I got home from work—a day and a half at the studio before they let us loose—when she knocked on my door. I needed sleep, but I fixed us a couple of iced teas, sat next to her on my sofa, and said, "To what do I owe the impromptu visit?"

Her lips trembled as she smiled. "I have some news too big to share over the phone. I stopped by your dressing room earlier, but you weren't there."

"This sounds serious." I studied the way she bounced a little in her seat, like she had too much pent-up energy. "Did you buy an ice cream parlor?"

"No."

"You left Dean for a secret admirer in France?"

"Oui. But he sent me home once he found out I can't cook or clean."

"Then what is it?"

"I'm expecting." She squeaked and enveloped me in a hug.

"Oh . . . my." I patted her back, but I was thrown. This isn't the kind of news that excites people in the industry. You know that. But as a man, do you really?

Because, for an actress, having a baby changes how the public sees her. All the time and money the studio spent making her fit a certain innocent or sexual image could be destroyed. It affects sales at the box office, which affects the studio's bottom line.

In short, it means problems.

"I've wanted to be a mother for longer than I've wanted to be an actress," Ruth said as she pulled back, eyes glassy with happy tears. "When I was a little girl, I had so many dolls—"

"As opposed to the reasonable number you have now as a grown woman."

"Then I'm not sure what you're going to think of the notebook I started at age ten with baby names in it."

"I will think several things—and keep them all to myself." I couldn't remember the last time I'd seen Ruth so ecstatic, and then it clicked. After so many years, I understood her love for all those odd dolls: Ruth dreams of being a mother. "What are you going to do?"

"Work up the nerve to tell Dean, for starters."

The man is head over heels for her. He'll come around. I hope. "And then . . ."

"We have to figure out what to do about my contract."

"You won't quit?"

"No." She adamantly shook her head. "I can't."

"Because you love it too much?"

She blinked, turning to stare out the window. "Dean has debts. If you haven't noticed, he's a bit excessive." A soft huff. "I suppose we both are."

Endless champagne. Ruth's mink coat. Over-the-top parties.

Yes, I'd noticed. But I had thought they could afford it.

"It was the greatest blessing when I got my contract," she said, turning back to me. Her face had fallen, and her tears no longer shone with happiness but with fear. "I can't lose it."

I chewed on my lower lip, the talk of money troubles making my body stiffen.

Ruth can hide it for a while. She has some time to figure out what to do.

Since I didn't have a solution, the best I could do was offer support. I took her hand. "You're going to make a wonderful mother."

I desperately want to help her and wish I could tell you the situation.

In some ways, writing about this makes it harder because I assume if I told you, you would know how to fix it. Do you have life figured out? Because it feels like I am still trying to catch up.

Love,

Vivian

———— ✦ ————

"What do you mean, the dress doesn't fit?" Dean's jaw clenched as he stared at me a few days after Ruth's visit. "Squeeze into it."

I had rushed over from my dressing room to our soundstage with the stunning mauve number I was supposed to wear for today's first scene draped over an arm. Dean sat in his director's chair as I quietly explained the dress didn't fit. I knew he would be upset, but I hadn't expected him to explode.

"I tried." Side-eyeing the crew, I bent closer. "Please keep your voice down."

"Every minute we aren't filming costs the studio money. You understand that, right?" He pointed at me, his eyes maniacal. "So if your costume needs altering, after you already had a fitting, it's going to cost hundreds of dollars in wasted time. All because you overindulged."

I wanted the ground to open up and swallow me whole.

Why didn't the dress fit? I'd been careful. Coffee at work, meals at home. Whenever we went out, I left food on my plate, even when I was still hungry.

Dean appeared oblivious to how everyone within a fifty-foot radius could hear him berate me. I didn't need him to give me special treatment because I was close to Ruth, but I thought we were friends.

Something on my face—likely sheer panic—made him snap out of it. His shoulders sagged. "Sorry. I've been under a lot of pressure lately." He rubbed his temples, and I wondered if he was thinking about his financial troubles or if Ruth had told him about her pregnancy. "When the studio loses money, it comes back to bite me."

"So what now?"

"We fix it." He called over his assistant. "Get Patricia to Vivian's dressing room. Now."

I went there to wait for her, pacing back and forth.

I had tried on the dress three days prior. What had changed? Was it bloat? Maybe if I did the grapefruit-and-cottage-cheese diet for a couple of days, it would make a difference.

This made me look so unprofessional.

Patricia knocked, flustered as she walked in holding a tomato pin-cushion and a notebook. A measuring tape hung around her neck, and a pencil stuck out of her poodle-cut hair.

I wiggled on the dress, showing her how I couldn't get it down my hips. "I don't know what happened."

She helped tug it back over my head, then slipped the measuring tape around my waist. "It's my fault. I know you wanted it taken in an inch, but it's hard to know without checking you myself."

My heart tripped over its next few beats. An *inch*? "I never asked for it to be taken in."

She peered up from jotting down a measurement, pencil still poised. "Helen said you had lost weight and wanted your costumes taken in. I only had time to do this one."

My eye twitched. "I didn't tell her that." I tried to keep my voice even. Helen was messing with me.

"She used to be a costume designer before getting her contract, so I believed her," Patricia said, measuring my hips. "Obviously, I shouldn't have."

I could have told Dean—I was five seconds away from it—but decided against it. I would look like a child running to her parent to tattle. And if Dean knew, he'd bellow it out like he had when I brought up the costume issue. I didn't need him reminding the cast to play nice like this was elementary school recess. Firing her would only cause more delays.

We pivoted and filmed the next scene while Patricia worked fever-ishly on letting out my purple dress. Only that wasn't the end of it.

A few days later, mid-swipe of my lipstick, I paused and flipped it over, checking the label. It should have said "Cherry Red," but it was the wrong color.

Enough was enough. I got out a piece of paper, scribbled a quick note, then strode over to tape it on Helen's dressing room door.

If you want to hurt this less talented Fanny Brice,

you'll need to try harder.

———— ◆ ————

"Viv!" Ruth snapped her fingers in front of me a couple of weeks later, bringing me back to the cushy red leather booth at the Formosa Cafe. Rows of black-and-white photos of stars hung on the walls and lantern lighting fixtures cast a warm glow on our faces. "Where'd you go?"

Ruth had decided we, along with Dean and Hugh, should go out for monthly dinners to catch up, starting when Hugh got back from Hawaii. Since he had returned earlier that week, we made plans to meet at our favorite Chinese restaurant.

"Sorry. I was thinking about something that happened on set."

"You look tired," Hugh said next to me.

I dug into my noodles, trying unsuccessfully for the millionth time to use chopsticks. "I'm fine."

My light tone didn't fool him, though—it never did—and he tipped his head as if to say, *Want to try that again?*

It was good to have him back.

Hugh nodded at Dean with a scowl. "He's working you ragged, isn't he?"

"We're on a tight budget. Time is money." Dean surveyed my plate. *Leave me alone.* I hadn't even had a bite yet.

"No more work talk." Anticipation glittered in Ruth's eyes. "Has Kit asked you out again?"

Right when my heart had eased into a gentle rhythm, it stumbled over a boulder.

"He asked you out?" Hugh paused his forkful of chicken halfway to his mouth.

"Sort of."

Hugh didn't comment, only rigidly shoved the food into his mouth. It highlighted one of the differences I'd noticed between him and Kit. I never had to wonder what Kit was thinking or if he censored his responses. While Hugh had layers I had to work to peel back, Kit embodied *What you see is what you get.* It was refreshing.

"For the record, I don't think you should have turned him down. I know you love TDH." Ruth gave a mischievous grin. "But the studio is probably going to make you go out with Kit anyway."

TDH? She did *not* just bring up Hugh's nickname in front of him.

I smirked. "I do. I want TDH on my tongue and in my bed. I'll want TDH until I'm dead. But TDH does not want me, so I now choose to let it be."

Ruth tipped her head back and cackled.

"You sound like Dr. Seuss," Dean said.

"Is TDH a prescription?" Hugh asked, concern narrowing his eyebrows. "Because it doesn't sound healthy."

I shot wide eyes at him. "Oh, it's highly addictive."

Ruth relaxed in her seat. "Why don't we tell the fellas all about TDH and see what they think?"

"Don't forget, I know where you live." I shifted my attention to Dean. "Don't be alarmed if you see me standing over your bed at night. Just know Ruth had it coming."

Dean slung an arm over the back of the booth. "Is it a diet pill?" he asked Ruth. "Because you don't need any, honey." He gazed at me pointedly.

"I have to tell you, Vivian," she said like a woman with a death wish, "every time I look in my closet, I picture you and Kit." She peeked at Dean, then back at me with that angelic look the studio had taught her. "I had to say something. He wanted to go at it in there, but I told him I kept seeing visions of Kit tearing your dress off."

"He was zipping. It. Up." Which, on second thought, didn't sound more innocent.

Hugh blinked. "I'm sorry, what?"

Dean tilted his head in Ruth's direction. "She caught Vivian and Kit in our closet."

Hugh didn't move a muscle. He gaped at me, then the table. "A lot happened while I was gone."

I dropped the chopsticks. I'd get the hang of them someday. "Nothing happened and you know it, Ruth."

"That's what you keep saying." She speared a broccoli floret, her voice light. "So when's the kiss?"

Hugh's fork clattered to his plate. His gaze snapped around the table. "Sorry."

"Next week," Dean said.

Six days. Eighteen hours. Thirty-three minutes. To be precise.

"He's not as terrible as I thought he'd be," I said. "I expected some puffed-up playboy, but he's actually pretty fun."

Ruth's eyes widened. "You like fun."

I pointed my fork at her. "I'm glad you're here to remind me."

She seemed in good spirits. While I hadn't pried to see if she had told Dean about the pregnancy, I was concerned.

Hugh pushed around his food. "What else do you like?"

I took a second to think about it. "I like how he's forthcoming. He says what he wants. I wish more people were like that." The second the words left my mouth, I pinched my lips shut. He'd asked what I liked and not specifically what I liked about Kit.

Dean took a gulp of his mai tai. "Well, Ruth's right. You won't have a say about the dates. The public needs to know who you two are to generate some buzz before the picture comes out. What you do otherwise is your choice."

After seeing Hugh's love life choreographed, I dreaded someone telling me who to spend time with outside of work. But the possibility of having dates arranged with Kit didn't strike me as a chore.

Hugh's chuckle didn't reach his eyes. "Choice? I didn't know MGM offered such a thing."

"It's different for you," Dean said. "You're too big a deal."

Hugh stared at his plate. "Lucky me."

CHAPTER SEVENTEEN

Vivian

then

I spun on a chair in my dressing room mere hours before my kiss with Kit.

The problem with Helen and my dress seemed over. I hadn't had any issues remembering my lines. We had minimal retakes, usually when the crew couldn't stop laughing. Everything was going smoothly: Eugene would be bonkers to turn down my desire for drama when my contract renewal came. I didn't want something like an embarrassing kiss to change that. Since we'd been short on time and sped through rehearsals, we'd only simulated it.

A knock sounded at my door.

"Come in."

Kit stepped inside. "So . . ." He crossed his arms. "Is it going to be strange for us to kiss?"

I studied my reflection in the vanity mirror, my cheeks a deep pink without any rouge. "Why? Because you want to sleep together? Or because you said you wouldn't be able to kiss me without imagining me in my bra and panties?"

"Both."

I waited to see if he would add more—take it back or say things had changed. When he remained silent, I shoved my brush and hairpins in a drawer and attempted to swat away the realization that I didn't want him to change his mind. "I'm more afraid of making a fool of myself in front of everyone."

"We could practice now how we're supposed to. It might make it less stressful later." He rested his hands on the back of my chair, so close to the neck of my robe, the hairs on my arms stood.

It'd been so long since I was kissed, I didn't want it to look unnatural. But ever since he mentioned wanting to sleep with me, a bigger, louder part thought about kissing him so often—driving to the studio, in the shower, lying in bed—my mind had wandered past considering it in a professional capacity and drifted toward fantasy.

I curled my hands over the arms of my chair as my heart pounded into a gallop. The warmth of him behind me spread to my shoulders, and I wanted to relax into it. My eyes found his in the mirror. "Maybe we should."

"Stand up." He spun my chair around.

I did, but he didn't give me much room, so there was barely an inch between us. He gripped my waist as I placed my hands on his upper arms like we were supposed to. For a few seconds, he held my gaze, and, good God, the papers were right. His eyes really were piercing.

"You're beautiful," he said in a low voice.

"That's not the line."

"It should be." Before the words fully left his mouth, he bent down and kissed me.

Kit's lips were soft and inviting, making me forget how my hands were supposed to keep still. Instead, I dug my fingertips into his arms, my worries over how natural it would look popping like soap bubbles, one by one.

His tongue grazed my lower lip, thumbs drifting higher on my sides.

My breath hitched. I wanted more.

But this wasn't part of the script.

I tore away. "You can't do that on set."

A short groan passed between his lips. "I didn't do it on purpose." He rolled his head to the side, his gaze catching mine. "Not at first."

"We have to try again." I sighed, willing the dull ache in my chest away. "Three seconds, Kit. It can only be three seconds and can't include anything spontaneous."

"I know, I know. Believe it or not, I do know how to do this."

Oh, I believed it.

His eyes were resolved as he gripped my waist and kissed me again. This time his lips were a firm, still press, his hands perfectly placed. Everything about it was technically right. Yet it felt like an itch you couldn't scratch. All wrong.

I wanted to be kissed. *Really* kissed.

My frustration built, doubling with each second, so when he started to draw back, a rumble sounded in the back of my throat. I fisted his hair and held his mouth to mine.

Kit smiled against my lips, his grip loosening to slide up my ribs, and then the kiss transformed.

No longer was it a rigid press but a nip at my lower lip like a thank you before his mouth slanted over mine. Each passing second he grew more eager, more demanding. When I met him movement for movement, he let out an aching groan I could feel all the way to my toes.

My back bowed, chest pressing his, and he eased me to the wall, his lips skating down my neck, igniting razor-sharp need through my bones.

"No wonder girls are always hanging on you."

"Hmm?"

"It's not just because you're an actor or because you're gorgeous. They want you because of how you kiss."

His teeth skimmed my earlobe. "Do *you* want me? Because that's all I care about."

There wasn't time to answer before his lips found mine again. He reached under my thighs, lifting me, my back against the wall. My robe parted below the belt, only a bra and panties beneath, as I hooked my ankles around his middle.

A knock came on my door. Our mouths tore apart.

"Miss Stone?" Sandy called. "Ready for Makeup?"

Not even close. "One second."

That had escalated quickly. It frightened me, how far we might have gone if we hadn't been interrupted. More than that, it frightened me how much I didn't want to stop.

Kit dropped his head to the wall next to me, our gazes locked as we caught our breath. I imagined we were thinking the same thing: How were we going to give a conventional Hollywood kiss after that?

———————— ✦ ————————

An hour later, Kit stared at his lines on set while Makeup finished last-minute touches. At the sound of my footsteps, he glanced up, his teeth catching on his bottom lip.

Dean called everyone to get started. Cameras focused. Lights brightened. Boom poles moved into place.

All the things I'd been concerned about—angles, how they wanted us to place our hands, whether I should brush my teeth or if a mint would do—disintegrated. The only thing that mattered was how Kit's blue eyes combed over me as I walked up to him.

Vaguely I remember Dean calling action and Kit and me reciting our lines. Each word pounded against my heart like a beating drum in countdown.

It shouldn't have been so attractive, the way Kit's chest heaved as he stepped closer, his gaze darting to my lips. With everyone watching, it should have been an unappealing atmosphere in which to imagine kissing. But I didn't notice them. Everyone faded away. Nor did it seem orchestrated when Kit swept one hand into my hair, the other gripping my hip. As his mouth came down on mine, I ran my palms up his arms.

A volcano erupted in my bloodstream for one, two, three glorious seconds.

"Cut," Dean called.

Lava collided with my nerves as I cupped his jaw and slanted my lips, demanding he give me more.

"*Cut.*"

Kit let out a light groan, setting my body on fire as he curled an arm around my waist and drew me flush against him.

"Anyone have a bucket of water?" Dean's words penetrated my mind. "Or a hose?"

I pushed against Kit's chest, splitting us apart. He stood there in a daze, dragging a finger across his lips.

How had we let that happen? It wasn't at all how the kiss was supposed to go.

I smiled. Which meant we'd have to do it again.

———————— ◆ ————————

That night Kit and I pulled up to Mocambo for the first of many sham dates the studio had planned. We weren't quite halfway through filming, which left plenty of time to drum up curiosity about us and therefore our film.

I stopped Kit before he could open his car door.

"Let's fix your tie." I reached over and loosened it, remembering how he'd dressed when I had first seen him at Romanoff's. "Our date needs to seem real. I can't imagine you looking so buttoned up to take out a woman. Now your coat." When he turned, I grabbed the collar to help pull it off. "Clothes tell a story. On you, a suit looks like armor. Like you're trying to build a wall between us. Which doesn't help the picture the studio wants to paint."

For my part, I had on a jade blouse with cap sleeves and a ruffled white petticoat under my black swing skirt. Exactly what I'd wear on a real date.

Smirking, he cuffed his shirtsleeves to his elbows. "Look at you, Stone. Acting like you know me already."

When he came around to my door and offered his arm, several photographers' cameras flashed. We shared surprised looks, only partially fake, as we hurried past the line and inside.

The place was packed, the band playing an upbeat song. Within minutes, Kit bumped into one of his previous co-stars, Arthur Davies. While they ordered drinks and caught up, I eyed the table where Hugh and I had once sat, an odd mix of satisfaction and emptiness forming in my chest. It felt like only yesterday but a lifetime ago.

I'd tried to move past my feelings for him and in many ways succeeded. My heart wasn't nearly as heavy as it had used to be. Maybe if we weren't friends and I didn't still see him, I could have put it behind me completely. That wasn't going to happen, though, so I'd accepted it: He was my friend. I deserved reciprocal love.

Arthur lifted his empty tumbler toward Kit. "Another round?"

Kit threw back the rest of his drink. "Why not? Night's young."

As Arthur retreated, Kit set the glass next to my nearly full one. "I can get you something else if you don't like it."

I shook my head. "It's fine. I don't drink often, so if I finish it too fast, I'll probably sing off-tune and embarrass myself enough to have to flee the country." I leaned in conspiratorially and whispered, "Tell me this, and it's serious: Do you know anyone who can charter a plane at a moment's notice? I'll also need someone who can forge identification papers."

Kit stared at me blankly. No laugh. Not even a smile.

I fidgeted with one of my hoop earrings. "No, but really, I stick with only one drink or else I worry about turning into my father." Maybe he'd been right all those years ago about me needing a muzzle.

"Is he a fugitive too?"

My embarrassment lifted. "Considering how fast he packed his bags, I wouldn't rule it out."

The band's tempo shifted to the opening notes of "Cheek to Cheek," and Kit took my hand, nodding to the dance floor. "Whaddya say?"

I'd been worried the date might be a little awkward, since it had been planned for us, but, maybe because of our kisses, there was a new level of comfort between us. In fact, I would have accepted a dance even if this night hadn't been orchestrated. "Sure."

He led the way through the crowd. When we found an opening, his hand reached my back while mine rested on his shoulder, our other hands locked.

"So is that why you wanted to be an actress?" he asked as we swayed. "To make something of yourself so you didn't end up like your old man?"

"No." Though I couldn't say he had nothing to do with it either. When he lived with us, I acted as a means of survival. Easing into another situation, I forgot my life for a while. "He used to be a big-shot stockbroker in New York, sitting high on the hog, until—"

"The crash?"

I nodded. "It happened right after I was born. My father lost everything and moved us to Long Island. He managed to find work, but he never returned to being the person my mother said he once was. He always found something to complain about."

"Some people are like that. Never happy. It's like their attitude eats away at who they are," he said. "The market crash affected my folks too. I've wondered if the pressure of it all took a toll on their marriage and who they became as parents."

I stayed quiet, giving him space to elaborate.

"They weren't affectionate. With each other or me. There were never hugs. No kisses. Not even a pat on the back or a 'Nice job, son.'" He stared at a spot past my shoulder, as if seeing somewhere other than the dance floor. "They were the same with my brother, John. I left home as soon as I could, and John is the only one who still phones once in a while."

"Are you two close?"

"Not really. Honestly, I've never really been close with anyone, to any degree, until . . . well, until I started acting."

My heart winced for him.

I wondered if that was why he had the reputation he did. Maybe he'd been so deprived of affection as a child, he took warmth wherever he could get it as an adult, even if only for a night. I imagined it was hard to trust someone, to open up, after growing up unable to rely on either of your parents.

As the song ended, the piano began another while a woman started singing "Dream a Little Dream of Me." When Kit raised his eyebrows in question, I gave a small smile and nod to keep dancing. Somewhere between the lake scene we'd filmed and tonight, we'd strayed past the professional relationship I had intended on, but I found myself not minding one bit.

"You mentioned your father," he said, "but what about your mother?"

"She's on Long Island now, but she used to be a ballerina in New York. My parents met after my father saw her onstage. He came to every one of her performances with flowers until she accepted a date with him."

"Impressive."

I imagined the photos I had used to study as a child of her wearing a tutu. "I would have loved to see her perform. But once they married, my father wouldn't allow it."

There was no need to ask why she hadn't defied him. We had lived in such a small neighborhood, where everyone knew everyone's business. There would have been no hiding it. While they were together, she was under his thumb. Anytime she asked to do more than join a garden club, it turned into an argument, ending with him drinking and knocking her around.

"She's the reason I never stopped pursuing my dream of acting." She couldn't escape, but I would give myself a better life for both of us. "I never give up, even if I have to pivot. Like with Hollywood. I ended up here because Broadway didn't work out."

"How come?"

"I wasn't good enough." It was the first time I had admitted it without my stomach twisting.

"So then comedy?"

"Another pivot. I came to do drama." What if I still wasn't good enough? The idea was too devastating to consider, because then I would have to face the truth: It didn't matter how much you wanted something or how hard you worked for it; it still might not happen. "But the longer I do comedy, the more ideas I come up with."

He held me closer. "Oh?"

Silly what-if scenarios and funny lines to go with them had been popping into my head. "I was thinking they would work for a movie, but they might be better for a TV show."

His eyes lit up. "Don't tell anyone, but I think I like TV as much as film. So, what, you want to write a script?"

I gave a self-deprecating eye-roll. "I don't think anyone would be interested."

"I am. Tell me."

I tipped my head to one side. "Okay, so we have this fella, right? And he's divorced . . . or maybe a widower." I tipped my head to the other side. "And we have this lady."

"It's a love story?"

"A comedy."

"*Romantic* comedy?"

A flash of heat ran across my cheeks. "I like a little hanky-panky with a storyline. Anyway, we have this funny lady in the part, and she's, I don't know, the housekeeper."

He gave a soft smile. "The housekeeper?"

"Something like that. I see this woman wrangling a man into all sorts of shenanigans week after week." With his blank stare, I couldn't tell what he thought of it. I hadn't realized I cared about his opinion until now. "What do you think?"

"It has to be you. Playing the housekeeper."

Because I didn't plan on sticking with comedy, it hadn't occurred to me to imagine myself in the role. "It isn't happening. It was only an idea." With his continued smile, I laughed. "Maybe it has to be you. Playing the divorcé."

"Maybe."

That night, in the seconds before I drifted to sleep, the comedy idea played out in my mind. This time, instead of faceless actors playing the parts, I saw Kit and me.

Confidential

Stone Cold Vivian Is Hot for Pierce

Well, well, well . . . it looks like perpetual bachelor Kit Pierce is hanging up his playboy ways for co-star Vivian Stone. The pair were seen out on the town several times already, including dancing the night away at Mocambo and sipping cocktails at the Pink Palace.

Ever since the curly-haired heartthrob came onto the scene a couple of years back, he's been bouncing from one gal to the next. Need we remind you of the time he walked into Trocadero with a certain blonde bombshell only to be seen necking with a bosomy brunette on the way out? But once he laid eyes on Stone, he was smitten, and there's no surprise she was with him too.

After she'd been single for so long, we'd wondered if her heart was made of ice.

CHAPTER EIGHTEEN

Vivian

then

"Don't buy another car."

"Do you have a better idea?" Hugh asked as we trudged up the stairs to my apartment after another monthly dinner.

He had renewed his contract with MGM. It was a smart move when the studio gave him a chance at action flicks. They had made an obscene amount off him playing a double agent in his last three spy movies. No one pulled off a black suit quite like him.

It might not have been in the stars for us, but he was a star, and I wasn't oblivious.

"I save a lot already," he went on, my mint green heels dangling from the tips of his fingers. Everything I wore matched, from my dress and heels to my undergarments. "And I'm donating to the soup kitchen you told me about. Now I want to indulge in something."

I could think of a few indulgences. "You could buy a castle in the South of France. A pair of shoes for every day." He smiled at my suggestions, but I was only getting started. "All the tulips in Holland. The Queen's Crown Jewels. Ten thousand pretty dresses. You'd make Ruth eternally grateful if I stopped looting her closet."

Not that I didn't have some money, but I still sent a good chunk of my spare income to my mother. While she rarely cashed the checks, I wanted to have the funds available in case she did. There was never any telling if the factory where she worked would have more layoffs.

We turned and went up another flight.

"Do you need new dresses?" he asked.

"I was *kidding*."

"Compared to a car, it's nothing."

"Buy a house."

"Sounds like a headache. I want to do something fun, and I've never seen someone get as excited about clothes as you." He gave me a pointed look as we reached the next landing. "Don't tell me I'm going to have to beg you to go dress shopping."

"Oh, I'd like to see that."

"You don't think I will?" He dropped to his knees and grabbed my hand, his next words coming out with gusto. "Oh, Vivian. You cannot refuse me. You simply can't. I'll perish. Please. *Please*."

I'd have been jealous of how effortlessly dramatic he was if it hadn't been so funny. "I think you ought to look into Buckingham Palace instead. See if they'd be open to negotiating a sale."

Someone's throat cleared. A man in a white T-shirt and jeans stood by my door.

Hugh got to his feet. "Is that—"

"Kit?" I strode over, panic building as I mentally checked my schedule. "Did we have a date?" Maybe another outing had been planned and I forgot.

"No, no." Kit's gaze shot to Hugh for a split second before landing on me. "I was hoping to take you to dinner."

"Oh." I had so many questions, all muted by the snag to his offer. "We already ate." If Hugh wasn't there to call my bluff, I would have pretended otherwise.

"Maybe another time." Kit pushed off the door. "I'll get out of your hair."

"You don't have to," I blurted, turning pleading eyes on Hugh. This was the part where he gave me a knowing wink and backed away as quickly as possible.

"Do you want me to leave?" Hugh asked.

"Yeah. Yes." I couldn't give Kit my full attention with Hugh there. "Thanks for the ride."

"Sure." Hugh's movements were stiff as he handed over my heels and retreated to the stairs. We stayed quiet until the echo of his footsteps hit the next landing.

Kit scratched his chin. "Was that a date?"

"Absolutely not." I exaggerated the words to compensate for his assumption and unlocked my door to drop my heels inside. "Do you want to come in?"

He rested a shoulder against the doorframe. "I don't trust myself not to kiss you."

The words were like a melody playing in my belly. "I thought that was what you wanted."

"I do, but I also want to go out with you. No shams."

"Why?" Kit Pierce didn't date.

He shrugged. "I like you."

Just like that. Simple. Easy.

"You do, huh?"

He bit his bottom lip, teeth skating free with his crooked grin. "Yeah."

"You're not dressed up." I pointed at his T-shirt.

"Someone once told me clothing tells a story. So if my suits are armor"—he used two fingers to puff out his shirt—"what does this tell you?"

Too much. "You said you weren't a sweep-you-off-your-feet kind of guy."

"I'm not." He held up a hand. "See? I didn't even remember flowers. But maybe you could tell me what kind you like in case I mess up and need to apologize for something."

"Mess what up?"

"Us." He skimmed his fingertips over the back of my hand, his voice less confident than usual. "I've never done this before—*really* done this—but I have a proposal."

"I'm listening." My ears were attuned to every syllable.

"You don't see anyone but me, and I don't see anyone but you."

A piece of my bruised and bandaged heart beat anew. "I could do that."

"Yeah?" He was close enough that I could feel the word on my lips, a flirtatious glint in his eyes. "So we're going steady now, Stone?"

"I guess so," I said, smiling.

All I wanted was to kiss him. To drag him inside. But he had come to take me out.

I toed on a pair of flats and locked the door.

"Where are we going?" he asked.

"I already had supper." I threaded our fingers and tugged him toward the stairs. "So you're taking me for ice cream."

———— ✦ ————

We crossed the street and went down the block to the closest soda shoppe.

A row of teenagers drinking malts and milkshakes sat on bright red stools along the counter while a couple of soda jerks in aprons and white hats filled orders and wiped trays. Two girls in poodle skirts and saddle shoes stared—probably trying to decide where they knew us from—while we waited for Kit's devil mint and my pineapple sherbet.

"Why's everyone into pineapple?" he asked as we stepped back onto the sidewalk with our cones, lampposts lighting our way. "I swear, pineapple upside-down cake is at every party these days. I don't see the appeal."

A kid sped by on a bicycle, a gentle purr coming from a baseball card hitting the spokes.

I licked my sherbet. "It's refreshing. And better than the after-dinner mint masquerading as ice cream you have."

He bit into his, making my teeth hurt on his behalf. "It's half chocolate."

"Like an Andes mint?"

"But better."

What would gossip columnists say if they got a picture of me right now? Likely there'd be at least one snide remark about how I

should put down the sweets. Ever since the tabloids started printing
our pictures here and there, I'd become acutely aware that potential
photo ops could happen any time. It wasn't always obvious until
there came a bright flash.

"I've been meaning to ask." He withdrew a folded magazine page
from his back pocket and handed it to me. "Do you happen to know
who this is?"

Between an article about Winston Churchill being knighted by
Queen Elizabeth II and one about Ernest Hemingway winning the
Pulitzer Prize for Fiction was an ad for coffee. A housewife was bent
over a man's knee, his hand raised like he was about to spank her for
buying the wrong brand.

I remembered the man's knobby knees digging into my belly. "I
can't believe they're still circulating it." Why couldn't Kit have found
one of me advertising a vacuum?

"That's going right on the fridge."

"You wouldn't." Though I kind of liked the idea of him having a
picture of me at his place, we could do better than that ad.

As he replaced it in his pocket, I reached for him.

He stepped back and wagged a finger. "Uh-uh."

Smiling, I reached for him again, and a cool sensation hit my
skin. A drop of sherbet soaked through below the Peter Pan collar
of my dress. "Oh, no."

He patted his pockets. "I don't have a hanky."

A hanky wouldn't help. It was only one spot, so maybe—

Another drop fell, and I groaned.

"Hey, hey, hey." Kit swirled his tongue around my cone, lapping
up the drips of an ice cream he didn't even like.

My shoulders slumped. "What if someone takes our photo?"

"It's so light, no one will notice." When I shook my head, he said,
"You don't believe me?" He glanced down at himself, then his cone.
Before I could stop him, he pressed the tip of the green-and-brown-
swirled ice cream against his white shirt. "There. No one will notice
yours when mine is so much worse." He positioned the cone again.
"Do I need another?"

"You're nuts, you know that?"

"Am I?" He came closer with a sly smile, and I backed up, a child-like joy coming over me. When he took another step, the fingers of his free hand dancing in the air like he might tickle me, I pushed my sherbet in his face.

A glaze of yellow spread across his mouth.

"Oh!" I laughed but stopped short when he returned the favor, his ice cream hitting my lips, making me gasp.

Both of us stood still, staring at each other. At the sight of his tongue darting out to lick away some sherbet, something snapped in me. Something desperate to taste the pineapple on his lips and the mint from his tongue. I threw an arm around his neck and rose on tiptoe to press my mouth to his.

When I remembered he didn't like pineapple, I stepped back. "If I taste terrible—"

"You're the best flavor." He splayed a hand across my lower back and drew me against him, his mouth finding mine.

I could feel it. How serious it would be between us, though it had only just started.

A car beeped as it drove past. "Hubba, hubba!" someone hollered out their open window.

I broke the kiss and pointed at my apartment. "Do you want to . . . ?"

"I'll walk you up."

We tossed our cones, and I wiped my mouth with the back of my hand while he used his shirt hem to wipe his, both of us quiet as we walked upstairs.

I held my doorknob. I didn't want him to leave. "Do you want to come in?"

He chewed his lip as he pressed against the railing across from me. "Don't people take things slow when they're dating? I wanted to show I like you by not coming inside."

I swung the door open and flipped on the lights, then strode over to him, more confident than I felt, and grabbed his arm. "You showed me that when you first got here."

Kit took a step, restraint fading. "You sure?"

"I wouldn't do something I didn't want to." Once I had him inside, I shut the door. "I want you."

The phone rang as Kit kissed me.

"Do you need to get that?" he asked.

I reconnected our lips in answer. My foot caught on something at the same time he stumbled a step, both of us breaking apart and laughing at the heels we had tripped over.

The backs of Kit's legs hit the sofa and he sank onto a cushion. He curled his hands around my hips, tugging me to him. My heart climbed to my throat as I slowly straddled his lap. One of his hands caught in my hair so he could bring my mouth to his, my fingers dragging up and down his chest and stomach as we kissed. When I shoved his shirt up, needing to feel more of him, he lifted his arms and let me pull it over his head.

He reached for the front of my dress and undid the buttons, one after another, so slowly I could have stopped him a dozen times before he pushed my dress down to my hips. My pulse sped up, a row of falling dominos, as he unclasped my bra and dropped it to the floor.

Kit studied me, his hands sliding over the dip from my hips to my waist, then up my ribs. "You're perfect." His thumbs grazed the curves of my breasts, then he cupped them fully, and a rush spread through me—a mix of fear and excitement like when I went on the Coney Island Cyclone as a kid.

I kissed him again, and he turned to lay me down on the sofa, my dress pooling as he settled between my legs, his mouth on my neck.

"Wait." I rested a hand on his shoulder, stopping him before my willpower took a flight to Rio. "I haven't done this before."

A devilish smile. "Fooled around with a co-star?"

"Slept with someone." In case that was where this was headed, he needed to know. When his smile fell, I cradled his face. "What are you thinking?"

"What a fool I was for propositioning you."

"You didn't know. And just because I haven't done much doesn't mean I'm ignorant."

After a quiet moment, he said, "We can stop."

CHAPTER NINETEEN

Margot

now

When the audio stops, I'm quiet, stunned she chose *there* to end the tape. What a tease.

"I found something about Kit," Leo says, scanning his phone like he's been doing on and off for the last ten minutes.

I sit up on the metal bench, where I've been reclined for most of the tape. "The way you said it sounds bad."

"You want to know?"

"Do you think it's something we'll hear on the tapes?"

"I honestly have no idea."

"Then don't tell me," I say, "and if it doesn't come out, share at the end."

He swings a leg over so he's facing the football field and rests his forearms on his thighs. "All that stuff about the studio rules—did you know it used to be like that?"

"Some of it. Years ago I went down a rabbit hole for a magazine article and learned about actors getting addicted to pills the studios forced on them. Some of them ended up seriously depressed. Suicidal. It certainly casts a dark cloud on 'Over the Rainbow.'"

He lifts his eyebrows and blinks at me. "Damn."

"So you think Vivian and Kit might be endgame?"

"I thought you didn't want to know."

I groan. "I know, I know. I want you to tell me but will let it play out." The shoebox isn't in sight, but maybe it's in his car. "Happen to get another tape cleaned?"

He winces. "Sorry."

◆

Over the next few days, between editing projects for work, I clean the attic until I have it completely cleared out. Downstairs, I make piles: donate, keep, sell.

I'm supposed to have more time for this. But with people coming to look at the house soon and David's mention of a fast closing, I'm rushing, and it's making this uncomfortable process harder. Especially because I still haven't come across the eighth tape or anything tied to Vivian. I'm running out of time to find it and places it could be, and I'm afraid maybe it's not here at all.

Leo and I have been texting every day. A couple of times I think of asking if he'd help lug out some of the heavier things, but I don't want him here when a memory of Gram hits so hard I get choked up.

One night we skip texting altogether and he calls. I rarely talk to anyone on the phone except my mom, and only because she thinks texting takes too long.

I connect my earbuds to my phone so I have my hands free to go through a stack of Gram's records in the living room. "Did you keep playing football in college?"

"Yeah." A bell jingles, then there's the clicking of metal I assume is him locking up the store. "Tore a ligament in my knee during my last year, which sucked. I went to physical therapy. Probably longer than I needed to."

I let out a huff of a laugh as I set a Monkees record I want to keep aside, since it was one of Gram's favorites. "Why would you go longer than you had to?"

"I met a girl." A car door shuts, then an engine turns over.

"Amy?"

"Yep." A few seconds pass. "Those early days were easy, you know? Before we had all the pressures of a house and student loans to repay. Marriage, wanting kids . . ."

"Hmm." The closest I ever got to any of that was when Ben took me to a jewelry store and asked which ring I preferred. I assumed a proposal would come soon after but it never did.

"How did you end up liking college? I bet you had a blast."

"Eventually, yeah." I settle against the couch. "For the first six months I contemplated coming home, like, every day." I remember sitting on my little bed in my dorm room, everyone having the time of their lives, while I felt like a baby for being homesick. "I lost count of the number of times I cried myself to sleep."

"Oh," Leo says on a breath. "I'd hoped your mom was right about you needing to spread your wings a little."

"I ended up being fine. I got close to my roommate. We started going out. I met Ben."

"What happened there?"

"Where to begin?" I shut my eyes, a time capsule with flashes of my relationship opening in my mind. "We were both into reading. The same movies—"

"*The Notebook*?"

"I *love* that movie."

He laughs, the sound warm and decadent. "You always had a thing for Nicholas Sparks."

I love that he remembers after all this time. "Ben liked to write, like me. I thought it made us a good match."

"And did it?"

"For a while. Then the differences in where we were in our writing felt like a bigger hurdle than the fact that he hated the beach or how I couldn't relate to his upbringing and the times he talked about 'summering in Europe.'"

"He was a better writer than you?"

"Writing is subjective. I'm not sure that he was *better*, but he was more successful. I think I started resenting him. Not for his success but that he had more time to dedicate to it than I did." It's easier to open up, to be vulnerable, when Leo isn't right in front of me. "I always thought if I'd been born with a trust fund, I'd have had more time to write, and then I would have gotten somewhere. Instead, I got bitter, I guess, and emotionally drained, so I gave up."

Leo stays quiet.

I dig the heels of my palms into my eyes. "He said I was a coward for it." I laugh to lighten the mood. "Not sexy."

"You've always been sexy."

I smile, appreciating his attempt at making me feel better.

Three hours later I'm in bed, yawning so loudly, Leo laughs. Before getting off the phone, we decide on a time to meet at his music store to listen to another tape.

I'm a few minutes early the next day when I reach the East Village. Leo said he'd be finishing a lesson, so I'm not in a hurry as I stroll down the sidewalk.

My gaze catches on the art store across the street. When did they paint a mural on the side of the building? I missed it on my last drive through. Without Gram here, who knows how long it'll be before I'm back. What else will I miss?

I reach the music store but stay outside to call my mom and give her an update on the house. I've been putting it off.

She answers on the second ring. "Hey, hon."

"Hi." I slump against the wall.

"What's wrong?"

She always knows. "Someone wants to buy the house. At least, they probably do."

"And you're not happy about it?"

"It's hard imagining someone else living there. Never going back."

"I know. If it's too much, I can help."

"How?" Her coming out again defeats the purpose of me taking care of it.

"I'll hire movers to put everything into storage. If you give the real estate agent the key, you can be done."

"I don't like that idea either." A storage unit still would leave Mom with an extra bill.

"Let me know. I'll help however I can." A keyboard clacks on her end. "Any update on those tapes? Did you find the last one?"

"Not yet." There's no hiding the uncertainty in my voice.

At least she doesn't try to console me by saying, *You will*. "Keep me posted. I'm curious."

We hang up and I walk into the store. Piano notes float out from the back. I wander over and sit in one of the seats parents use while waiting for their children.

"I'm really impressed," Leo says from a lesson room when the song comes to an end. "I knew you could do it, but it must have taken a lot of work."

Chair legs scrape the floor, and a boy of around ten with square-framed glasses walks out. Over his shoulder he says, "My mom doesn't let me play video games until I practice."

Leo laughs as he follows, the sound so masculine, I feel it in my chest. "Video games. An incentive that hasn't changed since I was a kid." Spotting me, he beams. "Hey, you're here. Gimme a minute, okay?"

A woman in a yellow sundress walks in the store and waits at the front counter for them. She curls an arm around the boy's shoulders while Leo goes over what they practiced before giving the boy a fist bump. The woman, around my age, nods, pride shining in her eyes.

In another life, that could have been me.

It wasn't too long ago I felt sure it was "the time"—my ideal window to get married and have a child. I had a vision for what my future looked like but kept telling myself, *Soon, soon*.

My chest caves in a little, not knowing what my future looks like outside the dreams I had.

The woman rests a hand on Leo's arm, speaking so low I can't decipher her words, and he laughs. There isn't a wedding band on her hand—the hand still on his arm—and the way she's looking at him has flirtation written all over it.

I wonder how many of his students' moms are single. How many signed up their kids as much for their own sake as for their kids'? It seems a ridiculous thought at first. Then again, how many good-natured, good-looking single guys in our age bracket are out there? Not many.

It's hot in here. I hold the collar of my shirt, puffing it out to get some air. Why is it so hot all of a sudden?

"You okay?"

I blink up at Leo, standing before me, and the bell over the door jingles as the child and his mom walk out. "Have you ever dated any of your students' moms?"

So that spilled out of my mouth. Yet he only stares at me for a few seconds. A telltale sign.

"You *have*," I tease.

"One time. All right?" He holds up a finger to defend himself, but he's smiling.

"She's interested." I nod toward the door. What the hell is wrong with me?

"Yeah, well, forgive me for not taking dating advice from the person who went with Tony What's-his-name to senior prom." Playfulness shines in his eyes. "The one with the red mohawk who listened to emo screaming music."

I lift my hands. "Tony was my lab partner. He needed a date after his girlfriend dumped him. I only agreed so he'd start pulling his weight on our lab project. I was struggling to pass chemistry as it was."

Tony turned out to be a pretty fun date. I don't remember how it happened, but we ended up daring each other to a push-up contest right in the middle of the dance floor. Everyone formed a circle around us as he shucked off his jacket, and I ignored the stretch of my beaded silver dress as I got to the ground. I was totally kicking his ass until the seam at my side split.

Leo was there, cheering me on, when he saw my wardrobe malfunction. He whisked me out and into the first private room he could find—an office at the venue. Being Mr. Fix-It, he picked through supplies on the desk. "Let's see what we've got to work with."

I sat on the corner of the desk and flicked on a lamp. "I would have beat him."

"Dude's arms were shaking so bad, I have no doubt he was three seconds from collapsing." He knelt before me, studying the rip. "How much do you care about this dress?"

"Not at all." I wouldn't be attending another prom, so it'd only take up space in my closet. "Wait, tell me what you're planning first."

"You trust me, don't you?" He came at me with a hole punch.

"For some reason."

Leo let out a light laugh, starting at the top of the tear, but both of us went silent as he touched the bare skin of my side. I glanced at the ceiling, trying not to focus on his every move, my breathing going shallow as he made his way down. Within minutes, he MacGyvered the rip with a hole punch, paper clips, and a stapler.

"There." His fingers drifted over his handiwork and the slivers of skin peeking through. A shiver zipped down my arm at the gentle touch. "It should hold."

I fought the quiver in my voice as I said, "Thanks. I guess I should get back out to Tony."

Leo's hand drifted from my side as he stood. "You deserve better than a prom date who's hung up on his ex and has shit taste in music."

We were so close, my chest grew warm. "I'll make sure to hold out for someone with better taste in the future."

He rested a hand on the edge of the desk. Above a whisper, he said, "You learned all the best bands from me, you know."

Everything came to a standstill, the muffled, upbeat music outside even quieter than our breathing. I swallowed hard as his gaze drifted to my mouth, my eyes, then my mouth again.

An inch closer. I thought I'd fracture in the second it took him to close the gap between us and brush his lips against mine. He drew back, giving us both a chance to change our minds. If he was waiting for me to stop him, he'd be waiting forever.

At the slide of my hand into his hair, my chin tipping up, his restraint snapped, and he fully captured my mouth with his.

Just like that, our friendship became more.

Leo stares at me now, his ears red like his thoughts wandered down the same path as mine. "He really did have shit taste in music."

"Yeah." The word comes out thick, like tar is stuck in my throat. I motion to the lesson rooms. "I didn't know you gave piano lessons. I thought that was your dad."

"Dad only does strings and vocals now. I do piano and drums."

"Since when do you play drums?"

"I don't know. For ten years now, maybe?"

We walk down a carpeted hallway, past a room with all-black walls and a drum kit in the middle. Broken gold cymbals decorate a wall like art pieces. He leads me into the next room, painted all cream. It's the one I used to get lessons in, with the same upright piano. Leo sits on the bench in front of the piano and pats the space next to him. My leg grazes his, sending electricity to my fingers and toes.

Think friendly thoughts.

He turns toward me. "Want me to teach you something?"

I lift a hand and shake my head. "I tried learning before, remember? I was *bad*." I laugh, but he doesn't join me.

"Sometimes people are lucky enough to be naturally talented at something. The rest of us have to practice our asses off. I'm sure it's the same with writing and surfing." His long fingers drift down the keys in what I think is "Bohemian Rhapsody."

"Sure, but I wasn't trying to *do* anything with surfing. It was only for me. For fun."

"Maybe that's the problem." He pauses. "When did writing stop being fun?"

I want to smile, to make light of this, but the truth spills out: "When I stopped writing what I wanted."

Ben wrote the kind of books that won prestigious awards. His first was listed as one of Obama's favorites. Oprah made his sophomore novel a book club pick. That had never been my goal until, little by little, he convinced me that was the legitimate way to go.

I can't take the pity on Leo's face. "Are we going to listen to a tape? I looked up some pictures of Vivian online. Kit too." I also looked up Hugh, not because I forgot what he looked like, but because it's Hugh.

"I looked up more too. Did you know—"

I wave to stop him. "No, no, no."

"You don't want to know how her love life panned out? Or her career? It's pretty juicy." He reaches into a reusable bag at his feet and withdraws a Cheez-It box. "And I'm not the kind of guy who says things like that."

"I want Vivian to tell me what happens. I want to feel like I'm there with her. I'm too invested to get the quick, spoiler-y version." Smiling, I take the box from him. "You know the way to a girl's heart."

"I aim to please." He turns in his seat and reaches for the boom-box. "Then let's find out what happens next."

Tape Four

CHAPTER TWENTY

Vivian

then

"No," I said, my back on the couch, Kit hovering over me. I caught the way his eyes dipped to my bare chest. "I don't want to stop."

His mouth curved into a hint of a smile. "You're supposed to kick me out and say this was enough for tonight."

"Then leave."

"Do you really want me to?"

"Not even a little."

"Thank God." Kit kissed me. "We'll take it slow, okay? I like you too much to check off all the boxes in one night."

Two sides of my mind warred: the grateful half, which appreciated how he sensed my apprehension, and the impatient half. Now that I'd decided I wanted it all, I didn't want to wait.

But the bigger half won out, the half that said I couldn't rush this. I had been used in the past at the whim of someone else and for their satisfaction. I needed time to learn how to share pleasure with someone. Someone I cared about. Something told me Kit needed it too. Despite his experience, being with someone he cared about and could trust was new.

He threaded his fingers through my hair as he dropped his lips to mine.

The time in my dressing room had been frantic, like we were on the game show *Beat the Clock* and had to complete the challenge before the seconds ran out. This time his lips were gentle as we pulled back and came together again. Lazy as we memorized each other's mouths and began to explore each other's bodies. We could savor this time.

And for the next hour, we did.

The phone rang again a little while after Kit left. I lifted the receiver from the cradle. "Hello?"

A long sigh came from the other end. "This is the fourth time I've phoned. I was about to come over and make sure you were still alive," Ruth said.

I propped my feet on the coffee table, crossing them at the ankle. "Why would I have perished between when I saw you at dinner and now? I was in the shower."

"Hugh Fox is why. You left your purse in his car, and by the time he turned around and got back to your apartment, you didn't answer the door. He got worried."

"I went out with Kit."

"Which is what I assumed when he explained what happened. But then I couldn't get ahold of you, and *I* started to worry."

That happened when a woman lived alone. "What did you say?"

"I didn't get a chance to say anything. Dean got on the line and told him to stop being overprotective. That it would be better for the film if you and Kit slept together. Something about you circling him like a dog in heat."

I shut my eyes. "He didn't."

"He did."

It was only natural for Hugh to watch out for me, like he used to watch out for his sisters. At his oldest sister's wedding, he'd said that when they were young he walked them home from school so no one picked on them and took the blame for accidents at home so they wouldn't get punished.

I twisted my finger around the coiled phone cord. "Speaking of Dean, did you tell him?" There could be no mistaking what I meant.

Movement in the background said she was carting the phone into another room. "Yes."

"And?"

"He's happy. Took a little while to come around, but we both wanted children someday, even if this isn't exactly the order we hoped to do it in."

Oh. I had been so focused on the career side of it, I hadn't considered the other aspect. They weren't married.

"We're going to schedule a meeting with Eugene," she went on, "and give him an ultimatum: Let us keep the baby or we both walk."

"You'd really walk?"

"No, but he doesn't know that."

I chewed on this information. Dropped my feet to the floor and rested my elbows on my knees.

In a very real way, we were characters that the studios dressed up and gave new identities. Where the public thought we were from, our families, our hobbies—all were decided for us.

My background, if anyone asked, was I'd had a comfortable upbringing in New York, attended an all-girls school, vacationed in the Thousand Islands with my family, and competed in equestrian events with my horse, Lucky. By inventing these stories, the studio made sure no one really knew me. My fans would never really love *me*; they'd love the image the studio fabricated.

Even now I haven't corrected these stories lest the public think I intentionally hoodwinked them. Would they like the real me?

Ruth's image, on the other hand, was angelically pure and hurts-your-teeth sweet.

Getting married would be wise and the default solution to a situation like this, but it was more complicated in Hollywood. While the public could put two and two together that *of course* a couple had sex, they didn't want to think about it, and they certainly would if they found out Ruth was pregnant. It was the same reason films and TV almost always showed couples in separate twin beds.

"In case he doesn't go for it, you could offer an alternative," I said.

"Like what?"

"Adoption. I heard Warner Bros. let an actress go to the hospital to get some 'rest.' We know what that means. Two months later she adopted a baby girl." The actress was a bombshell, so it wouldn't surprise me if the studio wanted to protect that image. Motherhood didn't scream 'sexy,' according to them. "Maybe you could do the same thing, if necessary."

"I'll take whatever I can get." Her voice lightened. "Enough about me: Now dish. What happened with Kit?"

"We went out for ice cream, then came back here and fooled around a little."

She shrieked. "Vivian!"

"Ruth." I knew she'd love that.

"You really like him, don't you?"

"Yeah, I do." I waited with the other information she'd squeal over. "He said he wants us to only see each other."

"He did?" She clapped. "You're going to marry him!"

"Don't get ahead of yourself."

I'd let myself think about it over the years, the kind of relationship I hoped for. One entirely different from my parents'. I'm sure it won't surprise you to know that, as a child, I looked to films for inspiration, combining the best parts of each hero into my dream man.

I couldn't help but smile as I brushed a hand across the cushion where only a little while ago Kit had made me feel adored. For once, I couldn't help getting caught up in the idea that real life was better than the fictional ones I used to dream of.

◆

A couple of weeks later, Kit and I were sitting in director's chairs at our soundstage between takes when a squeal came from behind us.

He propped an elbow on the back of his chair and twisted. "Was that a pig?"

"It's Ruth." I'd have known that noise anywhere before her blonde bob even came into view.

She dodged cameramen and leaped over lighting cords as she practically galloped over.

I waved frantically as I stood. "The British are coming! The British are coming!"

"More likely the Russians." Kit threw his arms over his head in a duck-and-cover motion like the schools made kids do.

"I said yes. I said yes!" Her hand flew toward my face. A huge diamond ring sparkled on her finger.

"Dean proposed?" Kit asked.

"And I said—"

"Yes," we replied in unison.

I embraced her. "I'm so happy for you. Dean, on the other hand, deserves a condolence card."

Stars shone in her eyes. "He did it last night and I couldn't wait to tell you. I nearly rang, but we got a little . . . preoccupied."

I almost asked if Dean had pretended to be Davy Crockett again but wouldn't mention their particular bedroom habits in front of Kit. "I can help you plan it, right?" I couldn't wait to see all the designer dress options. She needed something spectacular, even if I had to convince her to try on dozens of them.

"No need. We're eloping."

My heart sank. "Eloping?"

No gown shopping? No gorgeous designer try-ons?

"Vegas, baby." Her exuberance couldn't be beat. "We're going to a chapel, then hitting the Strip. I need you there."

"I *love* Vegas," Kit said.

I turned to him, and there it was: even greater exuberance.

"Then you have to come too," she said. "We're going in three days."

"Three days?" I scanned the soundstage. "Where is Dean? He might listen to reason."

"Don't you dare, Vivian Mackenzie, or I will tackle you to the ground."

I sucked a breath between my teeth and side-eyed Kit. "She used my real name. She means business."

"Under the circumstances"—Ruth exaggerated the last word—"it's what makes the most sense."

I couldn't argue. "I don't want you to miss having the wedding of your dreams."

"It doesn't matter anymore. I want to marry him, elaborate ceremony be damned." She gave me puppy dog eyes.

I was mush at the sight. "Okay, okay. I'll be there. Of course I'll be there." We were only a little over halfway through filming, so it couldn't wait until we were in postproduction, but I imagined Dean would carve out an opening in our schedules to make the wedding possible.

She squealed and hugged me. "Thank you, thank you, thank you."

Over her shoulder, I glanced at Kit. He lit up and mouthed, *Vegas*, with a smile.

———————— ✦ ————————

Three days later we were on a private jet—owned by a friend of a friend of Dean's—and settled in our seats when Hugh boarded. Without his new girlfriend.

Relief rolled over me at not having to pretend to be friendly with someone I would most certainly not consider good enough for him.

While in Hawaii, he got the studio's blessing to end things with Peggy, claiming she wanted more than he could give. Not too long after he returned, the photogs caught him out with a new starlet alongside an article headlined, "Things Are Heating Up!" Peggy had been so distressed, seeing them together at a party, that she stepped in front of traffic to get his attention.

Don't worry, Peggy was fine. Though a few years later she did fake her own death to get out of the spotlight and—

Damn. I wasn't supposed to say that.

"Hey," I said as Hugh sat in the seat across the aisle. "Fancy seeing you here."

He fumbled with his seat belt, metal pieces scraping but not finding purchase. On the third try, he got it latched, then shut his eyes and rested his head back. "I hate flying."

"Weak stomach?" Kit guessed. At the *Be nice* look I shot him, he gave a playful grin and gently squeezed my knee.

The plane taxied toward the runway as I turned back to Hugh. Beads of sweat coated his forehead, his complexion an unnerving shade of green. His big hands strangled the armrests.

My chest ached. What a great friend to suffer this for Dean.

"You're watching him like a hawk," Kit said quietly enough for only me to hear. "He's a grown man. He'll be fine."

"Of course." After one more peek at Hugh, I reclined in my seat.

We landed, checked into our hotel—separate rooms for Kit and me, though I hoped we'd end up in the same one—and settled on meeting in a little over an hour.

While the men planned to change, then meet in Dean's room for cigars, Ruth and I got ready in my room. I wore a beautiful halter dress in pastel pink with a matching hat, and she shimmied into a white dress she'd pulled from her closet.

"Are you nervous?" I fixed her veil, both of us standing before the bathroom's small mirror.

She rested a hand over her heart. "Just excited."

I leaned in so our faces were side by side, mentally taking a picture of this moment and how beautiful, how happy, she looked. "Then let's get you hitched."

We headed for the chapel, a small room where rows of empty chairs flanked a white runner, the minister standing at the front wearing a tacky red-and-blue-plaid suit. A mix of cologne, cigarette smoke, and sweat hung in the air, reminders of the people coming and going on a quarter-hourly basis.

If Ruth or Dean minded the smell or the cupid cutout decor, they didn't act like it as they exchanged vows while Hugh and I stood by their sides, Kit in the front row.

The ceremony was over in ten minutes.

As Dean kissed Ruth, dipping her in a way that would make her swoon, I knew this wasn't what I wanted. A quickie wedding in Vegas, no family or other friends around. No time to pick out a gown or decide the first song my husband and I would dance to. I wanted to be more intentional about my wedding.

Neon signs lit the Strip, cars zipping past, and thousands of people roamed the street. We walked into the first casino we found.

Cheering came from crowded tables to the left while coins clinked, slot machine arms cranked, and bells announcing winners rang out on the right. A waitress took our drink orders and I asked for whatever Kit was having. Within a few minutes, she brought me something citrusy.

Ruth twirled a finger. "I don't know about the rest of you, but I'm doing the slots." She headed in that direction.

"Happy wife, happy life, right?" Dean said before taking off after her.

Since neither of the fellas next to me had been married, they could only shrug.

"What are you thinking?" Hugh asked as we surveyed the room. "Roulette, blackjack. I think I'm going to play poker."

Several people stole looks at him as they passed. A few women giggled and whispered behind their hands.

"I hate cards. I'm going for craps." Kit loosened his tie.

They were all intimidating. "What's craps?"

"You place a bet and throw the dice," Kit said. "No skill. Just luck."

I turned to Hugh. "And poker?"

He hesitated, which didn't bode well for how easily I could pick up the game. "There are different combinations of cards. You have to decide which—"

I waved to stop him. "Craps it is."

"Good luck," Hugh said.

"I make my own, remember?" I kicked a leg behind me to point out the heels he had gotten me.

Looping his arm around my waist, Kit led me away. We stepped up to a table and watched until the round ended. Everyone placed their bets.

After a couple of people had had a chance with the dice, Kit reached for them and held his open palm toward me. "Blow."

"Excuse me?"

He smiled, irresistible dimples on display. "It's for good luck."

Everyone watched. Waiting. My heart pounded as I blew across his broad palm.

Kit tossed the dice against the table wall. "Yes!" He shook his fist.

After a few rolls, he lost his turn, and I took the dice. His hand rested on my lower back as I flung the dice.

Yes! I threw my arms up.

Thank you, lucky heels.

I flung the dice again and again. People crowded the table, forcing Kit behind me. Soon he wasn't the only one cheering.

As suddenly as my luck was up, it was down, and I handed the dice over to the next player. But with the gentle press of Kit's chest against my back, it didn't feel like losing.

We played for an hour. At the end of another round, after we lost all we'd won, Kit bent close and said, "Do you want to stay, or . . . ?" His breath brushed my ear, trickling heat through my body.

I relaxed against him, feeling fresh as I set my empty glass next to his. "Or we could leave?"

He gave a small smile and a nod. "Or we could leave."

Desire pounded through me. I wanted him and couldn't wait until we got back. Except my feet hurt. And my stomach churned, the citrusy drink too acidic. But otherwise? I would ravish him.

As we walked into the hotel lobby, I kissed the doorman's cheek, leaving behind a big red lipstick print. Kit and I laughed all the way upstairs.

I rested against the striped wallpaper next to my door while he stood a foot in front of me, both of us quiet. His eyes latched on to my mouth, all it took for me to fist his shirt and tug him close. I had barely tipped my chin up in invitation before his lips came down on mine.

Like the other times, we fit perfectly together. A push and pull that sent sparks down my arm. Magnetism beyond my control. I rucked up his shirt, freeing it from his slacks, while he hooked one of my legs around his hip.

"Can we check off a box?" I asked as his lips traveled down my neck.

"Sure." He dragged his hand up my thigh, catching on the top of my stocking. "How's the 'getting caught' box sound?"

Oh. *Oh.*

We couldn't do this in the hall.

I dropped my leg and turned in his arms to unlock the door. Adrenaline rushed through my veins as he followed me into the room, the door clicking shut behind us. We both stared at the bed with its satin coverlet in a pink-and-yellow floral print.

Behind me, Kit skimmed a finger from my elbow to my shoulder before resting his hand there—and my breath froze.

The touch was innocent and should have been sweet but in an instant, I was in Walter Row's office. My stomach burned with the memory of his belt buckle clicking seconds before he glided a finger up my arm and put mounting pressure on my shoulder, sending me to my knees.

I squeezed my eyes shut. *Stop, stop, stop.*

"Are you all right?" Kit asked.

Not at all. I was bad. Worse than bad.

Sick.

I scrambled for the bathroom, making it to the toilet in time to empty my stomach.

"Do you want me to get something?" he asked from the doorway.

A lobotomy, so I would never have to remember this humiliation.

I kicked the door shut. "Leave, please." The only thing more mortifying would be if he listened.

A few seconds later, the front door clicked shut.

I rested my head against my arm on the seat. The lights were too bright, but I couldn't stand to turn them off. I breathed in through my nose and out through my mouth.

The drink hadn't been sitting right before we left the casino, but it was the touch—the harmless touch that was so much more—that pushed me over the edge. My body's violent reaction might have happened even if my stomach hadn't hurt.

It was ten minutes or maybe an hour—who knows?—before my stomach settled as much as it was going to. I crawled to the bathroom door. As it swung open, Kit's gaze met mine from where he sat against the wall.

"You're still here."

He blinked away sleepiness and helped me to my feet. "Did you think I would leave you alone?"

I shut my eyes. "I still don't feel right." From the pounding in my head to my tense stomach to my flushed face, I wanted nothing more than to curl up and die.

"Water, aspirin, and time will help." He led me to the bed, where the first two were set out on the nightstand.

I popped an aspirin and washed it down. "How do you feel?" He'd had a couple more drinks than me at the craps table.

"Fine."

At least one of us was.

"Everything's spinning." I flopped back, the lights too bright for me to keep my eyes open.

"I know." He took off my shoes and untied my halter dress.

"Don't try anything." I wanted to be coherent for that.

"Wouldn't dream of it."

"Really? You wouldn't even *dream* of it?"

He peeled my dress off, then helped me under the covers. "I'm usually awake when I think about sleeping with you."

"Mmm." Good answer. When he stepped away, my eyes flew open. "Don't leave."

"I won't." The bed dipped next to me. He slipped off his shoes and tie before lying on top of the covers. "Vivian? What happened back there? When I touched you, you said the name Walter. Who's he?"

I hadn't realized I'd said anything.

I turned and pressed my face into the pillow to block the light. "My agent in New York. He was a bad man."

"What do you mean, 'bad'?"

I didn't consider holding back, the fatigue and my spinning head making me vulnerable to opening up when I might not have normally. "He locked me in his office until I repaid his favor." Again and again, my debt never cleared. A chill ran over me, Walter's phantom touch still on my shoulder.

Kit tentatively draped an arm around my middle while he kept quiet. Maybe he expected me to say more, but I preferred getting lost to the safety of his warmth.

"I'm really glad you're here," I said.

He kissed my temple before reaching over to turn off the lamp. "There's nowhere I'd rather be."

CHAPTER TWENTY-ONE

Vivian

then

My head throbbed the following morning like a battle was being waged from the inside.

I threw the blanket over me to hide from the light streaming in while I tried to drift back to sleep. But images from last night crept into my mind. My blood warmed the harder I pulled at the pieces until I pressed a fingertip to the spot on my temple where Kit had kissed me goodnight.

I liked him. A lot.

I dragged the blanket down. The other side of the bed was rumpled but empty. It might have been a dream, but I swore he said he'd stay.

The door clicked open. I drew the sheet under my arms to cover myself while Kit walked in with a tray, wearing a white T-shirt and the black slacks he'd had on last night. His button-down lay over a chair.

I sniffed the air. "Is that bacon?"

"Yes, ma'am." He smiled, setting the tray down. The sight made me at least one percent better.

I took the lid off a plate and released a contented groan. "Bacon cures everything." I grabbed a piece and bit into it, salt gliding across my tongue.

Sitting cross-legged opposite me, he handed me a mug, then removed the lid on a second plate filled with pancakes and sausages. "Coffee will help if you have a headache."

"Do you ever have trouble sleeping after drinking coffee?" Probably because I guzzled so much, I tossed and turned at night. I thought over the delivery of my lines from that day on set and worried about oversleeping and missing my call time.

"No." He dug into a pile of eggs. "The sedatives they give us to come down from the pep pills would help."

The idea was intriguing. I would love knowing I could fall asleep without difficulty. I had never bothered with sedatives because I assumed the two went hand in hand: If I didn't take the pep pills, I wouldn't need the sedatives. "Do you do that?"

"I don't take pills."

I smiled at our camaraderie. "I don't take them either. They seem too similar to diet pills. I tried those and felt like my heart was shooting out of my chest."

His gaze hovered around my shoulders, bare except for my bra straps. "You don't need them anyway."

A stack of rejections from directors in New York and LA told another story. "I stopped taking them because I hated how they affected me. I didn't feel like myself. It's the same reason I don't have more than one drink at a time and hate seeing people drunk." I had too many memories of my father volleying condescending words at my mother and raising his hand to her—something he never did while sober. "What about you?"

"What about me?"

"Do you drink much?"

"No."

I hoped it was true. I took a long sip of coffee, then lifted a pancake and bit into it.

His mouth fell open. "What kind of barbarian eats a pancake without syrup? Or cutting it up?"

"The impatient kind. But a barbarian? How dare you, sir." I straightened while adopting a British accent. "You've taken it too far. I'm a lady."

I had hoped for a laugh but got nothing.

He cut into a pancake. "Speaking of taking things far: Last night . . ."

I dropped my head. "You're never going to look at me the same, are you?"

"No, but not for the reason you think. What you said when you were asleep?" He tapped the side of his head. "Permanently branded on my brain."

"What'd I say?"

"I'm not sure if I should tell you. You might try to take it back." He gave a devilish smile. "It was sexy, though."

I brandished a butter knife at him. "Out with it."

Still no dice for any laughs. I needed to stop trying an accent.

"You said you were mad about me. Then some sounds led me to believe you were"—he considered it for a second—"having an intimate dream."

The knife fell from my hand, clattering against the plate.

He tilted his head, meeting my gaze. "If it helps, I liked it. And, actually, I've been curious about something. At your apartment, after we went out for ice cream, you said you knew about things when you hadn't done them. How? Do you read romance novels or something?"

"Ruth's told me a lot, especially when we lived together. She'd come home and tell me, in far too much detail, what she'd done the night before. So I learned from her."

Kit groaned his frustration. "Now I'm thinking through what we've done, and it's giving me images of Dean I can't erase."

If only he knew about the coonskin hat Dean sometimes wore in bed.

I drained the last of my coffee. "That helped."

He took my mug and dragged the tray aside with a suggestive look in his eye. "Since you're feeling better . . ."

I almost wrapped my arms around his neck but jumped back at the last second and covered my mouth. "I have to brush my teeth."

"Hurry."

I slid my legs out to stand and noticed my dress draped over a chair. "You undressed me." I'd forgotten that detail.

"If you'll recall, it's nothing I haven't seen before." He studied me as if picturing what was under the sheet. "You looked like a pinup."

My pulse took off like a rocket. I was nearly confident enough to stand up without covering myself. Instead, I tucked the sheet around me and headed for the bathroom.

There came a knock on the front door as I walked back out. Kit answered.

Hugh stood in the hallway. He looked so put together. First thing in the morning, he smelled like soap, he was freshly shaven, and even his casual attire was clean and crisp, whereas my day-old mascara had given me raccoon eyes and I wore a sheet.

His eyes widened slightly, taking us in before scanning the room, our clothes strewn about. "Hi." He shoved his hands into his pockets while Kit retreated, leaving me to hold the door. "I wanted to check on you. I didn't see you leave the casino."

"Then how did you know I got in okay?" I smirked, attempting to lessen the awkwardness. "I could have been abducted."

He pursed his lips as if thinking about it for a second. "They would have returned you by now."

"Nope. No refunds. Once someone takes me, they're stuck." It was a joke but hit close to home, my stance on never quitting including people. I couldn't understand when someone claimed to love another person and then walked away.

"What terrible customer service." He did the scrunched-face smile. "As far as knowing how you got in all right, I checked with the doorman. Your lipstick was on his cheek."

"I forgot about that."

"*He* sure didn't."

Kit came through with our tray, breaking the conversation. He set it outside the door before turning around.

Hugh focused on it as he ran a hand through his damp hair. "I was going to see if you wanted to grab breakfast, but it looks like you already did. Need help with your luggage?"

"I've got it." Kit shoved an arm through his shirt.

Hugh nodded, peering down the hall, before returning his attention to me. "I guess I'll see you out there."

I lifted a hand in goodbye.

Hugh was accustomed to swooping in to help, and I always let him, even when I could handle it myself. What did it hurt to let him feel useful?

Kit being part of my life was a dynamic we'd have to adjust to.

I sat on the bed and dragged my suitcase over.

Kit crossed his arms and propped his hip against the dresser. "I know you two are friends, but was it ever more?"

"No." When he worried his bottom lip between his thumb and forefinger, I smiled. "You're jealous."

He dropped his hand. "In my experience, there are only two situations where a man can be strictly friends with a woman. The first is he's not attracted to her." He pushed off the dresser, coming to stand before me. "Which can't be the case."

My mouth went dry. "And the second?"

"He knows he can't have her." He knelt to come eye level with me. "I couldn't do it."

"What?"

"Just be friends with you." He brushed a kiss against my lips. "You're everything I've always wanted. You know that?"

"You're only saying that."

He shook his head resolutely. "I wanted you when I couldn't have you. I would even if I could never be this close to you again. It's all . . . it's a big deal for me."

I brought a hand over my heart. "I feel honored." But he deserved more than jokes, so I rested a hand over his heart. "It's a big deal for me too."

There was a tether between us, and it tugged with every look and touch and kiss. It'd tugged so hard, it was knotted in place.

CHAPTER TWENTY-TWO

Vivian

then

One evening a couple of days after we got back to LA, I called my mother, as I did weekly, holding the receiver between my ear and shoulder while I tidied up the living room.

"You can stop sending checks," she said. "I have a dozen sitting here."

"I have a solution: Cash them."

"Vivian."

"What? You provided for me. Why can't I help you now? Why won't you—"

"*Enough.*"

The word wasn't loud but came firmly enough for me to freeze. My mother and I had a good relationship. I wasn't used to her snapping at me.

A little calmer, Mom said, "It makes me feel inadequate when my daughter sends me money."

"That's not my intention."

"I know. I've just . . . I've been doing this on my own for a long time now, and even if it's hard, I manage."

"Why can't you accept a little help?" I asked. "It's me, not Dad. I'd never tell you how to spend it. I'd never ask you to repay me."

"I like knowing I don't have to rely on someone else. But if it makes you feel any better, money won't be an issue soon. I'm moving out of my apartment."

I stuffed magazines into a side table. "Moving? Where're you movin' to?"

She laughed. "Your accent came out just then."

"Mom."

"I met someone. And before you say anything, I didn't tell you only because it all happened so fast."

"How long have you been seeing him?" I asked, sitting down. "What's he like? What's he do?"

"That's an awful lot of questions."

"Let's start with a name."

"Ted." There was a smile in her voice. "He's good to me. Kind, hardworking. I'm happy. I really am. He owns his house, so I'm going to sock away what I would have spent on the apartment. I'll still have my own money to do with what I like."

Kind. That was all I cared about. She deserved someone kind. What the neighbors would say about the two of them living together without being married was their own business.

At the rev of a motor, I glimpsed out the window behind the sofa. Kit got out of his car and lifted his gaze from the sidewalk to wave.

"Hold on." I set the phone down and ran over to unlock the front door and open it a couple of inches, then settled back on the sofa. "Kit's here, so I should go."

His steps echoed as they reached my landing. He knocked lightly on the open door and stepped inside wearing a white T-shirt, blue jeans, and a black leather jacket. My insides purred.

"What are you two lovebirds getting up to?" Mom asked.

I dropped the receiver from my mouth as Kit walked over. "My mother wants to know what we're doing tonight."

He leaned down and kissed my cheek. "Dinner?"

"Oh, he's got a nice voice, Vivian."

"Yeah, he does." He had a nice smile too. I wanted to kiss it. "I'll talk to you soon, okay?" As soon as we hung up, I cupped Kit's face and pressed my lips to his.

He rested his forehead against mine. "Have I told you I really like you?"

"I really like you too."

"Have I told you I love you?"

My belly fluttered like it'd been filled with fireflies. In a singsong voice, I exaggerated the words, "You *love* me?"

He shut his eyes. "I'm serious."

"Sorry." While we goofed around on set, I'd learned Kit was not like that outside work. "I love you too." I reached for the collar of his jacket and pushed it down his arms so it fell to the floor, then fisted his shirt, pulling him to me as I lay back.

I'd never considered love to be a choice but rather something that couldn't be fought, like in the movies. But that wasn't what had happened with Kit. I cared about him deeply, and the attraction between us was so strong—electricity crackling under my skin whenever his lips touched mine—I decided to give in to loving him back.

He propped himself on a forearm as our mouths connected, my body aching as the hardest parts of him pressed against the softest parts of me. He dragged his free hand up my thigh, my dress falling around my waist. A rumble came from his throat as I wove my fingers into his hair, our lips catching fire.

Between kisses, we lost his shirt and jeans. My dress. Undergarments. Restraint.

He stared down at me. "Are you sure?"

"Completely."

———————— ◆ ————————

Ruth sat at the vanity in my dressing room a week later. The bright lights surrounding the mirror highlighted every red splotch on her face and eyes on the verge of tears.

"He said no." She dropped her head into her hands, voice above a whisper. "We had our meeting with Eugene, and it wasn't even a conversation. As soon as we told him the situation, he said he'd cut off both our salaries until it was 'dealt with' overseas."

My heart slunk back in an attempt to protect itself. Not that it did any good. Her pain was mine. "Did you mention the idea about—"

"Adoption? Yes." She wiped her nose on her sleeve. "Apparently I'm not special enough to warrant that kind of allowance."

"But Dean is." In the studio's eyes, Ruth was not special. There was no use sugarcoating it. "How can Eugene just—"

"Because he can!" Her eyes turned feral. "He thinks he's the ruler of the universe, and we have to bow to him." She let out a desperate cry and folded her arms onto my vanity to sob.

My stomach tightened. Hugh was right: Eugene owned him. He owned all of us. We could go to another studio, but what would be the point? It would be the same song and dance with another exec.

I laid a tentative hand on her arm, wanting so badly to fix this for her. "I'm so sorry." The words felt hollow. This was her dream. "Have you reconsidered quitting? Temporarily?"

"I can't. He said he'll blacklist both of us. We'll lose *everything*."

If I could have taken her pain away, I would have, but I had no more ideas.

Anger radiated in my chest so strongly, I could have spit fire.

I hated Eugene Mills. Hated him.

"He's sending me to London at the end of the week." Her voice broke like a twig. "Can you tell Hugh we have to cancel dinner tonight?"

"Of course."

When I called Hugh after I got home, I revealed nothing.

"Ruth and Dean have to cancel tonight. Something came up." I hated lying to him, so I chose to be vague.

"No. Really?" He let out a disappointed hum. "All dressed up with nowhere to go."

"I know. Me too." I dragged a finger over the lace edge of my nightgown.

"Hey, what do you think about going out anyway?" Enthusiasm returned to his voice. "I hear *Monster from the Deep Sea* is playing at the Gilmore Drive-In. Have you seen it?"

"Not yet." I needed a distraction, something to momentarily cover the wound of Ruth's loss. "You know what? Sure. Let's go."

I threw on a pastel orange-and-yellow-striped playsuit, the skirt open below the waist to reveal a pair of matching orange shorts.

With me wearing a headscarf covering my hair, we took off in Hugh's Cadillac convertible. It was his newest car, the paint strikingly similar to my lipstick.

I loved reaching out for the speaker from the stand next to where Hugh parked and clipping it to the inside of the car window. Buying popcorn from the snack service fella who came by. The added level of privacy, being in our own car instead of sitting near strangers in a theater.

Apparently, I wasn't the only one who enjoyed the false sense of seclusion. Halfway through the movie, I peeked to my right. A couple in the next car pressed against the inside of the driver's door, necking no more than two feet away.

Hugh followed my gaze. "So *that's* why drive-ins are getting so popular."

"Maybe if there'd been one in my neighborhood growing up, I would have had more than pecks by the time I graduated."

"But then you wouldn't have needed practice." He gave a small smirk as his hand dove into the popcorn bucket in my lap.

I faked dismay. "Are you saying I was a bad kisser?"

"Can I plead the Fifth?" When I smacked his arm, he laughed a little. "I'm kidding! No, you were perfect."

Thank God it was too dark to see how hot my face got. "In any case, I'm sure I've improved."

His eyes dipped to my lips.

Don't overthink it. It was a natural reaction to talking about kissing.

"Where's Kit tonight?" His tone held an accusation.

"Out with friends. I invited him, but he thinks drive-ins are for families in station wagons with crabby kids." I threw a piece of popcorn at him, hitting his cheek. "What, don't you like him?"

He tossed the popcorn back. "I don't think he's good enough for you."

I never thought anyone Hugh went out with was good enough either, but those relationships were never serious. Studio setups and short-term flings. What Kit and I had was more.

"I appreciate your concern, but I love him, so stop being overprotective and start being happy for me."

He gaped at me. "You *love* him?"

"Yes. I do."

On the big screen, a woman treaded water while a sea monster reached out to touch her feet. As soon as he got close, he drew back. A moment later, he did it again. My pulse raced as the background trombones got louder. The creature finally grazed the woman's foot with the tips of his claws, and my heart flung itself up my throat. I gasped, jumping enough for popcorn to fly out.

Before I could think better of it, I erased the distance between us. My head accidentally brushed Hugh's hand, his arm slung over the back of the seat.

Grinning, he tilted his head to meet my gaze. "Really? It wasn't even scary."

I pressed a hand to my chest. "My thundering heart would beg to differ."

"Don't worry. I won't let any big, scary monsters get you." His fingers absently played with a lock of my hair.

He was so comfortable in our friendship, he didn't think anything of the touch. But it felt intimate, goosebumps shooting down my arm as a finger accidentally skimmed my neck.

I eased a foot away. "I'm better now."

His expression went blank, unreadable.

After a few seconds, he sighed, reaching for another handful of popcorn before turning back to the screen.

Confidential

Dean Keller's Double Life

Anyone who caught the spread in *Photoplay* about director Dean Keller's marriage to newcomer Ruth Phillips had to be thrilled for the happy couple. They revealed how they couldn't wait a moment longer to exchange vows, jetting off to elope in an intimate ceremony in Las Vegas. Photos show the couple bashing around London, all smiles, where they say they've planned an extended honeymoon.

If that's true, then why, only days after the article's publication, was Dean seen ducking in and out of MGM's lots—and Vivian Stone's dressing room? Vivian's been bosom friends with Ruth for ages, but we suspect that will end soon.

And where is Dean's blushing bride? One dame swears she did, in fact, see the sweet starlet in London. Though Ruth wasn't gallivanting around town but alone, her eyes red-rimmed, like she'd been crying.

Sorry, Dean. Looks like the cat's outta the bag.

CHAPTER TWENTY-THREE

Vivian

then

That autumn, while our film was in postproduction, I tried on several premiere dress options at the studio. Each was analyzed by an MGM rep and checked from various angles. In the end, it came down to two: a navy blue strapless with a ruched waist or a black silk with a square neckline and a layered skirt.

They left me to make the decision, so I called Ruth to help. She sat in a green tufted chair several feet from a round platform while mirrors formed a semicircle in front. She'd gotten back from London a little over a week ago. While her smile said everything was fine, you could never tell.

Actors. That's the point: We're good at pretending.

I didn't bring it up right away but waited until after I came out in the blue dress and we'd weighed its merits. "How are you? Really."

I'd phoned while she was away but could only talk to an assistant, whose updates were short. *She's recovering. She's not ready to talk. I'll let her know you called.* There was nothing I could do. No comfort I could offer. Not even a reassuring verbal word to let her know I was thinking of her. Only my love sent in a letter.

Frankly, it was progress to see her. After returning, she'd spent several days holed up in her house. Dean had said she'd hardly spoken.

"Not as good as I could be." She stubbed out a cigarette in a glass ashtray, the third she'd had since getting here. "Did you hear the rumors about it?"

The London honeymoon was, of course, a cover story. While Dean did stay with Ruth for a few days, Eugene had him back to work sooner than he'd have liked. The photos the studio shared with the tabloids were taken on set before they left to make it look like the happy couple was sightseeing abroad.

"Dean *was* in my dressing room. But only because he wanted to talk about you, and—"

She waved me off. "I mean Harriet's, where she said I was expecting."

Everyone in Hollywood hated Harriet and her gossip column. I'd heard that an actress confronted Harriet at her home one day about a damning article she planned to run, and Harriet wouldn't let the actress leave until a call confirmed that the article in question had gone through. She had a high percentage of accurate—and scandalous—stories. Which, in Ruth's case, made me angrier than if they were fabricated. Because if it was *Confidential*, we'd roll our eyes. Wonder if a photographer got a less-than-flattering photo or if the gossip was spewed by a jealous co-star.

But this? The truth was painful enough without adding the public's whispers. Ruth had been through so much. Her heart was still raw. It made me think of my mother's shame when the neighborhood gossip spread stories about what she must have done to make my father leave.

When someone I loved hurt, I hurt. Now frustration rippled down my spine. "I didn't see it. What's the studio's response been?"

She shrugged, the nonchalance unconvincing. "The fixers are working on quieting the gossip and shifting the narrative in another direction. All I can do is focus on distractions." She motioned in my direction. "And this is the perfect distraction. Let me see the other one."

I would have changed into a swamp thing costume if it made her happy.

I went behind a dressing screen and slipped into the black gown. When I walked back to the platform, Ruth pointed from her seat. "That one!"

I should have known. "You always want me to show cleavage." I stared at my reflection, lifting my straps. There was no tugging the low neckline any higher. "If I could give these to you, I would, so you could see how annoying they are."

She crossed her legs. "I'd take them off your hands in a heartbeat." Her eyebrows shot up. "Or off Kit's hands, I suppose."

"Hush, you." I broke into a grin and twirled.

"You're glowing. A relationship looks good on you."

If I knew Ruth, that remark was only a segue.

"Five bucks says marriage would look even better."

And there it was. "Ruth."

"What?" She wiggled her fingers, her rings catching the light. "Don't you want to join the club? You know the studio wouldn't give you any grief. They *love* you and Kit together."

I'd imagined what waking up next to him every day would be like. It wouldn't be all breakfast in bed and passionate romps between the sheets. It would be sharing our successes. Having a shoulder to cry on during hard times.

I knelt to ease a foot into a heel. "Even if I wanted to, I don't think he would." It was a big enough deal for him to be open to dating. Marriage? I wouldn't broach the subject.

"You don't know that. If he asked, would you say yes?"

I slipped on the other heel. "Of course."

Ruth didn't say a word. Not a peep nor a laugh. There was only my heart picking up speed as awareness prickled over my skin.

I lifted my head and met Kit's gaze in the mirror.

"Nice dress," he said.

I turned. "You heard all of that?"

He nodded.

Ruth got to her feet, smiling. "I should go."

"Traitor," I called as she walked out.

Kit took a step closer.

"I don't expect you to feel the same way."

Another two steps. Silence.

"Really, we can forget I said anything."

He stood before me. "I don't want to forget it." He got down on one knee.

"What are you doing?"

Kit withdrew a velvet box from his pocket. "Exactly what it looks like."

"Are you sure? You know what you're proposing, right?"

"I haven't quite had the chance to propose anything yet," he teased, "but, yes, I know what I'm doing. Now, are you going to let me do it, or do you have another question?"

"Yes. Yes, go on." It was hard to stand still.

"Vivian Mackenzie, I don't have an elaborate sweep-you-off-your-feet speech planned. I've never been that kind of guy and never thought I could be. But you make me want to try."

"You're doing pretty well so far."

He opened the box. An emerald-cut diamond ring glittered under the lights. "I can't promise to be perfect, but I can promise you this: I will always love you."

Those were the most perfect words he could have said. I flung my arms around his neck. "Yes. Oh, yes, yes, yes."

He laughed into my hair. "You didn't let me ask."

I released him, my cheeks now aching from smiling. "Whoops." I rested the back of my hand on my brow. "A girl could get dizzy, being swept off her feet so hard."

Straightening his shoulders, he said, "Will you marry me?"

"Yes! A thousand times yes. A million times."

He grinned as he took the ring out of the box, then slid it on my finger. God, his dimples. I kissed one.

This was it. My forever. Our love story would be so different from my parents'. Because we were more than lovers. We were partners. The paths of our careers made us equals. Or as equal as a man and woman could be at the time.

A squeal came from the doorway, and we pulled apart.

"Sorry, sorry." Ruth hurried over and hugged me. "I couldn't hold it in anymore."

Of course she'd been listening. "You planned this, didn't you?"

She pointed at Kit. "He planned. I facilitated."

"I wasn't sure you'd say yes. Ruth was pretty confident."

"I know my friend well," she said. "When do we go dress shopping? I know you've been drooling over Christian Dior."

I nearly swooned again. "I don't know. We'll have to talk. Set a date."

"Buy the dress of your dreams," Kit said. "As soon as it's ready, I'm ready."

CHAPTER TWENTY-FOUR

Vivian

then

A week or so after Kit's proposal came my meeting to discuss my contract renewal.

Eugene's secretary let me into his office, a room as big as my apartment in New York, though instead of being musty, it smelled sweet, like cigars, and was outfitted with a large mahogany desk cluttered with awards and stacks of paper. On the walls were framed photos of Eugene with his top stars alongside movie posters.

He glanced up from his desk, big brown eyes crinkling at the corners. He had to be in his sixties, his hair almost entirely white and greasy, practically plastered to his head.

"Come in, come in." He motioned to a chair. "Have a seat."

I did as he said, resting my hands in the lap of my checkered skirt. It matched my jacket, open over a blouse. "Thank you."

Be patient, I reminded myself. *Calm. Professional. Ladylike.*

Eugene rocked back in his chair. "How'd you think filming went?"

Butter him up.

"Wonderful. You assembled a group of incredibly talented people—from director to cast to crew. It's gone more seamlessly than any other picture I've been part of. More than that, it's been fun. Audiences will sense that."

All true.

He rocked a little in his chair. "We're full of opportunities here, perfect for go-getters. Is that how you'd describe yourself, sweetheart?"

Be humble, but don't miss opportunities to highlight my strengths.

"Absolutely. I've always been a risk-taker." I crossed my legs, recalling my prepared speech. "It took a leap of faith to move across the country with nothing but unflinching determination. And it's paid off: Two of the films I worked on were nominated for awards, and as for *Sunday Circus*, Dean Keller took many of my suggested script changes and ran with them."

"And what is it you want now? To continue at MGM?"

I contained my smile so as not to look too eager. *Remember, he would be a fool to say no.* "I'm open to it under the right circumstances."

The warmth in his eyes dimmed. "Such as?"

"Drama."

He studied the paper in front of him, which I assumed refamiliarized him with my backlist of films. "You do comedy."

"That's not where my heart lies. It's not why I started acting." My cool professionalism weakened alongside my voice's higher pitch.

"But it's what you signed your contract for." He jabbed a finger against the paper in front of him with each word like a hammer, the sound reverberating in my ears.

"My old contract, yes." It'd been my foot in the door. "I hope to sign a new one as—"

"You're a comedienne. That's your role type."

"It doesn't *need* to be." Tension strained my shoulders as I grasped my mental checklist, the reasons I never got a dramatic role: talent, accent, body. "I've made great improvement in my acting since signing. Ask any director I've worked with." I dropped a hand toward him. "You've been on set. You've seen me."

Eugene only stared.

I swallowed and pulled out the accent I'd learned to bury. "And you wouldn't believe it if I told you, but I'm from Long Island."

A heavy sigh left his lips.

Shit. This was going downhill.

Figure it out!

"And I mean, honestly"—I forced a small laugh—"did you see the article about me in the last issue of *The Hollywood Reporter*? I'm basically MGM's brunette version of Marilyn Monroe."

His gaze dipped to my chest, hovering there for several seconds. Though I was completely covered—my outfit feminine but professional—I felt exposed under his eyes.

All I meant was I'd become curvy like Marilyn. My weight had been an issue in the past, too high or low, but I'd reached what I hoped was the right balance.

He leaned back, hands behind his head, and I softly smiled, ready to talk business.

"You think you're the only knockout with a nice rack we got around here?"

I shook my head. "That wasn't what I—"

"Let me explain how things work, honey. After this film comes out, people will know your name and have a perception of what to expect from you in the future."

My stomach sank, tears pricking my eyes. "But I thought if I proved myself—"

"Stop." He shut his eyes, pinching the bridge of his nose. "All you'll be proving is you're good at comedy."

"But I can do more than that."

"Them's the breaks. If you're not interested in continuing, then quit."

Quit?

How did it go so wrong? I'd had a strategy. Everything I'd done was to get to *this* point. I didn't have a plan B.

Eugene walked over and held out a hanky. He smelled of grease, reminding me of my waitressing days. "It's not all bad, right? I'm offering another contract. Five years this time."

I blew my nose with a loud honk, and he laughed. I glared at him. The gatekeeper to my dreams. I wasn't the first to cry in his office and wouldn't be the last. For him, it was another Monday, but for me this was the end.

He tipped my chin up. "How serious are you about drama, doll?"

I gripped the thread of hope like it was a red-and-white life pre-server. "Very. I'd do anything. Small parts. B movies. Longer hours. Temporary relocation to the moon, if such a feat were possible."

Eugene let go of my chin, his finger drifting down my neck to stroke the bare skin of my collarbone. "Anything?" When I didn't, *couldn't*, speak, he slid his hand under my blouse and cupped my breast. He let out a contented hum. "There are other ways to get what you want, y'know."

I froze. Every muscle turned to ice.

No. *No.*

He had the power to destroy my career. Soon I'd be waitressing again. Or a housewife whose life revolved around making sure supper was on the table by six.

I could go to another studio . . .

But if our film flopped, no one would want me. Could I say for certain it'd be a success?

Eugene's breath skimmed hot and rank across my cheek. In an instant, I was back in my agent's office, the scent of onions wafting off him as he locked the door behind me and led me to his desk.

I couldn't stop the rising bile at the memory, and I didn't want to. At the sound I made deep in my throat, Eugene hauled back, while I pitched forward, vomiting into his trash can.

"Shit." He took a step away and yelled for his secretary. She scur-ried in and circled an arm around my shoulders, leading me from his office to the waiting room. While she fetched a cup of water, Eugene came out and tossed my contract. "This is my offer. Take it or leave it."

It fluttered to the floor. I didn't give him the satisfaction of picking it up until he shut the door.

CHAPTER TWENTY-FIVE

Vivian

then

After I got home from my meeting, I took out a piece of paper.

Dear Hugh,

I wish I could tell you what happened with Eugene, but I can't. I'm so mortified, I don't think I can tell anyone.

Do you remember the time you stormed out of his office and said he owned you? I don't know what you wanted, but whatever it was, I understand. Eugene won't give me what I want either. He took away what Ruth wants too. He's probably doing it to so many others in one way or another.

I used to tell myself I didn't quit, I pivoted. But the truth is, I settle. First, I settled for Hollywood instead of Broadway. Then friendship with you when I wanted more. Comedy instead of drama...

Sometimes I wonder if I'll always be settling.

Love,

Vivian

I reached for the red shoebox in my closet, the one from the lucky heels Hugh had given me, and set the letter inside.

I decided against phoning my mother. We'd already made plans for her to visit, and she would be here within a week. I could complain about the meeting then, when I had her shoulder to cry on. Not that I would tell her what Eugene had done—that would only upset us both—but I wanted to tell her about the rest of it.

Since I knew she was coming, I hadn't told her about my engagement and instead planned a dinner for her to meet Kit. My hope had been to share twofold good news: We were getting married *and* I had landed the contract of my dreams. Only now I couldn't, and I needed to think. Regroup. Figure out my next move and if I should sign the new contract.

The phone rang on Mom's first night while we were getting ready.

"Any chance we could push back dinner?" Kit asked. "Arthur invited me to his wrap bash, and I want to swing by quick. Offer my congrats."

"We're going to Chasen's."

He kept quiet.

"One does not simply *push back* a reservation for Chasen's."

"Right." A long pause. "It's only that this was his first lead, and he sprang the party on me—"

I made a sound, cutting him off as I checked my wooden cuckoo clock. "Let me think." I didn't want him to miss something important to him, even though dinner was more important. Still, we could make this work. "Our reservation isn't for an hour. As long as you're not more than fifteen minutes late, it should be fine. My mother and I will peruse the menu at the table while we wait."

He let out a deep breath. "I thank you. I love you. See you soon."

"Love you too."

About half an hour later, Mom and I were ready to walk out the door when the phone rang again. If Kit needed more time, he could forget it.

Except it wasn't him.

"I didn't get the part." Hugh's pain was palpable. "I just got off the phone with Dean. He's with Ruth at their vacation cottage, but he just heard and wanted to tell me."

"*No.*" I sank to the sofa. "Heathcliff?"

While Hugh enjoyed the action movies he'd been doing lately, as soon as he had heard about the casting for *Wuthering Heights*, he'd angled for the lead. And they gave it to him. At least, they said they would. As they should. Who better to play the tall, dark, and broody?

"I thought it was a done deal," I said as Mom nodded toward the door as if to say we needed to leave. "Who'd they give it to?"

"Ricky Boone."

"*Boone*? The fella with the receding hairline? Didn't he get in trouble with the cops over some indecent exposure ruckus?"

"Yeah, but they covered it up."

"The exposure charge or his hairline?"

"Both. Now they're trying to make him the next—"

"You?"

He cursed under his breath. "Can you meet up? I'm going to drive myself nuts sitting here all night."

I twirled the phone cord around my finger. How could I leave him alone after a blow this big when he desperately needed company? I couldn't cancel our big dinner, though.

"My mom is in town and we are meeting Kit at Chasen's," I said. "We're actually leaving now. I'm not sure if you have time—"

"I'll be there."

I'd planned on saying *later*, as in after dinner, but how much worse would he feel if I corrected him?

When we hung up, I checked the time. Kit would be at the party. There wasn't a way to update him.

We'd make it work. It would be a surprise. Which was how Mom and I came to be sitting in a nice booth at Chasen's, where she futzed with her new, thick fringe for the tenth time.

I was so proud to be sitting next to her, the strongest woman I knew. And beautiful too. She'd aged so gracefully, people said we looked like sisters.

I smiled at her. "Mom, you look great."

Her gaze drifted past Alfred Hitchcock without realizing it. I almost told her, but it would have made her more nervous.

"Why did we come somewhere so nice?" she asked. "I feel out of place."

"You're not. You look stunning." My cocktail dress fit her perfectly. It was the only one of mine she'd deemed modest, which would have made me laugh except I knew her self-consciousness stemmed from when my father controlled her wardrobe. He said showing skin was her trying to attract men's attention.

"But I don't need all this." She twirled a finger. "A burger and a milkshake would have been fine."

It took the wind out of my sails. She didn't appreciate how hard it was to get this reservation.

Hugh would be there any minute; Kit in fifteen. We couldn't change locations.

"They have burgers, but I'd recommend the chili. It's Liz Taylor's favorite." I stood and pushed my chair in. "I'm going to the ladies' room. Be back in a jiffy."

I made my way across the low-lit restaurant only to get stopped by Evelyn Summers out with Montgomery Clift. Thankfully, she didn't look as twitchy as she had while filming *In Your Eyes*, though everyone was saying she kept causing problems on the set of her new movie. Showing up hours late because she was nervous. Demanding multiple retakes when she wasn't happy with her performance. Apparently she was getting put on a slew of prescriptions to manage her stress and temperament.

It took an extra few minutes to get back to Mom, but when I spotted her, I smiled. Hugh was there, the two of them chatting.

"Sorry, I got caught up talking to someone." I kissed his cheek and scooted back into the curved booth. "Looks like you found Mom okay."

"She's practically your twin. It wasn't hard."

Her eyes glowed under the table's candlelight. "We were catching up. You've told me so much about him."

I knew she'd like him.

"Vivian is one of my favorite people," he said. "You did a nice job raising her, Sue."

She shook her head. "It wasn't always easy."

I rolled my eyes. *Here we go.*

Hugh gave a warm smile. "I have no doubt." He eyed me. "She's pretty stubborn, isn't she?"

Mom's eyebrows shot up. "And how. Once she gets something in her head, there's no changing it. Has she told you about the time she didn't give up on the gumdrops she wanted?"

"Don't tell me she stole them." He rested an elbow on the table and dropped his chin in his hand.

Mom waved like she couldn't wait to tell him. "She spent hours busking outside the five and dime, singing songs to earn a penny."

His eyes widened. "But she has a terrible singing voice."

I fell back against my chair and covered my hands over my heart. "*Et tu Brute?*"

Mom ignored me. "I think they paid her so she'd stop."

He shook his head and let out a warm laugh, the sound enveloping me like a blanket. I loved how they were getting on and hoped she would like Kit as much.

Mom relaxed in her chair, finally at ease, and turned to me. "He's a keeper."

"For putting up with me?" I scoffed and pointed at Hugh. "I'll have you know, I've grown on him."

He smirked. "Like a barnacle." His attention dropped to my hand, still pointing, and homed in on my ring finger.

My stomach flipped. I had meant to keep my hand in my lap.

Mom gasped. "You're engaged?"

There was no hiding it now. "That's usually what a diamond on that finger means."

She threw her arms around me while Hugh continued to stare at my hand. I didn't expect cheers, but even if he didn't like Kit, he should have offered his congratulations.

My mother released me to grasp Hugh's hand across the table. "You're perfect for my daughter."

His body went rigid.

"Mom, no." Even though his face was still as stone, I smiled, trying to get him to see the humor in it. "This is my friend Hugh."

"*Oh*." She let him go and motioned toward the entrance. "I'm sorry. He came over and asked if I was your mother, so I assumed this was Kit."

I took for granted that everyone knew who Hugh was. But Mom had never been one to read the gossip columns, and the only pictures she went to these days were mine. It'd always been me dragging her to the cinema when I was young.

Didn't I tell her Hugh would be here before Kit? Maybe in the rush to get here I'd forgotten.

"Don't apologize." Hugh pushed back his chair with a loud screech. "Will you excuse me?" He stood and strode toward the exit, angling past Kit, who was heading our way.

He had a right to be upset. I had told myself I'd kept the news from him because I wanted to tell my mother first, but that wasn't true. His opinion was important to me, and I was afraid he'd disapprove.

"I'll be right back," I told Kit as he reached our table, and then I headed for the doors and into the night air.

Hugh stood next to the wall, lighting a cigarette.

I went over to him. "Listen, I know you don't care for Kit—"

"That's an understatement."

"Fine. But you should want me to be happy."

A muscle jumped in his jaw. "I do." He focused on the road and the cars rolling past, taking a drag. "Do you remember when we got the flat tire and had to sleep in my car?"

"Of course."

"You asked me to tell you something I'm not good at." He flicked off the ash. "I'm bad at sharing my feelings."

That wasn't news to me. He rarely showed strong emotions or shared his deepest worries. "How come?"

"My father . . . he's a good man. Provided for us and gave us a stable home. But whenever I scraped a knee or got scared of the dark, he told me to buck up. That men don't make a fuss. So I learned to keep it inside. Pain. Fear. Wants. Needs. I repressed it all."

I pictured a dark-haired little boy falling off his bike, eyes burning with unshed tears. "Your father was wrong."

"It's hard to unlearn."

"I won't judge you. If you can be open with anyone, it's me."

For nearly a minute, he didn't move. I waited, patient as he worked through what was obviously a big step. Finally he sighed, shifting his attention from the road to me.

A sensation lodged under my ribs and tugged.

He wasn't going to tell me he cared for me, right? Not when I had been single for over a year after meeting him but before dating Kit. Not when it wouldn't matter now that I was engaged. The possibility was ludicrous.

The door swung open and Kit stepped out, his gaze darting between us. "What's going on?"

Hugh stomped out his cigarette. "I'm leaving. Apologize to your mother for me." He headed toward the valet.

Kit came over, holding a glass of whiskey, both of us quiet. When Hugh drove off, Kit turned to me, eyes piercing as ever. "Why the hell was *he* here?"

His sharp tone surprised me. "It was a last-minute decision."

"So it wasn't a coincidence? You invited him to meet your mother the same time as me?"

"Only because he called and was upset."

"Which makes it okay for him to be here like he's family?"

My hackles rose. "He *is* like family."

"Then you went ahead and shared our announcement without me?"

My mother must have told him. "I wouldn't have if you'd been on time."

"I told you I'd be late!"

I rested my head against the wall. He had told me.

Kit let out a heavy breath, reining in his frustration as he rested his head against the wall too. "It was *our* news. It's not like my parents care about my life."

"Did you try calling home again?" He'd phoned a few days ago to tell them about our engagement, but his father immediately handed the phone to his mother, and she only stayed on the line long enough to describe a tiff she was having with Kit's aunt before abruptly ending the call. He hadn't gotten a sliver of time to tell them.

"Why bother? Just send an invitation. They can find out that way." His gaze was intent on mine. "You're my family now. Your family is my family. I was looking forward to celebrating with your mom and didn't expect another man to be here."

"I'm sorry. The news came out by accident. I meant to wait for you." I grabbed his hand. "And I'm sorry for abandoning you and my mother without so much as an introduction."

His fingers curled around mine as our first real fight disintegrated. "It's fine." He drained his glass. "Let's go back in."

CHAPTER TWENTY-SIX

Vivian

then

On the night of our premiere the following month, I sat in a limousine next to Kit, my hands shaking. The door opened, and a round of flash-bulbs popped as Kit got out. I put my hand in his, standing to meet the bright lights of photogs. Handprints and footprints of celebrities, set in concrete, paved the forecourt of Grauman's Chinese Theatre. Two red columns at the entrance held a bronze roof, while above the doors was a dragon carved in stone.

"Vivian! Show us the ring!" someone shouted as we reached the red carpet. "When's the big day?" We paused to smile and pose. A man yelled, "Was it love at first sight?"

I should have been happier. My name was on the tip of everyone's tongue, like I'd dreamed. But I couldn't stop thinking about my contract. Eugene's secretary had phoned to say it was due on his desk the following morning or he'd cut off my salary.

My stomach was in knots. Was it better to accept an offer I didn't want or to find an alternative? Radio, maybe? Except I didn't want that either.

Inside, most of the cast and crew, along with their guests, were seated, and we found our reserved spots. It may surprise you to know, some actors don't like seeing themselves and skip watching the film at their premieres. But I always liked it.

The room darkened, and the movie rolled.

Fifteen minutes in came the series of scenes we'd ad-libbed here and there, starting with the one where Kit threw me over his shoulder and I reached desperately for help, like a cat forced into a bath.

A bout of light laughter erupted from the audience. A woman cackled. A man a couple of rows in front of us turned to the woman on his left, wiping a tear from his eye as he smiled.

My heart stirred. They liked it.

Kit grabbed my hand over the armrest. "I know you know this already, but you're really good."

On-screen, he stood in the lake and yanked the rope attached to the front of a car, his pant legs soaked to the knees. With another heave, he slipped with a great splash. The camera focused on his face as he emerged with a scowl and spit out a mouthful of dirty water. A lily pad sat on his head. It earned him a round of laughter.

"*You're* really good." I was so proud of him.

In the next scene, I snuck a dozen eggs out of the neighbor's chicken coop by stuffing them down my shirt. Kit found me at home before I could get the eggs out and coerced me to tango. As he held me close, I angled back in an attempt to keep distance between us, then stomped on his foot to show what an inept dancer I was and why we shouldn't continue. He recovered and, his face set in determination, twirled me out and back in.

With each twirl, we got a little closer. The third time, he spun me in so fast, my body slammed against his, the sound of a dozen cracks along with it.

The audience exploded in laughter, the sound dragging out at the way I winced while Kit's jaw dropped, his eyes traveling over the mess soaking both our shirts.

Slapstick was much more common back then. Even though people suspected what was to come, they loved it anyway.

Electricity crackled under my skin as they kept laughing.

It was a familiar feeling, like the time I made Hugh laugh as I climbed the pretend flights of stairs. Or how the crew hooted at each of our funny bits. Only this time the sensation was multiplied by a hundred. I'd have bottled up the sound if I could.

Kit squeezed my hand. "See?"

Each scene and each laugh elevated me higher and higher, until finally I did see. I saw what Hugh and Judy and Gerard knew all along.

I wasn't amusing.

Not funny.

I was *hilarious*.

I sat back in my seat, stunned. All along, I'd misunderstood. I'd thought, since I didn't take comedy seriously, since I didn't have to try hard, it wasn't worthwhile. But that wasn't true. I didn't have to try hard because I was a natural. Few days on set had felt like work. It'd been fun.

From my seat, I smiled, my blood humming. My heart racing. My fingers and toes tingling with the greatest elation I'd ever experienced.

This was what I was meant to do. I needed to make money, yes, but what I needed most was the fulfillment comedy gave me.

I couldn't wait to sign that damn contract.

———— ◆ ————

Hours later, we left the after-party, and Kit and I returned to my place, still high on the evening, and mused over whether MGM would put us in another movie together.

He uncorked a bottle of wine and poured two glasses while I stood in the bathroom and took the pins out of my hair.

"I can't imagine doing a film without you now. It will never be as funny with anyone else. And the idea of seeing you kiss someone?" I visibly shuddered. "I'm not watching."

He handed me a glass and loosened his tie. "You'd skip my premiere?"

"You'll have to warn me when to close my eyes."

"Like a horror movie?"

"Exactly." I covered a hand over my face and parted two fingers to peek through. "Tell me when it's over."

He smiled, turning around, while I finished taking out the pins.

"Hey, you have any smokes?" he called. "I left mine in the car."

"Top drawer of my vanity."

Kit came back to the bathroom holding up a pack—and an envelope with Hugh's name scrawled across it. It was the one I'd written the night Hugh accompanied me to my first premiere. The one that said I loved him.

The sight of it in Kit's hand crashed into me like a wave.

"What's this?" he asked.

Bad. That's what it was.

"Before I got my contract, Hugh paid my power bill and for some meals. I wanted to repay him, but he wouldn't take it." Those were pieces of the truth, at least. I nodded at the envelope, praying he wouldn't open it. "I've been holding on to it in case."

He flipped it over and squinted like he might be able to see through the paper. "Good friend."

My pulse pounded as I took the envelope and returned it to the vanity. I needed to get rid of it, and the others in the shoebox, at some point.

"We didn't toast." Kit held up a glass as we sat on the sofa.

I pushed my shoulders back and sat up straight. "To successful reviews and a successful marriage."

He clinked his glass with mine. "Cheers."

Reviews filtered in the next day. Ruth read one to me as I tried on wedding gowns.

Critics raved about my comedy ("Miss Stone's performance is a belly-laughing good time"), while they focused more on Kit's charisma ("Look out, James Dean. There's a new hunk in town!").

Ruth wasn't quite back to her usual self yet, but there was an encouraging glimmer in her eye. "I'm so happy for you; it's like *I'm* getting the paper's praises."

Even the gossip about me had been getting better. There were fewer comments about my weight, and most stories centered on my relationship with Kit: pointing out restaurants we frequented, saying we had been canoodling in the corner of a club. Speculating about what was next for us.

She brought over a veil. "How did your mom and Hugh take the news of your engagement?"

"Mom is thrilled." I stood on a platform, my embroidered train reflecting in the mirror.

"And Hugh?"

"Less than thrilled. I'd hoped Kit would ease into our friend group. Dean likes him. You like him. But if Hugh never does, we can't all go out together without someone being uncomfortable. I don't want to abandon our dinners, though. I love them."

"We won't. Hugh will come around. Eventually he'll find someone to get serious about and introduce her to us. Then he'll see it's not simple, joining an established group, and that he should have been easier on Kit." She took a step back and circled her finger. "All right, now spin, and if this dress doesn't give you a 'This is the happiest day of my life' feeling, we're moving on."

I raised my arms and twirled. When I stopped, I gave a wiggle-shrug. "So-so."

Ruth cupped a hand around the side of her mouth and called over her shoulder, "Next!"

The only aspect of our wedding I had a say in was my dress: a strapless Christian Dior gown with lace detailing and layer after layer of tulle. The studio planned the rest.

MGM loaned me a necklace with teardrop diamonds and matching earrings. I wore my hair in an elegant chignon, and while violins played, I walked down the aisle in the backyard of our new home. It was a Spanish-style nestled at the end of a cul-de-sac, the yard beautifully landscaped with fruit trees, and had the one thing I'd told Kit I wanted: my own bathroom.

I hardly heard a word the minister said, too consumed with calming my heart. As soon as I locked eyes with Kit, my grin did more than ache. It shook.

Everything about our pairing made sense. Our stars were rising at the same time and with the same momentum. Then there was our chemistry, undeniable on-screen because we had so much of it off-screen.

We could be Hollywood royalty someday.

After we exchanged "I dos," the evening became a blur of dancing and laughter.

Mom's boyfriend, Ted, tall and slim, with gray-streaked red hair, led her to a table with a couple of slices of cake, while Ruth and I abandoned ours in favor of more dancing. Over to the side, Dean made small talk with Hugh and Eugene.

Kit put a hand on my elbow as a song ended and turned me toward an older couple. I had seen a picture of his family, so I recognized them.

"Vivian, I want you to meet my parents, James and Dottie Pierce."

James looked like an older version of Kit but with wrinkles and a rounded belly, whereas Dottie was slim and petite.

"Nice to meet you." I took a half step forward, expecting an embrace, but Dottie only blotted the sweat from her upper lip with a cloth napkin.

"It's so hot, isn't it?" she said. "I don't know how you can tolerate it."

I didn't know if "you" meant me, Kit, or the whole state of California, but Kit jumped in.

"It took some getting used to, but, coming from where it's cold half the year, I love it."

"You better. Looks like you're stuck here." Ice cubes clinked in James's tumbler. He glanced at me while nodding in Kit's direction. "So you're like him, then? You like to play."

I cracked a smile, picturing children playing cops and robbers. "Pardon me?"

"He means *plays*. Musicals," Dottie said, like the two were synonymous.

James brought the glass to his lips. "I meant what I said the first time."

Clearly, they disapproved of actors. Kit had told me his father wanted him to work at the family furniture business in North Dakota.

Kit deserved more respect. I was determined to give him enough love to make up for their shortcomings.

Dottie attempted to fan herself with the napkin. "I feel like I'm melting."

An image of the Wicked Witch of the West flashed through my mind.

Hugh came over with a small wrapped box. "Sorry for interrupting, but I'm about to leave and wanted to say goodbye to the bride."

"Of course." I smiled at Kit and his parents. "If you'll excuse me."

When we were several paces away, Hugh lifted the box in my direction.

I took it without hesitation. "You didn't have to get us anything."

"It's only for you."

When I tore back the paper and lifted the lid, my insides wobbled. "My mother's heels."

They were the same but different. Pink and white crystals adorned the toe portion, while a black ribbon attached to the back, meant to tie around the ankle.

"They were in rough shape." Hugh grinned, clearly pleased with himself. "But with some time and care, broken things can be mended."

I could only stare at him.

His face fell. "Maybe I should have asked first, but Ruth liked the idea and offered to get them. I only planned on having them fixed, then I thought they could use something more—"

"I *love* them." I'd never seen such stunning shoes. It was the most thoughtful gift anyone had given me. I rose up on my toes to kiss his cheek. "You have impeccable taste."

"I've learned a thing or two since we met." He peered over my shoulder. "So you're happy?"

I followed his gaze to Kit, who was laughing with his brother over a couple of drinks and cigars. "Yes."

And I was. I really was.

For about two weeks.

CHAPTER TWENTY-SEVEN

Margot

now

"I figured it out. Why I couldn't find Ruth Phillips when I looked her up before." Leo scrolls on his phone from where he's sitting on the floor in the music store lesson room, his back against the wall. He turns the screen toward me, showing a picture of a laughing, middle-aged blonde woman. "She used her married name for most of her career: Ruth Keller."

I recline in a swivel chair near the piano, spinning a few inches to one side, then the other. A question has been pricking me ever since we heard it. "Do you think Kit was right when he said there are only two ways a man can be friends with a woman: not being attracted to her or knowing he can't be with her?"

Leo is an enigma. The sudden breakup. The renewed friendship. How did he see me before? How does he see me now?

"Pretty much. But I think he oversimplified it."

"How so?"

"Some men aren't attracted to women—period," he says. "Which, I suppose, doesn't make what he said wrong."

"What about the second option: knowing he can't be with her?"

"Kit failed to mention the possibility that one or both of them could already be in a relationship. Again, it doesn't make what he said wrong, exactly, though I'd rephrase it to 'someone or something standing between them.'"

I plant my feet, stopping the chair. "Who stood between Hugh and Vivian before Kit came into the picture? Peggy?"

"Hugh could have been standing in his own way."

"What do you mean?"

"Fear of rejection, for one."

I roll my eyes. "Vivian was *not* going to reject Hugh. At least, not back when she wrote those first letters. She loved him."

"He didn't know that." Leo laughs at the *Give me a break* look I aim at him. "What? He wasn't getting the play-by-play of what was going on in Vivian's head like we are. He didn't know how she saw him. There's also the possibility he didn't think he was good enough for her."

"Now you're just making things up."

He raises his hands. "It doesn't make it impossible."

I think through the options. "Which was it?"

He lets out a stream of breath through his mouth. "I have a hunch—"

"Not for him. For you." When Leo's gaze darts to mine, I wish I could rewind time and take it back, because I don't think I'm ready for this conversation after all, but it's too late. "We were friends for nearly two years in high school before you made a move. Why? Because you weren't attracted to me?" To smooth over any worry about hurt feelings, I add, "I wouldn't blame you. I wore braces when we met and hadn't learned to tame my curls."

"No, that wasn't it. I was young and overthought everything. All the ways I could stand in my own way, I did."

My heart warms. Since he was being open with me, I decide to be a little vulnerable back. "For what it's worth, if you'd had a play-by-play of what was going on in my head back then, you would have known you had nothing to worry about."

Leo gives a soft smile, opening his mouth to say more, but a faint jingle comes from the front of the store. He shoves his phone in his pocket. "I have another lesson, so we'll have to stop for today."

Disappointment seeps in, but I try not to show it. "A piano prodigy?"

"A retired schoolteacher. She said she's always wanted to learn." He catches my eye. "It's never too late."

I hum, ignoring the obvious connection he's trying to make. Though I can't help but check the corkboard on my way out, scanning the short story contest he'd mentioned, before shaking my head and striding out the door.

◆

I'm following Leo to his apartment a couple of days later. We planned to walk around the East Village, but a sudden rainstorm swept in as I got there, so he offered his apartment as a place for us to listen to the next tape.

Sitting in the car, thinking about him, brings back memories of another rainy night.

Our kiss at prom was only a taste of the summer that followed. We were inseparable, unable to keep our hands and mouths off each other.

Two weeks before I left for college, we sat in Leo's old Dodge Neon as rain sprinkled the windshield, my lips kiss-swollen as I rested my hands on his cheeks. "I'm not leaving."

Amusement danced in his eyes. "Your grandma is going to poison my next batch of cookies if you're out past curfew."

"I mean UC Santa Barbara. I'm not going. I'll stay here and go to college locally. I don't want to leave. Maybe I can go to Cal State Long Beach with you." I'd thought about it for weeks now and finally decided, though I hadn't told Mom or Gram yet.

Leo smiled. I swear he smiled for a second. Only I must have been mistaken, because his face went blank.

"What about your deposit? Your plans . . . ?"

"I'll figure it out." I let my hands fall from him, my tone confident despite his less-than-enthusiastic response.

He stared out the windshield.

I tried to meet his eyes. "What's wrong?"

It was the longest minute in existence before he replied. "I actually think we should break up."

I waited for him to laugh at the most terrible joke ever told. But he only kept his attention on the raindrops.

Rejection gripped my throat. "You're serious?"

I wanted to shout at him that if distance was the problem, it didn't matter anymore. Not if I stayed here. Except that wasn't it, was it?

When it came down to it, we had fun together, and he liked the physical side of our relationship, but when I tried to get closer—stay here, with him—he shut down.

"I'm sorry." He heaved a heavy sigh. "I don't think it's the right—"

"Who *are* you?" Who was this cold person? Where did the Leo I'd known go?

"I'm still me." Pity flashed in his eyes as he turned back to me. "Good luck in Santa Barbara. I mean it."

He was my first love. It took a long time to get over. It was nearly a year before I considered going out with anyone else. But what hurt worse than our relationship ending was not having him in my life anymore.

Now I follow Leo to an apartment complex and take the parking spot next to him. He opens my door before I have my phone and keys in hand, and I hurry so he doesn't have to get more soaked because of me.

We run, laughing as we dodge puddles to reach a three-story white stucco building.

He holds the door for me, leading to a quaint lobby. His shirt is damp, sticking to him. "I'll get you a towel as soon as we get up. Stairs or elevator?"

Droplets run down my back. "Elevator."

The silver doors open and shut behind us, and I'm not expecting the way my heart ricochets against my rib cage. In a matter of moments, I'll be in Leo's apartment.

He relaxes against the wall next to me, arms crossed, one foot resting over the other. The carefree stance has become my new favorite thing about him.

"Ever since Ruth's grilled-cheese talk, I've been craving one," he says. "What do you think?"

"That sounds—"

The elevator comes to a halt. I grasp the railing.

"What the hell?" He reaches for the emergency phone button.

A voice like sandpaper echoes from the speaker. "Everyone okay in there?"

"Yeah, we're fine," Leo says. "Just stuck."

"Let me get a couple of my guys on it. Stay put." The speaker cuts out.

"*Stay put?* Yeah, no problem." Leo studies me. "You gonna be okay?"

I've never considered myself claustrophobic, but now I'm unsure. "As long as it doesn't take too long to get out." I slide to the floor. "You?"

He follows suit, stretching his long legs next to mine, clad in dark gray shorts. "Believe it or not, this isn't the first time the elevator has broken down."

Side by side, I'm struck by how much larger and taller than me he is. "Your legs are really hairy."

"They're averagely hairy, I think?" He knocks his knee into my leg. "You're just used to your smooth ones."

"You don't know how smooth they are."

His gaze roams from the hem of my cutoff shorts to my sandaled toes. "They look it."

At the slight rasp to his voice, my heart makes itself at home at the base of my throat.

A slew of responses flit through my mind. One where I say, *Why don't you find out for yourself?* and another where I brush my leg against his to show him how smooth it is.

Think platonic thoughts, I remind myself.

"It's been nice having you back." Leo tucks a damp strand of hair behind my ear.

"It's been nice being back. I thought, since I visited Gram, I haven't really been away, but staying for an afternoon isn't the same as *being* here."

His eyes dip to my mouth as I'm talking. "No, it's not."

"We're trying to be friends, right?" It's impossible to hide my growing breathlessness with the way he's staring.

"I'm being friendly."

"*Too* friendly." I give his chest a gentle shove. "Please tell me Long Beach hasn't made you head of the welcoming committee."

"If I'm doing something wrong, you're going to have to be specific. Tell me, what would be too friendly for us?"

Nothing. Everything.

He glides a fingertip over the back of my hand. "Is this okay?"

Sensation blooms at the spot. "Yes."

"And this?" He sweeps my hair off my shoulder, his touch grazing my neck.

Electricity runs down my arms. "It's fine."

Leo reaches under my hair to the back of my head, strong fingers raking against my scalp, making my eyes momentarily slink shut. "Too much?"

"No."

"How about this?" He leans in, slow, and presses a soft kiss to my cheek.

Goosebumps fly down my legs. "Maybe if we're saying goodbye."

His gaze locks on mine, so close his breath tickles my lips as he whispers, "What if I only want to say hello?"

There's no holding back. I'm physically incapable of anything except throwing my arms around his neck and kissing him.

It's reckless, and I'm positive it will get messy and lead to regrets. But those thoughts get lost when Leo lets out a small groan that has my blood rushing, answering my kiss with one of his own. His mouth is entirely possessive as he urges me to move at his fervent pace, like he knows this may all slip away before he's ready to let go.

I let my palms trail down his chest, memorizing all the muscle that wasn't there before. He grips my hips, fingertips digging in.

"More," I say against his lips, even though it's the exact opposite of what I should do. There's probably a security camera in here I should worry about. But that thought vanishes the second he reaches under my thighs, calluses from decades of playing instruments skating across my skin as he pulls me over his lap. Each point of contact along our bodies, each brush of his lips against mine, forces my reservations to the background.

He moves to my jaw, kissing a trail down my neck. One arm encircles my waist, holding me to him, while the other drags up my leg.

"As smooth as they look?" I ask, because apparently I've become a masochist.

"Mmm" is his only answer, the sound coming from deep in his chest.

It's never been like this with anyone else. Never have I kissed someone who made me so dizzy, my knees would buckle if I tried standing.

We're going to have sex in the tiny space of this broken-down elevator. It's the only outcome of the kind of frenzy happening between us. In the back of my mind, I knew if I gave in and got my hands on him again, it would teeter on primal.

I shove up the hem of his shirt, only he's faster, his hand reaching under my tank and pushing it over my head.

"You're beautiful." He says it with such reverence as his gaze glides over me, I could weep. His eyes lift to mine. "You've always been so beautiful."

"Stop talking." Otherwise I'm going to think too hard about this.

We're kissing again, regressing to the hormonal teenagers we were the last time we were together like this, and—

A screech comes from the speaker. Our movements stall.

"Everyone still okay in there?" a crackling voice says.

Leo catches his breath, chest heaving. "Yeah."

"We'll have this thing up and running in a minute." The speaker cuts out.

I stare at my position on Leo, his hands still on me. *What did I do?*

"That wasn't good." I ease off him and reach for my damp shirt.

"The kiss?"

"*No*, Leo. The kiss was great." I stretch my shirt over my head. "Five stars. No notes. It deserves a glowing review in *USA Today* and a fan club."

He gives a cocky grin. "Then what's wrong?"

"I wanted to be friends again, but now that feels impossible."

The humor leaves his eyes. "Margot."

"Why did you kiss me?"

"Technically, you kissed *me*." When I roll my eyes, he's quick to add, "But I wanted to kiss you. I've wanted to kiss you since you stepped foot inside the music store. As teens *and* adults, in case you're wondering."

I can't look at him. Because I know if I do, I'll see the same sincerity in his eyes that's in his voice, and I don't trust my resolve when my neurons are still firing from the feel of his lips. "How does that get us back to being friends?"

"It doesn't."

The elevator doors open. I stand and stride out.

"Why is that such a bad thing?" His voice takes on an edge as he follows me. "I'm not a mind reader, but it seemed like you enjoyed what we did back there."

"I did." I move at a clipped pace down the hall, though I don't know which apartment is his.

"And I think you like spending time with me."

"I do."

"Then *tell me*." His voice isn't close anymore, and I stop, turning to find him a dozen feet back. "What are you afraid of?"

You. The thought comes automatically.

It's because I enjoyed what we did so much and because I like Leo that I'm afraid I wouldn't be able to keep things between us light. And light, no strings attached, is all I can do. Entertaining more would immediately have me anticipating it ending and all the hurt that would go with that.

He takes a step, then another, until he's in front of me. His face is all harsh lines as he levels me with a stare. "Why won't you go after what you want?"

"Because," I say, "I *don't* want it."

It's not true, but it's not a lie either. I'm dealing with enough, wading in grief as I sort through Gram's things. Readying myself to say goodbye to my childhood home. Spending time with Leo was supposed to distract me from everything else going on in my life, not complicate it more.

His eyes dart between mine, a haze of hurt forming in them. "Oh."

That one word guts me more than if he'd said I was a coward.

We're quiet as he leads me to his apartment. I settle onto his couch and reach for the cassette player on the coffee table, then hit *play* to prevent further conversation.

CHAPTER TWENTY-EIGHT

Vivian

then

After the wedding, the studio gave us a couple of weeks off for a honeymoon. Though rehearsals hadn't started, I endlessly read over the script for my next film. With my second lead, I needed to answer the question: Could I do it again?

I tried to ignore my worries by attempting a casserole when Ted phoned to say my mother was sick.

"She didn't want to bother you, but I'm worried."

I set the knife on the cutting board. "She looked fine at the wedding over the weekend." Hadn't she?

"She didn't want to mention it on your big day. It's been going on for a few weeks now and getting worse."

A vein pulsed in my temple. I'd rarely had a hard-to-kick bug last that long.

Bubbling came from the stove. Water boiled over a steel pot, sizzling as it hit the flames.

I crushed the phone between my ear and shoulder.

"Are you all right?"

I turned off the gas and fanned away the steam. "Yeah, fine."

I was not fine, and I'd never forgive Betty Crocker for her part in this. This new cookbook was called *Good and Easy*, but it should have been called *I'm Full of Bologna*.

He sighed. "I don't want to leave her alone, but I can't afford to take any more time off from work."

"I'll book a flight to come out tomorrow."

Mom probably needed fluids and rest. I had a little over a week before rehearsals started to nurse her back to health. Heating canned chicken noodle soup was well within my abilities.

As soon as I hung up, I abandoned the casserole and went upstairs to pack. I knelt next to the bed and reached under it, dragging out one of two identical brown suitcases we had gotten as an engagement present. It was heavy as I threw it on top of the bed.

My gaze caught on the tag. I'd accidentally grabbed Kit's. He must not have finished unpacking.

I flipped open the latches and pushed back the top.

His clothes were inside—seasonal ones he didn't need yet—next to a bottle of gin.

I stared at it.

We had a few bottles of wine in the kitchen, given to us as wedding presents, which I planned to save for guests and special occasions. Having more felt excessive. We had agreed on that. Kit knew I had issues with alcohol in my home—my safe place—since, when I was growing up, my home didn't feel safe because of my father's drinking.

My instinct was to dump the gin.

Instead, I shut the suitcase. I would talk to Kit more specifically about what I was comfortable having in the house when everything with my mother had passed.

◆

When I arrived on Long Island, Mom had a fever and a cough that made my chest ache. I did everything I could think of over the next several days, but when nothing helped, I called the doctor and made an appointment for a house call. He'd be coming the following day.

"Sit with me," Mom said from her bed, dark circles under her eyes. "You're flitting back and forth so much, you'll wear down the carpet."

"After I finish putting away the laundry." I hated feeling useless. The least I could do when not taking care of her was the chores that usually fell on her shoulders.

Two steps away, I noticed a dresser drawer wasn't pushed in completely. I reached for it, my back leg lifting behind me.

"A little higher," Mom said. "And point your toe."

I smiled and humored her, stretching a little more. "Like this?"

"A rusty écarté derrière, but it has potential."

I sat next to her feet on the bed. "Remember when we used to dance in the kitchen?"

Mom settled her head more fully on the pillow. "Those were the days. It always ended with you attempting to work it into a storyline."

"Otherwise you'd have me breaking my toes in some grueling ballet position." I rested a hand over her feet. "Have they ever recovered from the strain you put on them?"

"Mostly, but I don't mind. Every scar, every imperfection, is a reminder. Not of how damaged we are but that we've *lived*. And that is a beautiful thing." She coughed into her fist. When it continued, she lifted the covers to her face and coughed again.

I chewed my lip while I waited for the fit to fade. "Water?"

She shook her head, teary-eyed. "I'm all right."

It didn't take a professional to know that wasn't true.

The next day, the doctor came and told us Mom's prognosis: He suspected she had bacterial pneumonia and would need to be treated at the hospital. He didn't mince words: It was bad. If she survived, she had a long road to recovery.

If.

I called Eugene to tell him I needed more time. With Mom in the hospital and Ted at work, no one was home to see me pace the kitchen.

"Vivian," he said, like he was talking to a child, "this is going to be my lead film for the year. I'm pouring a lot of money into it and don't have room for setbacks. Either you get on a plane *today* or you're fired."

No B-list movies. No loan to another studio. Fired.

I couldn't leave my mother, the one who loved me enough to keep going when she could hardly see the light after my father left. The first one to believe in me and who kept believing in me even when I didn't. The woman who was the motivation for my dreams in the first place and gave me everything she could to help me succeed.

I couldn't leave her. But I couldn't lose my contract.

"Surprised?" he said when I was silent. "Thought you'd get off with a suspension? You'll cost me an unforgivable amount if I have to recast the role."

My heart ached as if held in a fist. "I know."

"So I'll see you tomorrow?"

I wanted to slam my head against the wall. "I *can't*."

Papers shuffled in the background. "Then you're fired."

The line went dead.

I held the receiver in front of me and gaped at it while tears slid down my face.

My contract was terminated. Just like that. *Poof.*

I cried because I was afraid of losing my mother. I cried because I lost my contract with arguably the biggest studio in the world. I cried over the loss of a dream I had only just begun to realize.

Eyes swollen, I went back to the hospital and sat beside my mother's bed while she slept. On a nearby table sat a vase of flowers. They were from Hugh. I reached for my purse and found a notepad and pen to write him yet another letter I would never give him.

Dear Hugh,

I'm more worried about my mother than I've let her see. Every day, I put on a brave face so she won't know how this is affecting me. But as soon as I'm in the guest room alone, I cry myself to sleep.

It is such a helpless feeling when someone you love is sick or hurting. Though I've complained about how much I shouldered in the past, I would do it again—and again, and again—to fix her, if I could.

I hate when things are out of my control, and this is completely out of my control.

Love,

Vivian

I tore out the page and stuck it in my purse, then grabbed my mother's cold hand. When she woke, I broke the news about being fired, and we both cried.

Days blurred in routine: I sat by her bed, held her hand, and withdrew my notepad and pen to jot down idle musings that had come to me the night before, completely out of context.

Soon, a scene took shape based on the television show idea I once shared with Kit about a widower taking care of his child.

That didn't sound funny at all, though.

It wouldn't be easy for anyone to care for a child on their own, let alone the breadwinner. He would need help. Perhaps not from a housekeeper, like I once imagined, but from a nanny. She would bring levity. I crafted scenes centered on her silly antics while helping to raise a little boy and falling in love with the father.

I named the script after them: *Bobby and Clara.*

So consumed by it was I that I didn't notice when several hours had passed. Then again the next day. And the next.

It reminded me of the times when I was a child and wrote my own stories. Back then, I didn't think, *I can't write* or *No one will take it seriously.* It was for fun and could be whatever I wanted it to be. My father left? I wrote a happily-ever-after. My mother couldn't afford to buy me new shoes for school? I invented a story about an heiress with a thousand pairs.

You know what bothered me? How few female writers there were in Hollywood. Sometimes one was brought aboard to give a female touch, should the script call for it. Why was it an afterthought? A "nice to have" but unnecessary? I wanted to change that. For the little girl I once was with a head full of possibilities. The girl who saw the magic of a blank sheet of paper.

When my mother's eyes cracked open, I set my notepad in my lap. "How are you feeling?"

She brought her free hand to her mouth to cough. "Good. I think today's a good day."

Ever the liar, my mother.

"You don't have to sit here every day," she said. "Get back to LA. Do some auditions. I'll have Ted give you updates."

Like hell I would leave her. Besides, I didn't want to do auditions. I had another idea.

"Actually, I wanted to show you something." I flipped the pages of the notepad to the beginning and handed it to her. She squinted, holding it a few inches away.

Her gaze flitted over line after line. Page after page. I kept quiet until she finished the entire pilot episode. Finally, she eyed me. "You wrote this?"

"Actually, Nurse Nancy has been stealing in here to scribble lines."

"I haven't seen you write since you were a child. Remember those notebooks you used to write in?" Mom turned to the beginning. "I love it. And it's for *television*. How wonderful."

God, it felt good to hear that she liked it, even if the prospect of TV wasn't thrilling.

You see, while more and more of the public was gravitating toward TV, most actors considered what aired foolish: game shows, cartoons, violence. Television was a step down. There was no going back to movies, though. Once word got out about Eugene firing me, no studio would hire me. I was untouchable.

"I want to play Clara. I don't know how or when, but I need you to get better, okay?" I held her hand, fighting to keep my voice from breaking. "Because I'll need to talk to you if this goes nowhere and I'm devastated. Or if it goes somewhere and I want to share the details."

Blue veins stood out along her temples and the backs of her hands. "Someone will need to tell you when you're wearing too much rouge." She swiped her thumb across my cheek.

I laughed, rubbing the corners of my eyes with the heel of my palm. "That too." I would have said anything so she had more reason to fight.

Every day, Mom and I talked about the script. Between discussing another episode idea and editing, I held her hand.

Slowly, her coloring got better. She coughed less. Sat up more and became a bit animated.

When she was released from the hospital, we continued the same routine at her house while she recovered over the next couple of weeks.

She recovered.

A Billie Holiday record played as she came down for breakfast on my last day. Both of us in our slippers, we swing danced across the linoleum like we did when I was a kid, albeit more slowly this time. I couldn't have been more grateful for that moment.

That night, when the long-distance rates were lower, I got ahold of Kit.

"What are your plans for the weekend?" Anticipation spooled in my chest at my plan to surprise him.

"A few buddies are swinging by." After a moment, he added, "I miss you."

I couldn't remember how many times he'd said that in the six weeks I'd been gone. If he missed me so much, he should have come out. Even a day would have made all the difference.

I tried not to let it bother me, instead focusing on how none of it would matter once I was back. Our time apart would be a blip we would easily smooth over.

Only nothing was ever that simple.

Los Angeles Examiner

HARRIET'S HOLLYWOOD
MARCH 8, 1954

TROUBLE IN PARADISE?

What is it that would keep a man from going home to his wife? It's an age-old question. What's even more baffling is when the wife is the sweet and stacked Vivian Stone. With Kit Pierce acting like a bachelor again, prowling the Sunset Strip, it seems like he's already forgotten their vows, made only a short time ago. But the truth is a stranger one.

The little missus hasn't been there to go home to.

Vivian has been notably absent from the Hollywood scene, and while we first speculated it was because she was in the family way, reports have circulated that she was fired from MGM. Looks like she left LA to lick her wounds.

Now, without her here to keep Kit in line, he's returned to his wild ways. He's been seen sharing drinks at the bar with Arthur Davies, Wayne Thompson, and Fred Healy till the joint closes down.

We sure hope wherever Vivian has been, she comes to her senses and goes home to her husband!

CHAPTER TWENTY-NINE

Vivian

then

Gravel crunched under the cab's tires as it pulled into my driveway that night after my flight. Headlights illuminated three other vehicles, which didn't surprise me. Kit had said friends were coming over.

The cabbie popped the trunk and grabbed my luggage while I paid the fare. Being separated from Kit by seconds and yards instead of weeks and miles had me shaking with excitement.

I walked up the steps and opened the front door.

Laughter and the overlapping voices of four, maybe five men hit me as I set my suitcase down. I toed off my heels and headed toward the sound coming from the kitchen.

Through a haze of smoke and the sweet smell of cigars, Kit and four others sat around our dining table, holding cards and tossing chips of various colors into the center. Dennis, a director fired from MGM last year, eyed me as he sipped a beer. I'd never worked with Dennis but heard he had gambled away his last film's entire budget. I rested a single finger over my lips, Kit's back to me.

I covered my hands over Kit's eyes. "Guess who?" I said sensually, an octave lower.

"Is it . . . Marilyn Monroe?"

"In your dreams."

"Every night."

I dropped my hands to lightly smack his shoulder. In one quick move, he twisted in his seat and looped an arm around me, hauling me into his lap.

"You're home." He held the back of my head, another hand clutching my hip, as he kissed me. One of the men whistled.

A chill raced down my arms, my body at odds. One part wanting to melt into his touch, even in front of an audience, and the other part fighting the shock over his voice's slower pace in the few words he spoke, telling me he was tipsy. I'd never seen alcohol have a noticeable effect on him. Even in Vegas. Did he have more tonight?

A memory surfaced of my father, slurring as he berated my mother about an overcooked steak. I ended the kiss, but Kit didn't relax his hold on me.

He nuzzled my neck. "Everyone out."

"No, it's all right." I set a hand on his chest and eased off his lap, needing a minute to collect myself. "You're all in the middle of a round of . . ."

"Poker," a man I didn't recognize with thinning brown hair offered.

I side-eyed Kit. He'd said he hated cards. "Right. Finish your game. I'll be upstairs."

Another whistle came from one of the fellas while I breezed through the kitchen, spotting a couple dozen beer bottles on the counter.

I went upstairs and sat on our bed, trying to relax. Within thirty minutes, the front door opened and goodbyes were exchanged as Kit's friends headed out. A round of engines turned over.

Realization shot my heart to my throat. Were any of them drunk?

Kit's feet pounded the steps, making his way to our room. He propped a hand against the doorframe with a wolfish grin. "I'll admit, I was hoping you were naked already. But I can help." My expression must have said that wasn't going to happen because his face fell. "What's wrong?"

"Are your friends okay to drive?"

He tipped his head slightly. "Yes . . ."

"Don't act like it's unreasonable to wonder, considering all the bottles on the counter."

He pushed off the doorframe and stepped closer. "I feel like there's something you're upset about, but I'm not getting it. You were gone. I was lonely. I spent time with friends."

"I'm not upset about your friends. I'm upset about the drinks." I scrubbed my hands across my face. "Before leaving for my mother's, I accidentally grabbed your suitcase and found a bottle of gin."

"So?"

"Then I come home, and it's obvious you drank more than usual. It's stirring up memories of my father. I can't be married to someone who reminds me of him. It's the one thing I can't get past."

He stared out the window for a few seconds, then came to sit next to me. "I think you're making this into a bigger deal than it is."

Was I?

People drank. There was nothing wrong with Kit having friends over for cards and some drinks as long as it didn't change how he acted. It seemed like he understood how I felt now.

When I lay back, he lay next to me.

I wanted to change the subject so I could relieve the tension caught under my ribs. "I had an idea while I was gone. What do you think about taking a crack at working together again? We work well together, don't you think?"

He turned to look at me. "Yeah, but you lost your contract."

"Which means I'll have to get another."

"You think another studio will sign you?"

"Even if I managed it, we couldn't convince anyone to put us together for movie after movie. We're not Judy Garland and Mickey Rooney."

He played with the top button of my dress, popping it free. "I don't have a solution."

"Television. Remember my zany housekeeper idea? I wrote a pilot about a widower raising his child. I changed the housekeeper to a nanny—me—who's hired to help the widower—you. We can pitch it to a TV network. If you're interested, that is."

The way his eyes lit up said exactly how interested he was. I knew the idea would get his attention. Kit had said he was partial to TV.

"My contract isn't up yet."

"You'd have to quit." I rested my hand over his, stopping him from moving to my next button before we'd finished talking. "Keep working until we pitch the idea and hear back."

"And if we don't get it?"

Oh, ye of little faith. "I'm not sure if you know this about me, darling, but I'm a very determined woman."

◆

Night after night, we pulled out the script for *Bobby and Clara*, marking it up until the wee hours rolled around and the ashtray was full. While I'd been afraid Kit would want to change my ideas too much, his suggestions merely helped refine a script he called "genius." If he was right, working together might be a gold mine.

Finally, we had a pilot episode we were proud to pitch.

Something about it was magical. The words glittered with possibility.

Rumor had it our old producer, Gerard Donovan, had stormed out of MGM in a blaze of fire over an argument with Eugene. He now worked at CBS. Kit rang him to invite him over for supper.

Which meant I would need to cook.

I'd have sooner jumped out of a moving vehicle than pore over another cookbook, but I wanted to sell the show partly by selling myself. Embodying the character, whom I saw not only as a nanny but also as someone involved in maintaining the house, could do that.

For the sake of giving our show its best chance, I cracked open a book. This one came with the delightful caveat telling wives to avoid "sissy" foods so as not to insult their husbands' masculinity. It sounded like a lot of power to give a meal. "Meat and potatoes" was touted as a classic.

I tied an apron over my floral dress and, with clenched teeth, made something resembling Salisbury steak. It was ready just as Gerard showed up.

The meal turned out fine. Edible. No complaints by either man as we made small talk. No compliments either. I'd given it the old college try, at least. Afterward, I set down slices of baked Alaska—which, no, I didn't make. I'd purchased the dessert from Perino's. Though I did specifically ask them to leave the torching to me.

Kit took a bite. "Listen, we wanted to talk to you about something."

"Oh, yeah?" Gerard said, mouth full.

I cleared my throat. "A proposition."

Gerard pointed at me with his fork. "I prefer blondes."

I humored him with a laugh and slid the script across the table. "We've been talking and would love to re-create the enchantment of *Sunday Circus* for a TV audience."

Using his forefinger, he dragged the script the rest of the way. He read the cover page, then flipped it.

A minute later, he chuckled.

So soon!

Kit and I hid our excitement under soft smiles. When he was halfway through the pages, I leaned over the table to check what Gerard was laughing at now.

"It's the scene with the balloon animals," I said to Kit over my shoulder.

"Oh, I love that part. Wait until you see how it ends."

I picked up Gerard's empty plate. "Let me get you another slice." When I came back, he dug in and continued reading.

Once he'd finished the last page, he glanced up. "It's good."

Kit's eyes widened. "Yeah?"

It's good.

I wanted to leap into the air. Do cartwheels across the table.

"Funny but heartfelt." Gerard rested the edge of his plate against his chest as he polished off his dessert. "Audiences would eat it up."

I couldn't temper my excitement. "You mean it?"

Gerard nodded in Kit's direction—"Housewives would love the idea of a handsome fella like him being a doting father"—then at me—"and there's no red-blooded man alive who wouldn't want to see you on their screen." To Kit he said, "Nice work."

Kit beamed a megawatt smile. "Thanks. I couldn't stop thinking about the idea."

As women, we're trained to compromise. So while I wanted to correct him and say that it was me who couldn't stop thinking about the idea—it was the very thing that helped me through my mother's illness—I said, "*We*, darling. *We* couldn't stop thinking about the idea."

Kit moved on. "So you think CBS might go for it?"

Say yes.

Gerard set down his plate, wiping the corner of his mouth. "What about your contracts?"

"She's already out"—Kit pointed at me—"but I'll terminate mine if you offer us a deal."

Gerard tapped the side of his glass, staring off like he was pondering the idea. "I'll think it over." He stood.

I couldn't let any uncertainty creep into his mind. "*Sunday Circus* was MGM's highest-grossing comedy this decade." It was 1954, so we weren't even halfway through the decade, but that was semantics. I followed him to the front door. Maybe he needed more. Something other than dollar signs. "Can you imagine what we could do together? Besides embarrassing the hell out of Eugene Mills for losing all of us."

Gerard huffed. "Bastard would deserve it." After a second, he clicked his tongue. "You know I don't have the final word on this, right? Best I can do is set up something for you two to come in and talk turkey. But we do have a time slot that needs filling, I can tell you that."

"Great," Kit said, casual and cool.

As soon as Gerard was out the door, Kit turned to me. "Do you think we're going to get it? Because it feels like we're going to get it."

I squealed and jumped into his arms.

<hr />

We got our meeting the following week and signed a deal on the spot.

Because we had already proven ourselves, we were given more leeway than actors usually got in designing the set and choosing the cast.

Kit and I agreed on a chubby-cheeked five-year-old named Rich Sullivan to play the part of his son, Charles. We worked with the network to pick writers, people we'd work closely with, since everyone loved the first script.

On the day we were to film our pilot, I was a nervous wreck getting ready in my dressing room. I'd had it outfitted with a blue velvet sofa and a credenza to display pictures: our wedding portrait, a photo Ted had taken of my mother fishing, a picture of Ruth and me in front of my old Ford when we drove cross-country. A snapshot of the monthly dinner gang holding black bowling balls: Ruth and me cradling them an inch from our mouths as if to kiss them for good luck while Dean and Hugh hugged theirs with one arm and made a muscle with the other. Then there was a photo Ruth took of Hugh and me on towels at the beach, both of us mid-laugh. A movie poster from *Sunday Circus* hung above.

Lit bulbs outlined the mirror over my vanity. I took in my reflection, scrunching my face behind round, thick-rimmed glasses. "And who do we have here? Is this young Charles?" I shook my head. With a deep breath, I did the line again.

A knock came on my door, Kit walking in a second later with roses. "I saw these and thought of your lips." He pressed a light kiss to them, careful not to smear my lipstick. When I didn't put in any effort, he stilled. "What's wrong?"

"What if the jokes fall flat? What if they hate us?" I'd been so confident, so sure of the script, but what if it was a silly little show no one could relate to? What if they didn't laugh?

I was used to filming in front of a crew. This would be a live audience. If no one laughed, I might not be able to go on.

We had so much to lose. Kit had given up his contract for me. For us. For this wild idea. And if it didn't work, I didn't know what we'd do. Our finances and careers rested on it being a success.

Kit took off my glasses and set them down. "They'll love you. You want to know how I know? Because you made me love you. Because people can't help it."

I relaxed a little. "You're not so bad yourself."

"I'm decoration. It's both our names on that script, but let's be honest: You're the star of this show." His fingers threaded through my hair as he kissed the side of my head. "And I wouldn't have it any other way. Now let's go knock it out of the park."

My hands trembled as he led me out of my dressing room and left me behind a set door. The announcer gave the audience the opening remarks, letting them in on how filming took place with the lighting and cameras and boom, then handed the microphone to Kit.

Kit thanked everyone for coming and introduced himself, then Rich Sullivan, whose squeaky voice made me smile and the audience laugh and clap. "And without further ado, playing Clara O'Reilly: the one and only Vivian Stone."

Showtime.

I straightened my shoulders and walked through the door, smiling while bright lights highlighted the set, warming my skin. The audience members were dark shadows of clapping hands. Somewhere out there, Ruth watched with Dean and Hugh. With a subtle kick of my heel behind me to point out my lucky shoes for Hugh, I came up next to Kit and gave a small nod to the left, center, and right of the crowd.

There was no clapping in pictures outside of premieres and award shows. But here, each one was a rocket to my confidence.

Once Kit handed the microphone off, the audience quieted, and we retreated off set and to our places. I shut my eyes, willing my heart to steady, but everyone's anticipation was an invisible weight I couldn't ignore.

Don't mess up.

"Action."

I walked out of an apartment to the hallway, where a long line of gray- and white-haired women stood outside a new neighbor's door. "What's all this? Free donut day?"

"Mr. Thorne's conducting interviews," a woman in a knitted shawl said. "For a nanny."

"You don't say." I pointed at myself with a bit of flourish. "Well, I need a job."

She turned her nose up. "The advertisement specifically stated he's seeking a grandmotherly type."

I squinted down at myself as if I didn't quite fit the bill. As I peered back up, I gave a Cheshire cat–like smile. That got me a couple of mild laughs. Enough to feed the adrenaline humming through my veins.

Music played to show the passing of time while I changed my costume. I came back, cane in hand, wearing a white-haired wig and thick-rimmed glasses. My ratty sweater and tweed skirt were mismatched.

Rich sat outside the door, pouting.

"Why the long face, pal?"

He stared at his shoes. "The boys outside are playing baseball."

"America's greatest pastime." I held my cane over my shoulder like a bat. "How come you aren't out there with them?"

His head fell against the wall as he looked up at me. "I'm no good. They'll laugh."

I knelt next to him. "You'll never know if you don't try."

Rich smiled, shooting to his feet as the apartment door opened, the other woman exiting. I used my cane to push myself up and, hunched over, walked in to stand before Kit, sitting behind a desk.

His head jerked back as he took me in. "Are you here for the nanny position?"

"You'll have to speak up, sonny."

Raising his voice and enunciating every word, he said, "Exactly how old are you?"

"Why, Mr. Thorne. You should know never to ask a woman her age." I scratched my head, the wig shifting. "But if you must know, eighty-two."

"*Eighty-two*?" More laughs as he wiped a hand down his cheek. "How about walks to the park? Are you up for that level of exercise?"

"Oh, yes sirree!" I lifted a bent leg and slapped my knee, the top of a sagging wool stocking showing. "These old things just need to get greased up once in a while."

Kit's eyebrows lifted high, horrified, while the audience laughed some more.

Rich came running in. "Dad, Dad! I did it! I hit a home run!"

I pointed at his scraped knees with my cane. "I haven't seen a gash that bad since my brother Frank stole a base and made mincemeat out of the second baseman with his spiked cleats."

Kit turned to me, indignant. "That's exactly why I didn't want Charles playing!"

"You know my brother Frank?"

Big laughs from the audience.

I took the kerchief off my wig, knocking it askew, and knelt to bandage Rich's knee. "We'll get Charles cleaned up in a jiffy."

With skill and timing beyond his mere five years, Rich reached and tugged off my wig.

Kit's reaction—intense wide eyes, slack jaw—combined with my exaggerated wince at being found out only intensified the laughter. We held the poses for several long seconds to get the most we could out of the audience's reaction. I nearly cracked a smile along with them. That shriek-like cackle had to be Ruth.

By the end of the episode, I was riding the highest of highs. Kit and I took each other's hands and bowed, then bowed again.

This could work. It would.

Kit found me in my dressing room afterward, both of us quivering with elation. We made love against the wall. Again when we got home.

The same chemistry we'd had on *Sunday Circus* translated to our show. Each week the audience followed Bobby and Clara as they fell in love and she wrangled him into different larks.

It turned out my mother was right when she said sometimes destiny found you. Comedy was my destiny, and in front of a live audience laughter became my fuel. It pushed me to ratchet up everything from the facial expressions to the movements to the execution of dialogue. Which bumped up the laughs. It was a delicious cycle.

One evening, I smoothed a newspaper out on the kitchen counter while on the phone with Hugh. The article open was one of several I'd read raving about the show's potential. While I shared my joys with Ruth too, she didn't let me simmer in the excitement like I wanted to. Hugh, on the other hand, let me go on and on for as long as I wanted.

"Those were some lucky heels you got me, huh?" It was silly, but I usually displayed them on a dresser in my bedroom. "I had them on for the pilot."

"I noticed." He had a smile in his voice. "But it was never about luck. You earned this. Now tell me what else the article says."

I traced a finger over the words, shaking so much I kept losing my spot. "'Stone is a rare jewel of the comedy world. Her character is mischievous but lovable, goofy yet charming. A looker who can keep a straight face through sharp dialogue.'"

"Yeah?" Hugh said. "I could have told them that years ago."

CHAPTER THIRTY

Vivian

then

One day during the second half of the season, Ruth lounged on the velvet sofa in my dressing room while I sat at my vanity. I took the top off my lipstick and twisted it up.

Maybe I'd try a new color. Give up the red and see what I'd look like in pink.

Nah.

"'Every week, nearly forty million Americans tune in to *Bobby and Clara*, making it a family ritual and the most watched television program in the country,'" Ruth quoted from the newspaper in her hands. "'When asked about her well of humor, Vivian Stone, who plays screwball nanny Clara O'Reilly, says she considers herself more brave than funny.'" She huffed. "Well, that's bullshit."

"Why, thank you." I swiped on the lipstick. "I do appreciate you keeping my ego in check. It's been running rampant these days."

"I mean the part about being more brave than funny."

"It's true. Half the time I'm in front of the audience I'm thinking past Vivian, who helped write the script, had no consideration for how brave future Vivian would have to be to do it."

I simply didn't know if I could pull it off, since it was even more over-the-top than my films. Yet, week after week, I pushed myself. My reward was soaking up the audience's laughter.

"Well, if you ask me," she said, "you're a shoo-in for an Emmy."

The door tore open. Kit's eyes blazed as he stormed in.

A weight formed in the pit of my stomach. Gerard followed him, shutting the door.

I sat straight. "What's wrong?"

"We're screwed." Kit lit a cigarette as he paced the room.

Gerard held up a hand. "Let's not get carried away. They're not out yet, so we still have time to come up with a plan."

"What's not out yet?" Ruth folded the newspaper.

"One of the gossip rags got ahold of some photos," Gerard said.

"Nudes, Vivian." Kit's face turned cold. "The paper says they have a bunch of them."

That weight in my stomach sank to my toes.

"Is it true?" Gerard asked. "I figured they were lying, but I have to ask. How we handle this will depend on your answer."

"Even if we deny it, they're going to print something, and the network's going to pull the show," Kit said. "The photos are obviously not her, but—"

"They are." I accepted the reality of my past and the choices I'd felt I had to make. "I mean, they probably are."

Kit cupped a hand behind his ear. "Say that again."

I'd told Kit a simplistic version of what had happened with Walter but skipped over the photos, feeling I'd already laid a heavy load on him. Too late now.

"They're real. At least, there are nude photos of me somewhere out there, so I assume they're the same ones." I turned to Gerard, wondering if he recalled my hesitancy on seeing the morality clause in my MGM contract. "I did have some skeletons in my closet after all."

Gerard crossed his arms, no judgment on his face. "When did you do them?"

"When I modeled in New York. It paid more than ads, and I was desperate for acting lessons." It was one thing for those close to me to know, but the rest of the country?

Ruth said to Gerard, "What can we do about it?"

"Best thing is to pay them off."

"Who's behind this? I will *bury* them." Kit's index finger pressed into the table, where my pictures were displayed.

"Probably my former agent." The heel. He must have seen me on TV and figured he could make a quick buck.

Someone knocked at my door.

Kit crushed his cigarette out in an ashtray. "Get lost!"

"Cool it," I said as Gerard went to speak to someone behind the door. Not that I was calm. Inside, my heart raced faster than a mouse in a wheel.

"I should cool it? The world's going to see you naked, and I don't have a right to be pissed off?" He pointed at the door. "You know what they're saying? The headline they're threatening to run with? '*Stripped-Down Stone*.'"

I swallowed the dread coating my throat. That headline had to be an exaggeration to get our attention. Even *Confidential* wouldn't print something that vulgar.

Ruth crossed her arms. "Hate to break it to you, but people have been thinking about her naked all along."

I sent a pleading stare her way. *Please don't.*

"I don't even know why you're here," Kit snapped at Ruth.

I wanted to raise a shield around her. How dare he speak to her like that! "She already knew about the photos."

"She knew? But your husband didn't?" Kit scowled. "Let me guess: Mr. Perfect knows too."

Kit had started making snide comments when I called Hugh to ask for his opinion, from details pertaining to interviews to radio spots to photo shoots. I had never dealt with success on this level, but Hugh had.

My silence was enough of an answer. At this point, Hugh knew the whole story about Walter too.

Kit snickered. "Of course he does. Better call to get his thoughts on all this."

Gerard shut the door. "They're ready for you in five."

Kit tilted his head back. "I can't go out there like this. I'll bite someone's head off."

"You're going to have to." In the mirror, my cheeks had a deeper flush, like a healthy glow rather than the more accurate frustration. We didn't have time to deal with this right now. "I think our only choice about the photos is to pay them off."

After dipping our toes in the television industry, it became clear that film studios had more clout and influence when it came to silencing slandering articles about their stars. Stopping this would be up to us. There was no way the network would let us continue if the photos got out.

I had once thought that television wasn't good enough, but now I couldn't live without it. Losing *Bobby and Clara* would destroy our dreams.

———— ✦ ————

The following evening, I wore a fit-and-flare dress—black on top and bright pink flowers on the bottom—with a matching pink beret and went to dinner with Hugh at the Brown Derby. Rows of caricatures of Hollywood's most famous were framed on the walls. Being among them was a sure sign you'd "made it."

Hugh was already sitting when the hostess led me to him. He gave a warm smile I couldn't help mirroring. Since I'd known him for over three years, it didn't often occur to me how handsome he was. But once in a while it struck me like how you could appreciate a work of art.

"I've always wanted to sit at Booth 5." I slid in across from him. "It's where Clark Gable proposed to Carole Lombard."

He braced an elbow on the table. "How do you know these things?"

"Well"—I peered left, then right—"don't tell anyone, but I'm a celebrity stalker. The actress thing is a front to get better access."

"Oh?" The fear in his dark eyes was fairly convincing. "Should I be worried?"

I waved him off. "There's nothing exciting in your medicine cabinet. But Rock Hudson's trash?" I whistled low. "Talk about burying some secrets."

Hugh pointed at the wall next to our table. "I don't think stalkers get their caricatures up here."

"Golly." I twisted in my seat to get a better look. "Would you look at that."

He grinned. "Now you'll always be at Booth 5."

"Where's yours?"

"Other side of the room." He tipped his head toward a table where a small group of diners peeked over and talked behind their hands. "But I'm not the one making someone's day."

I scoffed. "They're staring at *you*."

Hugh was the epitome of a star. Last year he had played an archaeologist on an adventure. Moviegoers loved watching him swing on a rope over a crumbling bridge and crack a whip.

Someone brushed my arm as I loosened my napkin from its silverware. A young woman walked past, glancing over her shoulder.

Hugh followed my gaze. "What is it?"

"She touched me. I don't know why some people do that." It was one of the most unnerving aspects of fame. One time, someone had pulled out a strand of my hair.

"That's the price we pay. There's no privacy. Did I tell you about the photos I got in the mail?"

I shook my head, taking a sip of iced tea.

"They were naked pictures with a letter asking me to send some back."

I pushed my drink away, disgusted on his behalf. It reminded me of my photographs.

"It's fine," he said. "I tossed them."

"Something happened." I tapped my red-painted fingernails on the table. "Do you remember the photos I told you about from my modeling days?" I emphasized "photos" so there would be no mistaking what I meant.

His posture stiffened. "What about them?"

I couldn't look at him, instead focusing on my dancing fingers. "They got out. One of the papers is threatening to print them."

Hugh cursed under his breath. "What now?"

"We pay them off."

"And you did?"

"Gerard is taking care of it."

"If there's anything I can do"—he reached across the table and took my hand—"tell me, and I'll do it."

There wasn't anything he could do, but I believed him.

Thankfully, Gerard phoned a couple of days later to tell me he had heard back about our offer to buy the photos. They wanted more money. Of course they did. What could we do but agree?

The following morning, when it was all settled and papers were signed, Kit made breakfast and brought it to me in bed like he did in Vegas.

"What's this?" I asked, sitting up.

He set a wooden tray in front of me. "An olive branch. I'm sorry for losing it over the photos."

With the relief of it being over, it was easier to rationalize his behavior. I would have been upset if it had been the other way around. "You need to apologize to Ruth too, you know."

"Does she like pancakes?"

"Everyone likes pancakes." I lifted one and took a bite. "Gerard says he'll bring the negatives over as soon as he gets them. I'm going to burn them."

I would never be able to scorch the truth of my past, but I would do whatever it took to keep it from dictating my future.

◆

I wore a stunning red dress by Hubert de Givenchy to the Emmys a month later. My leg bounced under the table as Kit and I waited to hear the results of our nominations.

Bright lights illuminated Ray Sanderson, star of the show *Keep 'Em Coming*, on stage as he went through each of the nominees for Best Actress Starring in a Regular Series. I was surprised he hadn't backed out. Ray had been under a lot of scrutiny recently over leaked photos of him kissing a model in a restaurant parking lot while his wife was still inside at their table.

Kit grabbed my hand and mouthed, *I love you*.

God, he was handsome. I hoped our children would have his curly hair or piercing eyes.

We'd stopped trying to prevent a pregnancy several months ago, though we weren't expecting yet. It might not have been the best time to try, given how busy we were, but there would never be a perfect time. I could only imagine it—playing a nanny so I could pay a nanny.

Writing a pregnancy into the show would be an issue. Some things simply weren't done on-screen. Thankfully, Bobby and Clara were getting married by the end of the season, so it was feasible they could also be expecting soon. All I'd need to do was help write a damn good script to convince the network to go for it.

A hush fell over the crowd as Ray opened the envelope. "And the winner is . . ."

My pulse pounded in my ears. I wanted this. I really wanted this.

"Jane Knox!"

I slumped but forced myself to clap.

Kit bent close. "You're wonderful, all right?"

I shrugged. "Maybe next year."

Ray went through the nominees for Best Situation Comedy. "And the winner is . . . *Bobby and Clara*."

Kit smiled, standing and offering his hand. I took it, convinced I must be dreaming. Everyone clapped as we walked onstage, looking at each other every couple of steps.

Ray drew me in for a hug and handed me the award. It was a bit heavier than I expected, and I let my hand holding it drop a foot, then scrambled to bring it back to my chest. Ray laughed along with the audience as I shot wide eyes at him.

He held up his hands. "Sorry!"

I turned toward the sea of people in the dimly lit room. "I should have been lifting weights in preparation, but no one told me how heavy it'd be." I motioned to Kit. "What did I marry you for?"

More laughter.

I took a beat to snap a picture of this moment in my mind. "I grew up being told I could be whatever I wanted. Well, what I wanted to be was a dramatic film star." I nodded in Kit's direction. "He's probably heard that more times than he'll admit."

The corner of his lips hitched like he was thinking about it for a second before he gave a quick shake of his head. "Nah, I'll admit it."

The crowd chuckled.

"But that's not true," I said. "You can't always be what you want. You can't always get what you hope and pray for. Sometimes life gives you something else."

I'd learned to write my plans in pencil. If at any time I had held too rigidly to one of them, I would have closed myself off to possibilities, experiences, challenges I'd never dreamed of.

I was surprised at the tears blurring my vision. "And if you're lucky, that something else turns out to be even better."

CHAPTER THIRTY-ONE

Vivian

then

The first time I woke to the other side of the bed still made and cold, fear engulfed me, and I raced downstairs to find Kit asleep on the sofa, still in his clothes, snoring. He must have been too tired to climb the steps. But looking at him, smelling him, I realized he'd also been too drunk.

Since starting the show, he went out with friends more, especially when we didn't have an early morning on set the next day. I never knew what time he got in, since I was already asleep.

If I confronted him about it, I might lose my temper, and we could have an unresolvable fight. Then all of this—the show, our marriage, the future I still hoped for—would tumble like a house of cards.

My stomach twisted as I paced the kitchen one night, waiting for him to come home. If I didn't have exciting news to share, I might not have been so frustrated.

On impulse, I picked up the phone, calling a number I associated with comfort, and slid down the kitchen wall to sit.

"Hello?" came a woman's voice.

Loretta Atwood. Hugh had been dating her for several months.

I dropped my head against the wall. "Hi, it's Vivian. Is—"

A shuffling noise gave me pause.

"Hello?" Hugh said.

Some of the tightness in my shoulders eased. "It's me."

"Give me a minute, okay?" he whispered in the background. There came a shifting of what sounded like bedsheets, and I imagined them basking in their postcoital glow.

I gently banged my head against the wall behind me a few times to erase the image. "It's fine. You're busy."

"No, it's all right."

A door clicked shut on his end while I stared at the knotted hardwood of my kitchen cabinets. "I'm thinking about changing out my cabinets. Or maybe painting them."

"What color?"

I squinted, picturing the options. "Pistachio."

"That's a flavor."

"The *best* flavor. Maybe then Kit will look forward to being here instead of skipping the dinner I made." I reached for an orange Jell-O mold, filled with nuts and cherries, and a spoon from the round table in the middle of the kitchen. "Now I get to eat all the dessert."

"Do you want me to come over?"

"You're spending time with Loretta," I said around a mouthful of Jell-O.

"It's fine. I was just reading a new script."

That was something I missed about working on films: the excitement of a fresh storyline. The surprise at how it ended. "What are you playing this time? A cowboy? Businessman? Pirate?"

"A pirate?"

"Why not? Tall, dark, and handsome men can play any role."

"It's also cliché and doesn't make me special. What you have is special."

"Oh?" I said it like I had no idea what he was talking about.

"Fishing for compliments?" His voice warmed with amusement.

Of course, he saw right through me.

Actors craved compliments. Every week there was a shiny new someone trying to take our place and make us old news. We had to continuously prove ourselves and show we were still beautiful. Still better than the rest. The best. So, despite the number of compliments I'd gotten over the years, yes, I still needed more.

"If I were there, I'd mime casting out a line and reeling it in," I said. "But please know I'm thinking it."

He chuckled. "I can only imagine. So, what, you want to hear you're beautiful? Because you are. I've loved watching the different versions of you over the years. From the Vivian Mackenzie with the Long Island accent, smiling for the camera, to the newly minted Vivian Stone, with that serious expression you've mastered, to the TV personality."

"You forgot to mention funny."

"So funny, I have to mute every one of your episodes."

"Hey."

"I'm kidding."

We sat in companionable silence while I eyed the script sitting on the counter. "I should go." Our conversation had helped me feel a bit better, but it was selfish to take his time away from his girlfriend.

As soon as we hung up, I dove into the script.

Kit and I had written the pilot together, but ever since, I'd been working with the writers. Sometimes my husband read an episode's script over and added notes.

I read his handwriting, scrawled in the margin: *I can't wait to see you do this.* I flipped a page: *I'm not saying we should change this, but I won't be held responsible if I can't stop laughing long enough to get through it.* Then: *Should we loop Rich in during this scene? I can see him looking at you in shock right here, which will only amp up the laughs.*

And on it went. Each line, each bit of encouragement, somehow increased my frustration at him still not being home.

The front door opened and closed. *Finally.*

I stood and crossed my arms as Kit walked into the kitchen with a stumble to his step—and blood dripping down his face.

It trickled from a cut above his eye while more ran from his nose. Red was smeared across his chin. His white T-shirt was stained in a few places.

My knees nearly buckled. "What happened?"

"I had an accident." He reached the round table and fell into a chair.

The second his words slurred out, any hope that he'd stumbled in only because he'd gotten hurt and not because he'd been drinking vanished.

I handed him a bag of frozen peas and opened a drawer to find a dishrag. I ran it under the tap. "What kind of accident?"

He pressed the bag to his eye. "I hit a telephone pole. Had to walk home."

I didn't know what kind of accident I'd hoped for. A slip and fall? Even a fight would have been better. His face must have hit the steering wheel upon impact. He couldn't have been going very fast, but what if he had been?

How could he do this to me? To himself? "You've been drinking."

There was no pretending otherwise. Not when he was right in front of me, still bleeding. At least he gave me the courtesy of not denying it.

Ice raced down my spine. "You could have died. Or killed someone."

He released a sigh. "No one died."

I wanted to scream. I wanted to shake him. I wanted to fall into a heap and sob. "Not this time."

"I'm *fine*." His tone said I was overreacting, which only made me angrier.

"Where were you?" I snapped, tossing the rag at him.

He lifted a hand to catch it, but his response time was too slow, so it landed in his lap. "Working."

"You do remember we work together, right?"

"It was other work."

Other work? Was that what he called all those nights out? "Then I have to tell you, darling, you deserve a raise with how hard you've been at it." I grabbed the rag from him and knelt. He wasn't doing a damn thing to clean himself up. "Hold still."

He dropped the peas to the table as I wiped his mouth, then above his eye. It was difficult to be as gentle as I needed to be when I was so livid, every one of my muscles tensed. "You need stitches."

"I'll go to my doctor tomorrow."

"No, *now*."

"At the hospital? Where photographers can get pictures? Hell no."

Who cared about photographers when the cut above his eye wouldn't stop bleeding? "We'll call Joe." He handled the network's crises.

"Joe?" He let out a hearty laugh. "What the fuck's Joe gonna do for my face?"

There was no reasoning with him. I dropped the rag onto the table. "I hate this. You know I hate it."

He ran his teeth across his bottom lip and winced as he grazed a cut. "I only did it because I was celebrating."

"Bullshit."

"I had dinner with a producer from a European studio. He offered me a part in a picture he's doing this summer while we're between seasons. I'm going to take it."

"Oh." I would never deny him an opportunity like this, but it bothered me that he hadn't talked about it with me first. "I suppose now is a good time to mention I'm expecting. The doctor confirmed it yesterday." This was not at all how I'd hoped to share the news, but here we were.

The joy in his eyes cut my anger in half. "Really?"

I motioned to the cold meat loaf. "It's why I cooked and wanted you home. To tell you."

Smiling, he stood and hugged me. I ignored my lingering frustration and hugged him back.

It wasn't unusual for people to drink when they celebrated. It didn't mean he usually got like this when he went out. Not that I was okay with it, even if I understood it.

He was not my father.

"We can talk about it more tomorrow," I said. "I'm going to bed. You can take the sofa."

Though I went upstairs, I couldn't fall asleep. An hour later, I came down to make sure he was sleeping on his side and not his back.

I had to take care of him. Because if I didn't, who would?

CHAPTER THIRTY-TWO

Margot

now

"Did you ever watch their show?" Leo asks from the seat opposite me on his couch. "*Bobby and Clara*?"

"I caught parts. Never the whole thing. Sometimes a rerun would come on—black-and-white, with the studio audience laughing at the right moments. Whenever Gram saw it, she'd say, 'Don't you prefer color?' and suggest one of her favorites, like *The Golden Girls*."

There's something unsettled in my stomach about it. Like I'm waiting for the other shoe to drop. A major secret at the end of all of this.

I glance around the room. "Where are the other tapes?" I don't want to wait any longer to listen to the rest. Finding a how-to cleaning video online shouldn't be too hard.

"They're not ready."

"I can figure it out. Did you ever get my player working?"

"No."

That surprises me. Leo used to fix more complicated things than that. "Any chance I can borrow that one?" I point at the cassette player we used today. "I'll bring it back."

"No," he says quickly.

"You said your dad has a collection. I'm sure he can spare one."

"We need them available for students so they can record themselves at home and listen back. You know, to catch their mistakes and—"

"Never mind." Why is he so adamant about listening to them? I stand and slip my phone into my back pocket, still a little off from what happened between us in the elevator. "Let me know when you have another ready."

———— ◆ ————

A couple I'm guessing are in their early thirties are touring Gram's place with David.

I'm sitting in my car, parked on the street with the windows down, texting Mom. It's been thirty minutes, so if they hated it, they would have realized by now. Which tells me they love it.

Of course they do. Sure, it's outdated. The floors are in desperate need of refinishing. The laminate counters in the kitchen and bathroom are chipped. The appliances are on their last legs. But it has good bones. A nice-size lot for the area. Potential.

Will they rip everything down to the studs? Will they pull out the poppies?

I try to assure myself it doesn't matter. I won't be here to see it. I can use my half of the profits to upgrade my living situation from a studio to a one- or two-bedroom place. I attend a monthly book club with women from college, and my colleagues and I meet for company parties, but I have never felt comfortable inviting anyone over. Soon, I might.

A text pops up from Mom.

> Sorry I took so long, I was looking into it. From what I can tell, he never remarried or had more kids.

It's been three days since Leo and I listened to the last tape, and I've continued to puzzle over the connection between Gram and Vivian. I already asked Mom if Gram ever lived on Long Island or if she worked on films. Did her father remarry?

No. No. And, based on her latest text, no.

It's a special kind of loneliness, knowing I can't ask Gram these questions.

I know her, though. I know black raspberry was her favorite flavor of ice cream and she loved murder mystery novels. She wore her independence like a badge of honor and considered sunrises superior to sunsets.

But do I *really* know her? I hate that now I'm unsure.

I type out a response to Mom, thanking her for checking, as David and the couple walk out, aglow. They stop in the driveway to talk, then the couple hops into their convertible and David, stout and wearing a navy pantsuit, walks over to my car.

I get out as the couple drives off. "How'd it go?"

He lifts his hands at his sides. "They love it. It's charming and exactly the neighborhood they dreamed of ending up in."

A lump settles in my throat, the verification like swallowing a stubborn pill. "Now what?"

"We're going to write up an offer, then you and I will review it. They don't want to waste anyone's time. They know you're only here to get everything cleared out, and they want to take ownership as soon as possible so you don't have to keep paying the mortgage."

I doubt they're moving things along for my benefit, but I give David credit for knowing how to butter me up. "I guess I'll hear from you soon, then." I pass him, walking to the house.

"Very soon."

Inside, I find my laptop and open a document I've been working on.

Maybe it's because I'm in a different environment, or maybe it's the break from my real life, but two days ago I started writing. Not something to submit to the short story contest. I simply had an idea I wanted to jot down, like I do sometimes, but my phone was charging in the next room, while my laptop was in front of me. So I opened a Word document instead of my Notes app. Once I began, the words poured out.

It was after midnight when I finally went to bed.

After my remote work the next day, I avoided my clean-out obligations and wrote some more. I wrote what I wanted without the intention of having anyone read it.

A nagging thought in the back of my mind says that if I analyze this, I'll panic. So I don't.

By the end of the week, Leo has another tape ready, and I ask if he wants to come over.

Lying out on the roof is his idea and one I probably should say no to. But this house is built like his parents', where we always used to sit outside, so I know it's doable. Still, I make him go first through the window of my old bedroom, then hold his hand as I climb out beside him.

I dig my fingertips into the shingles as I lie down. "We're a little old for this."

"What are you talking about?" He turns on his side. "We can't be more than eighteen."

"How long ago was high school?"

"Just yesterday?"

I smile. Before he can ask, I say, "I haven't found the other tape. I have a feeling I won't." My gaze locks on his. "I really needed it, you know? One more thing."

"You have so many memories of your grandma to hold on to already."

"Not the last one." I tell him about our phone call and how I was so invested in a book, I hardly listened to Gram. "She lived by herself and must have been lonely, so I made sure we had weekly chats, but I rushed her off the phone that last time."

"I don't want to diminish what you're feeling, but you know she went out all the time, right? Practically every day she'd pop into one of the stores in town. Everyone loved her and wondered why there wasn't a wake. Maybe you didn't realize how much she went out after you and your mom moved away. It doesn't mean she was never lonely, but she didn't sit inside all day."

"I didn't know that."

"Took her a while to come back to the music store after everything happened between you and me, but she came around," he says. "She talked about you all the time. When you worked at the magazine, she got copies and gave them out. I still have them at the store. Then you got your new job and she told everyone you were a professor—"

A laugh bursts from me. "I work *with* professors. On their textbooks."

"I figured something like that when I googled you."

"You googled me?"

"A few times." He smiles a crooked grin. "Don't let it go to your head."

Hearing that Gram was so loved warms my heart, but somehow it makes me miss her more. "As much as I'm enjoying Vivian's story, a big part of me had hoped Gram would be on those tapes. I'm already forgetting the sound of her voice. What if I forget her laugh?"

"You couldn't forget it if you tried."

The sound comes to me—high-pitched, nearly a shriek—and I smile, remembering earlier this year when she told me a story she could hardly get out, she was laughing so hard. "It was pretty memorable, wasn't it?"

He reaches up to run the pad of his thumb over my cheekbone. "It's your laugh too."

"What? No it's not."

"You're kidding, right? I used to hear you coming to the music store from around the block."

I remember walking around town with Kiyana or another friend and all the times I made them stop at the store with me to see Leo. I never over-thought the way he was smiling before I fully walked through the door.

"No matter what happens with the house or the tapes," he says, "you'll carry your grandma with you forever. One more conversation, as nice as it would have been, wouldn't change that."

That truth settles over me. Gram is part of me, from my laugh to my love of books to my belief in *everything in moderation*, even if it means spoiling your dinner with an ice cream sundae. She taught me that one when I was nine.

It doesn't take away my grief, but it does ease my guilt over that last conversation.

"Thank you for reminding me."

He nods, quiet for a moment. "I've been thinking about the other night. Is the reason you aren't interested in being more than friends because of how it ended between us before?"

"It hurt like hell when you didn't want me anymore, but that's not the only reason."

He stares at me, an intensity reflected in his eyes. "I still wanted you."

The admission startles me so much, I sit up, forgetting for a second we're on a roof. At my little yelp, Leo slings an arm over my waist to pin me down.

"Shit, Margot."

"I'm going to need you to expand on what you just said."

He pulls a deep breath in through his nose and forces it out pursed lips. "That night, in my car, when you said you wanted to stay here with me instead of going to UC Santa Barbara? I'd already been thinking of *leaving* Long Beach."

Something inside—my heart, my every organ—dips.

"I wanted to be here eventually, but seeing so many people leaving for school got me wondering if I should too," he says. "You remember my friend Caleb Hill? He was going to the University of Texas at Austin for accounting and kept talking it up."

"Why didn't you tell me?"

"Because I was embarrassed to be two weeks from classes starting and already thinking about transferring. Because I didn't want anyone to know until I'd decided for myself. Because I thought you might suggest UC Santa Barbara, with you, and I worried I'd say yes without knowing if it was right for me . . ."

I'm so stunned, I can't speak.

"Then you said you wanted to stay, and it felt like I was a deciding factor. And I couldn't be—not when I didn't know what I was doing. Not when you staying could make me second-guess leaving. Not when I worried your mom and grandma would blame me for you upending your plans. And definitely not if it wasn't right for *you* to stay here. I didn't know what was right for you, but I trusted your mom did. So I ended things, hoping—assuming, really—we'd both come home after college. Then we'd get our chance. Only you didn't."

My chest aches for the heartbroken girl who didn't understand what had happened. "You should have told me. We could have done long-distance." As I say it, though, I'm not convinced we would have. I was young and in love. I might have followed him anywhere.

He nods. "Remember when I said I stood in my own way by not telling you how I felt about you sooner? I did the same when I broke up with you, thinking I was doing the right thing. The mature thing. Turns out it was the opposite."

"I'm convinced we don't think like adults until our mid-twenties."

"*Late* twenties for me." Leo props himself up on an elbow, still holding me around the waist with the other arm. "After you left, you got so quiet, I assumed you were having the time of your life and forgot about me."

"I never forgot." I reach a tentative hand against his chest, right where his heart beats fast. "Anything else? Any other secrets to share?"

Uncertainty creeps into his eyes. "I suppose I should fess up to some deception when it comes to a certain cassette player."

I squint at him. "You fixed it, didn't you?"

"Yeah . . ." He draws out the word with a cringe. "I was afraid if I didn't do something, you wouldn't involve me anymore. Then I wouldn't get time with you."

I want to kiss him. And I know I decided that was a bad idea because then I might not be able to keep things between us light. But we have a history and a connection. Ignoring it is impossible. Maybe going into this knowing it has an expiration date will keep me from getting attached.

"In the spirit of honesty, I didn't mean what I said in the elevator about not wanting this." I motion between us. "It's a lot, getting ready to sell my childhood home and sorting through Gram's things. But pretending I don't want this when I do isn't making it easier."

"I don't want to complicate anything for you."

"You're not. Spending time together is making everything I'm going through more bearable. And the truth is . . . I think I need it."

"What is 'it,' exactly?" His voice lowers, a caress down my spine.

"Us, here, for the time we have together. Not overthinking it, not fighting it. Just letting whatever happens happen." I skim my hand down to the hem of his shirt and reach under it, my fingers sliding along the waist of his shorts.

He lets out a jagged breath. "And what do you want now?"

I tangle my hand in his shirt, tugging him to me. "Everything."

And then I kiss him.

Leo needs no time to recover, and his mouth immediately opens for me. With the first brush of his tongue against mine, all remaining hesitations become sinking speed bumps. I cup his jaw, our lips hot and slick as they work together, a push and pull that has him letting out a soft groan.

If someone would have told me in high school, when we used to sit side by side on his roof, that someday we'd be here, doing this, I'd have said they had lost their mind.

Then asked precisely how much longer I'd have to wait.

"Let's go inside," I say as his lips sear a path down my neck. "If things progress like they did in the elevator, one or both of us are definitely falling off this roof."

We stop kissing, then start again three more times before making it inside my room.

I glide my hands up his chest, taking his shirt with me. He barely gives me a second to look at him before he's peeling my top off and working his mouth over my collarbone, the swell of my breasts, like he's made it his mission to give every inch of bare skin attention.

My heart pounds so hard, he must feel it under his lips, alternating between nips at my skin and sweet kisses that soothe the sting.

"Stop playing." My desire is inching toward needy. "Touch me."

Leo lets out a soft laugh between the kisses he trails down my stomach until he's kneeling. "Margot, the problem tonight won't be me not touching you." He frees the button on my shorts, then finds the zipper, his gaze locked on its slide down. His fingers dip into my waistband and ease the shorts down. "It'll be getting me to stop."

A shiver rushes over me, and I reach behind my back to unhook my bra, letting it fall with the rest.

Hungry eyes rake over me.

"You're staring," I say, more than a little breathless.

"Haven't you noticed?" He drags his hands up my thighs as he stands and backs me up to my bed. "I'm always staring at you."

Leo's mouth and hands explore my body until my blood flows so hot, it's like I'm on fire. And when I can't wait anymore, I lock my legs around him.

It's not until noon the next day, when we finally leave my bed to find something to eat, that we listen to another tape.

CHAPTER THIRTY-THREE

Vivian

then

The summer Kit filmed in Europe was peaceful. Which probably should have been a big red flag waving over the Atlantic. But we talked a couple of times a week, and it was good. He told me about the cast. I updated him on my pregnancy. We went back and forth about names. If he drank while there, I never heard.

Maybe we simply needed this reset.

About a week before Kit was due back, I invited Hugh over for supper. I had learned to accept that my culinary skills lay in salads: garden, fruit, ambrosia. Toss some chicken in a salad and you have the base for chicken Caesar.

Really, I wished I'd learned that long ago.

When I opened the front door, Hugh was standing there in a burgundy sweater and a beige fedora, his hands in his pockets. The whites of his eyes shone brightly in contrast to his irises and the night sky.

He stood there taking me in. He hadn't seen me since our last monthly dinner. I was in a strange stage now where my stretchy dresses still fit but were tight in the middle.

"What?" I motioned to myself in a green wrap dress, belted above the curve of my belly. "This is the most presentable I've looked for weeks, so don't tell me I still look like a mess."

He stepped inside and removed his hat. "You do *not* look like a mess. You have that glow people talk about."

I became a little tongue-tied. There wasn't a pregnant woman alive who didn't want the reassurance that she still looked good. "I don't feel it. My boobs are sore, and I get leg cramps at night." Where was a muzzle when you needed one? I could never keep indiscreet thoughts to myself.

He motioned to my chest. "Well, they look good." His eyes widened as he caught himself and curled his hand. "I mean *you* look good. Overall. Not your boobs, specifically."

I tilted my head, smiling.

"Not that they look bad. It's just that I shouldn't be talking about them." He let out a short laugh, glancing away. "I'm going to stop now."

Flustered Hugh was without a doubt the most adorable thing I'd ever seen. "It's fine. Really."

We walked toward the sound of "Mr. Sandman" playing on the little green radio in the kitchen. He dropped his hat on the table and followed me to the cutting board, where I'd been chopping chicken when the doorbell rang.

"So you went with yellow for the cabinets. Not pistachio."

While we talked almost every week, Hugh rarely came over.

I sliced an uneven chunk of chicken. "It's called 'lemon chiffon.'"

"Hey, let me do that." He went to take the knife.

"You're the guest."

"I don't mind."

I propped the fist holding the knife under my chin. "What you mean to say is you're afraid to eat my cooking."

He quirked an eyebrow. "It's a little unnerving, you looking like a sweet housewife while holding a knife like that."

I used it to point at the salad bowl. "I'll have you know, I've learned to cook." Sort of.

Hugh raised a hand, the corner of his mouth lifting. "All right, Lizzie Borden, I believe you. But I know you don't like doing it."

He had a point, so I handed the knife over. "I'm supervising." I positioned a stool next to him and caught a whiff of his aftershave.

My insides warmed with nostalgia, remembering when we first met. After a handful of very even slices, I said, "You're very particular."

"Anything worth doing is worth doing well."

A fluttering came from my stomach. I rested a hand over it, sitting straight.

He stilled. "Are you all right?"

"The baby's moving."

He set down the knife, staring in awe at where my hand rested. The fluttering got stronger. I reached for his hand on instinct and pressed it to the spot.

I couldn't remember how many times Ruth had rubbed my belly like she could encourage movement strong enough to feel. I let her continue trying, even when it bordered on obnoxious, because I knew in many ways she was living vicariously through me. Eventually, she made me promise to grab her hand and put it on my belly whenever the baby kicked. She had yet to feel anything, though.

Hugh moved closer. His breath brushed my cheek as we both waited. As the fluttering came again, his eyes lit up. "I felt it." He rubbed his hand back and forth, and the baby rewarded him with a kick. "Holy cow."

I laughed.

During so much of my pregnancy, I'd felt alone because no one else could experience or feel what I did. Not the nausea. Not the tenderness. This was the first time someone could share the joy of what was happening inside me in the moment.

He tucked a hair behind my ear. "I can't wait to see the mom you become."

My heart soared. "Thanks."

He shifted his attention back to the cutting board and added the chicken to the salad bowl. "I wanted to tell you something."

"I'm on the edge of my seat."

"I proposed."

I rubbed at an uncomfortable sensation in my chest. "Really." It came out as a statement rather than a question. My pulse matched the rhythm of his chopping as he started on another piece of chicken. "I didn't realize it was so serious."

"People are wondering why I'm not married already. They're saying things."

"Like what?" I turned down the Elvis Presley song starting on the radio.

His lips formed a thin line. "There was an article in *Confidential* implying I might be homosexual. The studio wants me to show them it's not true."

I didn't know anyone openly gay, but I had accidentally walked in on two actresses in a bedroom at a party once. It was the kind of information that would destroy a career in Hollywood. The fact that someone would start a rumor about Hugh, knowing its consequences, made my ribs ache.

MGM had gotten the heartthrob years out of him. Women had swooned over Hugh as a bachelor. Now, as he neared thirty, they wanted to see him as a loving husband.

"So you're marrying Loretta because the studio wants you to?" I scoffed. "How long are you going to keep doing what they tell you?"

"You act like there's another choice. This is my career."

"And years ago you said you were sick of them owning you." There had to be another way.

A muscle jumped in his jaw. "It's not like they shoved Loretta into my arms. We're already together, and I care about her. It was probably going to happen anyway."

I almost said, *Care isn't love*, but he deserved my support. I simply didn't have it in me to congratulate him yet.

After supper, I walked him out. I didn't like being in the house alone and wanted to draw out having his company as long as I could. When we reached his car, he hugged me, and I rested my head against his chest, his scent a comfort, easing a stress I didn't realize I was carrying.

We hugged less than we'd used to. When he got married, it would probably be even less.

"You smell nice."

His chest rumbled against my cheek with his laughter. "I remember the first time you said that."

The night we met.

"I felt so pathetic." The memory was as fresh as if it'd been yesterday. "You were this movie star, and I was the nobody you were stuck talking to."

"I never saw you like that."

"I know you didn't." I let go of his middle. Continuing down memory lane would only stir up old feelings. "Thanks for coming over."

He pressed a kiss to my cheek, lingering for a second. "Goodnight."

◆

A week later, the front door opened as the clock on my nightstand read 2:05 a.m.

I'd tried waiting up for Kit, but he had a late flight in. I didn't make it past ten.

Footsteps creaked on the stairs. A silhouette darkened the doorway, and then he was next to me.

"You're back." I reached for him.

"I missed you." Kit lifted the blankets and got in next to me. "God, I missed you."

"I missed you too." I'd missed waking up to him every morning and how he sometimes mumbled in his sleep. I'd missed the warmth he radiated in bed for me to curl into.

He kissed me, and we found a rhythm between his eager lips and my tired ones. He tasted of lime and something else I couldn't quite place, my senses still waking up.

A fluttering came from my belly. I drew back and rested a hand over the spot. "Kit."

He flicked on the bedside light and homed in on the spot. "Did he . . . ?"

I smiled, removing my hand to let him touch. I'd been looking forward to this all week.

"Do you think I'll be able to feel him yet?" He splayed a hand on my belly.

My back tensed. He'd been drinking. It was obvious based on the unfocused look in his eyes and his slower speech. "You should. Ruth could."

"She did?" He bit the corner of his lip. "Is it ridiculous that I'm a little pissed she felt it before me?"

It hadn't occurred to me not to let her.

He dropped his hand from me. "Did anyone else?"

Kit would get mad if I told the truth, but he was already mad, and so was I. Maybe I was looking to pick a fight, because I answered honestly. "Hugh did when he came over for supper."

"Seriously?" Kit narrowed his eyes. "What else did he do while he was here?" He patted his T-shirt sleeve, searching for the pack of cigarettes he often kept rolled there.

The accusation made anger sizzle and snap through my veins. *What else did he do?*

While Kit had been on the other side of the ocean, pursuing a project he was passionate about, I'd been here, pregnant and alone. Not once did I complain. Not once did I ask who he was spending time with.

He pushed out of bed and walked over to my vanity, his body rigid as he threw open a drawer. He swept aside compacts and lipstick, searching for the cigarettes I usually kept there, only to pause on an envelope with Hugh's name on it.

"Why are you still holding on to this?" He raised it. "If he doesn't want your money, get rid of it."

My pulse throbbed. The other notes were in the shoebox in my bathroom closet. Kit never went in there, since we kept separate bathrooms. I'd foolishly forgotten the one in my vanity.

What I should have said was *You're right. I'll get rid of it*, then calmly taken it back. But I panicked.

"Wait." I stood and reached for it. If he read it, he would jump to conclusions. I wouldn't be able to explain it enough for him to believe me.

"I want to know why."

Instead of answering, I twisted around him, angling for it again, but he lifted it higher and squinted at me.

Above his head, he tore open the envelope.

My vision blurred with the stress. "*Stop*."

"It's a check, right?" Kit pulled out the letter. "What's this?"

"A stupid note."

"Let me read it." He unfolded it, still out of my reach.

Willingly? Not a chance.

When I jumped for it, making it impossible for him to concentrate on the words, he stormed into the hallway, then downstairs.

For the love of God.

I rushed after him, losing sight of him in the darkness. A single light from a Tiffany lamp led me to the living room, where he sat on the beige-and-pink floral sofa, reading.

My heart beat so fast, I felt sick. I sat next to him and dropped my head back. There was no point trying to get the letter anymore. It wasn't particularly long, so he must have been on his second read-through.

After a minute, he lowered the paper. "What's TDH?"

I'd forgotten I used to call Hugh that. Yet there was my handwriting. *My Dearest TDH.*

"It was this completely juvenile nickname."

He said nothing, waiting. He wouldn't let it go.

I searched my mind for an alternative that would make sense, failing to come up with something fast enough. Above a whisper, I said, "Tall, Dark, and Handsome."

Kit tossed the letter in my direction. "Cute. So you love him."

I shrugged a shoulder. "Years ago."

"But you don't anymore?"

"No."

"Vivian."

"I *don't*."

"I can't keep doing this." He scrubbed a hand over his face.

"I'm not sure why—"

"Because he's in love with you!" A vein bulged in his forehead.

Assumptions of a jealous husband. The letter combined with Hugh feeling the baby kick had blown this out of proportion. "You don't know that."

He dropped his head into his hands. "Anyone with eyes knows it. I just didn't know you loved him back."

Hugh had had the chance to pursue me but hadn't done it. He'd had a million opportunities to tell me he loved me but had never said it. Now he was engaged, for crying out loud. He didn't have feelings for me. I imagined explaining that wouldn't change Kit's mind, though.

"I love *us*," I said.

"Then why did you lie about what was in the envelope?"

Defensiveness clawed up my back. "Why did you lie when you said you weren't a drinker?"

We both sat quietly with those accusations for a minute.

Finally, he gazed at me. "I didn't know I had a problem, okay? I can't stop. I've tried."

I couldn't speak. It was the first time he'd admitted it.

"Before leaving for Europe, I tried getting help." He dug his wallet out of his pocket, withdrew a card, and handed it to me. "It's not like I can go to AA meetings. People would start coming in for autographs or sell the information to tabloids."

The card had a handwritten name on it: *Don Stedman*. Next to it was a phone number. "Who's this?"

"There are these people, sponsors, who've quit drinking. I can call if I need to talk." He pointed at the card. "Ring him if you want. He'll tell you it's true."

I'd had no idea he'd been trying to get help. That was how rarely we opened up to each other.

"How was it in Europe?"

He freed a breath. Cracked a knuckle. "Bad. It was bad."

My instincts had said something was off since finding the gin, but I had chosen to ignore it, wanting to believe him when he'd made it seem like I was overreacting.

"Thank you for telling me. I want to help. I want you to get better. But we both know this isn't working. The only way I can see fixing us is if you stop drinking. Actually stop."

He nodded slowly, the wheels in his mind turning. "Then I want you to stop talking to Hugh."

"What?" I gaped at him, not comprehending how we'd gotten here. "We're talking about how to help make things better for you. For us."

"That *will* help."

"You're being ridiculous."

"I just found a love letter you wrote a man you still spend time with. A man who was in our home, touching you, while I was gone." A humorless laugh escaped him. "Talk about driving a man to drink."

I understood his frustration, his worry, but Hugh was a structural wall in my life. How could I cut him out?

He pointed at his chest, his eyes wide. "Quitting drinking will be the hardest thing I've ever done. All I'm asking is for you to quit talking to someone. I should mean enough for you to do that."

We had a baby coming. A show we loved. A future. All the things I'd dreamed of but never knew I would get. I wasn't going to lose them now.

"Fine," I said, fighting the bite in my tone. "I'll stop talking to him."

SEPTEMBER 18, 1955

HUGH FOX AND LORETTA ATWOOD ARE GETTING HITCHED!

Hugh Fox and starlet Loretta Atwood celebrated their engagement with friends and family at a small celebration near Fox's childhood home in San Diego.

Noticeably missing from the festivities was longtime friend Vivian Stone. Come to think of it, we haven't seen the pals, who used to paint the town red before Stone's marriage, in a while.

Could it be Viv doesn't approve of Loretta? Though it seems more likely Loretta doesn't approve of her fiancé being so close to the bosomy comedienne.

CHAPTER THIRTY-FOUR

Vivian

then

One night we went with four of Kit's old co-stars to Musso & Frank. The restaurant pushed two tables together in the back for us, and the waitress came around to take our drink orders. I asked for a virgin gimlet, while Kit ordered coffee.

When the waitress came back to drop them off, the man to Kit's left did a double take. Arthur Davies was one of his fair-weather friends, with salt-and-pepper hair—more salt than pepper.

"Coffee?" Arthur patted Kit's shoulder. "What's going on with you, my friend?"

It struck me as sad that Kit's not drinking was evidence that something was wrong.

Kit fumbled for his words. "Nothing." He patted his belly. "The other stuff started affecting my body, you know?"

I reached for his thigh under the table and gently squeezed, giving him an encouraging smile.

Back when Mom and I packed the house to move into an apartment she could afford, we discovered my father's hidden bottles. I could still recall her whispering to herself in another room, "How did I not know these were here?"

But it is a truth universally acknowledged that an alcoholic in possession of a suspicious wife must be in want of a good hiding spot. So after Kit and I made our deal, I thoroughly combed our house. I checked closets. Threw open desk drawers. Scoured cabinets. Rummaged through the attic. His cars. The shed. Until I was confident I'd gotten it all.

For over a week, we went through hell getting him clean, but we found our way to the other side. It had been weeks since then, and so far he'd been holding it together.

I sipped my drink while everyone at the table droned on about who was working with whom, or was screwing whom, or should get out of the business altogether. They talked about money and Oscars and second homes and vacations.

Did they even *enjoy* the business? Or was it all about amassing things?

Kit stared longingly as drinks for the rest of the table were dropped off.

Sitting next to him while he thirsted for alcohol was too much. I dabbed my mouth with a cloth napkin and stood. "I'll be right back."

Kit chewed on his lip without looking up.

In the ladies' room, I swiped on a coat of lipstick in the mirror and smiled at my reflection.

The tube slipped into the sink as I curled my hands around the porcelain, needing it to steady me.

While Kit had done what I wanted, I didn't feel better about us like I'd hoped. Our relationship had changed down to its marrow.

Once I got it together as best I could, I walked out the door, my attention on returning my lipstick to my purse.

Someone held my arms, stopping me. I glanced up and my heart tripped over itself as I latched on to a pair of dark eyes.

Hugh.

Of all the restaurants in all the towns in all the world, he walks into this one.

"Viv. Hi."

A lump clogged my throat. I couldn't be there with him. Couldn't talk to him. "Hi. Sorry, I have to . . ." I nodded ahead, loosening myself from his grip, and angled around him, but he caught my arm again.

"Where are you going? I haven't talked to you in over a month."

Had it only been a month? "I know. I'm sorry."

"I should have phoned, but—"

"You were busy getting engaged."

He flinched like I'd poked a bruise. "You didn't come to the party."

"I'm sorry about that too." I hated that he didn't know why. Hated that I wanted—needed—to talk to him about everything I was going through but couldn't. "I really have to go."

The men's room door flew open. Hugh guided me to one side to let the man pass.

"Do you want to get dinner?" He stepped closer so I could hear him over a round of laughter in the dining room. "I'm free Friday."

"I can't." The words sliced like shards of glass over my tongue.

"It's fine. I'll call you. We'll figure something out."

"You *can't*," I gritted out. Why did this have to be so hard?

He tipped my chin up, his eyes searching mine. "Something's wrong." His voice softened. "You can tell me."

I wanted to. He deserved an explanation.

Kit rounded the corner, coming to a halt as he took us in.

I stepped back, freeing myself from Hugh. "Darling, look who I found as I came out of the ladies' room."

My voice had gotten higher, my nerves eating at me. I hated how it made it sound like I was hiding something.

Kit looped an arm around my waist, tugging me to him, and stared the politest of daggers at Hugh. "What a happy accident. Congrats on the engagement. About time you were off the market." He didn't wait for a reply, instead leaning close to my ear. "Our friends are waiting."

They weren't my friends. Hugh was.

I lifted a hand in goodbye as Kit ushered me away. "Nice to see you."

Nice to see you? This was all wrong.

"I'll call," Hugh said.

Kit led me between tables. "Was that planned?"

"What? No, it was a coincidence. He saw me, and I couldn't very well run away."

His eyes flickered with hurt as we sat back down. "You would have told me, right? If I hadn't seen, you still would have mentioned it."

Probably not. "Of course."

This was where we were. Lying would be less damaging than the truth.

———————— ◆ ————————

Dear Hugh,

Remember when my second film came out, and we went to see it at the theater so we could hear the audience's reactions? We put on disguises. You wore the mustache you stole from your set, and I had on a wig. Not that anyone knew me back then.

My role was small, but at the end, when people clapped, you said, "They love you."

They didn't love me. They loved the film or the leads. But you made me feel like someday I could be the kind of actress people clapped for.

A few days after you and I ran into each other at Musso & Frank, Ruth sat in my dressing room, eating bonbons. I'd say I'm kidding, but it's the truth.

"What's going on with your phone?" she mumbled around a mouthful. "I called to tell you I was coming, even though I know you love my surprises, but it's out of service."

I secured a lock of hair with a bobby pin. "I made a call this morning."

"Huh." She tucked another bonbon in her mouth. "Maybe you got a new number?"

Ice rolled through my belly. I knew the truth deep down, but I had to ask.

At the end of the episode, Kit and I took a bow while the audience clapped.

"Did you change our phone number?" I smiled. No one knew anything was amiss.

"I'm helping."

"How?"

"The same way you did." He waved at the crowd. "By removing temptation."

I'd assumed once Kit was clean, he'd appreciate all I did to help him. Instead, he was resentful.

And he wasn't the only one.

Have you tried calling? I have no way of knowing. I wish I could tell you what's going on, but I worry that will only make things worse.

Love,

Vivian

CHAPTER THIRTY-FIVE

Vivian

then

You might be wondering where this is all going. Or maybe you think you know. Stick with me a little longer, and it'll all make sense.

Two months after the incident at Musso & Frank, Kit attended an AA meeting associated with a celebrity rehab center, which he went to daily after work. It left me with more free time.

About a year after my father left, I called every Stephen Mackenzie in our local phone book, the only one I could get my hands on at the time. We'd never learned where he'd gone, so he could have been living one town over or on the other side of the world.

I'd wanted to know if he was happy without us. Sometimes I fantasized about asking if he'd ever loved me. I pictured him having another family and wondered if he had changed for them.

I never found him, but I didn't have any regrets, because over time I realized answers wouldn't heal me.

Now Hugh was lost to me too.

I wanted to ask him how filming was going. I wished I could get his opinion on a scene the writers came up with that I wasn't sure about but Kit thought sounded fine. I was curious what he thought of the talk of Alaska becoming a state and if we might not be better off having one more for an even fifty. I imagined saying, "The nifty fifty. Rolls off the tongue, doesn't it?" He would reply with some smart aleck comment sure to make me smile.

I picked up the phone in the kitchen and dialed.

"Hello?"

Ruth's voice was instant balm for my soul.

I sank to the parquet floor. "Thoughts on Alaska becoming a state: for or against?"

"Sounds like a political question. You know I don't do politics."

It wasn't the kind of answer I'd hoped for, but we didn't talk about the same things I talked about with Hugh. I couldn't substitute one friend for the other.

"I know." I twisted around to open a cabinet door and stuck a hand in a stack of mixing bowls. Empty. I never found more alcohol, but I routinely checked. "I had this nifty-fifty line I was hoping to use on Hugh, but it's all right."

Her end was quiet for a few seconds. "You know, the last time I talked to him, he mentioned you."

My hand caught on the glass bowls, making them clank. "What'd he say?"

"He asked how you were. Kind of out of the blue, he visited me on set."

My patience waned. "Well, what'd *you* say?"

"I didn't say you aren't allowed to talk to him, if that's what you're asking. I told him to give you time. I figured everything would have blown over by now."

Not even a little.

I shut the cabinet door and rested against it. "Do you think he's happy?" More than anything, that was what I cared about.

"You know how he is. It's hard to tell what's going on in his head. Are *you* happy?"

There wasn't an easy answer. "Sometimes. On set, mostly. Or when I'm thinking about the baby and what he or she will be like." I covered a hand over my rounded belly. "My greatest joke is my life. I can make millions laugh but never feel content."

"Then leave Kit. I don't say it more because I saw how good things were in the beginning. But the good's not worth the bad anymore. I know you, Vivian. You're probably thinking you're resilient enough to handle this. But just because you can endure a painful marriage doesn't mean you should."

"That would mean ending the show." There was no show without both of us. "I can't do that. We have a contract. We're in the middle of a season. Besides, I don't *want* to give it up. I love it. So many people would be disappointed in me if it ended."

"Not the ones who matter."

America thought of me as one of the funniest women in the world. They called me the "Queen of Comedy." But few would understand me leaving someone as handsome and charming as Kit, especially not while expecting his child. They would never forgive me.

Metal scraping against metal came from her end.

I winced. "What are you doing?"

"Making grilled cheese."

"With tomato soup?"

"Dipped in ketchup."

The combination still made me scrunch my nose. "That's a crime against sourdough."

Especially since Ruth and Dean had overcome their money troubles—but not their taste for luxury—and hired an Italian housekeeper. She was a gem. Always made sure I left with melt-in-your-mouth baked goods.

"Enough about food when we should be talking about you," Ruth said. "At some point, you need to take responsibility for your happiness."

If only I knew how to do that.

No matter what, I would sacrifice something. No matter what, I'd be unhappy.

After I got off the phone, I found a piece of paper.

To the friend I miss the most,

The next time I see you, I'll probably have a baby.

I want my child to know you. I want you to be as important in their life as you've been in mine. I'm not sure if that will be possible, though.

I've been worried about how well I can take care of a baby, but then I remembered how much I've taken care of over the years. When my mother got a job, I had to take care of things beyond what a child should. I made sure we had milk and bread in the house. I got myself to school and fixed my own meals (not that they were any good).

When she got sick, and I took care of her, I tried to remember a time when she took care of me like that, and I couldn't. I'm sure she did when I was really little. For all the years I remember well, I took care of myself.

Don't get me wrong: I was glad to take care of her. She did so much for me, I can't fault her for being too busy with work. But you know all of that. You also know I took care of myself in New York and paid most of the bills for the first couple of years Ruth and I lived in LA. I took care of Kit when he stopped drinking. Soon I'll have a newborn to take care of.

The pressures of life can get so heavy sometimes, I think they'll crush me.

They're not as heavy when we're in front of an audience. And the weight becomes nearly nonexistent when I'm near you. Then I can just be me. You give me that.

Love,

Vivian

The shoebox in my bathroom closet, next to the spare towels, wasn't easy to reach, but I managed to pull it down, fold the letter up, and leave it with the others. I replaced it as the front door opened and was under the covers by the time Kit's feet hit the stairs.

CHAPTER THIRTY-SIX

Vivian

then

One night, near the end of my pregnancy, I drove up to the Chateau Marmont in my black Chevy.

Kit had gone to dinner with his brother, John, who was in town visiting. When he wasn't home after a few hours, I phoned the restaurant. I didn't want to hover, making sure he didn't relapse, but it'd only been three months since he'd stopped drinking. I couldn't help but worry.

The bartender who answered said he'd seen Kit leave an hour earlier with Arthur Davies and another man—Kit's brother, most likely. He thought he'd heard mention of the Chateau.

Some of the most scandalous Hollywood parties took place at the Chateau Marmont hotel.

While I didn't want to change out of my nightgown and drive over, I also knew I wouldn't be able to sleep until I had him safe at home.

My kitten heels clicked over the parking lot and down long, narrow steps, surrounded by greenery, toward the sound of music and laughter. At the bottom was a wide concrete pad with a pool in the middle.

String lights draped from one tree to another. Waiters held trays of champagne. A man stumbled over the leg of a lounge chair and fell into the pool. A few people laughed as they helped him out. On the other end, a woman danced through the crowd, arms swaying in the air as she belted out a song alongside a record.

I took a couple of steps forward, scanning the area. My gaze halted on a head of curly brown hair near the bar.

Kit tilted his head back, a shot glass to his lips, while a woman with strawberry blonde hair stood next to him. She recoiled from a man with a thick mustache.

I recognized them both. The mustached man was Mitch Michelson, an MGM producer I'd never worked with but who had a reputation for being a slimeball, and the woman was Helen. As in the one who got her kicks messing with me on the set of *Sunday Circus*.

Kit sneered like he wanted to clobber Mitch and slung an arm around Helen, then pressed a swift kiss to her lips.

I blinked, sure my eyes were playing tricks on me. Yet there they were.

As if he could feel my stare, Kit's attention swung in my direction. He swayed. "Vivian?"

His surprise rang like sirens in my head.

My throat closed up.

I couldn't breathe. *I couldn't breathe.*

I would not break down in front of everyone.

My legs wobbled as I turned and pushed past the blur of people. Kit called, chasing after me as I reached the stairs, but I didn't slow down.

Step after step, I shook my head as if I could clear from my memory what I had just seen. But it kept popping back up, brighter and more vivid.

Footsteps fell several paces behind. "Damn it," Kit said.

I stopped, whirling to find him using the railing to haul himself up from where he'd tripped. No one followed us.

My father had fallen on the stairs more times than I could count. I had lost sympathy for him years before he left. I was struck by the irony of seeing Kit in a similar position, eyes glistening as if his heart were the one breaking. A humorless laugh almost escaped me but came out as a wheeze.

I pointed toward the party. "You're having an affair?" My words scraped like gravel across my tongue.

"What?" His bewildered gaze shot to the bottom of the stairs, then back to me. "No."

Years ago, I'd left Helen that note after she messed with my dress and lipstick, the one saying, *If you want to hurt this less talented Fanny Brice, you'll need to try harder.*

She hadn't forgotten. She'd succeeded.

Kit drew close to me. The scent of alcohol made my stomach turn, grinding like the thick cogs of a machine. I tried to pull away, but his arms held me so tightly, even the air caged me in.

He bent to meet my eyes, his breath wafting in my face. "I can explain."

"You're drunk." I gripped his arm, trying to loosen it from me. "How could you?"

"Vivian, stop."

All his meetings. All my patience. All the effort to make our marriage work. Gone.

I dug the heels of my palms into his chest. "Get away from me!"

His grip slackened, relenting at the same time I pushed with all my might.

My body tipped over the edge of a step, and I fell back.

Pain laced my elbow and head. Knees and hip. Face. Stomach. Down stair after stair after stair.

All the way to the bottom.

Stars danced behind my eyes, my vision distorted at the edges.

Movement came hurtling toward me. Between seconds of clarity, Hugh was there.

I thought I had to be imagining it when he cradled my neck with one arm, his other arm under my legs, as he held me against him and said, "I've got you."

Then all became the blackness of night.

◆

Bright lights shone behind my eyes, so sore that it hurt to crack my lids open. I moaned as I attempted to sit.

Ruth rested a hand on my shoulder. "Don't try to get up."

Sound advice, given my cramping. My body ached like it'd been through a taffy puller.

Realization gripped me. "Where am I?" I took in the basic metal frame bed and cubicle curtain in the corner. Everything so sanitary and simple.

"The hospital. Do you remember what happened?"

It came back to me in waves. Showing up at the Chateau. Seeing Kit and Helen. Smelling the alcohol on him and shoving him away. Falling down all of those stairs.

"My baby?" I rested a hand over my belly.

Her chin quivered as she stood. "I should get Kit."

I reached for her, panic clawing its way up my back. "*Tell me*. Is my baby okay?"

A glance at the door. Her eyes glistened as they flicked back to me. "I'm sorry, honey," she whispered.

No.

Agony shredded me from the inside, a sob breaking free.

No, no, no.

She enfolded me in her arms so I could weep against her. "Oh, Viv."

A sound came from me I'd never heard before. Pure anguish.

As much as I wanted to deny it, I could feel it. My insides were hollow, and I would happily have fallen into a void if by doing so I could have saved myself from the pain.

The door creaked open. Kit poked his head in. "You're awake."

His eyes were bloodshot. From crying or drinking, who the hell knew.

My pain doubled over as I let go of Ruth. "I don't want to be."

He took a few steps forward. "I know. I—"

"You let go." I clenched my teeth so hard they could have cracked. "If you hadn't, I wouldn't have fallen." Grief rang through my body, taking on a life of its own.

"You pushed back."

"And you didn't try to catch me!" I couldn't shoulder the blame. I'd mentally collapse.

His head dropped, voice small as he said, "It happened so fast."

Ruth eased a step toward the door. "I can come back."

"No." I reached for her, desperate. "Do you know what I was having?"

My body tensed like a rubber band, stretching my stability to its limit. It would tear me apart no matter what, but I had to know.

My heartbreak reflected in her eyes, but it was Kit who answered. "A girl."

Two words. That was all it took for me to snap.

A girl. My girl.

He stepped closer.

"Get the hell out," I said in a voice so low and sharp, I didn't recognize it.

"You need me." The way he took another hesitant step, he wasn't entirely confident of that. "*I* need *you.*"

I didn't answer. I couldn't. There was nothing left of me but a tightness like I would never be comfortable in my own skin again.

Kit turned pleading eyes on Ruth, but when she kept silent, a muscle flexed in his jaw and he stormed out.

The second the door slammed shut, I sobbed again, unable to hold it in. The physical and mental pain took turns dominating my racking body.

This wasn't my life. This hadn't happened to me. It was a mistake. The universe had to know I couldn't handle something like this. I'd never recover from it.

When my cries grew so heavy I couldn't catch a breath, Ruth got a nurse, who gave me medication.

My thoughts became cloudy as I drifted toward the numbness I craved.

CHAPTER THIRTY-SEVEN

Margot

now

Our half-eaten sandwiches sit on the kitchen counter, both of us needing to digest more than the peanut-butter-and-jellies.

Where had we imagined this story would go? Not here. I had thought perhaps an affair or a secret baby.

I was fine until Vivian's voice shook while she described her reaction to hearing she was having a girl. Then I lost it.

God, I can't imagine what she went through. I wonder if, with modern medicine, the baby would have lived.

I can't go there.

"Leo." I point at the shoebox. "Do you think that's—"

"Where Vivian kept all the letters? Yeah, I do."

My phone buzzes with a text. It's David. Again.

> Free for a quick chat?

No, I'm not. Which should be obvious, given that I ignored one of his calls already.

My phone rings, David's name popping up.

"Way to give you a chance to respond," Leo says.

I can't keep putting him off. "Hello?"

"Margot, hey, I couldn't wait to share the good news: We got an offer. Seventy-five grand over our planned list price. They don't want to take any chances that you'll put it on the market."

Seventy-five over? "That's . . . a lot." Yes, we have to pay back what Gram owed on the reverse mortgage, but Mom and I will still come out with quite a bit extra. Enough for me to get a new place.

"Sure is." David can't hide his delight, probably imagining his fat commission check. "They're going to take good care of your grandma's house. Making plans to gut the place and bring it back to life."

Gut the place? Bring it back to life?

It isn't that bad. Some new paint, sure. Maybe update the countertops. Refinish the hardwood floors. "Like what?"

"They mentioned during the walk-through that the two bedrooms at the end of the hall would make a fantastic master bedroom en suite. They also talked about an addition."

This is the biggest lot in the neighborhood. I loved having the extra space as a kid. Bumping the house out would destroy all of that. And that en suite idea? It's my old bedroom and Gram's they'd be tearing apart.

"No." All I can think of is the house I grew up in torn to pieces.

"No?"

What is the alternative here?

People love visiting Long Beach. Maybe I could keep Gram's place and rent it to tourists.

Except then I'd have to go back and forth to clean it between visitors. Hiring a cleaning service is possible, but it'd eat into the profits.

I could rent it out to a tenant to cut down on the cleaning and traveling. Except I have seen firsthand how much of a pain that can be. Ben's family had investment properties. You need to be available to handle problems at a moment's notice, and sometimes tenants don't take care of the property. The idea of anything happening to Gram's house makes me sick.

"I really don't think you're going to get more by listing it," David says, his excitement draining.

"I need to talk to my mom about it, since we're splitting the profits. I'll get back to you."

"We have to answer them soon or they might start looking elsewhere."

"Got it." I don't bother with a goodbye, ending the call and tossing my phone onto the counter.

Leo follows the path of the phone. "What's wrong?"

I cross my arms. "Someone wants to buy the house."

"It's not even listed."

"I know."

For a long moment he stares at his feet, in thought, then his eyes reach mine. "Do you want comfort or advice?"

"What?"

"It's something my mom said years ago. When someone is upset, ask if they want comfort or if they want solutions. My nature is to fix things—in whatever way I think is right. I've done it a lot. I did it with us when I shouldn't have. But I'm working on getting better. So tell me: comfort or advice?"

I like that idea. "Comfort."

Despite how much I know he wants to help me work through the house situation, he only nods.

"How about tea?" Leo turns and opens a cabinet, retrieving a mug. Lucky guess, or did he remember where we kept them? "Your grandma always made you tea when you were sad."

I smile on hearing that he remembers that detail. "Sounds nice." I haven't had any since being here.

He reaches for the boxes of tea, his shirt rising and baring a sliver of his stomach. I still need to find a stool so I can clean out that shelf.

Leo grabs one box, then another. "I'm not sure which—"

Plastic tumbles to the floor with a *whack*.

A cassette tape.

We both stare at it by our feet.

"Margot."

"I know." My heart stumbles as I pick up the tape and open it: *8 of 8*.

The last one. It was standing against the side of the shelf, the boxes of tea keeping it upright.

"What's that?" Leo points at something stuck between the tape and the case.

I pull out the tape. A small square of folded paper falls onto the counter.

My hands shake as I unfold it. The edges are creased in different places, like it's been opened and then tucked away several times.

Dear Ginger,

If you can find it in your heart to reach out, I'll be here.

Sincerely,

Vivian

Under her name is a phone number.

My pulse thuds as I stare at the loops and swirls of Vivian's handwriting.

"These really were for Gram." Part of me still wondered if they were meant for someone else. "That's her name. Ginger."

For the first time, a clue.

The letter couldn't have come like this, stuffed next to the last tape. It must have been separate. Maybe in the shoebox. Did Gram listen to the recordings, then stow the note away?

A queasiness settles in my stomach. "What could Vivian have done to my grandma?" It's not like Gram was an unreasonable person. I don't think Vivian is either.

He reaches for my cell and holds it out for me. "Why don't you try calling?"

"It's probably an old landline number. I doubt it's still hers."

Leo scans the page. "There's no date, so who knows when this is from. Maybe it's not as old as we think."

Vivian has yet to reveal any connection to Gram. Calling might be my best hope for the truth.

I bite my lip, taking my phone. "What if she answers?" I know: unlikely. But— "What if she's angry I listened to the tapes?"

I have to check myself for a second because I've come to feel like I know Vivian.

He shrugs. "Then she's angry, and you never have to talk to her again."

"Okay." I carefully dial the number from the letter, take a steadying breath, then press call.

A moment of silence, and then it rings.

My heart rate rockets. On the third ring, a woman answers.

"Hello?"

I open my mouth, but my words stick to my throat. This should have been planned better.

"Hi. Um, yes. Hello." Off to a great start. "My name is Margot DuBois, and this is going to sound strange, but I found some tapes in our attic. I think they belong to Vivian." She doesn't say a thing, so I clarify, "Vivian Stone."

Again, not a word.

"There's a letter with them addressed to my grandmother." My chest tightens, second-guessing this. "You know what? I probably have the wrong number, I'm sorry for—"

"Wait."

The word is like a shot of caffeine to my bloodstream.

"You have the right number," she says. "I'm Christine."

Leo leans in, so I switch the call to speaker.

"Would you like to meet Vivian?" she asks. "Tomorrow morning? Say, ten o'clock?"

Would I like to—what? I'm too starstruck to speak.

"She'd love to," Leo helps me.

"Yes. I'd love to," I manage.

And it's true. I really, truly would.

"All right, dear. Do you have a pen? I'll give you the address."

"You're going to tell me where she lives?"

"Well, how else would you get here?"

Holy shit.

As I write down an address in Bel Air, about an hour away, a voice in the back of my mind whispers that something else is at play here. Not the part about the address. It would make sense that, if Vivian was desperate enough to talk to Gram that she shared everything about her life, giving an address wouldn't be a big deal.

What pokes at the very edges of my mind is how Christine took no time to confirm who I was. Besides her particularly long pause at the beginning, she acted like this whole thing was perfectly normal.

Did she mute me to talk to Vivian? Is Vivian listening right now?

"Can I bring someone?" I'm not going without Leo. When I glance at him, he nods.

Silence. Then: "Yes."

As soon as I get off the phone, I reach for the shoebox. We don't have much time left, and there are still two tapes to go.

Tape Seven

JANUARY 1956

HUGH AND LORETTA CALL IT QUITS

Say it ain't so! Hugh Fox and Loretta Atwood have decided to go their separate ways.

The two met while filming *Rise to Glory*, and it looked like a match made in Hollywood heaven. Take a hunk like Hugh with a chiseled jaw, glossy black hair, and corded arms that make the dames swoon, and pair him with the statuesque Loretta with her regal beauty and grace. What could go wrong?

According to insiders who know the couple, a lot. While Hugh apparently didn't fall victim to the typical vices that would irk his future wife—other women, gambling, drinking—friends of Loretta say he is at fault.

Poor Loretta clearly tried to make it work, but it appears she wasn't foxy enough for that Fox.

CHAPTER THIRTY-EIGHT

Vivian

then

Our house was dark when I walked in. Quiet.

It'd been a month and a half since I'd been here. A month and a half since my fall.

We had filmed extra episodes, back before Kit left for Europe, that were supposed to air after I delivered to give me maternity leave. The network ran with those while I grieved at Dean and Ruth's vacation cottage. The one they went to when they needed to get out of the city.

Around the corner, a Tiffany lamp bathed the living room in a faint, buttery glow. Kit slept on the sofa in a white T-shirt and boxer shorts, a full ashtray on the coffee table next to a near-empty vodka bottle and a glass. The sight soaked through my soul.

I sat near Kit's feet, the movement making him startle awake. Bags made shadows beneath his eyes as he blinked several times.

"You're home." His tone had more than a little hope. Thankfully, he seemed sober.

"I want to talk." Though I'd already made up my mind about us while my mother visited me at the cottage, I deserved to know how it had come to this. "What happened that night?"

"Don't start." He ran a hand across his face as he sat up. "I still feel like shit about it."

My blood simmered. "I thought you and John were only going out for dinner."

He tilted his head back, staring at the ceiling like he needed divine intervention. "We were, but then Arthur sees us. Tells us about this party. He pestered me to go."

The second hand of the little square clock on the side table *tick, tick, tick*ed the seconds by.

Stay calm.

"You've been in that situation before," I said. But ever since getting clean, it'd never been without me or another dry ally. "You know what to do."

"Yeah, and I feel like a chump every time. No one drinks coffee or seltzer at parties. So when I do, it looks like I have a problem."

"You *do* have a problem."

"I'm not doing anything different than anyone else." His words were clipped.

My muscles tensed from my shoulders down my back. "We made a deal."

"I thought I could handle one, all right? It got out of hand." He jabbed a finger toward the door. "What about *your* promise? Your boyfriend was there."

"Thank God. Someone had to take me to the hospital." I sighed, my ribs straining under the pressure surrounding my chest. "We tried. We both tried, didn't we? But it didn't work."

He reached for my hand, face falling, and I let him take it, not having it in me to be heartless. "It still can."

Some people might have given him another chance. He had managed to stop drinking for a time. He could do it again, and the next time it could stick. But I was done, and once I was done, there was no going back.

"No. It can't."

"You're going to divorce me, then?" It didn't come out sarcastic. It was a real question, with real hurt in his eyes. The words punctured my heart like pinpricks. Just because I'd stopped loving him didn't mean this wasn't painful.

"Aren't you tired of it all? It shouldn't be this exhausting."

"What about the show?"

"We have a contract." I stood, letting his hand go. "We'll have to finish the season, but then that's it."

I needed to come up with a plan. How could I re-create myself yet again?

Kit's face paled. Within a heartbeat he sank to his knees and wrapped his arms around my thighs, the side of his head resting against my belly. "Please don't do this." His voice cracked as he repeated it again and again. "I love you."

A boulder knocked past my heart and plummeted to my stomach as his tears soaked my shirt.

This wasn't how I had expected him to react. I'd assumed he would be angry. I had thought he'd get caught up in yelling about all we'd worked for or how good we could still be together.

It did nothing to sway me, but it did awaken sympathy. For the broken boy who only wanted to be loved.

After he'd gotten it all out, he brushed away the tears and sat back on the couch.

"I can go to Ruth's," I offered.

"No. I'll go."

Without another word, I went upstairs, packed him a bag, and left it by the front door.

By morning, Kit was gone.

———— ◆ ————

That March I won the Emmy Award for Best Comedienne. It was plastered in the headlines. I had so much I'd wanted yet had lost an equal portion along the way.

Over the next several weeks, Kit and I found a new normal. We only spoke when it involved work—the audience never realizing we'd separated—and eventually the strain between us morphed into civility.

All the while, I wrote a script for a new show.

Not as a distraction this time. I did it because, even amid heartbreak, I never gave up on my dreams—or on the possibilities of a blank sheet of paper.

The premise was entirely different from that of *Bobby and Clara*. Instead of a couple, this show focused on two single friends who went to great lengths to pay the rent.

I had a slew of ideas: starring in a commercial where they had to eat something foul and pretend to like it. Wrapping peppermints at a factory while the conveyor belt moved too fast for them to keep up. A matchmaking business, setting up different people in their apartment building, only for one of their clients to fall madly in love with them.

And on it went.

Drawing from the strength writing gave me, I woke up one morning and summoned the courage to pack the baby things. I didn't feel like the earth might fracture and swallow me whole. Hopelessness had faded; in its place a nearly healed wound. It would never go away, but I could move forward.

While I was packing, the doorbell rang.

I wiped away tears and pulled open the door to find a woman around my age. A little younger, perhaps. She wore thick eyeliner, red lipstick all wrong for her complexion, and a halter dress that clung so tightly, it left little to the imagination. *Wrong neighborhood.*

"Yes?"

She shifted on her feet, peering behind me. "Is Kit here?"

"No." I crossed my arms. "Can I help you with something?"

"Do you know when he'll be back?"

I pursed my lips. I didn't have patience for this today. Not only did I want to be left alone, but I hated when a fan somehow discovered my address and showed up at my doorstep. It happened from time to time, though less often than when someone swiped my used napkins.

"I'm afraid I'm going to have to ask you to leave." I rested a hand on the door to close it, realizing I still held a cream knitted baby bootie. My lips quivered.

She pressed on the door to stop me. "It's very important I talk to him."

"And if he wanted to talk to you, I'm guessing he has a way to get in touch with you?"

"Yes." Her hold against the door eased, but when I went to close it again, her eyes widened. "It's just . . . I'm expecting. It's his."

Over the years, there were articles saying Kit was out flirting with other women. Hell, I'd been in a sleazy tabloid or two where my fidelity was called into question with completely asinine rumors. We all dealt with it. People would say and do anything to make a buck.

But this particular comment—right there, right then—cut deeper.

"If you're looking for a payday," I bit out, "you're not going to find it here."

"You think I want money?"

"Don't you?"

Her gaze dropped from mine. Not a denial.

I bunched the baby bootie into my fist. I would not cry. It would make me look weak when I was getting better every day. So I replaced the sorrow with anger and let it burn inside.

"I'm sick of this," I snapped. "People think because I'm in the public eye, I owe them something. I owe you *nothing*."

I understood not having money. Probably better than this woman could imagine. What I didn't understand was invading someone's privacy like this to get it. I'd never stooped so low.

"Leave." I pointed behind her.

She backed up a step. "I think I made a mistake."

At least she could see it. Maybe she wouldn't come back again.

With another step, she wobbled in her scuffed white heels.

My stomach knotted, thinking of my mother's old heels, back when they were falling apart.

I held up a hand, attempting to rein in my anger. "Wait here."

"You're calling the cops?"

I waved her off and went to grab my purse. This woman was desperate. I couldn't turn her away.

By the time I came back, she was gone.

CHAPTER THIRTY-NINE

Vivian

then

"There you are." Hugh pressed a warm hand to my lower back, smiling down at me. He redirected his attention to the couple I'd been talking to. "I'm afraid I have to steal Vivian. There's someone I'd like her to meet."

It'd been a month since I'd kicked Kit out, and when Hugh asked if I would join him at a house party for a co-star's birthday, I agreed. Not because I cared for these parties much but because it was good to get out and do normal things again. I was still getting used to having the house to myself. It got so quiet sometimes and my thoughts became so loud.

"Who are you introducing me to?" I asked as he led me out of the living room.

"No one." He had a conspiratorial glimmer in his eyes. "I was saving you. You looked ready to flee the scene."

Wise guy. I nudged him with my elbow, and he exaggerated a groan, grimacing as he reached for his stomach.

"Never mind," he said, strained, like I'd knocked the wind out of him. "You can go back."

Laughing, I slipped my arm around his. "You're cruisin' for a bruisin'. Don't you remember? Once someone takes me, they're stuck."

Hugh had visited me weekly while I grieved at Ruth and Dean's cottage. He made me pancakes, we played cards. He taught me poker. Many times we simply walked the quiet streets.

Sometimes I'd talked about the baby. My life. How it felt like I'd been convinced I was doing things differently than my mother only to wind up falling into some of the same patterns. Married to a man who was wholly different from yet far too similar to my father.

Hugh had let me work through it, often without saying a word, until, little by little, I came back to myself. An altered version, at least, with a new scar on my heart.

My mother had visited too. So had Ruth. Even though the cottage was a regular retreat for her and Dean, they'd said I could use it as long as I wanted. But those visits with Hugh were particularly special because, for a while before then, I didn't know if we'd talk again.

"What do you say?" Hugh nodded toward the dining table, where a deck of cards sat. "Find another pair for a round of canasta?"

It was so loud inside, I could barely hear him. "How about the pool? Dip our toes in?"

He smiled. "Let me use the john, then I'll meet you out there."

We separated, and I squeezed through the group in the kitchen, packed tight like sardines, to reach the patio door. As I opened it, a breeze lifted my dress to my knees, and I pushed it back down as I stepped out.

"What are we going to do about her?" came a woman's voice from outside. She wore a silvery-black cocktail dress and blew out a puff of smoke from her cigarette. "The little tart didn't deserve the lead. Mitch promised it to me."

"Ethel Ritz is on the blacklist now after a radio broadcaster said she was a communist." This from the woman next to her in a red off-the-shoulder dress.

They stood at the pool's edge. A light reflected from the bottom, while a row of shadowed lounge chairs lined either side.

The first woman took a drag, then flicked her cigarette into the pool. "Wouldn't take much to do the same to Helen."

These were the pariahs of Hollywood.

I could have minded my own business. I could have, but I didn't.

"Oh, put a lid on it. You two sound like a couple of phonies. Sour because another actress showed you up." I no longer worried about speaking my mind. I'd gone through too much to care.

They pivoted, and the first's surprise almost made me laugh. "Why, if it isn't Vivian Stone." She took a step forward like we were old pals, though I'd never seen her before. Since most of America knew who I was, sometimes they acted like I should know them too because I was on their television. "We were only gabbing."

"You were running your mouths."

The second woman screwed her lips up like she had sucked a lemon. She tugged the first's arm. "I'm a bit chilled. Let's go inside."

They eased through the patio door while I turned back to the pool. The cigarette butt floated in the water alongside an orange pool float.

Movement came from the shadows of one of the lounges. I hadn't realized anyone else was out here, and I doubted the other women had either. Someone stood and came into view.

A rotten taste formed on my tongue at the sight of cat-eye makeup and strawberry blonde hair.

Helen walked up to me in a collared lavender dress, cocktail in hand. "You're the last person I expected to stick up for me."

"In my defense, I didn't know which Helen they were talking about." The irony wasn't lost on me that what those women did to her was a lot like what she did to me when I beat her for a role.

She laughed, coming closer, but there was no humor in her eyes. In fact, they looked devoid of life altogether. "I always liked you."

It was my turn to laugh. "No, you didn't."

"I respected you, though."

"I don't believe that either."

She let out a light hum. "Well, I did, even back when you showed me up at our audition. I was as sour as those two." She motioned at the house. "You were remarkable, and I hated you for it."

"There's always someone better. For me too."

My mother used to tell me that when I was a girl. *There will always be someone prettier than you or smarter. But you will always be prettier and smarter than someone else.*

"Was it worth it?" Helen asked. "Everything we had to do to get what we wanted: Was it worth it?"

I hesitated, not knowing her journey. "Yes."

Helen took a sip. "You know the night of the party at Chateau Marmont? Your husband kind of saved me. Mitch wouldn't leave me alone. Everyone within thirty feet could hear it."

It took a second to recall. Mitch Michelson was the man in Helen's face at the Chateau.

"Kit whispered for me to play along, then became that playboy everyone remembered him as. And it worked. Mitch backed off." She glanced at me. "Until you showed up."

"Really?"

"Mitch is persistent." She tilted her head back to finish her cocktail. "Finally, I realized I could get a lot further if I went along with it instead of being a wet rag. Now I'm starring in his picture." She gave the saddest smile I'd ever seen.

The implication hit me with the force of a battering ram.

Mitch had pushed Helen into doing what I couldn't when Eugene insinuated I could have a drama contract. Like Walter did when I desperately wanted my big break. Like countless others were doing in studios and theaters and agencies across the country.

Helen had learned like I did that looks trumped talent in the film industry. If you didn't have enough of either, there was one other way to get ahead.

But it didn't stop with a contract. There would always be another role to chase—and someone who could help you get it.

I couldn't imagine how many Eugenes and Walters and Mitches there were who were getting away with traumatizing women like Helen and Ruth and me.

"I saw you in *Over the River* last year. You were really good."

She crossed her arms as the patio door slid open. "Is that a compliment?"

"It just might be."

Hugh stepped outside. "Vivian?" Even from several feet away, I could make out the stiffening of his body at seeing me with Helen. A woman he knew I detested.

"I should get going," I said. "You know, some actors are going freelance. No studio contracts. You decide who you'll work with and what roles to take."

I had to add that last part in case she didn't think she had anything to offer another studio without giving away pieces of herself. In case she loved acting as much as I did and couldn't see simply not doing it.

"There will always be people thinking they can tell you what you're worth." I met her gaze. "Don't let them."

CHAPTER FORTY

Vivian

then

My dearest Hugh,

You will never believe what I did. I can hardly believe it myself.
I talked to a reporter.

About a week after seeing Helen again, I decided to reach out
to Agnes Wright. One of her columns got my attention last year
when she exposed a scandal involving poor working conditions for
factory women. It made me think of the years my mother was one.
Do you remember me telling you about that? She used to work
with industrial parts up until recently, when Ted convinced her to
open a ballet studio.

Anyway, I told Agnes I had a story for her, so she came over.
But I had a feeling by the way she sighed from my sofa, wearing a
pencil skirt and a frown, she wasn't particularly looking forward to
interviewing me. I was more frivolous than her usual subjects.

She held a pen to a pad. "Is Kit . . . ?"

"He won't be coming."

Her only show of confusion came from the slight arch of an eyebrow. "Your season finale is next week. How exciting."

The way she said it, a fleck of dust floating through the air would have been more fascinating. Not that I blamed her. She wanted to report on something important. It was why I'd called her.

"It will be our series finale, actually. I'm working on a script for a new show."

"With your husband?"

Perceptive.

It was too soon to share what I had in mind, so I simply said, "I'm a comedian and a writer. Not just the wife of Kit Pierce."

For a second, Agnes' face relaxed in what I took as a mix of surprise and respect.

"I imagine you could think of a million more interesting topics, though." I lifted a hand. "Not that I blame you. So how about we talk about something else? Or someone else. Eugene Mills."

"The head of MGM?" She leaned forward. "What about him?"

He takes advantage of women.

He makes the higher-ups push diets and pills on his actors.

He uses his clients' vulnerabilities to get them to do what he wants—dictating their relationships and forcing them to make impossible decisions.

And so much more.

"Vivian?" Agnes pushed.

I would do this for myself. For Ruth. Even for Helen. I'd do it for the thousands of people afraid of the repercussions of speaking the truth. I'd blow the doors off the seedy underbelly of Hollywood, starting with its head honcho.

Maybe Agnes wouldn't find writing a story worth the potential consequences, but I would tell it anyway.

"Eugene takes advantage of his female employees."

Love,

Vivian

HARRIET'S HOLLYWOOD
APRIL 30, 1956

Eugene Mills in Hot Water

Controversy over a recent article in the *LA Times* has put the widely respected Hollywood mogul Eugene Mills in the spotlight. For once in his career, that's not a good thing.

The article detailed a laundry list of the powerful exec's toxic workplace habits, including sexual advances offered to boost careers and horrifying ultimatums related to his actresses' bodies and personal lives. It paints the picture of a monster who preyed on every power imbalance in the book.

Representatives declined to comment, but when Mills was spotted leaving court on Friday, he said, "This is nothing more than a misunderstanding purported by a disgruntled ex-employee."

That ex-employee? None other than Vivian Stone, former MGM princess turned CBS queen.

"It looks idyllic from the outside—awards and fame and money," she said in the article. "But on the inside, it's an old boys' club so ugly it would make your skin crawl."

CHAPTER FORTY-ONE

Vivian

then

Ruth dragged me into her closet like old times to pick out a dress for our monthly dinner that May. She deliberated between two while I took off a peach one. It was the fifth I'd decided against.

She pouted at the heap on the floor. "That one looked great on you."

"The color washed me out."

She went back to the dresses and found a formfitting dark green one with a sweetheart neckline. "Wear this. If his eyes don't pop out the second he sees you, I'll be a monkey's uncle."

"Who?"

"Hugh. That's why you left a pile of dresses in your wake, right? Because you want to look good for him." She tipped her head and blinked at me. "I wonder if you even realize you're doing it."

I turned to the mirror and held the dress up to myself. It was a showstopper. "Why would you say that?"

"Oh, I don't know. You've only been drooling over him for nearly five years."

"I never drooled."

She stared, hand on her hip.

"I told you, that was a dribble of water." I unzipped the dress and threw it over my head.

Ruth jabbed a finger at me like *I* was the one talking nonsense. "You consistently have that look in your eyes like you're a dog and he's the bone."

"Even if I used to do that, it's all in the past."

Yet . . . *yet*, when I thought of the times I didn't have to hold the world on my shoulders or be what someone else needed—the moments I felt like the very best version of myself—his face stood out.

It was Hugh to whom I wanted to tell the details of my life, even when I could only find the courage to do it in a letter. He was the one who made me laugh. He could pull me out of despair. Hugh knew my past, saw me when I was nobody, and liked me anyway.

It was what made me fall in love with him in the first place.

Back when my feelings for him were so deep it caused me pain, I had put a wall of thorns around my heart. But now, when I tore aside the brambles to inspect what was beneath, I found affections that had never died.

"Even if I wanted him to see me in another light," I said slowly, "I'd probably have to do something extreme, like dress as a French maid." Using my big toe, I pointed at a cream tufted seat, which doubled as storage when you removed the top. I'd once made the mistake of peeking inside and found Ruth's collection of bedroom attire.

She lit up and clapped. "Oh! I have the feather duster too!"

"What do you use that for?" I raised a hand. "On second thought, I don't want to know."

She tossed a dress over her head and motioned to the back. "Could you?" As I zipped it, she said, "You should see yourself when you're near him. You get this glow like you're lit from the inside."

I stepped back, finding my stockings, and gave voice to the truth. "I don't think I ever stopped loving him."

"You don't say."

To Hugh, I was probably nothing more than his goofy friend.

A thud behind me drew my attention, and I turned to find Ruth slumped against the wall, a hand over her mouth.

My heart did a backflip. "What's wrong?"

"Oh, you know. Just a little nausea."

My face slackened. "Are you . . . ?"

"Pregnant?" Her hand dropped from her mouth. "Yeah, I am."

I could practically see the dark clouds rolling in. I embraced her.

The memory of what she had gone through before had to be tearing her apart. She couldn't go through that again, but, like last time, I didn't have a solution. Eugene was still Eugene, and while Ruth and Dean's finances had improved, she shouldn't have had to choose between two things she desperately wanted and loved.

"Do you know what you're going to do?" I pressed my cheek against hers.

She took a shaky breath. "Not yet."

Though I hadn't been able to see it through, I'd planned how to have a child while working on a TV show. Scripts were written to handle it. Episodes prerecorded. There was no reason Ruth couldn't do the same.

The show I'd come up with about two friends came to mind.

"How would you feel about working in television?" When she stilled, I put a few inches between us to gauge her reaction. "I wrote a new pilot and, to be honest, I can't picture anyone else doing it besides us."

"You want to work with me?"

"I would *love* to work with you."

As we walked downstairs that night, Hugh glanced up from where he and Dean were talking in the living room. His mouth was open on an unfinished word, taking me in, and a yearning stirred inside me. One I hadn't let myself indulge in ages.

◆

At the end of our last episode, as Kit and I did our usual closing bows and the audience clapped, a few people stood. I smiled and bowed again. A few more stood. Then everyone else.

To them, this was the last episode of a season, though Kit and I knew better.

My heart exploded with gratitude. I'd never taken it for granted, not once, and I knew that all my hard work would have gotten me nowhere if I hadn't had fans.

Rich Sullivan, who'd grown so much taller since the pilot, came out with a bouquet. I bent down and kissed his cheek. We all took a last bow.

Thank you, I mouthed on shaky lips.

I went back to my dressing room afterward and waited until I assumed everyone had left. When it was dark and quiet, I walked onto the set for what would be the last time.

Kit sat on the sofa with his chin resting on his fist. Apparently, I wasn't the only one who needed a minute with our set.

I sat on the other end, both of us quiet for a minute.

He wet his lips as if wrestling with the weight of his thoughts. "I want you to know I'm sorry."

"I know." It didn't erase anything, but I believed he meant it.

"You deserved better than me. You deserve the whole damn world."

"Who, me?" I teased.

His eyes were earnest as they reached mine. "You did. You *do*."

I focused on the empty rows of the audience's seats. I'd anticipated an emotional goodbye but hadn't expected this. "You do too, you know. You deserve better."

"Than you?"

"Than *this*." I gestured toward him. "Better than what you've given yourself." It'd gotten cloudy, but I still remembered what I first saw in him. Kit was smart and talented and charming.

"I really did love you, you know. I always will. And I think I could have made you happy for the rest of our lives if I hadn't loved drinking more." He stared at his shoes. "I'm going to keep trying. One of these days, I'll conquer this thing."

I hoped he would. But if he did, he'd have to do it because he made the choice.

In the story of our lives together, Kit wasn't the villain. We didn't get a happy ending together, but I still wanted him to find it somewhere.

He gave my hand a light squeeze, holding my gaze, and I squeezed back.

After he left, I continued to sit, trying to soak up all the good memories there to pluck out in the future when I felt nostalgic. I took in the front door I'd ambled through with a cane during the pilot episode. Then the kitchen, where Rich and I had had funny skits making messes, including one involving a homemade bread business. There was the staircase, which led nowhere, where Bobby and Clara had shared their first kiss.

We always remember our firsts. First job. First car. First friend.

I'd held on to this first so hard, with such resolve, I couldn't imagine how another show would compare.

But it might.

"Goodbye," I whispered, taking it all in one last time.

When I strode out the door, I didn't look back.

CHAPTER FORTY-TWO

Vivian

then

Gerard sat at his desk across from me as he read the last page of my new script. He'd laughed a few times since starting, so I knew he didn't hate it.

Finally, he flipped the stack over. "It's good. But what does it mean for you and Kit?"

I squared my shoulders. "I'm going to divorce him." I'd practiced saying it aloud a hundred times before it came out with absolute resolve. "But I want to continue on TV."

"Without him?"

"Yes."

He raised an eyebrow like this was an unreasonable request and shouldn't need explaining. My mother had given me the same look when I was six and she had to explain why kittens didn't use kiddie pools. I imagined Gerard was second-guessing signing us season-to-season instead of locking us in for longer.

"You're the star"—he rested his elbows on the desk—"but another show wouldn't be the same without him."

"We can figure it out." Calmly, I pointed at the script. "I did figure it out."

"And it's fantastic, but audiences want both of you." He motioned to the wall, where framed copies of magazines hung, including one of

TV Guide with Kit and me on the cover. "If you start a new show, it'll look like you abandoned him."

My hard shell cracked. I didn't want to disappoint anyone, especially not the people responsible for me being able to do a show I loved week after week.

"I mean, what's the alternative?" I asked. "What option do you see?"

"Don't divorce? Keep *Bobby and Clara*?"

I rolled my eyes. Of course. Easy.

He lifted a hand. "Hear me out. You aren't living together anymore, yeah? Last week you two filmed the finale, and the audience was none the wiser about your marital troubles."

"We're far past troubles."

"I get it, but the public doesn't need to know. Think about what's best for your career." He pushed the script back. "Divorcing will sour people's opinions of you."

My insides shriveled. I'd never in my life quit anything until deciding on the divorce. Sure, I'd pivoted, but that'd put me on the path to finding what I was good at, what I loved. And now I *had* it.

"Listen"—he reclined in his chair and folded his hands over his belly—"I can't make this decision for you. I can only guide you on potential outcomes. You're going to have to figure out what scenario you can live with."

As for the best way to dissolve my marriage, that would take more time. When it came to my career, though, there was only one way forward.

"We're ending *Bobby and Clara*, and I'm not stopping until this"—I stood and shook the script—"gets off the ground. We both know it's going to be a hit, so I think the question is: What scenario can *you* live with? Will you be all right knowing you passed this up?"

If he said no, I'd go to another network. There would be no stopping me until I'd exhausted each and every avenue. Once I was through, this would make money for whoever took a chance on it, and he knew it.

Would fans think I'd abandoned Kit? Maybe—but only on TV. Until we divorced, everything else would be speculation.

Gerard's gaze flicked to the script, then back to me. "Who else you got in mind for this?"

TV Guide

That's a Wrap

Fans will be grieving the loss of their favorite television family, and, quite frankly, we think we'll all be mourning the end for years to come. It's reported the famed *Bobby and Clara* is ending the series with the conclusion of this season.

We here at *TV Guide* want to thank Vivian Stone and Kit Pierce for bringing laughter into our homes. During the half-hour segments, no matter what happened in our days, we could count on them to give us a break from it all.

As for what's next for the pair, no word yet, but whatever it is, we can't wait to find out.

CHAPTER FORTY-THREE

Margot

now

We were lying on the couch by the time the tape finished last night, and I kept telling myself I would get up to grab the last one in a minute. But being in Leo's arms was so comforting, I fell asleep, and he must have too. It was the first time I didn't have a fitful night of sleep since Gram passed, and I'm already wondering if I can convince him to stay over again tonight. Now, not only didn't we listen to the last tape, but we forgot to set an alarm, so this morning is a blur of rushing around, like something out of *Home Alone*.

I'm patting my back pocket as we head out the door, checking to make sure I have my phone. The shoebox is under my other arm, the player resting precariously on top.

"Let me carry something." Leo catches up, taking the player and the shoebox.

"My keys. I don't have my keys." Hands on my head like I might be losing my mind, I spin around, scanning the driveway.

"Around your finger."

I bring my hand down. My index finger is in the key ring.

"Don't be nervous." He takes my keys, locks the front door, then nods toward his car. "It'll be fine."

I'm not sure he's right. I feel like I know Vivian. I care about her. I grieved for her as she grieved. I mentally cheered her on as she started writing again. I nodded alongside her talks about exposing Eugene. I am so, so proud of her and how she refused to give up. No matter how many times life threw her down.

But she doesn't know me, and I still don't know how she knew Gram. What if this all goes terribly wrong?

My thighs stick to the leather seats of Leo's vehicle. He starts the car and rests a hand on my knee, which has been bobbing since we sat down, and reverses out of the driveway.

It's a common misconception that living close to LA means seeing celebrities. I've never seen one in my life, and I can't relax. I think about getting the player going with the last tape as we drive but decide I wouldn't be able to concentrate.

About an hour later we reach the tree-lined streets of Bel Air. The homes grow farther apart, and as we curve around a bend, the GPS has us pulling up to a black gate between two stone pillars. Attached to the one on the left is a speaker, a camera, and a number pad.

Before Leo can roll down his window, a mechanism cranks and the gate swings back. He rolls up and around a circular drive, a fountain in the center, coming to a stop at the front door of a stunning white-sided mansion with big, black-framed picture windows.

A woman stands by the front door as Leo parks and shuts off the engine. She has to be in her fifties or sixties and is nicely dressed in a blouse and knee-length skirt.

"It'll be okay," Leo says, collecting the shoebox and player. When he sees me frozen in my seat, he reaches over and cups my cheek. "Just breathe. I know you look up to her and you're scared of what's coming, but—"

"Does this end with you telling me celebrities are real people too?"

A smirk slowly forms. "I was working up to that part, yeah. Planned a little speech on the drive over."

I give him a quick kiss, then open my door. "No time for speeches."

He has successfully gotten me out of my head enough for me to peel myself out of the car.

"Margot DuBois?" The woman steps closer, the fine lines around her mouth and eyes deepening as she smiles. "I'm Christine. We spoke on the phone."

"Nice to meet you." I motion to my left. "This is Leo, my . . ." What the hell do I call him?

"Boyfriend." Leo reaches out to shake Christine's hand. "Hi."

The base of my spine tingles with the title despite my knowing it's not true.

Christine reaches for the doorknob. "Please, follow me."

Leo leans in, both of us trailing a few feet behind. "I hope that's okay. Sounded easier than explaining—"

"Everything?" When he's silent, I say, "Sorry, part of another speech?"

He pinches my side, and I yelp, fighting a laugh as Christine glances over her shoulder.

"I should warn you, Vivian isn't in the best of health these days. She tires easily, so I wouldn't push the visit too long."

"Of course." I can see she cares for Vivian beyond simple employment. I want to tell her not to worry: I care about her too.

We walk through the marble entryway, past a grand staircase, and into a sitting room. It's larger than my studio apartment, with vaulted ceilings and pristine vintage furniture. Tasteful and elegant.

"She'll be out in just a moment. Make yourselves comfortable." Christine gestures to a couch and leaves.

We sit on a blue velvet love seat while Leo sets the cassette player and shoebox on an oval coffee table.

"This is surreal." He studies a side table where records and a player sit, then a bookcase filled with a hodgepodge collection of VHS tapes and DVDs, books, and rows of cassettes and CDs. Framed photos line a few of the shelves.

"Christine seems like a protective assistant. Or whatever she is."

"That's an idea."

"What is?"

"Maybe your grandma was Vivian's assistant at one point."

"She was a switchboard operator," I remind him. "Mom said Gram used to be wild in her younger years, whatever that means. But I don't think an assistant would qualify as wild."

"Maybe she was Vivian's own secret switchboard lady," he says, and we both laugh.

A sound draws my attention toward the doorway, my gaze shooting up to the person standing there.

It's her. Vivian Stone.

She's shorter than I expected. Softer. Gone are the sharp lines of her cheeks and collarbones. The hourglass figure and voluminous hair. Her skin is speckled with age spots, and her hair is neat and white.

Despite all of it, the woman from TV is still in there. Vivian holds herself as tall as she can, emanating a vibrancy beyond the structure of her tailored dress pants and purple sequined blouse. She's a star, through and through.

Her mouth is slightly agape as her eyes roam over me. "I couldn't help but overhear your conversation." She walks closer. "You don't know who your grandmother was to me?"

Of all the ways I had imagined our introductions, this hadn't even ranked as a possibility.

It's strange to go from listening to her for hours upon hours, nothing but words flowing from the tape player, to having a person accompany the voice, albeit a little deeper now.

Vivian sits in a plush chair. "You are Margot DuBois." She says it without hesitancy. "I thought you listened to the tapes."

Leo grabs my hand for support.

"I am, and we did. All except the last one. I'm sorry if we weren't supposed to," I say. "I found them in my grandma's attic after she passed. We didn't know what we were listening to at first and then couldn't believe it was you."

I can't tell if she's angry or sad when her whole body stiffens. Despite my need for answers, I'm not going to push her.

"Or"—I motion to the shoebox—"I can leave them? And we can leave?"

"Relax," Leo whispers.

"I *can't*." My stomach is in the middle of an eternal somersault finale, each spin even more spectacular than the one before.

"You haven't finished the last one?" Vivian's sparse eyelashes flutter with her double blink. "We should listen to it before we say more."

"Now?" I ask.

"It's a miracle I've lived this long, darling. Time is of the essence, as they say. Besides, if you go home and listen, you may never come back."

Her ominous words cause my pulse to pound in my ears.

Whatever Vivian has done, whatever connection she has with Gram, it couldn't possibly be so bad that I would refuse to see her again. She's *Vivian Stone*. It's not the Emmys or fame or how she's a comedic legend that's caused me to like her so much. It's everything I've learned about her. I've come to care about her.

I know her. *I know her.*

When Christine walks in, Vivian lifts a finger. "Some lemonade and cookies?"

"Of course," Christine says, leaving us again.

We all sit, mute. It's so quiet, even my breathing seems to be at an exaggerated volume.

"Let's get started." Vivian's fingers curl over the arms of the chair.

Leo pops in the last cassette. The second it starts, Vivian sighs and closes her eyes.

Tape Eight

CHAPTER FORTY-FOUR

Vivian

then

One day in July, I sat on the edge of my pool, clad in a white bikini, while I kicked my feet in the water. The patio door opened and shut, and my eyes caught on the unmistakable high shine of rich black hair.

There's a difference between rich black and true black. I've never been an artist or had a reason to learn color science, but when I met Hugh, I wanted to know why his hair seemed darker than the black suits he favored.

What makes rich black so distinct is it has other colors in it, and I found myself wondering how much blue hid in his strands to make them so fluid, it was like you could drown in them.

When he walked out wearing fitted navy swim trunks and a T-shirt, my heart played a jagged melody fashioned by chipped keys and out-of-tune strings.

It'd been through battle, but it still worked.

He yanked his shirt off, displaying broad shoulders and the ridges of his stomach, and tossed it onto a lounge chair along with a bag.

Over time, I'd trained myself to stop paying attention to details that ventured beyond friendship. But now I let my eyes linger.

"Why aren't you in already?" He strode to the pool.

"I actually invited you here under false pretenses. You said you were a lifeguard in high school, right? I was hoping I could get a lesson."

His gaze narrowed. "You can't swim?"

A beach ball floated across the water. "I can. I'm just not good at it." And by "I can" I meant in the shallow end.

"We can try. I taught kids back then. They're a lot easier. Adults have so much in their heads, they're tougher to get through to."

I had a fair bit going on in my head as my eyes roved over his muscled chest, very little of it having to do with swimming.

Hugh jumped in, causing a spray of water to land on my thighs. More flew when he broke the surface and shook wet hair from his face. I dipped a leg into the water as he came close. Apparently it wasn't fast enough, because he gripped my waist and pulled me in.

My breaths scraped up my chest as I clung to him.

"You're okay. I'm not going to let anything happen to you," he said softly. We were deep enough for the surface to hit the tops of his shoulders. If I touched the bottom, it'd be over my head. "You really can't swim, can you? How did I not know this?"

"My aversion to stepping in the ocean whenever we went to the beach might have been an indication."

"Can you tread water?" He moved me a few inches from him to get a peek at what my legs were doing, but I dug my nails into him when I sank a little, and he drew me close again. "I guess not. I'm surprised you got a pool."

The water gently ebbed and flowed from our movement while I worked to calm my nerves. "I didn't want to let fear hold me back."

His thumbs drifted the faintest bit, skimming the waist of my bikini bottoms, and my heart shuddered. "Good for you. Fear holds me back from a lot of things."

I wasn't quite as adept as he thought, fear once again keeping me from saying how I felt about him. Our friendship had been in a neat box for so long; how would I begin to modify it? Would it all come crashing down if I tried?

Our legs brushed against each other, sending a jolt through me. I adjusted my hold on his arms. "Where should we start?"

"How about floating? Lean back." He tried to ease me down, but when I didn't stop gripping him, he smiled. "It's okay, I have you."

"You won't let go?"

"Never."

I trusted him, so I released a slow exhale and let my arms rest on the surface while he slid one hand under my shoulder blades and another low on my back.

"How's that?"

I shut my eyes against the sun. "Okay."

"Taking and holding a full breath makes the stomach float. Why don't you try it?" When I did, he said, "Now, spread your legs—" I cracked an eye open, and the corner of his lips curved, eyes glittering with amusement. "And your arms, like a starfish. It'll help you stay up."

He was right. My body was more buoyant, giving me some confidence. "How am I doing?"

One of his hands slipped from my shoulders to the middle of my back, pressing to encourage my belly up, while his other accidentally grazed my bottom and gently lifted my thighs. "Good."

"You're only using this as an excuse to get handsy."

He smiled, white teeth gleaming, and rolled his eyes. "I'm going to take one hand away, okay?" When I nodded, the hand under my legs disappeared, but he came a few inches closer, his chest touching my side. "This is good."

"You're a good teacher." We stayed like that, quiet for a minute. "How's the house?"

For five months after his split from Loretta, Hugh lived in one of the bungalows at the Beverly Hills and let her have their apartment. He finally moved into his new place last week.

"It's private, so I like it." After a second he said, "Eugene was talking the other day about how my 'mourning' period has gone on long enough and I need to get back on the market. I told him flat out I wasn't having it. He's dictated enough."

"You did?" I was always proud of Hugh, but his finally standing up to Eugene was more than I expected. He deserved to go after what he wanted without fear of repercussion. "Good for you.

Though I figured you'd date soon anyway. You didn't seem too sad when your engagement ended."

"I'd known it wasn't right for a while."

"Oh?"

"You know the last picture I did? The one with Grace Lightly?"

"Of course." I'd seen it six times. They had fantastic chemistry. "I love you and Grace together. I've always wanted to meet her. Wait, did something happen with her?"

"What? Who, Grace?" His tone lightened like I must be joking. "No. She's dating Max Collins, the fella who directed the film. You didn't know?"

Hugh had such a way of easing my worries without even knowing it. "I haven't been keeping track."

"Yeah, well, we had a kiss to shoot, and it wasn't working."

That surprised me, because the final product was *very* convincing. The kiss made it look like he'd die without her.

"I thought you knew how to kiss," I teased, remembering him telling me that when we first met.

"What do you think?" he said low, gaze latching on to mine.

I swallowed as I tugged at the memory. It felt like a lifetime ago. "Touché. So what happened? Max had to give you pointers on kissing his girlfriend? Did he tell you what mints she likes?" As the striped beach ball came near, I batted it away.

He chuckled, and my insides tightened, the small sound bringing me to a high like I only got in front of a packed audience. Of all the laughs I'd ever heard, Hugh's was my favorite.

"When you say it like that, it doesn't sound as professional as it was," he said. "No, Max tells me, 'This isn't just some woman; this is the love of your life. You have to kiss her like that.' And I say, 'I thought I was.' So he goes, 'No. This is how it's done.' And he kisses Grace. Then he wants me to try."

I smiled. "Lucky Grace."

"He still wasn't happy with it. He goes, 'When you kiss her, pretend you're kissing someone you're in love with. Pretend it's Loretta.'

This was back when we were still engaged. The thing was, for it to be convincing, I couldn't kiss her like I kissed Loretta."

My eyebrows shot up. "Did you come up with a solution?"

"Yeah, I managed to work out what to do." He stayed quiet for a minute. "Have you talked to Kit?"

"Not since we filmed the last episode."

"And you're okay with it being over? No regrets?"

"I'm more than okay. I'm *relieved*."

I'd thought over my relationship with Kit and realized what had brought us together was passion and business. Lust and drive. My love for him had been a decision.

A drop of water ran down Hugh's neck, demanding my attention. I'd never had a choice about loving him.

"That's enough for today," he said, helping me to the ledge. "It's best to start slow."

I pushed myself out and grabbed the striped towels from the lounge chair as Hugh got out too. After wrapping one around me, I tossed the other to him.

Half of it landed in the water.

I cringed. "Oh, sorry. You can have mine."

He used the dry part on his legs and feet. "It's fine." He wrung it out and laid it over the back of a chair.

"I have more in the bathroom if you want to get changed."

"Sure." He scooped up his shirt and bag.

Upstairs, I pointed out the bathroom closet, where he could find spare towels, then headed down the hall to my room.

The closet door gave a gentle creak. A moment later came a loud crash.

I propped my hands against my bedroom doorframe and dug my nails in, my body going rigid.

My mind slowed to visualize my bathroom closet, where rolled beach towels sat on a high shelf—right next to the shoebox full of letters.

No.

My heart lurched as I twisted and rushed back to the bathroom, the mere ten feet stretching out like ten miles. At the open doorway, I took in the shoebox on the floor, its lid popped off, dozens of papers scattered at Hugh's feet—

And one in his hands.

An envelope sat on the sink, the one Kit had torn open with Hugh's name on it. The one I'd finally stashed with the rest.

I wanted to stop him, his eyes flying over the lines in the letter, but I was frozen in place.

He peered up, his face blank. "What is all this?"

The air thickened as I coaxed breaths in and out.

It would be easy to explain that, yes, I had written them, but that was years ago. I'd had a silly crush that had long since been put to rest. That way, we could keep the neat box of our friendship intact.

Or I could tell him the truth, the whole truth, and let the cards fall where they may.

When I left home, I promised myself and my mother I'd have the life she couldn't—in my career *and* in love. And I never stopped, not one single time, pushing forward in my career. At every roadblock and dead end, I paved a new way. Why should I stop there?

"They're letters I wrote you over the years," I admitted. "It became a habit."

"A habit?"

"Any time I wanted to get something out, good or bad, I would tell you. Like a diary. There's one I wrote while my mom was sick. One after I lost my contract. There's another when Kit and I were fighting, and so many more in between."

He glanced at the folded papers at his feet, then set the letter on its envelope. "You know that story about how Max told me to kiss Grace?"

"You figured out what to do. And it worked beautifully. It looked like you couldn't live without her."

His eyes caught mine. "Because I can't live without *you*."

A steady *whoosh* of blood pounded through my body while the words on my tongue broke apart like tiles on a shaken Scrabble board.

"Years ago I talked to Eugene about us. I didn't know if you wanted to be with me, but . . ." Hugh paused like it was an effort to drag the thoughts out from where he'd kept them under lock and key. "He explained the strategy he had for my career and said it made no sense for us to be together when we weren't on the same level. I tried reasoning with him, but he wouldn't hear it and said if I mucked up his plans, he'd tank both our careers."

I remembered the day Hugh stormed out of Eugene's office.

Kit's words from years ago, after Hugh showed up at our Vegas hotel room, resurfaced. The reason he said a man could be strictly friends with a woman, even if he found her attractive: *He knows he can't have her.*

"So many times I almost said something but couldn't because I didn't have a solution." His voice was strained, like the thoughts sliced him from the inside. "It was one thing if it was only my career on the line, but it was yours too. You'd just gotten a contract earlier that year. I couldn't let him take it from you. But I knew once you got a lead, people would love you. Then Eugene could be swayed." He lifted his hand to my face, his thumb drifting across my cheekbone. "Only you met Kit. I hoped it'd fizzle out, but—"

"We got engaged."

"I was close to saying something at the restaurant after I found out, but it would have been selfish. There was no going back."

My head spun, still catching up. "Are you saying you care for me?"

"*Care for you?* I *love* you. Through the misery of watching you be with someone else, I've loved you. No amount of time or logic has ever been enough to dissuade me. You walk into a room, and my soul screams, *There she is.*" His gaze was intent, his voice a song in my veins. "When Max told me to picture kissing someone I was in love with, all I saw was you."

Those words. They wrecked my heart and pieced it back together at the same time.

"If I'm too late," he went on, "if you've gotten over what you felt in that letter, I'll be whatever you need. Friend. Lover. But if you let me, I'll give you everything."

I reached up and ran my fingers through his hair. When he leaned into the touch, his eyes closing briefly, I said, "I love you too. And I want all of it."

Hugh inhaled sharply. When I smiled, he focused on it, then my eyes, before returning his gaze to my lips, like he was convincing himself it was allowed. He could look as long as he wanted.

He reached for my hips, his fingertips digging in as he eased me to the wall. My heart pounded so hard as my chest pressed against him that he must have felt it, our breaths mingling, his mouth a hair's breadth away.

I tipped my chin up to let my bottom lip brush against his, a tease, featherlight, and only a fraction of a second passed between his groan and his mouth capturing mine. Pouring years' worth of yearning into a single moment.

The fear that we would never reach this place melted as I became lost to his touch. Like he'd opened a thousand-page book on wanting, wishing, waiting. Our lips drew the time out in languid pushes and pulls. His hands drifted up, bracketing my ribs.

"I've been living on the memory of kissing you," he said between the ones he peppered along my jaw. "I've replayed it in my head so many times."

"Is that all you thought of?"

A laugh, light on a breath. "No."

"Show me."

With one arm around my back, he dipped to slip the other under my knees, scooping me into his arms, then kissed me again. He carried me to my room, our mouths only separating when he set me on the bed.

Everything that came after that happened slowly, like we had captured all of eternity and could dedicate it to the slow exploration of each other's bodies.

Hugh tugged at the ties of my bikini top until they gave. My hands dove into his hair, lost in the inky strands, while his mouth sought my breasts. I memorized the appreciative sounds he made kissing down my body. One on my hip, easing my bathing suit bottom off.

He touched me with purpose. Like someone who'd spent a lifetime fantasizing about a dream destination, knowing exactly where they would go and what they would do, without ever expecting to get there.

He dropped his swim trunks to the floor and settled on top of me.

"All this time"—he traced a fingertip along my cheekbone, down my nose, over my cupid's bow—"I've been so hopelessly in love with you."

Hugh made love the way he kissed, the way he touched: thoroughly. It reminded me of the time he had said, "Anything worth doing is worth doing well."

It was like putting the last piece of the puzzle in place. The most satisfying feeling I'd ever known.

Downstairs, we puttered around the kitchen, comfortable with each other and the shift in our relationship. Like it was always meant to be this way.

Hugh handed me a cup of coffee and gestured to the pages sitting on the counter. "What's *Two Girls and a Dog*?"

"A script I've been working on."

I'd wanted to call it *Two Girls*—short and sweet—but Ruth thought it needed more oomph, so she added *and a Dog*. Which meant we had to go back to the script and add a dog. I came around to the idea, though. It'd worked for *Lassie*.

"Yeah? So who are the two girls?" He smirked. "And who's the dog?"

I poked his stomach as I passed him to find the sugar. "It would be an *actual* dog."

He did the scrunched-face smile I loved. "And the girls?"

"Yours truly, of course, and Ruth. I talked to Gerard about it, and he wants us to do some editing before presenting it to the execs. Hopefully they go for it."

"They'd be blockheads not to." He took a sip from his mug, watching as I added two spoonfuls of sugar to mine. "So I might be getting ahead of myself, but how long do we have to keep this quiet?"

"What do you mean?"

"When's your divorce finalized? I'm guessing you'll need to wait a little while before publicly jumping into another relationship."

"I . . ." I rested a hip against the counter and stared at him. "I didn't file."

He waited like I might add more. "Yet? You haven't filed *yet*, but you have the paperwork?" When I didn't say more, his eyes widened. "Please tell me you really did leave him."

"Of course. When I'm done, I'm done. And I am."

"*But*."

"But Gerard said divorcing him would sour America's opinion of me."

Hugh tensed, shaking his head as he set down his coffee with a thud. "So you're not getting a divorce?"

"I am."

"When?"

"I don't know! I have to figure out the right timing." I hugged an arm around my middle, so frustrated with the situation I could scream. "You did the same thing, remember? Put your career ahead of a relationship."

Hurt flashed in his eyes. "No, I put *your* career ahead of a relationship back when Eugene threatened it. If you're talking about my old girlfriend from back home, then yes. I told you I saw my mistake. I saw it so deeply, it made me afraid to love someone again."

It looked like I hadn't been the only one who had put a barrier around their heart.

He pointed at his chest. "But I do love you, Vivian. And it was one thing when we were friends and I didn't know how you felt. When you were married and trying to make it work. Now? After those letters and what we did, I *can't* only have a piece of you."

"I'm afraid the public won't forgive me for leaving Kit. Over the years, we've become a package deal. A married couple assumed to be as madly in love off-screen as they are on-screen. To find out we're divorcing might make people feel like we'd fooled them."

The strain in his face gave way to disappointment. "I don't think you're giving your fans enough credit. They love you because you make them laugh and have become part of their lives. Not because of who you're married to."

"Maybe. But I have to handle this the right way. We have to keep us a secret for now." The backlash if it got out would be worse than news of my divorce.

Hugh let out a deep breath. "Fine. I don't like it, but I get it. You need to do this on your own terms." His gaze reached mine. "I want to tell the world I love you. I want to plaster it on billboards and declare it on national television. But I can wait a little longer."

CHAPTER FORTY-FIVE

Vivian

then

Refining the pilot with Ruth was completely different from what it'd been with Kit. It involved a lot of laughing so hard, we cried, with me demonstrating, in the middle of my living room, how I pictured a physical comedy routine going while Ruth furiously scribbled it down.

For the record, climbing the half-inch ledges of a stone fireplace like a ladder is ill-advised and comes with scraped legs.

After what happened the last time I had gone to Gerard with a script, I worried he would veto anything I slid across his desk that wasn't *Bobby and Clara*, despite the door he'd left open about the new show at our last meeting. But with pilot season over, and Kit and me refusing to sign on for another season, there was little time for the network to find a new show to fill our slot. I had a history of making them money, so I shouldn't have been surprised when CBS green-lit *Two Girls and a Dog*.

And though it wasn't a deciding factor, Gerard relished sticking it to Eugene by poaching another MGM actor. Which only added insult to injury: Kit had released a statement about how he was leaving TV not because of any burned bridges but because he missed films. His first movie back wouldn't be with MGM but Paramount.

With our success on *Bobby and Clara*, studios probably would have welcomed me too, and maybe I would do another film someday. But for now, life had me exactly where I wanted to be.

The night of our pilot, Gerard rapped his knuckles on my open dressing room door. "Ready?"

I stared at my reflection, the color drained from my face. It didn't matter how many times I'd done this; it was a new show, and the idea of going out there filled me with exhilaration and terror.

"As I'll ever be." I shucked off the robe covering my costume, draping it over a chair, and met Gerard in the hall. "Is Ruth out there?"

"Waiting for Roger to hand over the mic so she can give the opening remarks." He walked me to my place behind a set door. "Knock 'em dead." He left to go around front, where he would watch near the cameramen.

I shook out my sweaty hands as Ruth spoke.

"We thank you, ladies and gentlemen, for coming to the pilot episode of a show we've poured our hearts into. First, I'd like to introduce a spunky and charming actress." She paused. "That'd be me." The audience laughed. "Ruth Keller."

I knew they'd love her. It didn't mean they still loved me.

"Soon you'll meet my energetic and gracious co-star. The dog in *Two Girls and a Dog*: Skippy!"

More laughs.

I twisted the doorknob and waited. Released a breath.

What if all my fans had left me?

"Finally, we have the loveliest person you could ever meet—and she's pretty funny too: Vivian Stone."

Here we go.

Smiling, I pushed open the door.

Lights blinded me as I walked through the set of our apartment and waved, the audience nothing more than a blur of shadows.

I took my place next to Ruth at the same time the light shifted, my eyes adjusting.

Row after row of people cheered and clapped. Hooted and hollered.

Oh, wow.

Tears clouded my vision while embers of doubt and fear fizzled out. They'd never left.

OCTOBER 30, 1956

Bobby Without Clara

Vivian Stone and Kit Pierce, household names and America's favorite TV couple, have put an end to more than their show. The pair, who met on the set of *Sunday Circus* and later made the move from MGM to CBS, have put out a press release stating the end of their marriage.

It's hard to imagine a couple who had it all on-screen had problems behind closed doors. But that's exactly what sources close to the couple say happened.

CHAPTER FORTY-SIX

Vivian

then

It'd been nearly three years since I was on MGM grounds, but Security still recognized me. I suppose everyone recognized me.

"I don't know which building," I said as I drove through.

"That one." Ruth pointed to the lot where my second movie had been filmed. "Dean knows to expect you. They're just rehearsing."

Hugh and I had been keeping our relationship a secret for six months. Long enough that he must have wondered if I'd ever be ready to make it public. But with the show's sky-high ratings, even a few months after the news of my divorce, it was clear that fans hadn't lost faith in me. I was more than my relationships.

Which was a good thing, because I couldn't pretend for a second longer that I wasn't a goner for Hugh Fox.

I parked and stepped out, my nerves tangled like television cords as I straightened my blush pink dress. It had sequins on it like the one I used to wear to auditions. The one I wore when I met Hugh. But the sequins on this one were firmly in place, cascading down my lower half from waist to knee. "I'm nervous."

Ruth got out of the car, a hand on her very round belly. Her due date was days away, yet she was already talking about wanting another. "Don't be. He'll probably be so excited, he'll scoop you into his arms like Superman again. I even have a cape he can borrow if that sounds appealing."

I rolled my eyes.

I might have gotten carried away sharing the details of Hugh's and my first time, but I knew she'd kill me if I skirted around them. Lord knew she had described far too much about her and Dean. At least my stories didn't include sundae supplies. After what she told me the other day, I would never look at Reddi-Wip the same.

"Shoulders back and chin up." She walked with me to the building door. "You're Vivian-frickin'-Stone. After all you've been through, you can do this too."

I loved her.

The soundstage was dark, save the set, modeled after the interior of a cabin. I spotted Hugh there, sitting on a cot and running lines with another man. With the crew focused near the front, no one noticed me.

I left Ruth and found a familiar face near the craft services table.

"Neely. It's so good to see you." Neely Kepner had gorgeous platinum blonde hair and had been an extra on our show once.

"Vivian." She covered a hand over her mouth as she chewed, her eyes crinkling at the corners. "What are you doing here?"

"I came to see Hugh. You're in the picture with him?"

She beamed. "My first lead. Isn't that something?"

"It really is." This was no time for chitchat. "Say, do you think I could jump in with your next lines?"

She shook her head, her forehead creasing. "I don't think Dean would like that."

"He's expecting me. A little impromptu show for the cast." When she didn't look convinced, I clasped my hands. "Please, Neely?"

She grabbed her script off the table. "Here's the next scene. If anyone asks, you took this without me knowing."

I hugged her. "Thank you."

I snuck around the side of the set until I reached the cabin door. My heart hammered as I found where they were in the script, each pound harder as they got closer to my cue. When the other man exited the cabin, I walked through.

Hugh's eyes widened as he stood. "Vivian—"

"You'll never believe who I saw in town today," I read from the script, lighthearted. Where'd that Southern accent come from? "Mr. and Mrs. Nelson drove through in their wagon with all nine of their children."

Smiling, he watched me, rapt.

"They acted like they'd never seen me," I said with flourish. "Like I hadn't saved their daughter's life when she had pneumonia."

For heaven's sake. I was still terrible at drama. I couldn't see it before, but now I did.

Hugh laughed, shaking his head. "You're something else, you know that?"

"I make *an impression*," I reminded him.

"I'll say." When Dean spun his finger in a *Go on* motion from his director's chair, Hugh checked his line. "You mustn't worry about them. They never loved you like I do."

I dropped the accent along with the script. "I love you too."

Shock ran across Hugh's face at me admitting this publicly for the first time.

I stepped forward. "If you think about it, I'm like these heels." Light reflected off the crystals on my shoes—the ones that used to belong to my mother and Hugh got repaired for me.

With my next step, the edge of my heel landed on a thick cord running across the set, and I tipped, my heart tumbling—

Hugh caught me around the waist before I could fall. "Whoa."

I gripped his shoulders, glancing up, and it was like seeing him again for the first time. *Tall, dark, and handsome.*

He steadied me, smiling at the way my gaze roved over him. "You were saying?"

Everyone else faded away. It was only us.

"I'm like these heels. They've gone through a lot. They've been damaged. And that hasn't changed. They're the same shoes beneath it all. But a special man once told me that, with some time and care, broken things could be mended. Someone found them, and me, worth the patience and love needed to see them at their best." I rested a hand on his chest. "I will never stop loving you for that and a thousand other reasons, and I'm prepared to methodically shout it from each and every rooftop. Trust me, I've mapped it out."

Hugh's eyes gleamed as he cupped my cheeks. "That was very dramatic."

"It's not my strong suit. But you have to admit, dramas have the best endings."

He shook his head. "The best endings happen after the curtains close." He bent his head and kissed me.

It lasted much longer than three seconds.

DECEMBER 28, 1957

SUGAR AND SPICE AND EVERYTHING NICE

It's a girl for Vivian Stone and Hugh Fox! The happy couple, who married earlier this year, didn't waste time adding a branch to their family tree. In a faux pas so shocking we had to fan ourselves, it's said Hugh insisted on being with his wife during the birth of their child. We'd give him a slap on the wrist, but our guess is that's exactly where Vivian wanted him.

Baby Beverly Sue's birth comes after an already busy year for the Foxes. Hugh's first film with none other than Twentieth Century-Fox broke box office records. Meanwhile, Vivian and Ruth Keller, who were both in the family way this season, wrote their bundles of joy into their show, a groundbreaking move in television history.

The Foxes made their debut as a family of three by pushing a stroller down the Walk of Fame to see Vivian's new star. With the adoring way Hugh looked at Viv, we imagine he already considered her a star.

Then again, by our count, he's always looked at her that way.

CHAPTER FORTY-SEVEN

Vivian

then

To say life was busy over the years that followed would be an understatement. Between two children, work, and my marriage, I hardly had time to breathe.

I still saw Kit on occasion. Usually at award shows, things like that. The first time I accompanied Hugh to the Oscars and saw Kit, it was a little uncomfortable. But we never lost the affection between us—not completely. It wasn't the same as before. Not a romantic kind of love, but one built on an appreciation for our experience working together.

Some people would think it's strange, but, even now, fifteen years after our divorce, Kit still sends me flowers on my birthday. He still signs the card *Love, Kit*. It didn't take long after we were over for him to date, yet he's never stopped sending those flowers. Never stopped calling once or twice a year to ask how I am. Ask about work. About my kids.

So I didn't find it unusual when he called one day, nearly two months ago. What was out of the ordinary was that he was in the hospital, asking me to come see him.

Visions of his car wrapped around a tree flashed through my mind the whole way over. But if it was that serious, he wouldn't have been able to phone, right? That was what I kept telling myself.

When I walked in, he was jaundiced and small, lying in his hospital bed. His eyes, his skin—God, I felt sick to my stomach at the stark difference.

The last time I had seen him in person was at a premiere six months prior. He looked fine. But the room was so low-lit, I could have missed a more subtle difference.

I sat in the chair next to him. "What's going on?"

"It's good to see you. How's work?"

"Fine."

"And Mr. Perfect? Still treating you well?"

"Yes. Now tell me what's wrong."

"Cutting right to the chase, huh?" He stared at his hands, folded across his belly. "I've been really tired lately, and Makeup has been telling me my coloring is off. I just asked them if they could cover it up, you know?"

"*Cover it up*? Kit, really?"

"Yeah, well, I guess I should have dealt with it sooner." He nodded, working himself up to what he had to say. "Turns out I have liver damage. It's pretty bad."

"How bad?"

"Shot. The doc said some transplants are being done, but they're still pretty experimental. I'd never qualify anyway."

"Why not?"

His gaze met mine. "Because of the drinking."

A familiar sensation of ice slid through my veins. I grabbed his hand, careful of a purple bruise on top. "There has to be something we can do."

"Nah," he said, entirely defeated. "They're giving me some medicine, but it's not going to change anything."

"That's unacceptable. There has to be—"

"There's not." The way he said it, so stern, made my heart stumble. "I have three months. Six if I'm lucky. I'm not going to spend them getting caught up in the 'Woe is me' bullshit."

No, that wasn't Kit's style.

"I have no kids," he went on. "No true friends. It makes you start to think."

"You've accomplished so much. That has to mean something, right?"

"You say that, but you have someone to share it with. I did, but I screwed it up. So many times, I screwed up."

With how vulnerable he was, I wanted to take some of the blame—to shift it off him. "We all make mistakes."

He laughed lightly. "You were a saint compared to me."

His tone gave me the sense he had something specific on his mind.

"Oh?" Maybe I wouldn't want to hear it, but if there was anything he needed to get off his chest, I would bite my tongue and listen.

Kit used his free hand to smooth the white sheet tucked around him. "After what happened with the baby, I was a wreck—"

"*You* were a wreck?"

So much for biting my tongue.

"Yeah," he snapped, his eyes piercing. "I'm kind of pissed at you implying I wasn't."

"Fine. And?"

He heaved a breath. "You were at Ruth's cottage for so long, I didn't think you were coming back. I was alone. Some days I drank myself sick. Others, I needed a distraction. Company."

I stared at him, expecting him to go on. When he didn't, the insinuation hit me. "Are you saying you were with someone else?"

I'd slept with Hugh while still married, but that was completely different. Kit and I were over. I'd already kicked him out. The only thing holding me back from filing for divorce was the fear of professional ramifications. Not because there was a chance for reconciliation.

Yet, back when I was grieving at Ruth's cottage, Kit didn't know we were going to divorce. In fact, as soon as I came home, he wept on his knees for me to stay.

I supposed his one-night stand, or affair—whatever he'd done—didn't mean he wasn't hoping I'd come home. Like drinking, it'd been another way he coped.

At this point, it was neither here nor there. We were long over. It still stung, though.

The only reason he was telling me this now was to ease his conscience.

"Who was it?" I asked, curiosity winning out. "Helen?"

"*God*, no. It wasn't a planned thing. I was at Arthur's house, and he invited some girls over." By the way he said "girls," I knew he meant call girls. "There was this one in white heels—"

"I don't need the details." I shifted in my seat. "If it helps, I forgive you."

I said it without really knowing if I meant it. But I knew I would eventually.

As I sat with Kit's revelation, the image of white heels flashed through my mind, and I saw a woman standing at the threshold of the house Kit and I once shared. A woman looking like life had beaten her down.

A woman who had said she was expecting Kit's child.

I brought a hand to the base of my throat, nausea rolling over me. *Was she actually pregnant?* I'd thought she made it up. She admitted to wanting money . . .

Of course she'd want money if she was going to have a baby and needed support.

Kit had said he had no children, so obviously he didn't know. Would it bring him comfort or pain at this point to learn he did?

If he did. I couldn't tell him without being sure.

Maybe I could find her. Verify that she'd had the baby, then explain the situation to her. If Kit had a child, they needed to meet.

I kept the information to myself, but as soon as I got home, I contacted a private investigator to help me locate the woman. Within a week, I had a name and address.

During the drive over, I kept rehearsing what I'd say. But as I pulled up to the beige bungalow not far from the ocean, every perfectly planned word slipped from my mind.

I parked at the curb and checked the house number to make sure I was at the right one.

It was small, like all the other houses on the street. I'd never known anyone with a house so small. I'd had a couple of tiny apartments in my life, but so much time had passed since then, it felt like another life.

Children played baseball in the street. A few more played hop-scotch on the sidewalk.

I walked up to the house and knocked.

I made a mistake, I repeated to myself while I waited. *I was wrong, and Kit is sick—*

A teenage girl with curly brown hair and sky blue eyes answered the door. I'd say they were the prettiest eyes I'd ever seen, except I'd seen them before.

They were Kit's eyes.

The sight stole the breath from me.

"Hi. My name is Vivian." Not that I had a huge ego, but I figured she would know who I was and braced for recognition to hit. It didn't. "Is your mother home?"

Before she could speak, a woman pulled the door open all the way, an apron over her dress and flour streaked across her cheek.

It was her. I recognized her from the photo the investigator had given me, even if I couldn't remember her from when she stood at my doorstep a decade and a half ago.

The way her gaze narrowed, she remembered me.

She shooed her daughter away, then held one hand on the door-frame and the other on the door. "Yes?"

One word very distinctly conveyed *What do you want?*

I don't remember everything I said. My mind was a blur. There was an apology. An appeal to talk so I could explain myself. The conveying of the importance of it all. I surely said something along the lines of *There's not much time* without getting into the nitty-gritty of it on her stoop.

I hadn't expected her to slam the door in my face. Though I probably should have.

And I probably should have known the letter I sent after, having meticulously pored over every word, would go unanswered. As did my calls.

I couldn't stop. This was my fault, and that girl was clearly Kit's child.

When I got nowhere, I phoned him to explain what I had figured out. I told him he had a little girl. Well, not so little anymore. I shared what had happened all those years ago, how I'd turned a woman away, and the connection I had made at the hospital.

"Are you fucking *kidding me*, Vivian?" he yelled, making my eyes water. Even more so when his voice broke on a sob. "You knew about this and kept it from me?"

"I'm so sorry. I didn't realize." I sank to the living room floor, my legs not sturdy enough to hold me. I'd never felt a pang of guilt so strong. "I'll fix it. I promise, I'll fix it."

But every call, each letter, continued to go unanswered.

After a month of it, I recorded it all. Everything I could think of to explain what had happened and how I'd gotten to this point. The way fame made it hard to believe people weren't using me to make a buck or trying to take me down in some way. How losing my baby had broken part of me, and I was still grieving when I had lashed out. My complicated relationship with Kit. All the reasons I'd chosen not to believe the woman who had shown up one day at my door.

Which leaves us here.

Now you know everything. The good, the bad, and the downright ugly. And I hope—I really, truly pray—it's enough that you'll give Kit a chance to meet his daughter.

Please, give him that peace, Ginger.

CHAPTER FORTY-EIGHT

Margot

now

The player clicks with the end of the last tape, the three of us sitting in heavy silence.

Condensation pools around our glasses of lemonade while the lingering taste of sugar cookies is too sweet on my tongue.

I shift in my seat. "Can you clarify what you said at the end?"

Vivian merely blinks at me. "Which part? The letters I sent or—"

I wave to stop her. "Are you implying I'm related to Kit Pierce?"

"The whole point of the tapes was full transparency, so let me be frank: Your grandmother appeared at our doorstep one day saying she was expecting my husband's child."

"A child, meaning my mom?"

The lines on her face deepen, ones telling a story of hardship. "When I went to talk to Ginger, your mother answered the door. She had such beautiful blue eyes. The same as yours. As Kit's. The ones the tabloids loved to say could pierce you to the core."

The words bring me to my feet. "Gram was a switchboard operator. What would someone like Kit Pierce be doing with a switchboard operator?" I exaggerate every word so she can see how unreasonable it is.

"She may have been, but before then"—Vivian lifts shaking hands like I'm a stray animal that needs to be approached with care— "Ginger was a call girl."

"Excuse me?" I don't shame sex workers, but it feels like a bold assumption on Vivian's part. Based on what, appearances? The way Kit said "girls"?

It must be the venom in my tone that has Leo resting a hand against the small of my back. "Your mom said—"

"I know what she said." She said Gram was wild. That didn't mean she was a call girl.

"Though it hurt to recount the details of my life, especially the more traumatic ones," Vivian says, "it seemed necessary for Ginger to understand the big picture. So your mother and Kit could meet before he died. I hadn't imagined his granddaughter would come across the tapes someday."

"Don't call me that."

As much as I liked Kit early on, I grew to dislike him after what he put Vivian through. Yes, he had a moment of redemption later on, and, yes, it hurt to hear how sick he got. But I'm not sure how I feel about being related to him. Instead, I focus on Vivian. The one who turned Gram away. Our whole lives would have been different if she hadn't.

"I took all the blame Kit sent my way," she says. "I saw how hurt he was to learn he had a daughter out there while he was dying."

"He died angry with you, then?" Leo asks.

"I think he died angry at himself more than anything. On the last day we spoke, in late 1972, he apologized for blaming me."

I assume she doesn't want me to blame her either. Unfortunately for her, I can't help it.

"You acted like it was so important to empower women, what with how you mended fences with Helen. Then that interview exposing Eugene. You were willing to risk backlash from one of the top film companies in the world so those details could come out. So other women wouldn't feel alone. Have you ever thought about how alone my grandma felt? How hard it must have been for her to tell you she was pregnant?"

"I've thought about it dozens of times."

"You *humiliated* her." I know it without Gram here to confirm it. It must have taken so much courage to go to Vivian's doorstep. To explain to a star like her what had happened. With her husband, no less.

"That's why I went to her when I realized I was wrong," she says. "But you have to understand: The tabloids made things up all the time. I learned to stop trusting the public. Ginger could have tried harder, though—tried again—and she didn't."

"Why did she go to your house instead of wherever Kit was staying?"

"No one knew we were going to divorce yet," Vivian reminds me. "She thought that was where he lived."

"I think," Leo says, "if she had wanted to find Kit badly enough, she could have."

How hard *did* she try? How hard did Kit try once he knew about Mom? "Was Kit too sick to reach out to Gram?"

"He did reach out. When she didn't respond to him either, I convinced him to get a lawyer involved. The fathers' rights movement had gained steam by then. He died before they were able to move forward with it."

"So he was willing to get a lawyer yet left nothing for us when he died?"

"Believe it or not, he spent it all. Kit died broke. I was going to pay for the lawyers."

My eye catches on photos sitting on the bookcase, and I walk over while Vivian keeps talking.

"I'm not the villain here. There isn't one. We all did something we could have done differently. Kit was the one who cheated on me while I was grieving the loss of our child. Your grandmother refused to give him a chance to see his daughter, despite knowing he was dying. And

I shouldn't have turned Ginger away when she came looking for help, but I had perfectly good reasons to doubt a woman who showed up at my door looking like she did."

"Like *what*?" I say over my shoulder, part of me daring her to say something hurtful.

"I understand if you can't forgive me for what I did. I've had to live with regret for a long time. I'll admit, I reached out to your grandmother in part to ease my conscience. But I also did it so your mother could meet Kit. So she could know how much Kit would adore her. And if he'd lived long enough, he would have adored you too."

Closer now, I take in the assortment of photos on her shelves. There's a black-and-white one of Vivian and Kit on set. Another of them onstage, holding an award. Vivian and Hugh on their wedding day. One of Vivian and Hugh alongside Ruth and Dean, all middle-aged.

Vivian comes up next to me. "They're all gone now. Dean died of heart disease. Ruth of lung cancer." She sighs, homing in on a family photo. "Hugh had a pulmonary embolism nine years ago. And now it's just me. Sure, I have children, and grandchildren, and great-grandchildren, but everyone's busy with their lives."

She might be alone in this big house, but she had an awfully big life.

Vivian reaches for a simple silver frame and holds it out for me. "If you'd like."

It's a photo of Kit. He's young and happy, grinning as he sits in a boat, his elbow propped on the edge.

"Your hair is like his," she says, scanning me with a small smile. "Silky curls. Your mother's is the same, from what I remember."

Mom. She didn't get to meet her father.

"So many absent men," I say, almost to myself. "My grandfather, my dad. *Your* dad. They all leave, don't they?"

"Hugh never left." Vivian pulls down a photo of her and Hugh with his arm around her as she holds a baby. "Dean didn't leave.

Ted stayed with my mother and made her happy until the day he died."

"My dad never left," Leo says, and when I look over, there's a glimmer in his eyes, like he's trying to convey something about himself.

"Of course some do leave. Some women leave too." Vivian replaces the photo on the shelf and straightens it. "The ending of any relationship or dream or could-have-been scars us. After what happened with my first marriage and show, I could have decided another wasn't worth the risk. But then I would have missed out on the things that turned out to be the best parts of my life."

I used to go after what I wanted. When they didn't work out, it crushed me, so I stopped taking chances. Now I wonder if by closing the door on the things that could hurt me, I've been closing the door on the ones that could make me happy too.

Leo pops the cassette player open.

Vivian focuses on it. "I still have no idea if Ginger listened to the tapes."

"I think she did." Leo replaces the tape in its case. "We found your letter folded up next to this one."

"I'm grateful for that, at least," she says. "That she knew the truth."

"It didn't matter in the end, though, did it?" I walk back over to Leo.

She considers it for a moment. "Except now you know too."

"What difference does that make?" Everything I heard, and it changes nothing.

"Sometimes we don't understand why things happen the way they do right away." Vivian places her hand on a bookshelf for support. "You know what, dear? I'm feeling a little tired." She laughs lightly. "I'm tired a lot these days. Regrets are heavy."

Leo closes the shoebox. "Should we leave these?"

"No, no." Vivian pats the air in our direction. "You take them with you. Do whatever you'd like with them. Hold on to them; sell them. I have no use for them."

I can't imagine giving them up. But I do leave her letter to Hugh on the coffee table.

"Let's talk again soon, Margot," she says as Christine walks in, ready to escort us out.

"You can't believe that's going to happen."

"I've never been one to give up, even when the odds were against me." She meets my gaze. "Why should this time be any different?"

CHAPTER FORTY-NINE

Margot

now

It takes until we get home for me to wrap my head around the conversation at Vivian's. I have spent all this time falling for a woman who was my grandmother's nemesis.

I feel betrayed. Not only on behalf of Gram and Mom but me too.

Leo pulls into Gram's driveway and cuts the engine.

"You can tell me now." I glance up from the framed photo of Kit in my lap. "What did you find out that I asked you not to tell me?"

"That Kit died. That they all died except Vivian." A sigh falls from his lips. "I guess it should have been obvious, considering how long it's been, but I could tell you were getting attached to them, so I stopped asking if you wanted to know." His attention flicks to the house. "I wasn't sure if the truth would hurt you."

Because of Gram. Because I've been dealing with her death, with grief, and he didn't want to burden me with more. Especially without my knowing the link between her and the tapes.

"I've been thinking about what you said to Vivian, about men always leaving." He turns to me in his seat. "Is that what you believe?"

"It's hard not to. I grew up thinking my grandfather and my dad abandoned us. Even when I took a chance on relationships, hoping my story would be different, they ended, and I was devastated. So I stopped trying."

"You don't date anymore?"

I shake my head. "Nothing serious."

He sits with that information for a moment. "In the tapes, when Kit told Vivian he couldn't only be friends with her, I felt it to my bones. Maybe that's because it's never been strictly friendship between us for me. Even before. I've always wanted more. The difference now is I'm not going to pretend I don't." His eyes reflect a hope that makes my chest ache.

"What if the person you want doesn't exist anymore? I'm not the same person you used to know. At a job I don't love. Quitting the things I do. I'm a mess."

"Not everything in my life is perfect either."

Of course. "I know. Your divorce."

"Do you know *why* we divorced? When it came down to it, it's because of me. We didn't realize until they ran some tests, but the reason we couldn't have kids is me." Lingering pain shadows his face. "I would have adopted—tried other options—but she wasn't interested, so I didn't fight it when she brought up divorce. I didn't want to hold her back."

"I'm sorry." His heart has always been in the right place.

"I don't have my life all figured out. It's okay if you don't either."

"I think I'm getting somewhere," I admit. "I'm writing again."

"You are? What are you writing?"

"Something for me. I'm not thinking about what I'm going to do with it. I'm just having fun. I think listening to the tapes inspired me. I mean"—I roll my eyes—"how many damn times did Vivian keep trying? At some point, she had to throw in the towel, right?"

"But she never did." Leo reaches for the ends of my hair, looping his finger around a curl. "I know who you are. You're the person I think about every day. The one I miss as soon as we say goodbye. I want to be the man who proves to you that not everyone leaves. If you'll let me. Because the reason it was never strictly friendship between us for me is because I love you. I loved you when we were kids, long before we were together. And I love you now."

I'm not expecting how good it feels to hear that.

The truth is, I never got over the boy who's had my heart since I showed up at the music store with a tin of cookies. Now I've fallen for him all over again. This time for the man he's become.

I decide to open the door on the chance at happiness. "I love you too."

The smile that lights up his face is devastatingly beautiful. He leans in, pressing his lips to mine.

Maybe Vivian was right when she gave the speech at the Emmys about how sometimes life doesn't give you what you want. It gives you something else. What did she say? *And if you're lucky, that something else turns out to be even better.* I can't deny that being with Leo is better than the friendship I thought I wanted.

My phone buzzes, and I break our kiss to check the screen. "It's my mom. I should talk to her." I hand him the house keys. "Will you stay?"

"Of course."

While Leo goes inside, I take the framed photo of Kit, sit on the stoop next to the poppies, and answer the call. "Hi."

"What's wrong?" Mom says.

She really does always know.

I let out the longest sigh in existence. "You know those tapes we've been listening to? They *are* Vivian Stone's. She sent them to Gram."

She scoffs. "Margot, honey—"

"It's true. There was a letter with them we didn't see at first. Addressed to Gram with a phone number. So I called. Vivian wanted to meet me." Across the street, two kids play hockey in their driveway. High-pitched laughs come from a couple of houses down. This has always been a quaint neighborhood. Even from Vivian's perspective over fifty years ago. "So I went to see her, and—"

"Excuse me?"

Thirty-eight years old, and I'm still being reprimanded by my mother. "I brought Leo." A pause. "You know Vivian's husband? Her first husband, Kit Pierce? He was in that sitcom—"

"*Bobby and Clara.* Your grandmother hated that show."

Did she? Thinking of the times Gram suggested I turn on something else makes more sense. "She says Kit's your dad. Vivian turned

Gram away years ago when Gram went to their house to tell them about you."

There's absolute silence on her end, then: "When I was a teenager, I found letters shoved in the back of Gram's nightstand from a man named Christopher. Isn't Kit a nickname for Christopher?"

My back goes rigid. "What were they about?"

"Asking Gram to visit him. For her to bring me. To call."

He probably wrote them from the hospital. "I never saw any letters when I was cleaning."

"No, you wouldn't have. She caught me snooping and ripped them up. When I asked if Christopher was my father, she said yes but that we were better off without him."

"So you knew."

"I didn't know Christopher meant Kit Pierce, but several years later I asked her about it again, and she told me she did some things in her younger years to make money. Things she wasn't proud of. She'd kill me for telling you, but there's no point in hiding it anymore."

"Hiding what?"

"For a while, Gram was a lady of the night."

"A sex worker?"

Vivian was telling the truth.

Mom laughs. "I told you she was a wild child before she had me."

"No one says 'wild child' anymore." It's my duty to tell her. I switch the phone to my other ear. "Kit died of liver failure. When he was in the hospital, he confessed to Vivian that he had cheated on her near the end of their marriage. She put it together that she'd made a mistake by not believing Gram and tried to make it right. When her calls and letters went unanswered, she went to your house."

"I think I remember," Mom says. "Mostly because your grand-mother made a big deal about it after, telling me I shouldn't open the door for strangers even though I was a teenager by then. I didn't recog-nize the woman. Then again, Gram didn't let me watch reruns of her shows either, so I wouldn't have recognized her at the time anyway."

Her end goes quiet again.

"Mom?"

"I'm processing."

I bet it'll take her a long time to process. It'll take me a long time too. She hums. "I'm Kit Pierce's daughter."

"It is kind of cool, isn't it?" I look down at the picture of him. "You're not mad that she kept you from your father?"

"Who, your grandmother?"

"No, Vivian. She kept you from having a relationship with your father."

"Maybe initially," Mom says. "But it's possible Gram never intended on me having a relationship with him. For all we know, she only wanted money to help take care of me. Your grandmother was an independent woman. After all you've told me, it's her doing more than Vivian's that I never knew my father."

It sounds more reasonable when Mom says it. I think because I know she's not hurt by it all. "Why don't you think she told you about Kit until you pushed her about it?"

"Shame, if I had to guess," Mom says. "It's okay. I think we did pretty well together, the three of us, wouldn't you say?"

I smile. "We did. We really did."

This house, though on the small side, feels more like home than anywhere I've ever lived. I can't imagine having grown up somewhere else.

The front door opens, and Leo takes a seat next to me on the stoop. I catch a whiff of his detergent, making my insides warm.

If anything in our lives had been different, I wouldn't have met him.

"I don't want to sell the house," I say before the idea is fully formed, and Leo peeks at me, hope in his eyes. "Would you care if I kept it?"

"To rent out?" she asks.

"To live in."

Nothing is forcing me to stay in Santa Barbara. Yes, I have memories there. But not like the ones I have here. I've been working at my job remotely. There's no reason I can't continue. If my boss doesn't want me to, there are other jobs. I'll find something.

For the first time in a long time, I'm willing to take some chances. Go after what I want.

"Santa Barbara is great," I say, "but Long Beach is home."

"Keep it, then. Gram would be happy to know you're there."

I can tell Mom is smiling.

It was a completely unplanned decision, but now that I've made it, I feel lighter somehow.

As soon as I get off the phone, Leo curls an arm around me, and I rest my head on his shoulder.

I'm home.

CHAPTER FIFTY

Margot

now

I scan the open document on my laptop, pride burning bright in my chest.

Tonight, I finished the first draft of the manuscript I've been working on.

It's far too short and full of plot holes, but it's done. The words poured out of me like all this time they've been filling a well inside my mind, and once I released them, they wouldn't stop until I'd let out every last one.

It's a special kind of satisfaction to finish a project you're passionate about. Over the years, I'd lost my passion. Now I know why.

In the writing community, they say to write the story you want to read. Some call it "the book of your heart." It's impossible to keep your passion when you're speaking to someone else's heart.

I don't know what will happen with the book, and I know I have a long road ahead, but maybe someday I'll see it published. And if not this one, it could be the next one. Or the next.

Maybe it will never happen.

But maybe it will.

The more I think about Vivian's story, the more strength I get from the notion of perseverance. She never once let something new, something challenging, hold her back from pursuing what she wanted. She never said it was too late or it would be too hard.

In some ways, I've seen how Vivian and I are similar, but in other ways, we're opposites. She considered quitting a failure and learned that sometimes it's okay to let go, whereas too often I quit because I didn't believe in myself and worried I'd get hurt. I suppose I'm learning to hang on.

Gram used to refer to herself as "no spring chicken," and while I'm unsure of the cutoff age for spring chickens, I'd lumped myself into that category too. But I shouldn't have. It's not too late to pursue something I want. It's not too late for writing. Or surfing. Not even for love.

While there might be barriers along the way, I'm not going to let my mentality be one of them.

The doorbell rings.

I stand from my seat at the dining table. Leo spends more nights here than at his own place now, and I don't think it's because of the shoddy elevator in his building. I've already told him several times he's welcome to knock once and come in.

When I open the door, I find a package sitting on the stoop. I bring it to the kitchen and tear back the flaps.

An envelope sits on top. I set it aside and go back to the box. Two silver objects—a Zippo lighter and a cigarette case—rest on black leather. I brush a finger against a dent in the case, and a chill rolls over me.

These were Kit's, weren't they? He had this case when he and Vivian walked the studio lots. Said it saved his father from a bullet during World War II.

I leave them on the counter and withdraw a black leather jacket from the box. It's worn and buttery soft under my fingertips, a faint musk wafting from it. I stuff my arms into the sleeves and pull the jacket close.

A pang tugs my insides at never being able to meet him. It's a change of heart I'm not expecting. I tear open the envelope.

Dear Margot,

I hope this isn't an unwelcome surprise, but I felt it important to get these to you and your mother. As you can probably guess, they were Kit's. I've kept them ever since he passed but wanted to give you the choice of having them if you wanted them.

All my best,

Vivian

A peace offering.

A month has passed since I saw her. How she knows I still own this house or that I'm living here now, I don't know. I can only assume she has the means to figure it out.

I reach for my phone and scroll through my recent numbers until I find hers. By the fourth ring, I don't think anyone is going to pick up, then—

"Hello?"

"Hi. It's Margot."

"Margot." There's a smile in Vivian's voice. "So good to hear from you."

"You answer your own phone? I thought Christine did that."

She laughs. "Christine only works until five o'clock. Besides, I don't get many calls these days."

Vivian is all alone in that big house. Despite hers being one of the most recognizable faces in television history, she's by herself. I imagine she has a lot of time to think.

"I got your package. Thank you." I walk back to the dining table and sit in front of my open laptop, jiggling the mouse to light up the screen again. "I've actually been thinking about everything since we spoke, and I think when my grandma had my mom, she made a choice to start over. Leave the past behind. But I think she knew you realized your mistake and tried to make it right. Only she was doing what she thought was right for her and my mom."

Vivian hums. "That's all we can do, isn't it? What we think is best. Sometimes we get it right, and sometimes we don't."

I've gotten it wrong in my life at least as many times as I've gotten it right. "You were right: The tapes might not have changed anything for Gram, but they changed something for me. I finished a novel for the first time in years, and I think it's at least partly thanks to you."

"You should be proud of yourself. What are you going to do with it?"

"I don't know yet, but I'm guessing whatever it is, you're going to tell me to fight for it until I succeed."

"No," Vivian says. "What's important is knowing which things in life are worth fighting for. I learned those are the ones you never give up on."

I nod. "I'm not sure if you're hoping for my forgiveness, but I thought you should know I do. I forgive you."

My gaze catches on the framed photo of Leo and me as teenagers, sitting on a side table. It's from the disposable camera I found in the attic and got developed last week. The shot is off-center and too close, but in it we're lying on his bed. While I'm smiling for the camera, Leo is smiling at me.

"My mom and I were happy," I go on, "so if this is a regret you're still hanging on to, you can let it go. You don't need to hold it on your conscience anymore."

The other end is so silent, I pull the phone back to make sure we didn't get disconnected. In a voice so weary it makes me ache, Vivian says, "Thank you. I . . . I think I've been waiting half my life to hear that."

This is all I can do. I can't take back how heartbroken Kit must have been when he didn't get to meet my mom. I can't fix how terribly it must have hurt Vivian to see him die, knowing there was nothing left she could do. But I can give her this.

"I was thinking," I say, "would you have any reservations if I wrote about Kit? Because I can't write about him without writing about you."

"As in a novel?"

"Yes. I think it could be cathartic to write about him. Do some research, talk to people." It would be harder than it sounds, but I'm willing to try.

"If you do, it might behoove you to go public with the fact that you are Kit's grandchild. I can corroborate it. People will still have doubts, of course. You must prepare for the attention that will come your way."

My stomach tenses. I don't know if I'm up for being in the public eye. "I'll think about it. But I want to write it regardless, even if it's only for me."

Vivian is still talking—telling me to call her anytime with questions—when there's a knock at the front door. Leo walks in, holding up a take-out box, and I bow like he's my hero, both of us laughing.

"I'm sorry, I didn't catch that." I try to focus on Vivian as I find plates.

"Oh, it's all right," she says, and I think she's smiling. "I won't keep you any longer."

"Okay." It's hard to put up a fight when the scent of tacos is wafting through the air. "Take care."

"You too, dear. You too."

I end the call and explain to Leo who I was talking to, including the box Vivian had delivered.

"What do you think about watching *Bobby and Clara*?" he asks once we finish eating.

I've never watched an episode all the way through. I'm curious. "Sure. Let's do it."

As we get situated on the couch, Leo loads the pilot episode to stream. The theme song plays and there she is.

Vivian Stone.

She's beautiful and curvy, with that raspy voice. In a matter of minutes, I'm laughing, and I see what millions of fans over the years couldn't get enough of. Despite her mistakes, I still like her.

I'm grateful. Grateful I got to know her story. Grateful I got to know her. Because now, regardless of the ups and downs that might come, I'm going after what I want with my whole heart.

I learned that from Vivian.

The New York Times

FEBRUARY 4, 2026

THE END OF AN ERA: VIVIAN STONE, TELEVISION'S COMEDIC GENIUS, DIES

Vivian Stone, the indisputable Queen of Comedy, died in her home. She was 96 years old.

Miss Stone, adored for her flawless timing, clever physical comedy, and witty dialogue, came to be known as a Hollywood legend. The curvy comedian cut her teeth at MGM, where she received praise and recognition for her leading role in *Sunday Circus* alongside her future husband, Kit Pierce. It wasn't until they headed to CBS to star in the sitcom *Bobby and Clara* that Stone became a household name. Best known as an "All American" couple both on- and off-screen, they enjoyed the success of the series for two seasons. Their collaboration ended with their divorce in 1956.

As a self-proclaimed tireless worker, Stone went on to star in *Two Girls and a Dog* alongside friend and fellow starlet Ruth Keller, which concluded after nine seasons. While she continued to act in various projects—even once alongside her second husband, Hugh Fox—Stone refocused her energy on elevating new actors, especially women, as a producer for numerous sitcoms.

She was a great supporter of the Los Angeles Centers for Alcohol and Drug Abuse as well as the National Coalition Against Domestic Violence, to which a significant portion of her estate is left.

ACKNOWLEDGMENTS

When I started writing this book, I was full of self-doubt and fear and frustration over whether I would ever be good enough to be published. This road is hard and filled with so many noes, you'd think I couldn't take a hint. But it's been my dream forever. I'm too passionate about it—and too stubborn—to quit. Sound like Vivian? Little did I know when I wrote her triumph that I would have my own. I didn't get here by myself, though, and I have many people to thank.

Johanna Castillo, my superstar agent: Whenever I think of the summer we brainstormed edits for this book, I remember the many hours we talked and laughed on the phone. Thank you for believing in me and this book! Sincere gratitude to Victoria Mallorga Hernandez for all you do behind the scenes.

Carrie Feron, my fairy godmother editor: Finding out you wanted to work with me was a pinch-me moment I still haven't recovered from. Thank you for seeing what I was trying to do with this book and helping me make it the best it could be. I would happily write a hundred more books with you!

To the lovely people at Gallery Books: Jennifer Bergstrom, Jennifer Long, Eliza Hanson, Ali Chesnick, Heather Waters, Fallon Mcknight, Ana Contreras, Nancy Tonik, Jane Phan, and Julia Jacintho. Getting a book into the world takes many hands, and I'm grateful to have the expertise of this dedicated team in my corner!

Thank you to everyone who talked through plot points with me and offered valuable feedback along the way: Shannon O'Brien,

Crystal Christie, Cari Polick, Jennifer M. Lane, Rachel Fitzjames, Jillian Michel, and Stephanie Downey.

Allison Hubbard, Cat Curry Hasz, and Kristen Power: I love our little group that started with writing and has grown into so much more over the years. Oh, and Cat: Promise to read this under the bar at a reggae concert like you did with the manuscript, 'kay?

Once I started getting Leigh Anna Knappick's feedback on a Friday night ("I'm just over here stuffing my face with page after page"), I knew I'd found a kindred spirit—someone who offers stellar advice and can make me laugh. I hope you see your fingerprints all over these pages.

A shout-out to the MJs: This group is one of the best parts about writing. Thank you for being there as sounding boards, shoulders to cry on, and the biggest cheerleaders around. Love you, ladies!

To Alicia: You read my first novel before anyone else, and I will always appreciate your kindness and encouragement.

Thank you to Michele Vidal for being gracious enough to share her family cookie recipe (you can find it on my website), which was my inspiration for Gram's cookies.

Mom, thank you for having made trips to the bookstore an adventure and for letting me read whatever I wanted. I wouldn't have wanted to write stories if I hadn't first fallen in love with reading them.

To my boys, Rowan and Kellan: Never give up on your dreams, no matter how insurmountable they might seem. I'll always be there, cheering you on.

Finally, to Shawn: You've taken care of so much over the years so that I could have space to write. Many times I decided I wouldn't succeed, but you never doubted it. Thank you for believing in me and for helping me become a better version of myself. With you, real life is better than the movies.

BOOK CLUB QUESTIONS

1. Vivian describes many horrifying parts of Hollywood. Which had you heard of before? Which were new to you?

2. There are many kinds of grief. Which types do the characters in this book experience?

3. Aside from their interest in acting, Hugh and Kit are very different men. What do you think Vivian loved about them?

4. Vivian says she chooses to love Kit, while she couldn't help but love Hugh. Do you think her love for Kit was real?

5. Leo admits he had made a mistake in how he handled ending his relationship with Margot. Can you think of a decision you made when you were younger that you would have handled differently as an adult?

6. When Vivian makes the move from film to TV, she's not thrilled about it because television was seen as inferior to film. If her story was being told in the present, do you think Vivian would have the same reaction about TV?

7. Vivian's letters to Hugh go on before, during, and after her marriage to Kit. Do you see them as her having had an emotional affair?

8. Loving someone who is an addict is challenging. Do you think, in leaving Kit, Vivian made the right decision? How was their relationship different from her parents' marriage?

9. In what ways does Margot change throughout her time listening to the tapes? What about Vivian's story encourages those changes?

10. How do you think Margot's life was affected by her not having a father figure? Did Vivian's relationship with her father, or lack thereof, influence her relationships?

ABOUT THE AUTHOR

Melissa O'Connor became obsessed with stories involving family secrets, betrayal, and forbidden love after being given a box full of used V.C. Andrews books at age ten. She lives in Buffalo, New York, where she can usually be found cheering on her kids' sports teams and sneaking words onto the page between games. *The One and Only Vivian Stone* is her debut novel. To learn more, and for bonus content, visit melissaoconnor.com.